Rogues of Regalia

The Rogues

Ruby Vincent

Published by Ruby Vincent, 2022.

Prologue

I'm sorry. I wish I had the words to express how sorry I am.

You always told me I needed to toughen up. You'd say in a world of wolves, you can either be a rabbit or a bear.

I wanted to be a bear. There were even days I thought I could be. That I was strong enough to see this through and reach the great new life that everyone said was waiting for me. Now I know that new life isn't possible, because it's for the wolves, and I was always a rabbit.

I'm rambling now. This letter is about one thing: saying goodbye.

I love you, Luna.

The stronger, prettier, braver sister. You are a bear, tiger, shark, and anything you want to be. You're fearless and you can't stand to see things done wrong when you can put it right.

That's the best thing about you, but not this time.

I'm telling you the truth of what happened so you and Mom won't spend a lifetime wondering if there was something you could've done. Know that you couldn't have stopped this, and you can't put it right.

Do not go to Regalia University, Luna.

Beneath the pretty facade is a hideous nest of lies, secrets, and betrayal, and there are people here who'll do anything to prevent the truth coming out.

Do not share this letter with anyone, do not confront the men named, and <u>do not</u> mess with the Royals.

Any law thrown at them will fall short. Any fight will end with you losing everything, and them walking away without a scratch. They're untouchable, and more dangerous than you can believe.

This letter is both a confession and a promise. I want you to know the truth as long as you swear to do nothing about it.

Swear on a million jelly beans.

Alright, it all started the first day of school when I ran into Owen Thasher...

I stopped there—folding the note and tucking it safely in my inside pocket. I didn't need to read the rest. I didn't need to read the letter at all. I had it memorized. Even so, I had to hold it in my hands, imagine my sister penning the words—drown in her pain with each teardrop that warped the ink... that way the hatred burned hotter.

"Morning, young lady."

Raising my head, I plastered on a smile. A middle-aged woman with striking streaks of gray in her brown hair smiled back at me. "Are you looking for your dorm?"

"Yes, I am. Abbott Hall?"

She pointed over my shoulder. "It's back that way, around the corner, and on the left. You can't miss it."

"Thank you so much."

"No problem at all," she said as I hitched my bags up my shoulders.

I moved back a couple of steps, making like I was heading for the dorm, when I stepped around to see over her shoulder to the face she blocked.

He laughed at something his friend said, tossing his golden mane from his eyes. The guys slapped backs and went opposite ways, him heading in my direction.

I placed my hand over my heart, hearing paper crinkle. Passing by me, Owen Thasher winked—seeing an attractive new coed and nothing more.

"Welcome to Regalia University," said the woman, reaching down to help with my bags.

I fixed on Owen, following a short distance behind him into Abbott Hall. *Crinkle, crinkle* went her letter.

"Sorry, sis," I said under my breath. "This is one promise I won't keep."

Chapter One

Mrs. Bryon helped me carry my things to the second-floor dorm at the end of the hall.

"Good luck. If you need anything else, your student guide should be along shortly."

I thanked her again, sending her off.

Fuck the student guide. I was going to my room and taking the longest, hottest shower. Whatever it took to kill the maggots under my skin. That's what it felt like. A million, billion creatures crawling under my flesh since I set foot on this campus.

Remember why you're here, Luna. This is for Winter. Just go inside and—

I swung open the door, blinking at the sight. A raven-haired vision in gold stretched out on the bed, her glittering pumps resting on the pillow. Her fingers were a blur typing on the phone, while the other hand twisted her locks.

"Oh, sorry. I thought this was my room." I backed out.

"Luna Sinclair," she said, stopping me in my tracks. "Nah, you're in the right room. I've been waiting for you."

I came in, taking in the space and the stranger who made herself comfortable in it. From the website and my sister's old photos, I knew I was walking into a dorm unlike the bunk-bed prison cells other freshmen suffered through. Still, I wasn't prepared for this.

Forget the cinder block, my walls were plaster painted a soft cream. Empty picture frames hung all over the room, waiting for me to give them their purpose. Heavy gray blackout curtains covered the windows and served another function of matching the gray-and-white fluffy rug under my full-size bed.

I set my stuff down on my massive oak desk, gazing heavily at the stranger in my bed. "Why were you waiting for me?" I prompted. "Are you with administration? Did I forget to turn a form in?"

"If you did, that's not my problem." She was kind enough to finally get her shoes off my pillow. "I'm your student guide, Katie. Not Kathy. Not Kathleen." She straightened to her full height—all five feet six inches of gorgeous. This close, I counted the freckles on her upturned nose and the stray strand stuck to pink cupid's-bow lips. "And not Kay-Kay. Katie, you got it?"

"Got it." I stuck my hand out. "My name's Luna. Nice to meet you."

"Nice to meet you," she mocked, rolling her eyes at my hand and picking up her phone again. "What are we? Fifty-year-old women at a rotary club meeting? Besides, did you miss that two-year-long pandemic we just beat? Who even shakes hands anymore? Ugh, gross."

My hand returned to my side. "Sorry." I fought to keep an even tone. Nothing wrong with not being a handshaker, but she didn't have to look at mine like she just watched me wipe my ass without toilet paper, while dirt smears from her shoes were on my pillow. "Thanks for getting up early for me, but I've got my map and orientation packet. I don't need a student guide."

"Tough. This shit counts as fifteen hours toward my mandatory volunteer hours. Unfortunately, too many people signed up as student guides, then blew it off. Now they make the freshmen take tests at the end of orientation to prove they were taught all they need to know. You fail and not only do I not get my hours, but they kick me out of the program and I'll have to do something disgusting like pick up trash or ladle soup to flea-ridden bums."

"Wow." I looked her straight in the face. "I don't think I've ever disliked someone so fast."

To my surprise, she smirked. "Everyone says that at first. Don't worry, Lu-Lu. I grow on you." She brushed past me. "Keep up. I've got a lot of shit to tell you, but it doesn't have to take all morning. Sooner we get this done, the sooner Dean is licking my pussy in the library stacks."

I gaped at her back. My sister warned that this place was like no other school I've ever been to.

It's a university for the wolves.

Quickly, I dumped my stuff and moved my pillow to the laundry basket. Giving myself a quick look in the floor-length mirror, I fussed with my windswept hair and straightened my clothes. The air-conditioning was busted on the bus, so the passengers rolled all the windows down. It barely made a dent in the sweltering heat.

The forty-minute drive in my stepfather's Audi would've been much more comfortable, but I couldn't put him or my mom through that—dropping another daughter at the gates of hell.

I caught up with Katie halfway down the hall.

"—like other schools," she was saying. "The first two years are general education classes and the last two are major classes. Since Regalia is super exclusive and each incoming class is limited to one hundred students, you're split into two classes and the people in yours are on the same schedule with the same professors—except for one or two major prep courses."

"I was wondering why I was sent a class schedule instead of choosing them."

We stepped out onto the lawn, soaking in the morning rays. A sea of green was broken by weaving concrete. Again, the brochures didn't do the place justice. The lawn was awash in stone fountains ringed by manicured gardens of azaleas, begonias, and daffodils. Students gathered on wood and iron benches, studying or talking over their phones. It looked like paradise.

My lips curled. "Where are we going?"

"Cafeteria." Katie strolled off, her gold-sequin dress glittering and reflecting on the path. "I'm not missing breakfast because of you."

"Is the food good?" I couldn't give less of a shit, but talking was something to do while I kept an eye out for Owen. I wasn't too worried since I knew where the guy slept. Even so, there were cameras in the Abbott Hall corridors. I had to learn his regular routine if I was to find the right place, and the perfect moment.

Katie shrugged. "It's decent. They make everyone who lives on campus pay for the meal plan. My parents let the staff go on vacation. Unfortunately, our chef decided she needed one too. It's eat this stuff or starve."

Katie pointed out buildings, classrooms, the gym, and the library on our way. "Show up to class on time. Profs don't do ridiculous crap like call roll, but they will notice if you're forever skipping and sleeping in class. They can get vindictive about it."

"Vindictive," I muttered. "Disturbing word choice."

Darby Hall rose in the distance. Students streamed in—some in designer jeans and dresses, and some in pajamas. Neither wardrobe choice could be right or wrong since college cafeterias didn't come with a dress code, and yet I was still underdressed.

Black marble floors filled the space, dotted all over with dark walnut tables with silverware and linen place settings. Fake lilies plopped in glass vases, and those vases sat atop each table as centerpieces. Katie got in line for a five-star buffet.

I left her—my jaw hanging open as I circled the food, reading the labels. French toast, ricotta pancakes, chocolate toast, pecan cinnamon buns, poached salmon, lobster frittata, and that was just the stuff on the buffet table. There was a separate list of items that were made to order. If this was a "decent" menu, I could only imagine what Katie's chef whipped up for her daily.

I joined up with her in the line. "This is all included in the meal plan?"

"Yep. Breakfast is served from six to nine. Lunch from eleven to one. Dinner from six to nine. Remember that," she ordered. "It'll be on the test."

I nodded, still taking it all in. I wondered if I'd ever get used to this life. Mom married my rich new stepdaddy four years before, but since he shipped me off to boarding school two weeks after the wedding—and the little mishap on his yacht—it's been uniforms, nuns, and strict routines for me. Sister Agatha wasn't taking anyone's order of poached eggs with hollandaise sauce.

"What's your deal, freshman?" Katie asked while munching on a slice of bacon. "Besides your appalling lack of fashion sense and understanding of germ transfer."

It was my turn to shrug. "No deal. I graduated from St. Thomas's Academy. It was a year-round school and the dress code was strict. Wasn't much sense buying a whole bunch of clothes I couldn't wear." I glanced down at my threadbare jeans, Crocs, and purple plaid shirt. "But I could do with a trip to the mall."

"Fuck's sake, that's putting it lightly. You look like a bored housewife who long since stopped being satisfied by her husband, and now gets her kicks masturbating behind a Dairy Queen while sneaking glances at the hot comanager on his smoke break."

"Super specific."

"Seriously," Katie said, dropping a croissant on my plate. "Yuck."

"I really get it. Anyway, what's your deal?"

Katie squared her shoulders, and inadvertently pushed out her cleavage. "I'm Katie Langford of the Regent Langfords—as in Regent Langford Jewelers. My family has lived in Regalia since forever. We practically built half this school. For real, you don't know how lucky you are that I'm even talking to you right now. We're in different stratospheres, Lu-Lu. Me among the stars, and you"—she tapped my nose—"in a Dairy Queen parking lot."

I hunched my back, trailing my leg across the tile. "It's an honor to be in your presence, mistress." I put on a dry, croaky voice. "May I kiss your shoes? After you wipe them on my back."

Peals of laughter spilled out of her lips. "You're such a freak." I could be wrong, but I detected a trace of something other than contempt in her voice.

We got our food and headed for a booth in the back. My butt sank onto plush, black leather.

"So, here's what you really need to know." Katie speared a bit of smoked salmon. "The only two classes there really are in this place are the Royals and the Dregs. I'll make it simple: I'm a Royal. You're a Dreg."

I ignored her millionth insult during the course of our short interaction. She was finally saying what I needed to hear.

"What makes you a Royal and me a Dreg? Money?"

She shook her head. "No. All of the Royals wear Prada, but wearing Prada doesn't make you a Royal. You get me?"

"Um, no."

Katie heaved a sigh. "Being a Royal is about status. It's about standing on and off campus. My name is a worldwide brand. A Regent Langford bracelet is wrapped around the queen of England's wrist. I have a reputation of class and elegance—"

I swallowed a snort.

"—that stretches back a thousand years. That doesn't compare with Adriana Goddard over there, who's the daughter of the dean's third wife and former personal trainer. She doesn't get a seat at the table just because her mom fucked her stepdaddy on it."

"I got it," I said simply.

Inside, my mind churned. This was good. I walked onto this campus thinking every rich prick was my enemy. It turns out the Royals are twice as exclusive as the admissions process. They were the ones Winter warned me to stay away from. The ones nobody could beat.

I watched Katie through my lashes. *A Royal like you.*

"Like I was saying, Dregs don't talk to Royals. They don't sit with them. They don't eat with them. Dregs don't take up more space than is necessary—and even then."

My fists balled under the table. "You buy into all that stuff? You really treat people that way?"

Katie waved that away. "Nothing to do with me. I'm just letting you know the rules so you survive here, Lu-Lu. Some of the Royals can be brutal to Dregs who forget their place. Personally, I think the whole thing is way over the top. Dean is a Dreg and the man fucks like a beast. Seriously, he has me coming so hard I see heaven."

"Didn't need to know that," I muttered, though my clenched fingers unballed.

"Imagine me missing out on the best sex of my life just because his family sells washing machines and he's new money. I deserve the best," she said. "Far as I'm concerned, you do your thing and I'll do mine. Either way, I sleep in a king-size bed inlaid with real gold."

"So why did you say I was lucky you're talking to me?"

She scrunched her nose. "'Cause you look like a homeless woman."

From Dairy Queen masturbator to homeless woman. How am I going down in this woman's estimation?

"It's super embarrassing even being seen with you right now."

"Then, let me give you a break." I got up from the table. "I saw a tea station up there. I'll need a soothing cup of chamomile to get through the rest of this."

"Make that two."

I hadn't made it two steps before she helped herself to my croissant. Apparently I was holding it for her.

I rejoined the line, sliding in as the doors opened. Swirling notes of leather, mint, and cedar hit me first, turning my head to a sight that struck me stupid.

Wow...

Piercing amber eyes set in ovals and rimmed with long lashes. A shadow's dusting covered his chin, cheeks, and above his mouth—matching the thick, coal eyebrows moving as constantly as he was. His long, pointed nose wrinkled, screwing up with his face as he mouthed the words. That did nothing to mar his beauty. Nor did whipping his wavy, sable locks about mess up a strand of his hair.

The wildly dancing stranger was in his own world—uncaring of his audience or the social norm of not dancing when you're the only one in the room doing it.

"It's a hundred to stare."

I jumped. His lips moved. Common sense said he was the one who spoke, but the deep, melodious voice was too angelic to have come from a mortal.

He slowed, shifting to a mellow bop, swinging his hips. "Two to touch."

"S-sorry. Didn't mean to stare." I spun around, and looked straight into green eyes and snarling teeth.

"Ruff, ruh, ruh!" He leaped, barking furiously.

Screaming, I flung back and landed within a pair of muscled arms.

"*...surrender to me...*"

His music floated into my ears, telling of how close we were, if his cologne, hard chest, and amused eyes weren't doing a good enough job.

"Racked up three hundred dollars before breakfast. Not bad." He flicked over me. "Easy, Cato. She's cool. We like her."

Heat licked my cheeks. I quickly straightened and got a look at the Cato in question.

The green eyes were real. Flinty, bottle-green pools narrowed to slits. His hair was thick short waves matching the color of the long-haired stranger. What wasn't real were the gleaming fangs. Those were painted on the metal mask covering his face. I tried to think of another word, but only one came to mind: muzzle.

"Where the hell am I?"

"Finest place on earth—or so you'll be told."

"Rafael," a voice called. "Clear?"

"We're clear," my new friend replied.

The door swung in and a tall, built vision in red, black, and blond strode in. It was the jawline that hit me first. Square sculpted perfection that would break my knuckles if I even thought of hitting it. Then he drew me higher to his soft-looking pink lips, Roman nose, blue eyes, and sweeping blond hair. He caught sight of me over Rafael's shoulder and moved so fast, I blinked and he was an arm's length away.

"Who are you? What do you want?"

My brows flew up at his suspicion, and Cato's sudden low growl. Even Rafael cocked his head, expression changing.

"Yeah, who are you?" Rafael grasped my chin between two fingers. "You look familiar."

My heart squeezed. Winter and I weren't clones, but if you looked hard enough, you saw we shared the same nose and eyes. Or at least, we used to.

Are you seeing into my sister's eyes like you did when you tortured her?

I tore away from him, walking off without another word. I had tea bags in my suitcase. I'd have some later.

There was no getting chummy with anyone in this school. My sister's letter named five men, but there were countless more who sat by, watched, and egged them on. I would find out who... and make every single damn one of them pay.

Katie's legs stretched out onto my spot when I came back. She saw no reason to move, so I helpfully lifted her feet off and moved them to the floor.

"Where's my tea?"

I ignored that. "Who are those guys?"

She followed my line of sight. "Ah, of course you sniffed out the freaks in under an hour. Like finds like."

"You are literally the worst person I've ever met."

Katie barked a laugh. "I'm telling you, you won't be saying that in a few days. No one who knows me for long enough can help but love me."

I hurt myself stopping an eye roll. "Are they Royals too— My goodness. Is *he* a Royal?"

He was the pale, slim figure that just walked in wearing a black waistcoat, matching tailcoat, and silver cane. If I wasn't absolutely certain it was impossible, I'd double-check to make sure we hadn't slipped years in the past to the Victorian era.

Long brown hair fell around a face touched by the gods. That was the only explanation for how this cosplaying man before me could be so handsome and his strangeness did nothing to lessen the effect.

"They are definitely not Royals," Katie said. "They're not Dregs either. We call them the Rogues."

"Rogues," I whispered. It fit. I couldn't say why, but I knew that was the name for them. "What do you have to do to get that title?"

"I usually don't spare people like that the honor of my talking about them, but when it comes to those guys, not even I can help it. They're so freaking gorgeous, it's a sin. Even Cato is, under that... you know."

I couldn't disagree. I tried to look away. Over and over, my gaze found them, following them through the line.

"The guy with the headphones is Rafael Dumont. That's his younger brother, Cato, in the mask. They should be a year apart, but Cato was put in the sophomore class because Rafael's the only one who can control him."

"Control him?" I repeated. "Why does he need to be controlled?"

"Because he's a dangerous psychopath who can practically start fires with his eyes. I'm not kidding. He's searched before and after he leaves a classroom to make sure he hasn't gotten his hands on lighters or a match."

"Very funny. Let's stop playing jokes on the new girl now."

She gave me a flat look. "I'm not joking. His last stint was in Seaview Psychiatric Hospital. You can look it up if you don't believe me. Rafael broke him out of the place. It was on the news."

Try as I did, I couldn't hear the trick in her words. The mocking and contempt were gone too. Katie was serious.

"I don't understand. My application for this place was a mile long. They asked for my extracurriculars from elementary school. How does a mental hospital escapee and his accomplice get in?"

"Most of us have a legacy around here, and not all of them are good. Their father is known and employed by certain Royal families—not mine," she added quickly. "But some of them hire Leon Dumont to make their problems go away. Rumors say he's made a few *people* disappear too. Of course, there's no evidence to prove it.

"All the same, when the guy who knows where the bodies are buried asks you to enroll his sons in your school, you do what he says. It's in everyone's best interest that Leon remains on good terms with the Royals."

"Long story short: blackmail."

She tapped her nose. "Pretty much. The twitchy, shifty-eyed guy behind them is Wilder O'Rourke. No one really knows what his parents are into, or if he has two of them. You can try to look him up but it's a waste of time. He's got zero internet presence, and Wilder isn't going to fill in the blanks.

"He won't tell anyone where he's from, what day he was born, his middle name, or what he likes on his toast. He's basically convinced we're all government sleeper agents out to stop him before he exposes our secrets."

"What secrets?"

"Ugh," she scoffed, reaching for her milk. "Pick one. Literally, any crazy-as-balls conspiracy theory. Wilder buys into them all, and he's going to expose them. He thinks covid was purposely released by the government to thin out the world's population. He claims another virus will be unleashed in ten years."

"I... I don't even..." Words failed me.

"Yep, and I haven't gotten to Lucien. Crazy steps off his throne and bows before Lucien Calais."

"Why?"

"You need to ask." She swept out a hand. "Look at him. He dresses like that every day because, and I'm not shitting you, he believes he's a vampire born in 1845, then turned in 1864."

"And now I know you're joking."

"Fine," she said, grinning. "You'll find out soon enough."

I shook my head. "Let's go back to the student guiding. Tell me more about the Royals. Who are they exactly?"

Katie turned out to be a wealth of information. She bragged on the names and history of every Royal in Regalia from the freshmen to the seniors. The freshmen weren't a concern. They weren't here when everything happened to my sister, but the rest... I had more names to add to my list of five.

Later that day, I pressed my hand over my heart, hearing the paper crinkle and the rush of pain and sadness that went with it.

A thousand jelly beans.

That was our promise between sisters. When we were little, the one thing we loved above all was the once-a-week treat our mother brought home after work—a bag of jelly beans, so what else could we swear to keep our secrets on?

A thousand jelly beans that I wouldn't tell Mom Winter accidentally broke her great-aunt's vase. A thousand jelly beans that Winter wouldn't tell a soul that I snuck out of boarding school to go to a Bruno Mars concert. A thousand jelly beans to hide how much we disliked our stepfather at first, so we wouldn't ruin Mom's chance at real happiness.

Eighteen years and so many promises, I've never broken a single one... until now.

"I couldn't keep this one," I whispered. "Everyone who hurt you. Who drove you to..." I trailed off, eyes welling. "They're all going to pay, Winter. That I can promise you. They'll regret every single second of their existence if it's the last thing I do."

"Did you say something, sweetheart?"

I shook myself, coming back to reality. The cabbie squinted at me in the rearview. "Are you sure this is the place?"

I fixed on Bowden Manor. All thirty-six acres, tennis court, swimming pool, greenhouse, and three stories of it. "This is the place."

He dropped me at the gate, leaving me to trudge the stone path alone. I let myself in and went straight upstairs, searching out the west wing master bedroom. A still mound lay among the pillows and red satin sheets. Slowly, I padded over to her.

"Mom? Mom, it's me. Luna."

The mound moved. Otherwise, there was no response.

Rounding the mattress, I climbed on, gently tugging the sheet down. Dry, scraggly hair appeared first—once my mother's crowning feature. A sallow cheek came next, and as I brushed her hair back, Mom's red-rimmed eyes.

She blinked at me. "Luna?" she rasped. "Is... that you, baby?"

"Yeah, Mom. It's me." I whispered as if a loud word could break her. I wasn't so sure it couldn't. "How you doing, Mama? Can I get you anything?"

"My beautiful girl." Bony fingers stroked my cheek. "My baby."

My eyes stung. Throat closing, I forced out, "I'm going to make your favorite. Oolong tea. Why don't we snuggle up on the couch and watch *Pride and Prejudice* while we drink?"

I tugged the blankets down farther. She snatched them short of her knees and pulled them back up. "I can't have tea right now, sweetie. I'm too tired." Her eyes fluttered shut. "I'm going to take a nap. But don't go." Mom laid her hand over mine. "Please... don't go."

"I won't." I lay down next to her, listening to her breaths even out. "I'm not going anywhere."

I don't know how long I stared up at the textured ceiling, sinking in the rare stretch of alone time with my mother. Since Winter's funeral, this was what we did. I lay next to her wishing up ways to get her out of bed, the whole time knowing there was only one sister who could do that, and she wasn't here.

"Luna." My stepfather filled the doorway. "Your mother is resting. Give her space."

That's all Mom does is rest, and that's all we do is give her space. It's been months. How long until we get her help?

I swallowed the reply. Jack insisted he was taking care of Mom and getting her everything she needed. When I pushed and asked how exactly he was doing that, he turned it around on me and said she needed to grieve in her own way, and my pushing her wasn't helping. I don't know if it wasn't helping, but it certainly wasn't working.

"Come, Luna. You have to get ready for the party."

My teeth clenched. Mom wasn't the only reason I came to the manor that night. I should be unpacking my room and then crafting my plan to get to the other guys in the note. Instead I was participating in my stepfather's ridiculous charade.

I closed the door behind me. My head came up to Jack's chin. Four years ago, he seemed so big and imposing with those unsmiling, thin lips and coldly handsome face. The only time I saw a spark of happiness in him was when he looked at Mom. He wanted Eloise Sinclair bad. The two kids she came with—not so much.

"Jack, I know I said I'd do this—"

"—and I will honor our agreement," he finished. "I hope that is how you planned to end that sentence. Luna, you refused to apply to another university even though your mother locked herself in our room for a week and a half after you got your acceptance to Regalia University. We begged you not to go, and then when I refused to pay the tuition, you said you'd do whatever I asked to change my mind. This was the deal," Jack said, voice hard. "If you renege, it's a simple matter to call the registrar and tell them I'm canceling the payment."

My lips pressed tight together, penning in my first response. It wouldn't be good enough to combat a single thing he said, since he was right. I told Jack I'd do anything for the tuition to Regalia. That place didn't give scholarships and Jack would have to cosign a loan.

What else could I do? If only Jack's price wasn't so high.

"Wear something formal."

I went downstairs to my old room. Band and model posters claimed the walls. Mom promised when we moved that I could decorate my room however I wanted. Quite a lot of power to put in a fourteen-year-old girl's hands. I painted the walls purple and put wallpaper on the ceiling. Everything from the chairs, to the couches, to the bed was soft, fuzzy, and plush.

A vision of me and Winter burrowed under the covers, drinking tea and watching movies flashed in my mind. I turned my back on the bed, facing the closet.

St. Thomas's was year-round, but Mom always let me come home for spring break and Christmas. The first meant bikinis and beach trips. The latter was balls and parties. As such, my wardrobe was composed entirely of two-pieces, ball gowns, and plaid skirts. Flicking through the sea of chif-fon, I settled on an ombre floor-length sleeveless stunner with a sweetheart neckline.

Thirty minutes later, I was showered, done up, and waiting for him at the bottom of the grand staircase. Jack came down in one of his gray be-spoke suits—alone.

"Mom isn't coming?"

He glanced at his watch rather than meet my eyes. "She's tired. She de-cided to catch an early night."

"Right."

"Shall we?" Jack offered his elbow.

I slid my arm through, accepting my fate. Tonight was a small price to pay if it meant getting justice for Winter.

Jack and I rode in painful, awkward silence. Once or twice we tried to start up a conversation. They fizzled out quickly.

"So," Jack began, trying again. "How did you get to the house?"

"I took a cab."

"That won't do. A cab driver drops you off at a home like ours and they start wondering if they should help themselves to more in your wallet than their tip."

I glared at him. "You know, you have a pretty low opinion of the work-ing class for someone who married a former housekeeper."

"Yes, and you have a rosy view of the world for someone who's been ex-posed to its hideousness."

Wincing, I replied, "Touché. I always wondered if that's what Mom saw in you. Give back as good as you get—unlike the other starched-shirt, wedgied-by-their-manners bores around here."

Jack laughed, shocking me. "That may have been part of it, but accord-ing to her, she fell in love with my humor and passion."

"What did you love about Mom?"

The lines around his mouth softened the way they only did when think-ing of her. "She was beautiful," he murmured. "Still is. The most beautiful creature I've ever seen. And when she laughs... it just about knocks you on your back."

I shifted to the window, the beginnings of my smile fading. "If I do this, do you think it will make Mom happy? Will she laugh again?"

Jack didn't reply, and I didn't look to see if the lines were back. We didn't speak for the rest of the ride.

I heard the party before I saw it. Music echoed through our small town, blanketing Regalia in sweet melodies. Our patch of earth was beautiful, but affluent communities tended to be. What set it apart was the entirely new way of separating people and putting them down. In the years since I'd lived part-time in Regalia, I never heard the words Royals and Dregs. Did they save that for the university? Another way to make college life harder than it needed to be?

Whatever the reason, the blanks were starting to fill in. My sister, step-daughter to an owner of a tire franchise, wasn't good enough for the old-money blueblood Royals. They singled her out—likely for breaking one of their idiotic rules. Then, they came at her relentlessly until she couldn't take it anymore.

Which begs the question, is it just a handful of Royals I need to take down, or the whole fucking system?

Jack pulled up to the valet who opened my door. Fancily dressed couples streamed around us, climbing the marble staircase into Wilson Mansion. Fairy lights strung along the banister and the columns, casting a shimmering glow on my gown.

Jack and I were almost to the door when I heard my name.

"Lu-Lu? Is that you?" Katie left a handsome middle-aged couple behind and bolted up the steps. Her gown was even prettier than mine. An A-line strapless number with layers upon layers of blue and gold. "It is you." Her eyes bugged taking in my dress. "Where the hell did you get that? Since when did the Wilsons pass Valentinos to the waitstaff?"

She locked on Jack, and our linked arms. "Ah, I see. This is your boyfriend. You know, you don't have to"—she waved her fist by her mouth, poking her cheek out with her tongue—"suck dick to get an invite."

Why did she mime it if she was just going to say it?!

"I would've slid you in on my arm." Katie pushed Jack off me. "Beat it, hairy balls. She's young enough to be your daughter."

Jack sputtered. "I beg your pardon."

"I am his daughter," I cried. "His stepdaughter."

"No shit? But— Hold on, you're Jack Bowden, aren't you? That means..." Katie's pre-programmed snobby smirk melted away as she beheld me with an expression I saw on her for the first time. "Sinclair."

My chest panged. Not letting myself think of the connection she just made, I reclaimed Jack's elbow, raising my chin as I faced the double doors. "Enjoy the party, Katie."

Together, the two of us continued on, passing by two butlers into one of the grandest homes in Regalia, fitting for one of its richest families.

My heels click-clacked on the marble floors, sounding in the cavernous white, blue, and silver space. Easy to hear as the music muted, signaling the start of something. A double staircase looped around and met at the top under a six-foot-wide crystal chandelier. People gathered near and beneath it, sipping champagne and trading pointless conversation. I looked at them with sharper eyes, picking out the Royals among us.

Releasing Jack's arm, I climbed the staircase, meeting the lone figure waiting at the top.

"You're late," he hissed.

"No, I'm not. I can't be late to my own party."

Cutting off a curse, Victor Wilson wrapped an arm around my waist, pulling me close. "Just smile. Look like you're happy to be here."

The MC cleared his throat. "Ladies and gentlemen, thank you all for coming. It's my honor to present to you for the first time since their engagement, Victor Wilson and Luna Sinclair. Join me in congratulating the couple and wishing them a long and happy marriage."

Cheers, applause, and whoops battered our ears. My fiancé and I cheesed till our faces hurt. I hoped our audience bought it, because we weren't fooling each other.

Chapter Two

Victor and I moved through the crowd, leading the way to the ballroom. The transformation was extraordinary. His mother spared no expense hosting the engagement party for her beloved son. Actually, I couldn't say if the pink rose centerpieces, votive candles, expensive spread, and our names spelled out in cupcakes were for Victor. It certainly wasn't for me since Martha didn't ask for my opinion on a thing.

For my contribution, Victor's mother put me through three rehearsals. Though she praised my getting a "proper" education at Catholic school, for some reason that didn't instill her with enough faith that I could remember the order of events, how to dance without stepping on Victor's toes, or how to eat with my mouth closed.

He swept me onto the dance floor—one hand holding mine and the other placed on the small of my back. We looked into each other's eyes as we waited for the music to start.

Victor Wilson was the opposite of me in almost every way. I was born to a single mom who cleaned houses like this to support me and my sister. He was born slurping from the silver spoons she polished. Victor's record was spotless. He never sank a yacht, got shipped off to boarding school, or so much as collected a speeding ticket. Victor Wilson was gifted by looks and talent.

His reddish-brown hair flashed amber when it caught the light. That was nothing compared to the effect of his mercury-gray eyes, seeing straight to your pounding heart whenever he smiled at you. If that wasn't enough, the man was an animal on the rugby field. Watching him play caused swooning in the stands—if you were into empty-headed jocks who can't hold a conversation or even look up from their phones long enough to have one. Or if they were into you.

"Don't step on my feet," Victor said as the music filtered out of the speakers.

"I'm not going to step on your fucking feet. I know how to dance—unlike someone who almost broke my back in half dipping me."

"If you weren't so stiff."

"If you weren't so rough!"

His cheeks twitched trying to hold his smile. "I'm not rough."

"You're a roided-up jock with meat hooks for hands. You'd break the bones in my face just trying to stroke my cheek."

"Like I would put my hands that close to your mouth. You're liable to bite them off, man-eating shrew."

"Oooh," I crowed. "Liable and shrew? Did Mommy hire another tutor to help you learn the big-boy words?"

"Did Stepdaddy marry you off to keep the big boys out of your pants?"

Victor whipped me around, lifting me off my feet. We smiled wider for the privileged mob cooing at us.

"You're one to talk. How many girls here have you slept with? And their mothers?"

Scoffing, Victor dipped me. "You shouldn't listen to rumors, Bowden. Then again, that's all you got since you're not one of us. What else do you have other than whispered scraps from people who didn't know you were in the room?"

"What else do you have other than a small dick?"

Victor choked—irritation briefly breaking his mask. "I fucking hate your ass."

"The feeling is mutual."

We straightened as the music wound down.

"Just remember why we're doing this," Victor said, releasing me. "It's so everyone gets what they want. After we're married, you'll live your life and I'll live mine."

I curtsied as he bowed. "Why wait until after? Outside of putting on a show for these fools, stay away from me."

"With pleasure."

We turned our backs on each other and walked off. I made it three steps when a missile in blue and gold seized me.

"Come with me," Katie ordered. "Now."

"What—? But— Katie!"

My protests were ignored. Katie marched me through a group of girls, two of them snapping at us to watch out. She dragged me all the way through the house to the back patio. Lights and linen-covered tables were set up, but the party had yet to venture this far.

Katie shoved me unceremoniously in a chair. "Out with it. Now. What the fuck are you playing at?"

"I'm not playing at anything." I stood and was pushed back on my ass. Add grabby to Katie's list of faults. "What is your problem?"

"What's my problem? You dressed up in that gross disguise and pretended like you didn't know about Regalia or the Royals. You're not Luna Sinclair. You're Luna Bowden." She folded her arms, hip cocked and eyes blazing. "Why?"

"It wasn't some trick. I did go to boarding school and, believe it or not, the history of Regalia's richest families didn't make the curriculum. I came back after graduation, but I've been staying in Jack's beach house up the coast. It's t-too hard to be at home." My voice cracked. "The only times I came into town over the summer was to see Victor. Since his parents didn't want anyone to know about the engagement until the invitations went out, they didn't go spreading my presence around." I matched her clench-jawed anger. "You don't need any more explanation, do you? You recognized my name."

She sniffed, flipping her hair over her shoulder. "Don't flatter yourself. I don't have *Sinclair* on web alert. Your sister was in my classes. We partnered on an English project. Professor Kensington announced it to everyone when she died."

"When she committed suicide," I corrected, getting in her face. "Right next to her in every single class, did you see it all, Katie? Did you watch your Royal friends torture her and say nothing because it had nothing to do with you? Why care about someone getting bullied when you're due to get your pussy licked in the library?"

Her lids fluttered, rolling her eyes. "Oh, please. I didn't know it was that bad. I saw a guy purposely spill a drink on her once. I told his ass off and gave her my jacket to cover up. Whatever else happened, I had no part in it.

I had my own shit going on last year—what with my mother battling cancer and all that. Outside of classes, I was barely on campus."

"I'm sorry to hear about your mom—"

"Shove your pity up your ass."

I heaved a sigh. "You're such a pleasant person."

"I get that way when people jerk me around. Why were you going around calling yourself Luna Sinclair when you're Luna Bowden? Why would you come to Regalia if you believe the Royals drove your sister to suicide?" Her eyes narrowed. "Why are you marrying one? Why did you ask me so much about them? Did you come back here for revenge?"

Got it in one, Katie Langford. You are many things, but not stupid.

"I came back here because I have to understand. Winter didn't leave a note," I lied. "I've been piecing together the time leading up to her death and all I know is she had trouble with people on campus. The only way to find out what happened was to come here, talk to people, talk to you. It's nothing to do with revenge and everything to do with closure. If someone you loved ended their life without a warning, wouldn't you need to know why?"

"Luna—"

"Wouldn't you?" I pressed.

Katie looked away and a tense silence swallowed us. "Fuck. Yes, okay?" she barked. "Yes, I'd need to know, but that doesn't make what you're doing a good idea. You may find out more than you want to know."

I already have. I swallowed past the needles in my throat. "I couldn't possibly feel any worse than I already do. At least this way, there's a chance of understanding why I'm living through hell."

Katie glanced back at the mansion. "What's all this crap, then, about you marrying Victor? I've known the guy my whole life. Fucked him twice over the summer. First I heard he was getting married was two weeks ago."

"You know, if we were secret star-crossed lovers, telling me he cheated on me over the summer isn't the cherry on top of my engagement party."

She shrugged. "Eh, whatever. If he used me to fuck around on you, you deserve to know. I'm looking out for you. Say thanks."

"Thanks?" I shook my head. "Good news is the marriage is arranged. That's not a secret. I'm sure most people figured it out since Victor never mentioned me."

"Why would you say yes to an arranged marriage?"

Because my stepfather refused to fund my tuition unless I did.

"Because the match makes sense," I replied instead. That was the line Victor's mother was giving people. It'd work for me as well. "Besides, from what Victor said, arranged marriages aren't uncommon around here. He said it's a say-I-do-or-lose-your-inheritance type thing in Regalia."

"Yeah, but only for guys whose parents are controlling shits who don't love them. Tough break for Victor." She patted my arm. "And you."

"You just insinuated my folks don't love me, but I have a feeling that was your attempt to commiserate and bond with me, so I'm letting it go."

She laughed. "Didn't insinuate it, Lu-Lu. This whole situation is garbage. Who forces their daughter to marry someone who cares so little about her he can't be bothered to keep it in his pants while the ring is on her finger? All the while she's grieving over losing her sister. Yeah, they're punishing your ass for something. Thankfully, I never have to worry about that. Just one of the many ways I'm blessed to be me."

"Now you ruined it, you asshole."

Katie only laughed louder. I was starting to suspect she was a sociopath.

"For real," Katie said, sobering. "I'm sorry about your sister. She was cool. When we worked on the project together, she brought me low-fat white chocolate lattes every morning because she knew it was my favorite. She wasn't sucking up either. She was just... being nice. The nice don't last long in this town," she said, sweeping over the landscape. "But that doesn't make it okay."

I swiped a tear off my cheek. "Thank you," I said softly. "Winter was the best person there ever was. Better than I could be. I'm glad to know at least someone stood up for her."

"Don't thank me." The edge in her reply made me look up. "I obviously didn't do enough. And though it may have sounded like I was, that wasn't an attempt to commiserate and bond either. That was a warning, Luna. Regalia University is brutal for those who don't attract the wrong attention, it's worse for those that do. If whoever bullied your sister finds out you're the new freshman, three guesses who they'll come after next.

"Driving a girl to suicide doesn't go up high on the résumé. They're not going to like you digging up what happened and ruining their reputation."

"What are you saying? I should keep my head down? There's no point hiding now. Winter went by Winter Bowden to make Mom happy, but it seems she let slip she's a Sinclair too. If you figured it out, other people will too. But it doesn't matter because I'm not going anywhere."

"I said my piece." Katie sauntered toward the door. "When shit turns bad and you're looking for who to blame, remember who warned you."

"I told you. There's nothing anyone can do to me now. I'm already in hell."

Katie paused, reaching for the door. If she was going to say something, she thought better of it and went inside.

I sank in the chair, dropping my face in my hands. Maybe there was a chance of me lying low if it wasn't for Martha and Jack insisting we announce the engagement to the whole fucking world.

I couldn't have hidden for long, sense said. *I hoped going by Luna Sinclair would give me protection, but in the end, I didn't come here to play undercover spy. I want those Royals to know who I am. They need to know exactly why they are being punished.*

"She's right, you know."

Jumping up, I spun around. Four ladies glided down the garden path, climbing the stairs onto the terrace. I recognized them as the group Katie and I walked through coming out of the party.

A girl in a long-sleeved sheer peach dress led the pack. Bold as well as beautiful, the dress's beading was strategically placed to cover her important bits. The rest of the dress left nothing to the imagination. Matching peach lipstick graced her full smiling mouth, and her long, blonde hair fell past her shoulders, adding up to the loveliest woman I've seen out of a magazine. I wished I could say she was the only one showing me up at my own party. Down the line, beautiful models in dresses worth as much as Bowden Manor surrounded me.

"I hope you don't mind that we listened in," said Peach Dress. "Your last name sounded familiar, so we followed you out to ask if there was any relation to a Winter Sinclair-Bowden. I guess we have our answer."

"I do mind actually."

She smiled, placing her hand over her heart. "My apologies. It was rude. Normally, I remember my manners, but we're quite surprised to find out Winter had a sister. How did she hide you from us? Are you full sisters? Half? Step?"

"Wow, you have forgotten your manners." I backed out of the circle they were enclosing me in. "You should at least give me your names before asking personal questions."

Her laugh tinkled with the bubbling garden fountain. "Of course, you're right. Forgive me, I'm used to everyone knowing who I am. My name is Saylor Burkhardt." She held out her hand palm down as if expecting me to kiss her fingers. "Pleasure."

"Gabriella Montana," said an Eva Longoria clone with black hair and red tips.

"Piper Alvar." Short blonde hair and pointed ears granted me visions of pixies. She winked at me like she saw what I did.

"Everleigh Starling," replied the final eavesdropper. She flicked her tawny brown fringe out of her hazel, dreamy eyes. I used to have bangs and then had to grow them out because they made me look younger. Everleigh didn't have that problem. If she told me she was a twenty-one-year-old international model, I'd have believed it.

"And you're Luna," Saylor drew out, closing the distance I put between us. "Did we hear right that you're Regalia University's newest freshman?"

"Correct."

Piper clicked her tongue. "Oh, no. What possessed you to enroll there after everything that happened?"

I tensed. Katie's warning rang through my head.

I'm just letting you know the rules so you survive here, Lu-Lu. Some of the Royals can be brutal to Dregs who forget their place.

Were they a few of the Royals she was talking about?

"If you were listening, you know why."

"Closure," Everleigh repeated like it was a foreign word. "That's it? That's all you want?"

"If it was us…" A slow, honeyed voice dripped from Gabriella's lips. "We'd want revenge."

I raised a brow. "Revenge against who exactly? Do you know something I don't?"

A smile stretched Saylor's peach mouth. "Us? What could we know? We don't concern ourselves with sad little Dregs and their problems." She said it so sweetly, the callousness took a beat to penetrate. "We do, however, make it our business to protect our own. Victor is one of us. So is his family. You better have good intentions for this little match. If you don't, well… engagements end every day."

I pointedly stepped back again, getting that woman out of my face. "Is there a reason you're threatening me? I wasn't aware we had a problem."

"Whether we do or don't is up to you." Saylor cocked her head. "You never did answer me. Was Winter Bowden your full-blooded sister, or did Jack Bowden slip the help an extra tip eighteen years ago?"

"I didn't answer you because that's a weird-ass thing for someone to ask. Winter was my sister, that's all you need to know." I picked up my skirt. "If you'll excuse me, the host can't spend all night talking on the porch. Enjoy the appetizers. Martha had them flown in from France."

"You should leave, Sinclair." Piper stopped me inches from the door. "You won't find closure here, and a nobody daughter of some tire seller isn't fit to marry a Wilson. Run away, little Lu-Lu. This isn't the place for you."

Turning, I gifted them a wide, beaming smile. "Ladies, I mean this sincerely: fuck you, you wannabe Regina George knockoffs. I'm not impressed by this weak intimidation routine, but I am amused by your false sense of superiority. Your nannies may have convinced you that you're perfect little princesses, but obviously they didn't notice your personalities rotting inside." The falsely sweet grins melted away. "So stop stalking my fiancé. Even if I left him, he still won't want any of you."

Lips curled, Piper advanced on me. Saylor swung out her arm, stopping her in her tracks.

I opened the door, passing inside. "One last thing, if my sister's name ever comes out of your mouths again, you're going to need another nose job."

The chandelier rattled with my slam. Steaming, I fled toward the party, thought better of it, and veered up the stairs. I had no idea where I was going. Martha and John, Victor's parents, gave me a tour, but we didn't make it higher than the first floor.

I stumbled down the hallway—chest tight, heart pounding. The noise, sounds, smells were pressing in, flooding my senses. I needed a break. I needed to breathe!

Throwing open a random door, I fell inside, almost running into a bookshelf. I found the library.

I rested my forehead on the cool wood, breathing deep and willing my heart to slow.

Those four were freshmen with Winter. They knew my sister. They know what she did, and a too big part of me suspected they witnessed what Owen and his friends did to her, and didn't blink an eye at the problems of someone who wasn't one of them.

"Rough night?"

Peering around the shelf, I landed on a figure cloaked in moonlight. He stretched out on a chaise placed beside a massive wrought iron window. Dangling from his long, tapered fingers was a decanter of golden liquid.

"Yes, actually."

"So rough you fled the joyous festivities downstairs? Shame."

Moving closer, a long face, neatly trimmed beard, and untamable curls unveiled in the soft glow. Irrational anger filled me. Another sinfully handsome rich prince appeared just in time to mock me. If these fuckers were so much better than everyone else, why couldn't they get it up without putting us down?

"Whatever turned your night sour," he said, "I bet all the priceless first editions in this library that it doesn't top mine."

My nails pierced my palm. "You don't want to make that bet. Trust me."

"You think? Pull up a seat." The stranger dropped his head against the window, gazing up at the ceiling. "I was told my genes are a ticking time bomb. There's a one-in-four chance I could pass a terrible illness on to my children, so I made what I still believe is the right decision to get a vasectomy."

I sat down, accepting the space he made for me.

"I talked to my fiancée about it. I told her what I was going to do. She disagreed with me. Said seventy-five percent were good odds, and I had to have faith." He shifted—eyes the color of his drink reflecting me. "Would you risk those odds? A twenty-five percent chance your kid would die slowly and painfully."

"No," I murmured. "I wouldn't."

"Neither could I, so I went through with it. Catalina threw my engagement ring at my head a day after I had the procedure. She told my parents an hour after that."

"Your parents? Why would she do that? You should've decided when you told them."

"See, that's what I said." He swept out the bottle, sloshing the contents over the rim. It was just hitting me he was drunk. "Catalina's response was to call me a selfish ass. My mother's wasn't too far off. My parents refuse to understand why I won't roll the dice. Honestly, they refuse to believe there's anything wrong with me at all," he said. "Nothing but healthy babies up and down my family tree. The first, second, and third doctor I went to all misdiagnosed me. They told me to reverse the procedure, get Catalina back, and work on providing them a grandson, or they'll disown me."

My jaw unhinged. *Okay, maybe this guy does have real problems.* "You're shitting me. They threatened to kick you out of the family if you don't have kids? What kind of sixteenth-century nightmare are we in?"

He snorted. "This is a twenty-first-century nightmare, except no one told my folks you're supposed to wake up from those and it's all over. This morning, they dissolved my trust fund, wrote me out of the will, threw me out of their house and said not to come back until I was ready to 'grow up and accept my responsibilities as their eldest son.'"

I made strangled noises trying to say something. Jack pushed me into an arranged marriage, but all he held over my head was tuition to a school we all hated. He'd never abandon or kick me out of the family—for my mom's sake if nothing else.

"I'm sorry. You had a heartbreaking decision to make. You were just trying to do the right thing."

"Alright." He closed my hand around the bottle. "Your turn."

It took me a second to realize what he was talking about. I had to share what made my night suck for all the first editions. Looking from him to the alcohol, I clocked the stranger as twenty-six—possibly twenty-seven. And too sloshed to notice I was a few years short of the drinking age.

I chanced a sip. Then another. Then five gulps. He shared an incredibly personal tragedy with me. If I was reciprocating, I needed what turned out to be fine scotch.

"You want my story? Here it is: four years ago, I was sent to a small Catholic boarding school in France. It was hard to keep in touch with my sister thanks to the lack of Wi-Fi, no cell phones, and internet usage restricted to the computer lab with a sister standing over my shoulder, watching me. Still, my sister and I didn't let that get in our way. We talked and video-chatted every week.

"But last year... she was different. She missed calls, and when we did link up, she didn't say much. Our two-hour-long conversations barely cracked twenty minutes. I *knew* something was wrong," I rasped. "But she wouldn't tell me.

"Two weeks before graduation, my sister jumped off Zibia Bridge and drowned."

His cloudy pools cleared. My friend was sobering up quickly.

"Mom collapsed outside the coroner's office. She couldn't go in, so an hour and a half after my plane touched down, I was driven to the coroner to identify my big sister's body."

"Fucking hell," he breathed.

"Couldn't have said it better." I swallowed a healthy swig. "But you asked what made tonight so awful. I'm marrying a guy who wants nothing to do with me, because he's tight with the people who bullied Winter till she killed herself. The same people who basically told me to fuck off or they'd drive me out." I hugged my knees to my chest, resting on the window. "I wasn't supposed to do this without her. Winter and I planned our weddings to the last detail—including her maid of honor dress."

I didn't know my cheeks were wet until he stroked them, staining his fingers with my tears.

"I wasn't meant to pretend life goes on with the very monsters who drove Winter to end hers." I laughed mirthlessly. "What do you think? Do I win? Because losing the family you have and the family you wished for all in one diagnosis is pretty fucking crushing too."

"I'm not so callous as to declare you a winner. I'm sorry I suggested a bet... and I'm sorry about your sister. If she's anything like you, she was a special person. The world is worse off without her in it."

My chest cracked on a sob. "How can you say that? You don't know me."

"Most of the crowd downstairs would agree with my parents' decision to disown me while you're here drinking with a complete stranger, saying what I wished to hear someone say since this nightmare started—that I made the right choice. That's enough for me to start with."

Despite myself, a tiny smile pricked my lips. "Names would be a good place to start too." I wiped my face, tucking my grief back into a place it'd do me the most good and fuel into hatred. I wasn't crying anymore. It was time for the Royals to do that.

"I'm Luna."

"Luna." Something flashed in his eyes, so quick I figured it was the remains of his buzz. "Nice to meet you. My name's Adonis."

My brows flew up my forehead. "Adonis? As in the Greek god of beauty? This time you are shitting me."

He laughed too loud, tugging giggles out of me. "I'm afraid it's true. They put Adonis on the birth certificate. Now you see the people I've been dealing with my whole life."

"Don't get me started. At least you weren't named after your parents' adventurous sex life. Winter for my sister because she was conceived while they were camping in the snow. Luna for me because I came along during a moonlit picnic."

"Got a thing for outdoor sex. Can't blame them."

"Ugh," I cried, clapping my hands over my ears. I forgot about the scotch and splashed half in my hair. "Imagine that being one of the only things your mother told you about your dad. He was handsome, kind, and—oh yeah, he drops his pants in the dirt."

We fell against each other laughing.

"I can't top that, but I've got my stories. When I was eight, my father left me at the zoo. He said forgetting me was a mistake, but I've always suspected he secretly hoped the chimps would adopt me. Park security popped that dream."

Cracking up, I helped myself to more.

"I feel compelled to ask if you're old enough to drink, Luna."

"Squash the compulsion. You just got disowned and I'm a commercial for antidepression meds. No one needs a drink more than us."

"I hear you." He said that but the decanter was suddenly out of my hands and placed on the floor beside him. "I was supposed to get married last weekend. I should be sailing the Mediterranean on a month-long honeymoon right about now."

I groaned. "Italy, France, Spain, Morocco. You should've gone without her."

"The only thing more pathetic than drinking your sorrows above a party you weren't invited to, is going on a honeymoon alone."

"No, the only thing more pathetic than drinking your sorrows above a shitty party is being the sad acts printed on the invitations, bringing the whole town out to celebrate two people who can't stand each other. You, Adonis, would have no shortage of young, nubile backpackers willing to help you forget about your ex-fiancée. On my honeymoon, my bedsheets will see as much action as a nunnery."

"Hmm." Adonis scrunched up his face. "Tell me more about these nubile young backpackers."

I nudged his arm. "Mindy, Tracy, and Belinda are going to tell you about themselves while asking you to rub suntan lotion on their backs for the fifth time."

A low chuckle rolled out of his chest. "I know. I get it. Feels like the end of my life now, but I'm young and I've got my health. One day, I'll meet someone who understands why I did what I did, and if she wants a family too, she'll explore the other options with me. Until then, I've got a degree and a job. I didn't need my parents' money before and I don't need it now that it's gone. I'll be okay." He laid his hand over mine. "Will you?"

"No." I didn't have to think about it, or look into some far-off future. The day the medical examiner pulled back the sheet on my sister's blue and bloated face, I knew I'd never be okay again. "But in a way, that's good. This pain is a part of me now. It drives me to honor her memory, and do for her what Winter couldn't do herself. If I can't live with her, then living for her is the next best thing."

"What kind of life will it be if you're married to a man you don't love?"

I inclined my head. "Not as regretful as you're thinking. I'm doing this for Winter too. As hard as it is, if I had to go back, I'd make the same decision."

The corner of his mouth tugged up, revealing a dimple. "You're an intriguing woman, Luna Sinclair."

"How did you—?"

"You're one of the sad acts on the invitations, remember."

That set off another round of uncontrollable giggling.

I don't know how long we sat in there, trading sad stories, and laughing till my full bladder threatened to burst.

"Wait here." I pushed up too hard and almost fell flat on my face. Adonis didn't move the scotch far enough out of reach. "I've got to go to the—the bathroom."

"Where am I going to go? No one's waiting up for me."

"Oh, Adonis." I cupped his cheek. It wasn't a conscious thought. One moment those kiwi-fuzz eyes were caressing me, and the next there was no distance between us. I kissed him—a quick peck that zinged electricity through my veins and flushed the alcohol out of my system. I was sober, and suddenly acutely aware of what I just did.

Jumping back, my hands flew off him. "I'm sorry. I didn't mean to— That was just to comfort you, I swear."

Adonis blinked at me, lips still parted.

"I really didn't— I'm just going to go." Picking up my feet, I rushed out of the library.

"Luna, wait."

I shot through the door and ran into a hard chest. "Luna, there you are. Heavens, what is that smell?" Jack cried. "Have you been drinking?"

Oh yes, my buzz was fading fast. "A little."

"A little? You smell like a brewery! Hurry up. Get in the bathroom and fix yourself up. It's time for toasts."

I did as he said, recalling our deal as I spritzed perfume on my head and prayed it covered up the scotch rinse. I played the good little fiancée and Jack didn't pull me out of Regalia U. All things were worth it, even the loathsome Victor Wilson, if it meant Winter got justice.

Plastering a smile on my face, I entered the ballroom, finding and draping an arm around Victor. We posed for flashing cameras.

"Where were you?" he asked out of the corner of his mouth.

On the other side of the room, Saylor, Piper, Gabriella, and Everleigh sipped champagne, making no secret that they were watching me.

"I was off remembering why we're doing this. You don't have to worry about me, Wilson. I'm seeing this through." I locked on Saylor's gaze. "To the end."

Chapter Three

Tuesday morning, I dressed in a spring break leftover outfit—a blue flowy cutout dress and silver wedges. I was due a shopping trip over the weekend to update my wardrobe, and get warmer clothes for the Regalia fall.

Mom used to love shopping with me. Maybe I can get her to come.

Moving down the line on my dresser, I tucked pepper spray, a safety alarm, a stun baton, and a self-defense key chain in my backpack. The last to go was Winter's note. I picked it up, continuing where I was forced to leave off the day before.

Alright, it all started the first day of school when I ran into Owen Thasher at a back-to-school frat party. The girls on my floor invited me. I thought it would be fun to hang out and make some friends.

Owen latched on to me the second I walked through the door. He acted sweet at first, asking me where I was from, what I liked to do, about my family, and what I was studying. When it got obvious I wasn't going to sleep with him, he turned into a skeeze, going on about how lucky I was he was wasting his attention on me. I told him I wished I was unlucky, so he'd stop blowing his rank taco breath in my direction.

Maybe that's why when it all started, Owen was one of the worst to come at me. Painting frigid bitch on my door. Leaving disgusting messages on my phone all day and night from hundreds of random numbers. Getting his buddies to follow me around, moaning and pawing me.

I changed my number six times and had to get campus security to walk me to and from class. By the end of the semester, I barely left my room. He was always out there waiting to call me a dime-bag slut who should've taken it like a good girl and shut my fucking mouth.

It escalated. Getting worse and worse between me and the Royals until they decided to put me in my place once and for all. The day I returned from spring break, Owen broke into my room, dragged me out of the shower, and

I stopped there. Sliding on my jacket, I put the note in the inside pocket where it'd be safe.

In the end, Owen Thasher wasn't satisfied with daily, constant harassment. When he saw my sister wouldn't be beaten, he set out to break her for good.

It was terrible for Winter that this school put everyone on a predictable schedule and those guys knew where she was every day... and that fact would be twice as misfortunate for Owen.

He's a sophomore. He's in general education classes this year. I shut off the lights, getting the last of my things as I made for the door. *Once I get my hands on his class schedule, I'll know how he spends the day and where he sleeps. Filling in the in-between will be easy.*

I stepped down and locked my door.

"Oh, Lu-Lu Sinclair, you're a Thor-damned tragedy." Katie posted up on the opposite wall, sipping what I suspected was a low-fat white chocolate latte. "Cutout dresses are so three years ago. How are you not ashamed walking around in public like this?"

"Good morning, Katie," I sighed. Katie's outfit was a tie-waist shirt dress and suede boots. "Sorry to hear another outfit doesn't meet your standards, but I clearly have good enough self-esteem to deal with it, or your constant put-downs would curl me up in a ball in that corner."

"This isn't about you anymore. I've got to walk next to you. Thor forbid anyone thinks I befriended some sad little Dreg who can't dress herself." She checked her phone. "Okay, I've got a thing at eleven, but the dean can wait. We're going shopping."

"I was going to do that later anyway. Make your meeting with the dean."

"At this point, I can't trust you. I'm taking you and I'm not hearing an argument about it." Katie strode off, tossing over her shoulder, "Money is no object."

"Are you asking me or telling me?" I cried.

"You should know me well enough by now to answer that. Keep up."

For the life of me, I'd never understand the person who accepted Kate Langford's application to guide innocent, unsuspecting freshmen and said she'd be a great fit.

I jogged to her side. "Thor forbid. I like it."

"Chris Hemsworth can give me his hammer any time. He's the god I worship."

My Catholic education forbade me from continuing the conversation. "What's on the student agenda today?"

"I've got to show you where your classes are and then you've got a meeting with your adviser to go over your academic goals for the semester. You're most likely going to miss it. Fixing you will take all day."

"What if I don't want to miss the meeting?"

She gave me a look.

"Yes, yes," I sang. "I know you better—"

Someone knocked my shoulder. "Oops, sorry." Owen Thasher swung in front of me, gripping my arm. "You okay, lovely?"

My skin crawled. Throwing him off, I snapped, "I'm fine."

His grin widened, raking me up and down. Hair shaved close to the scalp and pale blond eyebrows made him look a bit like a hairless monk. It disgusted me that he was handsome regardless. Wicked grin, strong jaw, and athletic body—the guy didn't understand no because people rarely said it to him.

From the glint in his eyes, he didn't think my outfit was a crime against humanity. "Haven't seen you around. Freshman?"

"Yes."

"Where you from?"

"A place where we execute people for being late." I snagged Katie's sleeve. "I have to go."

I sidestepped him, dragging Katie after me. She freed herself outside at the bottom of the steps.

"Do you know who you just blew off? Owen's father sells the luxury cars your stepdaddy wishes would wear his tires."

"My stepdaddy doesn't need Owen or his father. That guy is the shit that shit shits, and someone's got to make him cry for it. You're worse than self-involved if you pretend you don't know what he is."

"Calm down, Sinclair." Katie pulled a compact out of her bag and puckered her lips at her reflection. "We've established your parents don't like you very much, don't go pissing away your only friend."

"Since when are we friends?"

"You love me. I'm still deciding if you're worth my time. So far, you're off to a bad start."

My jaw worked for a full ten seconds trying to form the words against that nonsense. I made no secret of my feelings for Katie Langford. When exactly did she turn that into love?

"I don't deny the guy's an ass," Katie continued. "He's got selective hearing. Funny that it only goes when a girl says no."

My irritation leaked out. Katie wasn't that self-involved. She saw what Owen was.

"This is me warning you again, Lu-Lu. You say you're not worried about him, but you should always worry about insecure boys with small dicks and big bank accounts. Piss him off and he'll make life difficult for you, and your life will be difficult enough when everyone finds out a Dreg bagged one of the most eligible guys around."

I couldn't comment on what she said about Owen being dangerous. Not without crying. No one knew that more than me... and Winter. "That's it? It's already decided that I'm a Dreg?"

She nodded. "There are only three kinds of people around here, Sinclair. The Royals—families that were established decades ago, their kids, and their kids' kids. Once in a while, new money claims the title, but that's for people who invent the iPhone or something. Kings of a tire empire and his stepdaughter don't make the cut.

"Then, like I told you, there are the Rogues. Four guys who don't have the standing of a Royal, but no one would think of fucking with them. Only an idiot would get on their bad side. Last year, Cooper Trace thought it'd be funny to play a prank on the paranoid Wilder. Cooper woke up the next morning, his family's bank accounts were frozen and he somehow ended up on the terrorist watch list. TSA tackled his ass in the security line when his family tried to fly to Saint-Tropez."

"I'm still eighty-two percent sure you're exaggerating about those guys."

Katie laughed. "The point is, if you're not a Royal or a Rogue, you're a Dreg. End of."

"Sounds stupid and the very reason why we don't have a monarchy in this country."

"You're getting my point, right? Like, I don't need to draw you a map or color you a picture in crayons." She knocked on my forehead. "Is this thing receiving me?"

Katie grabbed my head, talking into it like it was a microphone. "Don't. Fuck. With. The. Royals," she shouted. "Someone should make Owen cry, but it's not going to be you. I won't have anything happen to you."

I untangled myself from her, smile tugging at my lips. "Won't have anything happen to me? Are you saying you care about me?"

Katie rolled her eyes. "Now who's self-involved? Look, your sister was cool." She raised her latte. "Her fashion sense wasn't any better than yours, but I kind of liked her. I don't want what happened to her to happen to her sister too."

"Seems like you think it will anyway. I'm a Dreg marrying a Royal."

"That's right, so don't make it worse."

Katie walked me to the English building and showed me Professor Anthony's class. Our next stop was supposed to be to the communications building for my speech class, but a guy in shorts and sunglasses called her name as we were walking out of the English building, and she was gone.

"Bye, Lu-Lu. I'll pick you up here in two hours for our shopping date." She ran into his arms, gifting a kiss that got everyone in the vicinity hot under the collar. I assumed that was the infamous Dean who fucked like a beast.

Shaking my head, I got my map out of my backpack and continued on. Classes started officially on Thursday, giving us three days of orientation. I was all for getting new students acquainted and teaching them the ropes before throwing them into their first day, but what happened to groups, perky tour guides, and silly icebreaker games?

Wouldn't want new students to bond and make friendships before the caste system assigned their worth.

I found where I was on the map and turned right, heading in the opposite direction of the communications building. I needed to get my hands on a class schedule. My first method was to go to the registrar's office and just ask. If that didn't work, I'd get creative.

"Luna Sinclair."

I jerked, heart shooting into my throat. Rafael Dumont strolled casually by my side, headphones snug over his ears. "Fucking hell! Where did you come from?"

"My mother."

"Cute." I dug my palm into my beating chest. "You scared the mess out of me. Don't sneak up on people."

"You're Luna Sinclair, correct? Winter Sinclair-Bowden's younger sister."

My face shuttered closed. "What about her?"

"I'm asking you," he said, grinning. "It's a simple question. Answer it already."

"Yes, she was my sister. Why do you want to know?"

Rafael's grin faded. "Because I'm sorry for your loss. Winter was good people. She treated everyone the same and was never weird around Cato." He gestured with his chin, drawing my attention to my other side and the guy with the skull muzzle walking silently next to me. My second fright of the morning. "We're both sorry. We wanted to go to the funeral, but your stepdad said it was family only. We sent flowers though."

"You did?" I slowed. "Which ones?"

"The carnations, chrysanthemums, and—"

"Orchids," I finished. "I wondered where that one came from. It was unsigned. Those flowers were all my sister's favorites. How did you know? Were you friends?"

"We were in the same class. She mentioned once that they were her favorites. I remembered."

The wide, cavernous pit where my heart used to be widened further. Tears pressed behind my eyes. "Th— Thank you," I croaked. "No one else in her class sent flowers. No one else c-cared."

"Everyone else in her class is a selfish, empty-headed fuck who thinks decency is a town in France."

"Yes." I seized his arms. "Yes, they are. You know. You saw what they did to her."

Rafael's face tightened and he looked away. "I saw enough. I want you to know we didn't all sit by and do nothing. When those shits started stalking her around campus, she asked for guards to escort her and the administration was going to say no. They didn't have enough to guard one student. I helped," he said carefully, "the dean find money in the budget to hire more.

"Wilder gave her self-defense gear. Lucien taught her some moves, and Cato threw Ian Bexley in a dumpster and tossed a match in after him when he saw Ian trip Winter coming down the stairs." Rafael shrugged. "He lived—if that matters."

My breaths came out too fast, making my head light.

"We tried to do more, but Winter told us to stay out of it. This was between her and the Royals, and she could take care of herself. We listened, and that was the biggest mistake we ever—"

I launched at him. Throwing my arms around him, I squeezed Rafael till he grunted, bawling into his chest. "Thank you, Rafael. You don't know— I thought she was all alone. That no one here gave a shit about her, or tried to help."

"We *didn't* help."

"You wanted to." I gazed into tortured, raging eyes. "That's more than can be said for everyone else on this campus, including the dean who had to be pushed into action. You wanted to," I whispered.

Releasing him, I turned on Cato.

Rafael rushed, "Hold up—"

His brother's low growl sounded its own warning. Uncaring, I hugged him, burrowing my face in his neck. He saw someone hurt my sister and risked jail or another psych ward to make him pay for it. If he wasn't wearing a muzzle, I'd kiss him.

"Thank you."

Cato was stiff in my hold. The growling stopped, though he didn't move or lift his arms to hug me back. Leather pressed against my cheek, soft and tickling, rubbing up and down. What was he—?

Hands grasped my waist. "You've tempted fate long enough, darling." Rafael peeled me off his brother. "And no more crying," he said, holding my chin between two fingers like before. He gently wiped my tears on his sleeve. "Making a lady cry first thing in the morning means I owe you a favor to make it up. Whatever you want."

"You don't owe me anything more."

"Where are you headed now?"

"The registrar."

"We'll walk you."

The guys fell in step with me. We walked a wide path lined with old brick buildings and freshly clipped grass. Everywhere I looked, twosomes went about campus—one talking animatedly and pointing things out. Freshmen and their guides. Where was mine? Doing things she'd likely tell me about in unwanted detail later.

I snuck glances at the Dumont brothers on the walk. Rafael turned his music back on at some point. He shuffled on his heels, head bobbing.

I tapped his headphones. "I've heard things about you and your friends."

"All true."

"They can't be," I said with a chuckle. "Someone said your friend Lucien thinks he's a one-hundred-and-fifty-eight-year-old vampire."

"Looks great for his age, doesn't he?"

"Come on. Be serious."

"The guy who turned him was some lonely old shopkeeper who got tired of living an eternity alone. Lucien started working for him, they became friends, and he decided eternity was for two. They had a falling out and split ways a hundred years ago. Lucien's been moving around ever since, collecting degrees. He finished architecture four years ago, so now he's studying history."

I waited for him to laugh.

Nothing.

"Okay," I drew out. "So, what's your story? People say some pretty wild things about your dad."

"Like what?"

"That he's a—" I cast about for the word. "A fixer, or something like that."

"He's not a fixer."

I bobbed my head, throwing up my hand. "See? I knew it was non-sense."

"Pops is a hit man," Rafael dropped. "Totally kills people for money. I'm only telling you this because if you repeat it, I'll deny it, and there are no bodies to link him to the crime either way."

I gaped at him. Swinging to Cato, he snapped at me from behind the mask. I didn't know what the fuck kind of reply that was.

Weirdos. Complete and total psychos like Katie said. Kind psychos who tried to help Winter, but it's becoming real obvious why she didn't accept their help.

"We're the fixers." Rafael shook a finger between him and his brother. "Got a problem, we'll take care of it. For the right price, of course."

The administration building appeared up ahead, and just in time. It was time to part ways. I appreciated these guys for everything they did, but the one thing I did not come here to do was make friends. I couldn't have distractions. People asking where I was while I tracked the Royals. Girls banging on my door begging me to party with them while I planned my revenge against Owen and his pals.

Katie was already getting in the way—dragging me out onto the balcony for a conversation that was heard by the wrong people, and warning me off Owen. The last thing I needed was the Rogues dripping their nonsense about Victorian vampire shopkeepers and hit men dads in my ear.

"Thanks for the escort and for what you did for my sister." I picked up the pace to the stairs. "I've got to..." My brush-off trailed away as the doors opened.

Piper, Everleigh, Gabriella, and Saylor filed out. Saylor wore long white pants, flats, and a satin one-sleeve top with a huge bow on her shoulder. The look should've turned her into a thirty-nine-year-old society wife. Instead she looked like that wife's hot personal designer.

"Luna Sinclair. What are you doing here? Putting in your transfer papers?"

"I'm afraid not."

"Oh, well then, isn't it a good thing we caught you?" She smiled and spoke like we were two chums sitting down for tea. "You *are* going to transfer out of this school, pack a bag, and put our town in your rearview mirror. You'll do it today. This is the last time we'll discuss this," she said lightly, smile reaching no higher than her mouth. "If you're not gone by the end of the week, Regalia University will become an unhappy place for you."

"Are you threatening me?"

She gasped. "Oh, sweetie, no. I never make threats. I leave that to un-cultured thuggish swine who say they'll break your nose if you talk about their sister."

Anger clamped my throat.

"No, that wasn't a threat," she said. "It was advice that you should take. I'm only looking out for you." Saylor dropped her voice to a whisper. "People around here can be really mean. I heard some pathetic little Dreg got picked on and ended up on a ledge. They fished her out of the lake three days later like a floating bag of trash. No one wants that to happen to you too."

I reeled my fist back. Something flashed out of the corner of my eye.

Rafael secured my hand, bringing it down by my side. He didn't let go.

"Morning, ladies."

Their demeanor changed instantly. Gabriella and Everleigh checked their hair. Piper tugged her tank top down, exposing more cleavage. And Saylor dropped her fake smile for a real one. I was surprised by their behavior but only a little. Rafael was one of the most handsome men I've ever seen in person or on the screen.

"Hey, Rafael." Saylor angled to put me at her back, sliding between us. "Did you have a good summer?"

"The best. Dad took us out on international waters. Two months diving and deep-sea fishing till the heat died down."

The four of them laughed. Saylor and Gabriella slid in closer, touching his arm.

"You ladies clearly spent your summer getting more gorgeous. Damn, give us weak, mortal men a chance."

Saylor giggled. "What would be the fun in that?" She flicked down to the hand he still had wrapped around mine. Her lips flattened to a thin line and the first flash of the person behind the sweet little heiress mask flashed through the cracks. "I'm sorry. I didn't realize you two were friends."

"We are," Rafael said without skipping a beat. "Close friends."

"Aww, Rafael," Everleigh said. She crowded in close behind Saylor, and in front of me. "I've always loved that about you. You do favors for everyone, even the lowliest Dreg."

"Charity work," Piper added.

I didn't see who it was. Out of nowhere, one of them grabbed my waist and flung me aside. I stumbled on the steps, crying out as I caught myself. The Royal girls immediately took my space and surrounded him. Cato disappeared somewhere, but they didn't mind in favor of having Rafael to themselves.

"You should run along," Saylor called over their heads. "You have something you need to do in administration."

"So, Rafi," Everleigh purred. "Are you doing anything this weekend? Owen's throwing an ABC party."

My ears pricked up. They had my full attention.

"It's a little back-to-school thing," Piper said. "Royals only. And you."

"What about my boys?"

"The invitation is only for one." Gabriella walked her fingers up his chest. "So don't even think about bringing a date."

"Yeah," said Saylor. "We—"

Raucous barking cut through the air. Cato burst through them, knocking the girls aside like bowling pins. Screeching, they took off running—Cato baying and chasing them down the steps.

Rafael dusted off his shirt, strolling up to me with a grin like nothing happened. "Anyway, like I was saying. We're a full-service operation. Anything you need." He slid his fingers through mine, turning up my palm. "Anything. Just call me." He placed a scrap of paper on my hand.

"Why would I need—?"

Rafael flicked his music back on. He skipped a jaunty dance down the steps, hit the bottom with a slide, then Charleston'd away.

"So much weird inside so much gorgeous," I mumbled, crumpling the paper and tossing it in the trash. "At least Cato drove the Royal Wenches away."

Putting them out of my mind, I tracked down someone in administration and asked for a copy of the sophomore class schedule. It was surprisingly easy. All I had to do was tell the lady I lost mine, and she printed out another with no more questions asked.

It was a good thing Katie ditched me. I scoped out all the buildings, but not the ones that held my classes. I tracked down the ones for Owen, his friends, Saylor and the rest of them. Of course, there were two sophomore classes and I couldn't be sure which one they were in. According to Katie, the schedules and class times were the same except flipped. If Class *A* has English Monday and Wednesday, Class *B* has it Tuesday and Thursday. I'd figure out where they all were after two days.

Katie was late to meet me for shopping after the big deal she made of it. I gave her a look that she ordered me to wipe off my face and replace with gratitude. It was a privilege to have Katie Langford as my personal shopper—her words.

Eight hours later, I staggered into Abbott Hall loaded with bags. Katie went wild tossing clothes at me. My input wasn't required. My putting things back wasn't allowed. It was a good thing my stepfather set up an account for me to make purchases throughout the school year. I just hoped he wouldn't find out it was almost depleted in the first week.

I closed in on my door, awkwardly fishing the keys out of my purse. I hooked my finger through the ring and it slipped off.

"I've got it."

My head snapped up as Owen jogged down the hall.

"No, don't. I don't need help."

"Come on. You're no less an independent woman just because a guy helps you with your bags." Grinning, he plucked my keys up and turned it in the door, sweeping a hand for me to go in. "After you, milady."

Jaw clenched, I edged around him.

"By the way." His whisper poured in my ear. "I know who you are, Sinclair. We all do."

A chill climbed my spine, stopping me in my tracks.

"What the hell were you thinking coming here? And with a Royal's ring on your finger? You gold-digging Dregs just don't know when to quit."

"Fuck y—"

He flashed, grabbing my neck and slamming my head against the doorjamb. "No, bitch, fuck you!"

My bags crashed on the floor. Grip tightening, he forced the air from my throat in desperate gasps. I fumbled at my zipper.

"I spent all of last year on your stupid slut of a sister, teaching her that this is *our* school and we make the rules. You'd think you'd catch the hint and know you're not welcome here, but it seems you need a lesson too."

I got my hand in, frantically scrambling for my gear. Black bled into my vision.

"The first time, it was to see if I could. This time I'm going to do it for fun." Owen's hot breath burned my watering eyes. "You're going the same way as your sister, *Luna*. I give you two months before you're floating facedown in the lake."

Owen shoved me away. I sucked in deep lungfuls, corrosive hatred scouring every breath. My fingers closed over the stun baton.

Turning his back, he marched off, trampling my bags under his boots. I jammed the baton between his shoulder blades.

"Ahhh!"

I couldn't tell who screamed louder. Owen seized—body convulsing as the electricity burned his veins. He collapsed, flopping on the floor, and I hit him again. And again.

And again.

Chest heaving, I bore over him, picking his head up by the hair. "You're messing with a different sister now, bitch."

Owen was out cold. He didn't hear me, but the students poking their heads out of their dorms did.

"You're all going to pay for what you did to her. Being stunned till you piss yourself on the hall floor will be Disneyland compared to what you've got coming to you."

"Hey!" Two guys thundered down the stairs, racing toward me.

Grabbing my things, I slammed into my room—bolting the lock and shoving a desk chair beneath it. Outside, they pounded on the wood, demanding I come out.

I slid down the wall—adrenaline and rage humming in my bloodstream.

I wasn't afraid, and I was far from crying. This was always going to happen when the Royals realized I was here to avenge Winter. It happened faster than I expected and Owen skipped from taunts straight to violence. It didn't faze me.

I came here to burn, destroy, lay waste to all in my path. Surviving the war didn't matter. Winning it does.

Blowing out a breath, I stroked my sore throat.

It begins.

THURSDAY MORNING, I chose a red turtleneck sweater dress from my closet and paired it with black boots. The bruise from Owen's good night hadn't faded.

It was the first day of classes. According to the sophomore class schedule, they had their first class of the day at seven and my freshman English class was at eight. It gave me an hour to walk free and eat breakfast without running into Owen or his friends.

I stuck my head out the door to be sure, hand clutching the stun gun. His friends swore while they were shouting through my door that they'd get me back.

No one was there. I left and headed for the breakfast hall. Heavenly smells wafted out the door, drawing me in with a grumbling belly.

The buffet selections changed every day because that's the world I lived in now. At St. Thomas's, we had three items available for breakfast: cereal, oatmeal, and frozen pancakes. That morning, I loaded my plate with a veggie quiche, chocolate chip monkey bread, and vanilla bean French toast. Hey, I put the veggie quiche on my plate. That's healthy enough.

Stepping off the line, I searched for a table. Mock whispers hit my ear as I weaved past the chairs.

"...she's that girl's sister..."

"...marrying a Wilson..."

"...heard she crashed a boat and got sent to a nunnery..."

"...total trash..."

"...worthless Dreg..."

"Gold digger."

Lifting my chin, I sat down at a booth in the back, pretending I didn't see the people who dropped their bags on the empty seats. I picked up my knife and fork and cut into my French toast.

A tray dropped next to mine. Victor pulled up a chair and got comfortable. I froze with my breakfast halfway to my mouth.

"Excuse me? What are you doing?"

"What does it look like?" He was fresh from a shower. Droplets clung to the nape of his neck, running free down his merry-go-round curls. Sweet scents of bergamot and candy apples hit my nose, wrinkling it.

"You smell like you just got out of some girl's shower."

"You smell like you just got off the food stamp line." He sniffed me. "Ah, yes, eau de poor."

"Will you get run over by a car already?"

To my surprise, he chuckled. "Ah, Sinclair. Our battle of wits is always fun, but now that we've announced our engagement, we need to set some ground rules."

My eyes narrowed to slits. Victor had a pleasant, even tone, but he never used it on me. "What kind of ground rules?"

"If we're going to fight or argue, we don't do it in public. Everyone knows that this is an arranged marriage, but they don't have to know it's an unwanted one. It'll start up all kinds of questions that we don't need."

I made a noise in my throat. "It'll start up questions from other people? I'm the one with questions, Victor. My stepdad and your parents arranged this whole thing, and I still don't know why. What is everyone getting out of this?"

"You know the answer to that. The Wilsons have a stake in almost every industry—including Formula One racing. Your stepdad is about to become an exclusive tire supplier for the big leagues."

"I did know that," I said, boring into the side of his head. "What I don't know is what the Wilsons get out of the arrangement."

He blew out a breath. "If I tell you the truth, will you agree to my rules?"

"Before I've heard them?"

"Yes."

I hesitated—a bit too long since he turned back to his breakfast.

"Guess you'll never know."

"Fine," I blurted. "I'll agree to the rules. Tell me why Martha Wilson is so eager to have me as her daughter-in-law."

Victor glanced around, lowering his voice. "Strategic, mutually beneficial marriages are common in Regalia, but not at eighteen. If we did this the right way, our engagement party would be held in our late twenties—giving us both a chance to study, date, travel, have flings, and enjoy ourselves before we settle down. For all the other eligible women in Regalia, they're attached to that tradition and aren't willing to give up their freedom eight years early." He grinned. "You, Sinclair, were."

"That's it?" My mind struggled with the explanation. "It was me because Jack was willing to enter me in the broodmare race first? What about you? Why would you want to get married now?"

"My father's sixty-eight years old. He has a weak heart, diabetes, and a bunch of other health issues. He needs to retire, but he won't because he won't appoint a successor to run Wilson Industries.

"He said I wasn't a man." Victor's grip tightened on the fork. "I didn't have a wife, family, or responsibilities. A few months ago, I was in high school, asking permission to use the bathroom. What did I know about running a multimillion-dollar company? He doesn't believe I can do this, and the stubborn ass is going to kill himself rather than give me a chance."

Victor gestured between us. "I will prove him wrong. Once he sees I can handle a wife, a home, and kids—"

My eyes bugged at kids.

"—he'll trust the company is in good hands. Mom is on board with this too. She's been begging him to retire for five years."

I studied him, searching for a trace of dishonesty. Victor held my gaze without blinking.

"Wow, Wilson. That's almost... noble."

He scoffed. "Don't go getting a crush on me. I still wish my parents arranged for me to marry literally anyone else. Our forty-two-year-old housekeeper, June, would've been a better candidate."

"If I was in danger of forming a crush, you just killed it dead. Actually, you killed any chance of me liking you when at our first meeting, you snapped your fingers at me and said to fetch you iced tea because you thought I was the help. You asked my net worth over dinner, and then after, I found you in the closet with said June's daughter on her knees, blowing you. Enough pompous ass to last me a lifetime."

"You're no caramel sundae yourself, sweetheart. I didn't know then that you were going to accept the proposal. I thought our families were still discussing. Last I checked, I wasn't required to be faithful to some random girl who *might* marry me. And afterward, I apologized and asked you out to make it up to you three times. Each time, you blew me off."

"Maybe because I was doing this thing called mourning!"

"We don't argue in public, remember?"

Steaming, I stabbed my breakfast—mentally blowing up his head. It's true we disliked each other from the very first meeting. He may have done this to help his father, and me to avenge Winter, but that did not mean we had to smile and kiss over becoming Mr. and Mrs. Wilson.

"What are your other rules?" I snapped.

"We put on the show at parties and banquets. Plus, at least three times a week, we eat breakfast together—act the part of engaged couple," he replied. "Friday nights, you have dinner with my family to prove to my father we're responsible and committed. We can date other people, but discreetly—no one else can know."

"What if I don't want my fiancé to screw around on me? Especially since people are already calling me a trashy Dreg and saying I'm a gold digger. I bet your hookups would let it slip to embarrass me."

Victor inclined his head. "You're right. It's too risky. Rumors get around easily on campus. Okay, no hookups."

"You mean it?"

"Yep," came out smooth. "You can meet my needs instead. That works out since I might as well find out now if you're crap in bed. I'll teach you to be the perfect wife in all ways."

"Leave."

Laughing, Victor stretched out, getting comfortable. "Damn, you can't take a joke. If I stick my dick in you, it'll snap off from the frostbite. Trust me, I'm delaying that for as long as possible."

I resisted dumping his mocha on his lap. "*Sweetheart*," I mocked, "that delay is not up to you, and you'll be lucky if it ends after the 'I dos.' But I have a rule too. Outside the regularly scheduled sham, you don't talk to me. You don't text me. You don't get in my way and I don't get in yours. Deal?"

"Agreed."

We shook.

We finished our breakfast in silence. Gathering up our dishes, Victor beat me to the tray return and took off though we were headed to the same place. Our deal didn't include strolling through campus together.

Walking to the English building, I picked up stares along the way. Word about me was spreading and malicious rumors followed in its wake. It started this way for Winter too. First the whispers, then the nasty comments, Owen and his buddies stalking her, and finally, the attacks. If they followed the same pattern for me, things were about to turn quickly. I had to get to Owen before he got to me.

I entered the English hall, soaking in the air-conditioning washing over me. Students led the way into the classroom at the end of the corridor. I followed them in, and stopped dead in the doorway, my binder slipping out of my hand.

A bearded man with slicked-back curls stood at the chalkboard, writing the name Professor Anthony.

"Adonis?"

He turned his head, frown marring features even more handsome in the daylight. Shock blew his eyes wide.

"What are you doing here?" I blurted.

Adonis flicked from me to the class. In a blink, his face smoothed out. "I am teaching this class, Miss Sinclair. Take your seat."

I marched up to him, face reddening as every detail of that night unfolded in my mind. I didn't drink enough to black it all out, and by the naked surprise that was in his eyes, he didn't either.

"Miss Sinclair?" I repeated. "Did you know who I was the whole time? Did you know I was your student?"

The night morphed—changing from a fun, open talk with a nice guy to... creepy.

"This isn't the time—"

"Just answer me."

He strayed over my shoulder. "I haven't looked at my roster yet. Sit down. We're not having this discussion now."

"But you said—"

"Hey, everything alright?" Victor sidled up next to me. "After class, can we talk?"

"What more do we have to talk about?" I asked. Then I noticed Victor wasn't looking at me.

"Bro? Come on, man," he said. "You know I don't agree with Mom and Dad."

The words were both the detonator and explosion in my mind. *Mom and Dad?!*

"Bro?" I hissed. "You did know who I was. My name was on the freaking invitation announcing that I was marrying your brother!"

His beautiful, once kind eyes were empty and cold as steel. "This is neither the time nor place," Adonis gritted. "Sit *down*. Both of you."

"Asshole!"

Silence smothered the room. Every eye in the class fixed on me—for a new reason.

"Sneaky, underhanded, lying sack of—!"

Adonis slammed his fist on the desk. "One more word and I'll have campus security escort you out of my classroom. Take your seats. I will not tell you again."

My jaw cracked, I clenched it so hard. He knew who I was the entire time. Adonis, if that was his fucking name, was laughing at me, asking if I was having a rough night. He got me to spill so many truths.

And I bet everything he said was a lie.

I trudged to my seat, humiliation leadening my steps. Of course it was a lie. If his parents disowned and kicked him out, what was he doing hanging around in the library drinking scotch? I walked in and he decided to have some fun with me. He just wasn't expecting his lie to come back and bite him on the ass when the school bell chimed.

Students eyed me climbing the stairs for my seat. Looking at them, it was obvious to tell who was Dreg and who was Royal. Regalia University didn't give out grants or scholarships, so the people with supermarket backpacks, department store clothes, and twenty-dollar sneakers were easy to pick out as the ones saving all their pennies to pay back the massive student loan debt they were racking up. Ditto the Fendi backpacks, Rolex watches, eight-hundred-dollar phones, and Prada sunglasses identified the Royals.

The curled lips were shared by both groups.

Purses and bags were dropped on empty seats one after the other as I got close.

Victor hit the fourth floor, smacked hands with a couple of jock types, and plopped in his seat good to go. Moving on, I claimed a seat at the top empty row.

Adonis cleared his throat. "Good morning, everyone. Forgive that earlier commotion. From now on until you leave my class, we'll conduct ourselves in an appropriate, professional manner."

My face heated. He didn't look at me, but the comment was for me all the same. Real rich talking about being appropriate when you screw with people's fiancées.

"My name is Adonis Anthony. You may address me as Professor Anthony," he said. "This is English Composition I. If you're surprised to hear it, you've mixed up your schedule and you're in the wrong class."

People chuckled until two guys got up and scurried out.

"Good," Adonis said, moving around the desk. "Now we're jumping right into it. This class is about writing on the college level. This includes essay writing, academic writing, and editing. Beyond that, you'll learn how to analyze and evaluate different works ranging from poems, to fiction, and academic essays. I know what you're thinking."

That your balls really should shrivel up and fall off.

"This is no different than what you did in high school—and did well. You had to excel academically to get into this school, so why are we treating you like you can't read and understand an essay?"

A few heads nodded. A few others tilted and twirled their hair around their fingers. More than a few students were hot for teacher.

"For one thing"—a smirk stretched his lips—"the papers you'll turn in this semester are four times as long."

If he wanted groans from that comment, he got them.

"They also won't be standardized, cookie-cutter essays written to get As and, in turn, get into a great school. You're in a great school. Now, it's time to write something that matters. It's time to be honest."

I bit my lip, penning in a snort. This guy was incredible talking about honesty. Was Regalia built by and for sociopaths? What other explanation was there for his ability to spout garbage with a straight face?

Professor Anthony went for his bag and pulled out a stack of papers. He waved them overhead. "This is your syllabus. Take one and pass it on. On it, you'll see your assignment for the day," he said. "Get to it. You have forty minutes."

It took eight of those minutes for the syllabus to make it back to me. The last guy flung it on the seat behind him, not bothering to get up and give it to me. I got it and carried it back, reading off the first page.

Write two pages on a topic that's important to you.

Simple and straightforward.

I got a pencil and paper from my binder, and got to work. My major was psychology—recently changed from communications. After all my sister went through without help, my mom's suffering and depression, and pain that swallowed me so completely, I didn't remember what it was to be happy. Well, there was only one thing to do with my life now.

But I didn't write any of that.

I wrote about my dream of opening a practice that helped young people navigating difficult times in their lives. I wrote about signs that are dismissed because some assume a young, pretty twenty-year-old has nothing to worry about. Then, I finished by saying a life helping others is the most rewarding life I could lead.

Students were getting up and handing in their papers as they finished. I kept mine on my desk. I'd hand it in after they left, and we had that discussion.

"Turn in your paper when you're done." Adonis fixed on me like he knew exactly what I planned. "Everyone."

Stiffly, I climbed down and placed it on his outstretched hand. The air charged as our gazes locked—sparking with electricity.

"You may return to your seat."

I went. Excuse or no, we were having that conversation.

During the rest of class, I stared him down, listening with half an ear. While I did, three girls in the sixth row stared at me.

I didn't notice at first. A giggle pierced my attention and I flicked off Professor Anthony. Two of them staring right at me, turned away quick when I looked back. The three leaned in close, whispering something, and then I saw one of them raise their cell phone. After, all three looked at me again—smiles I didn't like twisting their mouths.

Passing nasty things about me in text? You'd think they would wait until they actually had a conversation with me.

"You three," Professor Anthony barked.

The girls, and I, jerked.

"Your phones," he said. "Bring them up here now."

"But, Professor, we didn't—"

"Class, this is my first lesson to teach on the English language. 'Now' doesn't mean when you feel like it, or after you've argued with me. It means immediately."

Their red faces lit up the room. They shuffled down the steps, handing over their phones. The satisfaction at their embarrassment didn't combat my irritation for him.

Adonis spent the rest of class going over the syllabus, assignments, and expectations.

"You'll have a ten-page midterm and final paper. Those are to be summarized and presented to the class. Are there any questions?" No one raised their hand. "You're dismissed."

I was slow packing away my things. Everyone filed out, leaving one other to lag behind.

Victor stopped in front of his *brother's* desk. They were too far for me to overhear what they were saying.

Maybe they're discussing the hilarious prank Adonis played on his drunk fiancée.

Taking my time, I descended and part of their conversation drifted to my ears.

"—give them time," Victor said. "They'll come around."

"It's too late for that."

"No, it isn't. Come on, Don. You practically spat in Dad's face by choosing literature over an MBA—or that's how he sees it. He raged for a while, then he accepted it. This time is no different."

Adonis shuffled papers, expression grim. "It's not about what he accepts anymore. It's about what I'm willing to accept. They crossed the line by continents. I'm not letting them run my life." He flicked to me. "And you shouldn't either. There are more important things in life than running Wilson Industries."

My muscles clenched. I didn't want to marry Victor, but it was a whole other thing standing there while his brother implied he should dump me.

"There are more important things, like our dad's health."

"Don't buy into it, Vic. That man will outlive us all."

"Whatever. Just say you're coming to dinner tomorrow."

Friday night dinner? As in the one Victor just made me promise to attend?

"We'll see. I may have plans," Adonis said.

"Cancel them. I'm telling Patrice to set an extra place." Victor headed out, leaving the two of us alone. Adonis picked an essay out of the pile and started to read.

For a beat, I just watched him, piecing together what I heard. So there was strain between him and his parents. If it was for the reason he said, I couldn't be sure, but Victor wasn't playing peacemaker for my benefit.

Even if he didn't lie about them falling out over his vasectomy, he did pretend he didn't know who I was to his brother.

"Do you need something, Miss Sinclair?"

"Why did you pretend not to know me?"

"I will say this once, and only once, because I admit my actions require explanation." He didn't look up from the paper. "The other night, I was going through a difficult time. We hadn't been introduced, so I didn't recognize you until you told me your name. At that point, I should've excused myself, but it had been a long day and talking to someone without the complication of who I was and who they were—appealed too strongly to my impaired judgment. I apologize for the boundaries that were crossed. If I'd known you were also my student, none of that would've happened."

"You mean giving me alcohol, flirting with me, letting me—"

He snapped his head up, eyes flashing. "Enough."

I swallowed the rest. No, I was not dealing with the same fun, cute guy from the night before.

"I'm your professor. You're my student. Our relationship will be strictly professional from here on."

"I'm not just your student. I'm marrying your brother."

"Engagements end every day."

I bristled—hearing Saylor's voice in my ear. "What the hell is that supposed to mean?"

Adonis sighed, pinching the bridge of his nose. "It means that my relationship with my parents has been strained for years, but not my relationship with my younger brother. I know this marriage is a business arrangement. If you two make it down the aisle, we'll find a way to get along as brother- and sister-in-law. Until then, we keep things professional."

"Professional? You can't even look me in the eye while giving me your prepared brush-off."

I didn't normally speak to my teachers this way. I could possibly accept his explanation, if he wasn't acting like I did something wrong by being fooled by his deceit. Snapping and shutting me down? This was less a conversation and more a scolding.

"I'm not looking at you because I'm reading your essay," he breezed.

"What? Don't do it in front of me."

"It's a good thing I did. This is terrible."

My expression froze. "Excuse me?"

"I'm only halfway through," he said, frowning at the page, "and I don't want to bother going on. This is uninspired drivel. Something you'd write for a college admissions essay. *A life helping others is the most rewarding life I can lead.*" He snorted. "Did you read that off an airport advertisement?"

"But— But I—"

"There's no heart here. No passion. You might as well be talking about a stamp collectors' museum or a yarn exhibit. I can't feel your excitement for the career you'll work for forty-plus years."

"I am passionate," I cried. "This is important to me. It's what I'm meant to do."

"This is English class, not speech class. There's no point telling me." Professor Anthony thrust the paper at me. "Redo it. Turn in a new paper by tomorrow. My office hours are three to five."

"Are you kidding me?"

He cocked a brow. "Your other option is for me to grade it as is. Spoiler alert: you'll get a D."

I plucked the paper from him, stuffing it in my backpack. "I like you better when you're drunk."

A vein jumped in his forehead. "Have a nice rest of your day, Miss Sinclair."

"You too, Professor Anthony."

The rest of my day was good because I didn't wind up with any other professors that I drunkenly kissed.

After English was biology class, lunch, and then calculus finished up the school day. For students moving up to premed, environmental science, or psychology, they needed a few specific classes in their general schedule. That's where the major prep classes came. I had to do anthropology as a social science with everyone else in the class, on top of the psychology intro class. Lucky for us Regalians, we took more credits per semester than the average college student.

I deflated on a bench outside the Cultural Diversity Center. The first day and I had an online calculus quiz, three chapters to read in biology, and a paper to rewrite. I didn't want to think about what the next day had in store for me especially since my weekend was full. I had dinner with my loathsome fiancé, and a party to crash.

Owen came out of the center walking in the middle of a bunch of sophomore guys. He didn't notice me on the bench as he turned in the opposite direction—his classes of the day over. I trailed a good distance behind.

Saylor said Owen was throwing a party and I doubted it was in his dorm room. The ones they gave us were pretty big, but if it was an all-Royals-and-one-Rogue party, they'd need more room.

That left one of his buddies' frat houses, or his folks' place. Breaking into a mansion was more difficult than a frat party, but neither would do me any good if Owen was surrounded by people the whole time. I'd be at that party, but just in case, I needed to know his routine as a backup.

The guys fanned out in a line, taking up the massive sidewalk and forcing people to walk around them. I was too far back to hear what they were saying, but from the disgusted look on the faces of girls passing them, it wasn't anything I wanted to hear.

Why? Why are they allowed to harass and stalk women without consequences? Is the dean too busy counting the Royal parents' donations to worry about the hell they put students through?

The group made it to Abbott Hall and kept going. I followed them to Greek Row where they descended on Tau Theta Kappa. That was one point in favor of the party held at the frat house. Why risk junking up his house when he's always at the frat and the boys love a good party.

With people everywhere, getting in would be easy. The trick is getting him out.

Icy, bitter hatred smothered my soul—pushing down the person who would never dream of doing the things I planned to. I wasn't that girl anymore.

Coming on to him won't work after our last electric encounter. I'd pay someone else to lure him away, but then I'd be the first person they point to afterward. Or I could cause a distraction that'll make him come running.

I shook my head. That was no good. How could I be sure Owen would run off alone? Or that it'd be him who came?

Maybe the party won't work. Depending on how late he hangs around with his frat boys, I could follow him to the dorm one night and—

"Lu-Lu! Hey, Luna. Is that you?"

Owen was on the porch kicking back with his friends. He whipped around at my name, landing immediately on me standing beside the hedge.

Shit! Shit, shit, shit!

Katie came out of the house across the street, waving goodbye to a shirtless Dean. I thought fast.

"Katie, there you are! I didn't remember what house." I ran across and hugged her, heart galloping in my chest. Was there any chance he bought that? Did he realize I followed him?

Katie peeled me off. "Okay, eww. Why are you pawing me?"

"It's called a hug. Can you not be yourself for a minute?"

"No." She popped her shades over her eyes. "Come along, Lu-Lu. The car will be here to pick us up in ten minutes."

"Wait, us?"

"I need you for something, and how psychic are you? You came without being called."

"I don't trail after you, Katie," I said, though I fell in step with her. "You're not my guide anymore."

"Don't be like that. We had so much fun shopping the other day."

"Fun? My stepdad told me he's not putting another cent in my account until the new year, and even then, only a little at a time to *keep me on a budget.*"

"Worth it."

"You're not allowed to decide if my struggles are worth it. I do that."

She groaned. "Moan, moan, moan. That's all you ever do."

Katie set a determined pace away from Greek Row to the campus entrance. I resisted the urge to look back and see if Owen was watching me leave. Doing so would give away what I really went there for.

If he knows I'm following him and goes on alert, it'll be ten times as difficult to get him alone.

He's already on alert, another voice said. *Maybe the direct approach is exactly what I need.*

"Hello? Earth to Lu-Lu." Katie waved her hand in my face. "Are you even listening to me?"

I shook myself. "Sorry, what was that?"

"I said there's a party this weekend and you're going to help me with my outfit."

Now she had my full attention. "Whose party?"

"Doesn't matter, you're not invited," she tossed over her shoulder, heading off. How the woman moved so fast in six-inch heels I'll never know.

"Why does that mean I can't know who's throwing it?"

"Just some guys. They're sophomores, Luna, don't worry about it."

I pressed my lips together, warning stopping me from pushing her. She's bringing me along to hold her bags and purse. Katie will naturally talk about the party while we're shopping.

Katie's driver picked us up in nine minutes, but instead of turning right for town, the car veered left toward the gated community.

"Where are we going?"

"My place."

"You said we were going shopping," I said.

"No, you said that. My housekeeper did the shopping and now I need you to help me put it together."

"Don't you have friends for that?"

"They're busy working on their outfits whereas *you* don't have friends or plans. You're free to help."

"I do have homework," I said, unable to refute the other two. "And I'm not seeing why you need me? You didn't even let me pick out my own clothes the other day. Why do you need my help to put together an outfit?"

"It's an ABC party. Anything but clothes," she explained.

Bingo. So she is going to Owen's party, and why wouldn't she? Katie's a Royal.

"Everyone else is wrapping themselves in caution tape or picking palm fronds off the lawn. My outfit will be original."

"What were you thinking?"

"Oh my goodness, it's going to be so cute. A dress out of candy wrappers with matching crown. We're about the same size, so you'll be my mannequin."

"I've never been to an ABC party," I said lightly. "People come up with some amazing outfits."

"It's going to be insane." Katie threw out her hands. "The first party of the year always is. It's like a challenge to all the parties to come that they'd better top it."

"Does everyone come out? I mean, are the parties open to everyone?"

"Nah. Dreg parties, yeah, but not Royal parties. Though the Dregs always try to crash."

"You know, you don't have to call us Dregs. It's just the two of us. No one around to witness you bucking the social order."

Katie threw her head back laughing. "What? You think I have a secret soft side? Aw, that's so cute. Sorry, Lu-Lu, but you're such a Dreg, it'd be wrong to call you anything else. Look at you dropping everything to be my shop window dummy just because I told you to."

"I mean this sincerely: fuck you." I got back a laugh in response. "And I'm only helping you because you are going to buck the social order and get me an invite."

"Actually, I'm not."

"Actually, you are."

Katie's brow crawled up her forehead. "Why would I do that?"

"Because I want to see them, Katie. I want to look into the faces of the people who watched, ignored, laughed, and tore down my sister." The smirk melted off her face. "It's only right I meet the people responsible."

She gave me a long, unreadable look. "No."

"No?" I repeated.

"I'm not getting you into the party."

Anger flared hot and corrosive, burning in my chest. "You said you liked Winter. You claimed you gave a shit!"

"I did— I do! But last year and this summer wasn't just a nightmare for her. I'm not comparing our situations," she rushed when I sprang forward. "I know it's not the same, but freshman year sucked for me. I barely hung out with any of my friends. I had to lie to everyone because Mom didn't want them to know what she was going through.

"Then Winter... died, and this dark cloud hung over the whole summer. It felt wrong to party and go to the beach like nothing happened," she said. "Maybe it makes me all the things you're calling me in your head right now, but I'm tired of being sad. So, *no*. I'm not going to let you crash the party and cause a whole drama that wrecks the night."

"Because heaven forfend that the princes and princesses take one night off from their champagne and caviar lives," I said in a high-pitched, snobbish voice. "The death of one lowly serf should never get in the way of a good time! Is that it, Katie?!"

She punched the seat. "No. I won't let you do it because then they'll come after you!" Her roar blew me back. "You'll start off a war that you won't win and I won't forgive myself if something happens to you too, you selfish asshole! Can I just have one damn day of not worrying someone close to me is going to die? Can I have one night to enjoy college like a reg-ular student? Is that too much to ask?"

We glared at each other, chests heaving.

"You call me a selfish asshole," I said in a low, calmer tone, "but there were a lot of *I* statements in the following questions."

She flipped me off, turning shiny eyes out the window. I almost cracked a smile. I almost understood her.

I was watching my mother be slowly crushed under grief, and there was nothing I could do to stop it. Katie wanted a break from pain and helpless-ness, and if there was anyone who could understand that, it should be me... but I had no sympathy to give while she stood between me, Owen Thasher, and the names on my list. Even if deep down it twinged something in my chest that in her own way, she was trying to protect me.

"I get it, Katie." I pushed my anger and that twinge down. "It's putting you in a tough spot and you've got your own stuff to worry about. I shouldn't have asked."

Despite my words, her eyes narrowed. "Don't ask anyone else either. I'm serious, Luna. You don't want a war."

"I'm not sure I have a choice." I dropped my head on the leather. "Peo-ple recognize Luna Sinclair as the sister of Winter Sinclair-Bowden. They're already laughing and pointing as I walk by."

She cursed. "Okay, well then, stick to Victor. Your engagement is offi-cial now, and even though you're a Dreg, no one has the balls to mess with a Royal's fiancée right in front of him. You're lucky you bagged a Wilson. That'll be what saves you as long as you don't make the situation worse. Lie low—let everyone see you're not here to stir shit up."

My sister wasn't here to stir shit up and that didn't save her.

I swallowed the reply. "Good idea. Stay close to Victor. That's what I'll do."

"And don't try to use him to score invites either. Royal or not, he's still a freshman. He's not going to the party either."

"I'm not going to score a thing." A smile stretched across my face. "So, tell me more about your outfit. Is it a dress? Skirt and top?"

She studied me, but my smile held. "It's a dress," she finally replied. "We're going to..."

The driver dropped us off in front of Katie's mansion. The place was twice as big as the Bowden Estate for three people and an army of servants. Katie didn't bother to introduce me to them or her parents as she led me through the sitting room, dining hall, study, and indoor pool to get to the pool house beside the *outdoor* pool.

Two floors of grand design, bold art pieces, expensive furniture, high-end kitchen, entertainment room, and clothes all over the floor to signal this was all Katie's space.

We talked, but not about the party as I stood in the middle of her bedroom, standing still with my arms out while she used me as a mannequin. No, she didn't talk about the party, but she did talk about her friends.

"Saylor is so lucky. Her dad's a senator, so she flies back and forth to DC all the time. She's for sure going to be the next first lady."

"Senator Burkhardt," I said. "I should've recognized the last name. Are you sure she wants to marry a politician? She was getting pretty cozy with that guy you told me about—Rafael Dumont."

She waved that away. "Rafael is the guy you fuck in the sand at a bonfire beach party. He's not the guy you marry. No one is trying to have his dad as a father-in-law."

I turned big eyes on her. "That whole hit man thing. That's not true, right?"

Katie suddenly got very busy gluing Skittles wrappers to my backside. "Anyway, then there's Everleigh. Her fam is in the furniture business. Making, shipping, displaying in Everlasting Furniture stores all over the country. She's set to get her MBA and take over the business as soon as her mother steps down."

I filed it all away. I had the official information I dug up online of the families of Regalia, but if Katie wanted to fill in the details, I wouldn't stop her.

"Everleigh is a pretty name."

"It's a passive-aggressive name. I can tell you because everyone already knows," she said, leaning in like someone does when they know something good. "Mr. Starling cheated on Mrs. Starling with her sister. To get back at him, she slept with both of his brothers, but it was the young and virile Everton Starling who knocked her up.

"Her husband decided to stick by her and raise the baby as his own, but that didn't stop her mom from naming her Everleigh after her uncle/bio dad as a warning to her husband. Don't fuck around on me."

"Wow. That's... wow." I reconciled the sneering model as the same person who called her dad Uncle and her uncle Dad. "Stories like that put your family drama into perspective."

"You're telling me."

What about the other two? I thought as Katie busied herself with the dress. *Keep talking about your friends.*

"Gabriella is the best," Katie continued. "Her grandfather invented something that's used in every plane that takes off from the tarmac. No one in her family has to work for the next twenty generations. Her grandchildren's great-grandchildren will be flush. So she's always around to chill, jet off to Vegas, or drive cross-country to hit a burger joint in California. My girl is down for anything."

"She sounds great."

"Last is Piper. Her family owns Alvar Extreme Sports. You wouldn't know it by looking at her, but she's insane on a skateboard. I bet you'd fall and break your face just from looking at one."

I barked a laugh. "An insult, yeah, but I can't even lie, I would break my face. Are pro skaters in her fiancé pool? Does everyone around here line up their prospects all the way back to when they sipped their juice on the preschool playground?"

"You're one to talk. You snatched up Victor Wilson before he could get in the pool."

"The match made sense," I said, repeating my ordered reply. "I'm not knocking you guys. It's just weird for me too that I have to think about all of this now. Friday night dinners with my future in-laws. Engagement parties. I'm doing it sooner than most of the couples around here, but doesn't it get to you sometimes, realizing that your life is decided for you?"

"Not for me. My parents would never force me into marriage. And you don't have to worry about the women of Regalia either. We can say no to a match. It's not social suicide or anything. Some guys snore or are crap in bed. Who's trying to suffer forever with that?"

Ah. So it's just me who's blackmailed into putting rings on my finger. Good to know.

"Did everyone around here grow up together? Same elementary, middle, and high schools?"

"Shouldn't you know this already?"

"Mom lived in Regalia when we were little. I was three when we moved," I said. "My mom used to come back to visit old friends, but it was a girls' weekend kind of thing. We didn't go with her. It was during one of those weekends that she met Jack."

"Ah." Katie worked her way toward the front, forming the dress bit by bit. "They have a torrid affair and then, one day, she springs on you that she's getting married and you're moving back home. Too bad you were home for all of a second before Stepdaddy shipped you off to the nunnery."

"That wasn't quite how it went down, but close enough."

She chuckled. "To answer your question, yes. Everyone knows everyone around here. Best part is that Regalia gossip is way juicier than normal small-town gossip."

My ears perked up. "How juicy are we talking?"

"No names, of course. But pretty much every scandal you can think of has gone down in the last five years. That guy ran off with the maid. That lady was caught banging the pool boy. The secretary drained the pension fund and took off to Tahiti. The girl in the grade above took five months off because she got mono." Katie shook her head, lips pushed out. "Secret adoption. Might've gotten away with the lie too if someone didn't peek her C-section scar."

"Wow. The most scandalous thing that happened in my high school was Callie Gilbert sneaking in cigarettes."

"No way. All those girls trapped in a nunnery, stewing in angst. I know you got up to something, Lu-Lu."

"First, it wasn't a nunnery. Second, we wanted to get up to something—don't get me wrong—but it was impossible. We were stuck in this little town that was basically a pretty countryside nursing home. As soon as the kids grew up, they moved away and raised their families by movie theaters, restaurants, and shopping. All things our town did *not* have.

"There was no one below fifty to hook up with. There was nothing fun to do even if we managed to sneak out. Of course we behaved ourselves. We didn't have a choice."

"Wow, you have such a sad life."

I looked away. "Yes," I whispered. "I do."

"Oh, I didn't mean—"

"I know what you meant."

Katie patted my arm. It could've been an attempt to comfort me. It was over too fast for me to tell.

"Let's get back to talking about me. Did I tell you how Dean and I met?" She plowed on, not needing an answer. "His sister was usually in the next bed over, receiving chemo. I pulled him aside to threaten his life if he told anyone at school that my mom was getting treatment. The jerk said I couldn't take him, so I informed him I was on the wrestling team for two years. He replied that he was captain of his wrestling team for four years, and I definitely couldn't take him. So I dragged his ass into a storage closet and I"—she winked—"showed him what I learned on the mat, if you get my meaning."

I rolled my eyes skyward. "Oh, I definitely get your meaning."

"Just making sure. Wouldn't want it to go over your sweet little virgin head."

"Who said I'm a virgin?"

Katie spun me toward the mirror. It was quickly dawning on me that she was amazing at this. The wrappers spun down my body in a rainbow of color, molding perfectly to my curves. It seemed she had other gifts besides turning people's hatred into love.

"Uh, you did. You were sent off to boarding school in the land of geriatrics. Unless you and your roommate were dipping in the honeypot, that cherry is ripe for the plucking."

"Is it serious between you guys?" I asked, steering the conversation back on track. "You say you don't buck the social order, but what do you call you and Dean?"

"Fuck buddies," she dropped without hesitation. "The only thing serious about us is how hot the sex is. And how quick I can get him over here. The man's like a bag of buttery popcorn—ready to go in minutes, all it takes is a push of a button." Katie held up her phone. "I send him this and he's tripping through my door with his pants around his ankles within the hour."

I looked down, and shrieked. "Joseph Collins, woman!"

On the screen was Katie Langford buck naked and doing things that I didn't even do to myself. My hand flashed, smacking the phone away before the image permanently seared into my brain.

Katie gave me a look. "Oh yeah, you're a virgin. Just wait until you see a penis. I bet you faint."

"Can we please not pretend you flashing me your nudes is normal!"

She cracked up. "Relax, Little Miss Prudey Pants. I'm not shy. There's a spot by Robin's Point where we all go skinny-dipping. Almost everyone in my graduating class has seen me naked."

"I'm going to bet they did not all see you do *that*."

"By the way, who's Joseph Collins?"

"He's who you shout in a Catholic school instead of a certain person with the same initials. Unless you want to spend your weekend cleaning the chapel floor grout with a toothpick."

"Ugh, you're so repressed. You don't know how lucky you are to have me in your life. I'll fix you."

I mumbled under my breath. "Does it matter at all that I don't want you in my life?"

"Nope," she sang, hearing me loud and clear. "I've gotta pee. Don't move."

Katie skipped off to the bathroom. I shot across the room as soon as the door shut.

Picking up her phone, I swiped off her Dean bat signal and pulled up her messages. Finding the group messages between her, Saylor, Everleigh, and the rest of them was easy.

Okay, I'd give it to her. I was lucky to have the Royal princess, Katie Langford, in my life. Who else would have the location, time, and all the details for the party ripe for the scrolling?

I tucked the information away, swimming along with my ideas for my ABC outfit. Fuck the no-Dregs rule, I was going to that party... and making it Owen's last.

Chapter Four

Music poured out the front door, playing its tune for people sleeping on the other side of campus. For those on this side, they put every party I attended to shame and I hadn't made it inside yet.

Multicolored lights decorated the frat house—flickering, strobing, flashing on the variety of outfits gracing the party. Couldn't say how many of them made their own as opposed to hiring someone, but once again it was proof rich kids did things on another level.

Newspaper halter dresses. Playing card tops. Skirts made out of bendy straws. Shorts, pants, and tie out of black-and-white tape. One guy strolled up in a mess of colored condoms covering his bits. And of course, a parade of caution tape dresses led by Saylor Burkhardt.

I hung off to the side, watching Saylor, Everleigh, Piper, and Gabriella climb out of their town car—all dressed in caution tape and boasting different styles from long, short, two-piece and one-piece. Last to climb out of the car was Katie, carefully slipping out and unveiling what took five hours of my life.

The wrapper skirt flared out and fell to her knees while the bodice clung tight to enviable curves. Gracing her collarbone was a necklace made of Skittles with matching earrings.

She looked amazing—and she clearly knew it as the five of them glided into the frat house, collecting wolf whistles as they walked by.

I gazed at my outfit, fingers twitching against my thigh. A strange, buzzing energy claimed me the night before as I bought the mountain of cotton and lugged it back to my dorm. After all the waiting, planning, researching, bribing, and sneaking, it was finally time.

Lifting my chin, I made for the house, and the wolf whistles turned on for me. They would. I looked damned good.

Wrapped around my bits was mesh and glued to those were my mounds of cotton—fluffed around my body and formed into two clouds. Tucked beneath them, battery-powered twinkle lights flashed their lighting.

I did an even better job with my hair. It was sprayed and teased into a wild, wispy style as if blown in a storm, then sprinkled with glitter. Completing the outfit was a mask made of clouds, covering most of my face.

After seeing Katie's outfit, I knew I'd need something wow to get me through the door. Anything less would give me away as a Dreg.

"Damn." Condom Boy leaned against the doorjamb, raking me up and down. "Nicely done. Give us a little spin."

I gave him a middle finger.

Laughing, he said, "What's the word?"

"Trust fund."

Access granted, he stepped aside, letting me into the party.

I took one step and jumped back, narrowly avoiding colliding with a band of hooting guys wearing nothing but empty cardboard beer cases to cover their bits.

A low whistle escaped me and smothered under the sound. Freshman Royals weren't invited to the party, but the ban didn't seem to apply to the upperclassmen. There were twenty-eight Royals in the sophomore class—I did my research—and a lot more than twenty-eight people dancing and spilling their beer in the living room, clogging up the stairwell, playing beer pong on the kitchen island, making out on the pool table, and taking the party outside.

All the better for me. With so many people around, no one would notice the cloud moving through the party who shouldn't be there.

Find Owen. Find the shit-faced bastard and make him wet himself twice.

I went into the living room, and got caught up checking the place out. I didn't have much experience with frat houses, but none of the ones I saw on television had expensive hardwood floors, chandeliers, Persian rugs, a mounted big screen longer than my body, or a spiral staircase leading into the living room from a loft.

Photos of handsome, smiling men circled the walls, gazing down with approval at the scantily dressed partiers. A deejay set up in the corner—professional setup and everything. Weaving through the crowd, guys dressed in heavy-duty trash bags offered their trays loaded down with shots. One of them came up to me.

Floppy, curly hair hung over his green eyes. Even in a trash bag he was cute. "Silver bullet?"

"Oh no, thanks," I shouted over the music. "What's the deal with the servers? Are you guys pledges?"

He scowled. "No, he's a pledge," the guy snapped, pointing at another trash-bag-wearer. "I'm a brother. But that doesn't matter if you're a Dreg."

"Oops. Sorry," I said, but he was already walking off.

I shook my head at the whole mess. Owen wasn't even in the frat, but he could come in here, throw a party, and force the actual brothers to walk around in a garbage bag serving drinks.

No wonder the guy didn't think the rules applied to him. Everywhere he went, he made the rules up for himself.

Pushing through, I headed for the kitchen. Everleigh, Saylor, Gabriella, Piper, and Katie lined up at the counter, pouring cocktails from the endless supply of alcohol. I brushed up behind them, rounding the beer pong game.

"—totally disappeared on us this summer," Piper said. "We texted you to come to the beach house for the back-to-school party."

Another back-to-school party? How many times did these people need to celebrate being young, pretty, and rich?

"Blew us off," Saylor said. She didn't need to shout over the music. Her prim, imposing voice was heard by anyone she deigned to talk to. "We were starting to think you were too good to hang out with us."

"I am too good to hang out with you guys."

I stifled a sigh. Katie was a peach to everyone she knew. I didn't know if that made me feel better or not.

"But that wasn't the reason this time," Katie continued. "My dad's been keeping me super busy with the internship. Says I had to work, take college seriously, blah, blah, blah if I want my outrageously generous stipend to stay outrageous."

"Harsh," Everleigh said. "I don't know why our folks waste our time with that bullshit. When one person catches you in last season's Caddell and the rumors start spreading the Langfords are broke, they'll dump all the money you want in your account."

"Seriously," Katie said.

"That's it?" Saylor pressed. "You were MIA because of the internship?"

"That's what I said, isn't it? Oh, there's also a new guy that I've been screwing. Love you ladies, but you don't beat orgasms."

"You're so crude," Piper replied, amused.

Saylor didn't let it go. "Internship and new guy. Sucky reasons to blow off your best friends, but at least it's not because of that Bowden girl."

I stopped dead.

"Yeah," Gabriella chimed in. "You were so pissed after she went and drowned herself. Yelling and going on about the way we treated her."

Blood soaked the tips of my nails as they pierced my palms.

"All those things you called us," Saylor said, mimicking something that was supposed to be distress. "You were super mean, Katie. You called us bullies."

I stood rigid, gaze fixed on a guy knocking back beer that had a dirty ball in it without seeing him.

"No," Katie said lightly. "I called you vicious, harpy cunts who'd become sociopathic serial killers if stalking and murder didn't cut so much into your shopping time. You know, if we're being specific."

A tense silence spread through the group, permeating my soul. *Katie said all of that? She told off her best friends in defense of my sister?*

Saylor burst out laughing. "Can't even be mad. We are vicious. Why pretend otherwise? But you're wrong about the serial killer thing. It's not because of shopping that we don't bother. It's because we're rich, boo. We've got people to take care of that for us.

"Let's go. I saw Dylan go upstairs."

A hard shove propelled me into a guy's back. "Ugh, get out of the way," Saylor snapped.

I held still, keeping my head low as they passed. It wasn't just Katie, and it wasn't only my sister. Saylor didn't know the person she tossed aside wasn't a Royal, so she truly was that heinous to everyone.

Vicious, harpy cunt was putting it lightly.

With them upstairs in search of Dylan, I moved free through the party, looking for Owen. I did two laps, looking hard at every guy in a mask. I didn't see him in the front yard, in the backyard by the pool, or inside dancing with the girls who heard "anything but clothes" and decided to wear nothing at all.

He has to be upstairs, I thought as I gripped the rail, making up my mind.

I doubted Owen was up there sitting alone in a dark corner, repenting his sins. He was either hooking up, snorting something up his nose, or messing around with his frat buddies. Bursting in on him during either of those situations didn't bode well for me. The guy still wanted my head, and I wasn't about to fight him when he was high, had backup, or a witness.

I'll just poke my head in, checking to make sure he's here and didn't blow off his own party.

I put my foot on the step. Someone circled my waist and carried me off. "Dance with me."

"Hey!" I pounded the arm, bucking to get free. "Put me down!"

Ignoring me, he carried me onto the dance floor—my flailing legs parting the crowd. He put me down in the middle of the circle, and I got a look at my captor.

The rant lodged in my throat.

Rafael Dumont stood before me in all of his glory. Like Katie, he decided he would stand out or he wasn't coming at all.

Creeping, painted vines climbed his chest, swirling around his nipples to draw my attention there, then disappearing over his shoulder. I tried to keep my eyes on his nipples—it was far less scandalous than drifting lower and—

I flicked down, unable to stop myself. A few big maple leaves hung on a string around his waist—the only thing standing between him and giving the women feasting on him their heart's desire.

Rafael encircled me before I found my voice, molding me to his bare chest. "On the first day, he created the heavens," he whispered in my ear. His fingers skimmed my clouds, popped goose bumps on my side, and rested on my hips.

"And he declared it was good."

Heat melted the flesh off me. I was on fire as he hooked one leg around his thigh, rocking me side to side to the music. It wasn't a slow song or one that was easy to dance to. Rafael did so all the same.

He rode every beat, chin bobbing against mine as his whole body moved—fingers tapping the rhythm, shoulders rolling, hips thrusting. That those hips happened to be thrusting against my thigh rocketed my pulse into the fainting zone. Katie was fucking right, okay? I was a virgin.

"What are you doing?" I tried to hiss it but the question came out more like a squeak.

"Dancing. What are you doing besides sneaking your hand toward my ass?"

I snatched it up, gripping his shoulders.

"Hey, no one told you to stop."

I turned my face to his neck, feeling the eyes on us. "Listen, I'm not whoever you think you're dancing with, so—"

"Sinclair," he said easily. "You think you can cover yourself in cotton and put some paper mâché on your face and I won't know it's you?"

The room spun. I blinked up at Rafael, leg tightening automatically around him as he dipped me low, smirking into my eyes. This close—so very close—I noticed under the crown of leaves on his head, his earbuds were in.

"I'll always recognize you, Luna."

I swallowed, fighting to keep my voice even. "That's not a creepy thing to say. Not at all."

Chuckling, he lifted me up, spinning me off my feet. "You've got dimples and a little beauty mark above your ass. Noticed them the other day. If you were trying to hide, my little crasher, you should've covered them up."

"I do not!" I blurted, sounding stupid because, of course, I did have back dimples and a beauty mark. "And if I do, you're not supposed to be looking that low."

"I didn't look any lower than you." His mouth twisted into a wicked grin. "I saw you checking out my... leaves."

"Goodbye." I slipped out of his hold and marched off, making it two steps before he grasped my elbow and spun me back. I bumped into his hard chest, inhaling his sweet lemony cedar scent.

"Touchy." Rafael grabbed my hips, grinding them in time with his. "You want to check me out but you don't want to be called on it. Cool with me as long as it goes both ways. Your ass is looking fine in that bed stuffing, girl. Uh-uh, say nothing. You won't shame me for my sexuality."

I snorted—too quick for me to pen it in. "You're an idiot."

Grinning, his eyes shone. "Not a very nice thing to say, but not the worst thing I've been called."

"I can manage something nice. You're a pretty good dancer."

"I'm an excellent dancer." He spun me out, but I twirled back in—lacing our fingers as my back pressed against his chest and we swayed. "You know what they say about men who can dance."

"Stay out of their way because it hurts twice as much when they stomp on your feet?"

His deep, sensuous laugh rose high above the music. "Clever. I think I like you, Cloud Girl."

My cheeks flamed. *What the hell is happening? I'm dancing and flirting with the half-naked guy I dismissed as a weirdo on the most important night of my life. I can't do this right now, and even if I could, I can't do it with* him.

I opened my mouth to say I had to go, and he flattened his palm against my stomach, holding me closer. All of him molded to my body—the leaves doing nothing to protect his modesty.

The rejection died as his cheek, soft and warm, brushed my temple. I didn't have to flip through my history to know this was the furthest I've gone with any guy, and an entire party full of people got to witness it.

You have to go, Luna. Sense cleared the fog. *You have to find Owen.*

"Rafael," I began, "I—"

"What's this?"

The fog blew away. A cold bucket of water to the face was its parting gift.

"I thought we told you that you didn't get a plus-one," said Saylor. She spoke from behind us, and sounded pissed. "Who the hell is that anyway?"

I didn't think. I didn't speak. I didn't turn around. Breaking free of him, I shot out of Rafael's arms, diving through a break in the crowd.

"At least she knows when she's not wanted."

"Wait," Rafael called.

"Let her go." I chanced a look back as the caution tape horde surrounded him, pawing him all over, cutting off escape. "We were waiting for you to show up."

My gaze flicked to the left, and locked with Katie. Her eyes narrowed.

Whipping around, I ducked behind the beer pong guys and ran outside.

Five minutes passed. Then ten. Then fifteen.

I got up from my hiding place behind a beer fountain. If Katie or one of the other girls was going to come for me, they'd have done it by then.

Taking a deep breath, I squeezed between the bodies coming out, hurried into the hall and made for the stairs. I don't know what made me stop and look toward the living room.

Rafael was right where I left him, dancing to put everyone around him to shame. Everleigh, Gabriella, Piper, and Saylor revolved around him like planets circling the sun—except Venus wasn't so obvious about copping a feel. They ground, giggled, and rubbed their breasts all over him. And his hands were going everywhere, but he wasn't touching them.

I couldn't explain exactly how, but I sensed Rafael was in his own world, dancing by himself. No one else mattered. Actually, if we all left right then, he wouldn't notice, or stop.

Shaking myself, I scanned for Katie and didn't spot her. She could be in the bathroom, or looking for the cloud girl.

I can't let her get in my way. I need to find Owen and get him alone now.

Picking up my feet, I padded up the stairs, finding the second party.

People lined the walls, knocking back beers and shooting do-me eyes at everyone who walked past. Smoke billowed beneath the door crack from the room closest to the stairs. Holding my breath, I stuck my head in.

Four guys smoked cigars and tossed chips across the poker table. Beside them, a couple screwed the crap out of each other, uncaring of the other people in the room. Of all of those people, none of them were Owen.

I left them to it and tried the other doors in the hall. Three of them were locked. Two had people hooking up on the other side. I rounded the corner and shot back, plastering myself against the wall. Owen didn't notice.

He pressed the girl in the bendy straw dress against the plaster—one arm propped over her head, and the other hand playing with her plastic skirt. Owen chose to wear wrapping paper with two bows covering his nipples. Because the fucker was a present.

My lips curled. As welcome a present as the one the plague leaves when it rips through the population.

Straw Girl giggled. "All the rooms are taken."

"So. We'll go in the bathroom."

"Ew. You think I'm getting on my knees in a frat house toilet? You must be joking."

She tried to walk away and his hand flew off her skirt and struck the wall, stopping her in her tracks. "Forget the bathroom. I know somewhere we can go. Private. Romantic." He kissed her knuckles, smiling into her eyes like he wasn't a loathsome son of a bitch. "Come on, Lindsay. I've had a crush on you since high school."

"Really?"

"Are you kidding? Everyone did. You were the hottest girl in school." Owen dropped on his knees, slapping his hand over his heart. "For all the hopeless geeks who dreamed you'd notice him, I'm taking my shot. Please, Lindsay, suck my dick."

She swatted his arm, eyes rolling. "You're so stupid," she said, but not in a tone laced with rejection.

I gagged. It was bad enough the shit stain thought he was charming. Watching women fall for it turned my stomach inside out.

Winter's note came back to me. Even then, I had it close—taped to the inside of my top.

Owen came at me hardest of all. Painting frigid bitch on my door. Leaving disgusting messages on my phone all day and night from hundreds of random numbers.

"Come on, hopeless geek." Lindsay sashayed down the hall, floating a kiss over her shoulder. "You said you knew somewhere private we could go."

I hurried away, racing down the stairs and into the living room. I hid just inside the entrance, watching the two of them come downstairs and head out the door. I made to follow them as something flashed out of the corner of my eye. I ran headfirst into sweaty caution tape.

There wasn't a chance to react before my mask was ripped off my face.

"You." Saylor's thick, cupid's-bow lips pressed into a thin line. "I knew it."

Gabriella, Piper, and Everleigh were on me in a blink, flanking their flaxen-haired leader.

I flicked between their curling lips, then over their heads to the door. Owen and Lindsay were getting ahead of me.

"Yes, it's me," I said, "and I was just leaving. Sorry for crashing your boring party. Next time, I'll do something fun with my Saturday night and watch my toenails grow."

I pushed through and was shoved back.

"Not so fast, Sinclair." Saylor snapped her fingers. "Turn the music off!"

The noise cut off with a jarring screech, drawing everyone's attention. The ping-pong ball bounced across the kitchen floor. The bare-chested players were too busy coming closer to notice.

"You don't have to rush off so fast." Piper came at me. I lurched back to stop her boobs getting in my face.

"Yeah," Saylor said. The curled lips morphed into a different shape, forming a smile that glinted in her eyes. "We're glad you're here."

She bumped me, moving me back. I sidestepped and bounced off Everleigh. They were herding me into the middle of the room.

"So glad," Gabriella purred. "We have an announcement to make and it's much easier with you here to help."

Saylor glanced around. "Where's Katie?"

Piper scoffed. "Upstairs getting fucked, no doubt."

"Good."

I planted my feet, refusing to move another step even as their sweat and Chanel perfume clogged my nose. "What announcement?" I gritted, looking over their heads. I had to go. Now! "I don't have time for this."

"Make time, sweetie." Everleigh flicked my nose. "It's important."

"Listen up, everyone." Saylor snapped her fingers again, but there was no need. Except for the noise from outside and upstairs, no one made a sound. "I want to introduce you to Luna Sinclair. She's Winter Bowden's sister. That sad little thing who threw herself off a bridge last year."

My lips peeled back from my teeth. "You better watch where the fuck you're going with this, Burkhardt."

"Oooh," she mocked. "So scary. Don't worry, I don't have anything to say about your sister. All that needed to be said about her... I told to her face."

Stiffening, my fists balled. Saylor circled me.

"No, this is about you." Her voice carried through the room. "You're the one who didn't get the message, and enrolled in *our* school where you don't fucking belong. You're worse than a Dreg, Sinclair. At least they know their place." She pointed at some poor guy in a trash bag. "And they make sure the world knows it too."

"The world also knows that you're a fork-tongued demon. Now get out of my way." I rushed Piper and Everleigh, and was thrown back again. "What the fuck is your problem! You want me out of your party, I'm gone."

Gabriella gave me a sickly sweet smile. "We don't want you gone. What we want is for everyone to get a good look."

"Burn this face into your memory," Saylor called. She grabbed my jaw, twisting my head toward the crowd. "Don't forget the name Luna Sinclair. Since she insisted on coming to school here, we'll have to look out for her. We can't have her slinking around campus unnoticed. Make sure she feels as welcome here as her sister did.

"We wouldn't want sweet Luna to go the same way as Winter."

Knocking her off my chin, I reared back and punched her in the mouth. Saylor's head snapped to three cries, gasps, and an "oh damn!"

"I told you to keep my sister's name out of your mouth! Keep trying me, Burkhardt. That smile won't be so pretty when all your teeth are broken."

She whirled on me, snarling. Blood stained her mouth, adding a horrifying effect to the burning hatred singeing me where I stood.

"Bitch!" Hands grabbed me.

"Don't," Saylor barked. "It's not her fault. All inbred, low-class sluts like her know how to do is lash out violently. We're not sinking to her level."

"You're so far below my level, the sun doesn't reach you down there." Strong, rolling energy washed over me, twitching my fingers against my thigh. How dare she speak so heartlessly about Winter. "You want to meet an inbred, low-class slut? Blow her kisses while you're covering up that fat lip tomorrow morning."

Saylor flicked the blood off her chin. "She opens her mouth and more filth comes out. We get it, Sinclair. You're trash—just like your pathetic sister and gold-digging mommy. But if you're going to our school and crashing our parties, the least you can do is respect the dress code. *That* is what you wear."

I had a second to realize she was pointing at a guy wearing a trash bag, then they were on me. Saylor, Gabriella, and the girls slapped, scratched, and tore at me, ripping my cloud outfit to shreds.

"Stop," I screamed as Piper yanked the mesh band underneath, nearly exposing my breasts to the hooting, cheering crowd. "Get off!"

"What's going on here?"

Rafael broke through the crush, stepping inside the circle. Saylor and her crew backed off me in an instant.

"We playing a game?" he asked lightly, beaming away. "Rip off the non-clothes? That was meant for me." Rafael grasped my arm and drew me behind him, standing between me and the harpy cunts. "I'll go next."

The four didn't move. Torturing me for the crowd was one thing, but torturing me in front of the guy they were desperately trying to sleep with wasn't so easy.

"Go on," Rafael prompted when they didn't move. He rolled his hips. "Tear off my leaves. Give everyone in the party a treat."

I didn't bother to stick around and see if they got their treat. I shoved through the bodies, racing onto the front lawn. Tears stung my eyes.

My cotton clouds were gone, leaving behind the lights—dangling off me and only hanging off from a few seams they hadn't ripped. The mesh I used was opaque, but there wasn't much of it. A thin band around my breasts and butt were all that was left. Another round of wolf whistles chased me onto the sidewalk.

Screaming, I ripped off the lights, flinging them away. I should've done more than punch that sneering bitch. Even after they ruined Winter's life, they mocked her. Crowed on the edge of admitting what they did to her, with a grin on their faces like it was all a fun game.

Standing there on the sidewalk, half naked and bleeding from dozens of scratches, I added four more names to the list.

But first, Owen.

I ran down the sidewalk, searching for him and Lindsay. They had too long a head start on me. I didn't see them anywhere.

Think, Luna. Think! He said he knew somewhere private and romantic. Is it his place?

If they went back to his dorm or his locked, gated, and guarded mansion, I had no chance of getting to him tonight.

But if it was his place, he could've just said that instead of going on about some lover's hideaway. He also seemed pretty desperate for that blow job.

Owen got on his knees and made an even bigger ass of himself. Plus, the party was still going and there was a house full of women for him to sleaze on. Would he dip out an hour before midnight?

The shadowy, romantic spot could be on campus. It could be close by.

I started walking, stumbling toward the back end of Greek Row. My mind recalled the map of campus included in my welcome packet.

The other way was dorms and empty classroom buildings. If he didn't walk over twenty minutes to the dorm, and he opted for a hookup spot nearby, that left the tree-shaded paths spiderwebbing from this side of campus to the soccer and football fields. Along the way, a small pond bubbled beneath a man-made waterfall. On the map, they dubbed it Fowler's Retreat.

A scummy pond beside a bench was the kind of place an idiot like Owen Thasher would call romantic. The best part for him—he could ditch his date at any time and walk eight minutes back to the party.

I changed my number six times and had to get campus security to walk me to and from class. By the end of the semester, I barely left my room. He was always out there waiting to call me a dime-bag slut who should've taken it like a good girl and shut my fucking mouth.

Be there, Thasher. You better be there.

My pulse slowed as I made the trek, falling into an even, steady hum. A calm in my chest that didn't spread to my fingers—jerking and drumming on my legs. They moved of their own mind, tugging on my hem, smoothing it down, scratching an itch, and twitching out of control.

It only got worse as I descended the fluorescent-lit path, a silent figure that couldn't compete with the singing cicadas. I swept the trees, recalling the way to the pond. It was just up ahead.

The grunts reached me first. Rough, primal sounds that sickened me. It was a sin against nature that Owen experience any pleasure, happiness, or satisfaction after what he'd done.

The day I returned from spring break, Owen broke into my room, dragged me out of the shower, and threw me at his buddies.

Owen stretched out on the bench, his head flung back. He didn't see me duck behind the sequoia. He wasn't paying attention to much of anything with Lindsay's head bobbing between his legs.

They pinned me to the floor and groped me, laughing themselves sick while Owen snapped pictures. It wasn't enough that they violated and assaulted me.

My twitching fingers traveled beneath my hem, finding the single page from Winter's letter that would give me strength... and the switchblade taped to my inner thigh.

Owen sent the photos to every Royal and posted them on WinterSinclairIsAFilthySlut.com.

I crumpled the page over my heart, wetness running down my cheeks. It was natural that I cry, but the emotion filling me wasn't sadness.

Despair, helplessness, frustrated rage were all I knew before I found the letters she left me and Mom. Those feelings lifted the barest fraction as I read, allowing an icy calm to chill my veins. I wasn't helpless. I knew the way forward.

I knew what I needed to do for my sister.

Everywhere I went they flashed the photos in my face, but because the guys were blurred out and the dorm's cameras were conveniently off that night, the dean refused to expel them. He said it was my word against theirs, and they all had statements from their lawyers swearing they were miles from my dorm.

Owen got away with it, Luna. After everything he did to me, he didn't suffer a single second.

"He will, Winter," I whispered. The blade slid free of its sheath. "All he'll know for the rest of his short life is suffering. I promise."

Owen grunted out his ejaculation, flopping back on the bench. "Nice, babe."

Lindsay popped up and climbed on his lap. "My turn."

"Next time." Owen held her at arm's length. "We should get back to the party."

"What? Why? We don't have to go so soon."

"Your friends will be looking for you."

"Screw them." Lindsay tried to wrap his arms around her waist. "I'd rather be here with you."

Owen threw her off. "For fuck's sake, you can't take a hint. I'm done with you and your sloppy blow jobs. Fuck off already."

The knife handle tightened in my death grip. This was the soulless cockroach my sister dealt with every day.

Lindsay stumbled away, eyes wide. "What happened to your big crush on me and all that shit?"

"What happened is I got what I wanted. You can go now."

"Asshole!" She swung and Owen caught her wrist, stopping her slap short of his cheek.

"Don't try that again." His voice dropped the temperature twenty degrees. "Get out of here, Lindsay. Now."

She stomped off, shouting and cursing him out. I stayed low as she stormed past.

I shouldn't have worried about getting Owen alone. His repellant personality drove people away all on its own.

Gripping the knife behind my back, I stepped out from the trees. If he turned around before I got close enough, all he'd see was another Sinclair girl to tear apart. It was fitting that's how he'd die—underestimating Winter and the people who loved her.

Owen was never going to get away with hurting her—not while I lived.

I closed the distance, bare feet padding soundlessly through the grass. Strange how quickly I accepted having to kill him and the others in her letter. Though it made sense, their lives in payment for my sister's life, I thought I'd have a moment of crisis when the time came. Everything I learned about right, wrong, moral, and lawful would come back to me, and I'd feel the drive to protect my soul, if not them.

Of course, I should've known that wouldn't happen. My soul was scraped out the day my sister died.

Owen belched, pulling out cigarettes and a lighter from the depths of his wrapping paper. The wind carried his smoke into my nose.

Five feet.

Two feet.

I reached out my hand.

Yank his head back and slice. In one smooth move, Owen dies alone in the cold and dark, just like Winter. One move—she rests easier.

My hands didn't twitch or shake. My heart slowed to a steady pace.

Winter... this is for you.

His hair brushed my fingertips. Raising the blade high, it fell in a graceful arc.

A hand clamped my wrist, stopping the knife short of Owen's blissfully unaware self. Before I could think, a gloved palm clamped over my mouth and a band circled my waist.

I screamed inside as I was dragged away from Owen, carried into the trees.

Chapter Five

"**M**hh! Mhhh!"

Screaming and thrashing, I twisted my neck, trying to see my captors. The tight clamp on my jaw kept me pinned to his chest, preventing me looking up.

Two men had me. They raced me through the brush, carrying me back toward campus.

Security? They saw what I was about to do to Owen and dragged me away.

Then why aren't they talking? Why didn't they holler and bluster, order me to drop my weapon and then myself?

I bucked harder, snapping at the gloves. They were not security.

We broke through the brush, coming out behind the psychology building. Two figures waited in the glow of the fluorescent light, I recognized them instantly.

Rafael leaned against the brick façade, a few leaves short of nature's loincloth. Beside him, Cato crouched on the back steps, flicking a lighter on and out.

"Oh good." Rafael clapped. "You got her."

"Mmmh!"

"Where was she?" he asked. "Did she get to him?"

"No," replied one of my abductors. "Close, though. We stopped her just in time. Thasher didn't notice a thing."

"Wow." The shadows stretched Rafael's grin. He plucked the switchblade from my grip. "You were really going to go through with it. I'm impressed, Sinclair. You've got titanium balls under that deliciously short skirt. A fact I should find off-putting, but it's making mine tighten all the same."

I tried to kick him but the hold on my legs was too tight.

"Put her down."

They let me go just like that—placing me next to Cato, who crowded me, his face muzzle uncomfortably close and his lighter closer. Heat tickled my chin as they towered over me—Rafael, Lucien, and Wilder.

Rafael moved to lean on the rail, cutting off that route of escape. On the opposite rail, the guy I had yet to meet in person, Lucien, adjusted his gloves, smoothed down his ruffle shirt, and flashed me a smile, sharpened canines glinting. You would've thought we were gathering for a chat and tea, if not for Wilder's burning glare. He stood between them—arms folded and bursting out of his shirt.

"What the hell are you mad about?!" I barked. "You weren't the one manhandled and dragged around campus like a futon! How'd you know I was there? Were you following me? You really are freaks, you creepy-ass, twisted, shit-licking, vomit bags! You're lucky I don't have that knife or I'd fuck you up six ways to Saturday!"

My rant went full steam, devolving into insults and curses I didn't know I knew. My stress was understandable. After months of planning, compromises, and the rending of my soul it took to get here, I finally had one of the men responsible for my sister's death within reach.

Rafael laughed. "That's right, love, get it all out. I'm not anatomically capable of doing half those things to myself, but if you want to give it a try, I'm up for anything in bed."

I launched at them. "Get out of my way!"

Wilder was a boulder. I bounced off his hard abs, ending up back on my ass. I didn't move him a centimeter but my efforts did gift me Cato's unsettling growling in my ear.

"Luna, please, calm down." Slow, honey-dipped speech flowed from Lucien's lips. "We apologize for the rough handling, but you understand we had to act fast. You were in the process of slitting a man's throat."

He said it so casually, a shiver trawled my spine, hardening my muscles.

I took a deep breath, skimming blank, angry, and amused expressions. "That's a cute joke, but I wasn't in the process of doing any such thing. Whatever you think you saw—"

"Save it," Rafael broke in. "We're in a blind spot. No cameras. No one in the building or out. And if someone comes, we'll see them long before they overhear what we're talking about. We're safe to talk here, Sinclair."

"I said I don't know—"

"Stop wasting our time," Wilder bit off. "You came here to get revenge on the Royals who drove Winter to suicide. If we wanted to stop you, we'd have sent the cops after you instead of picking you up ourselves."

"You—" I halted, part of what he said penetrating. "What do you mean, if you wanted to stop me?"

Rafael sighed loudly. "You're seriously asking that? I dropped how many hints."

"Hints?"

He bobbed his head, eyes wide in mocking and brows up. His earbuds stuck in fast despite the motion. "Told you I was the son of a hit man. That I'm the go-to fixer around here. If you need anything, call me... Any of this ringing bells?"

I stared at him.

"Let me help, Rafa. You can be quite opaque." Lucien bent, smiling at me. "What he was trying to tell you is that he has the lack of morals one acquires when they're raised by a hired gun. He's in the habit of doing things society frowns on in exchange for favors, and he has a brother and a few friends who are too. In summary, Rafael was offering you our help in taking down the Royals who hurt your sister."

"Help," I repeated slowly. Saying it out loud didn't help either.

"Yes, help," Rafael said, "and damn, do you need it. You're begging to be caught, girl. Wilder, how many people know she stunned Owen till he wet himself the other night?"

"Everyone on campus."

"How many people know Owen led the worst of the bullying against her sister?"

"Everyone on campus," he said flatly.

"How many Royals know she crashed his party tonight?"

"Almost all of them. The freshman Royals will know by morning."

Rafael nodded, sweeping out a hand. "And how many people clocked her racing off in the same direction as Owen and his hookup?"

"Five," Wilder said. "Not including me and Lucien."

"So, when he was found murdered on a bench, who do you think the police were going to question first?"

"Luna Sinclair," the three said at once. Cato bumped my shoulder.

I opened my mouth and nothing came out. What was I supposed to say? Their logic was solid. If I was a cop, I'd connect those dots too, but they can't—*these guys can't.* No one is getting in my way. Not after all I did to get here.

"Murdered on a park bench?" I forced a laugh. "That's a bit dramatic. I'm sure it looked bad, but I wasn't going to kill the guy. I planned to cut his hair. Let's see him strut around all full of himself with a bald spot."

"Cut his hair?" Wilder repeated. "With a switchblade? Scissors were invented in 400 BC, sweetheart. Try again. The details are everything in a trial."

I flushed. "I wasn't going to hurt him. You have it all wrong."

"You have a story and you're sticking to it," Rafael said. "I respect that. Cato and I were sailing the Atlantic this summer, and you won't hear me say otherwise. But we're not kidding, Sinclair." The joking leeched from his tone. "We'll help you—whatever you ask. You have no idea the hell we were going to rain on Owen, Levi, and the rest of them. They would've wished they never met your sister. Then, we bumped into you on the first day, and there could only be one reason why you're here."

Jaw clenching, I looked away.

"She was your sister. Revenge belongs to you," he said. "We won't take over or get in your way, but you do need our help. Without us, you'll be sleeping in a jail cell before Levi and the rest ever know you were after them."

I didn't speak for a long time. Neither did they, waiting me out.

"Let's say," I began, "that I do want revenge. Why would you help me? You knew my sister, but you don't know me. There's also the fact you're cozy with the Royals," I flung. "Have you fucked Saylor and her crew yet, or are you waiting until your schedules are clear so you can have the orgy at once and knock it out?"

He laughed. "That right there is how we'll help you. You actually believe I can stand those four. There's a reason Cato chases them off when they're pawing me. A man can come up with only so many fake compliments."

"What? You mean you don't like them either?"

"They're four pairs of matching Fendi wallets and no more, but if some terrible accident were to befall them, no one is looking at me." He beamed. "Why would they? As far as anyone is concerned, I worship the ground they walk on. That's rule one, Sinclair: the people you hate are the last ones to know."

"Not a bad rule," I said lightly, edging away from Cato.

"As for why." Something flashed in his eyes. "I was paid to get a woman named Katherina out of an arranged marriage between her and Josiah Thompkins."

I bared my teeth at the name.

"The business merger was going to make her folks millions and bring better pay and benefits to their employees. Katherina couldn't face telling them she wanted out. She tried manipulating Josiah into ending the engagement himself, and when that didn't work, she went to my dad."

I stopped trying to get away, listening.

"My dad doesn't deal with trivial matters like that unless they come with a higher price tag. He passed the job to me, and I took care of it. Her parents were sent photos of Josiah with three hookers. The shit they were getting up to made my eyes water, and I told you I'm an open-minded guy.

"Her folks ended the engagement on their own. Katherina was so happy she passed my number on to her younger sister. When Katherina's parents started talking about hooking sister number two up with Josiah's younger brother, Levi. Emily warned him not to pull any shit because she could end the whole thing and make it his fault with one phone call."

"What does that have to do with Winter?"

"Josiah Thompkins's younger brother is Levi. That marriage was going to make his family a shitload too. Not only that, his future wife put him on notice." Rafael met my eyes. "I don't need to tell you what a violent, vicious bastard he is."

No, he did not.

"Levi rounded up his buddies and set fire to our place over winter break," he dropped, widening my eyes. "Campus was deserted. We always stay while everyone else clears out to the ski resorts in Aspen. The fire would've smoked us out. Ten of them were waiting with bats and brass knuckles. That's if the fire didn't flat-out kill us."

"That's what would've happened," Lucien said softly. "If Winter hadn't overheard their plans and warned us. They set fire to an empty building and Wilder recorded it. The dean expelled everyone except for the guy sharing the name with Thompkins Hall. Levi got off with probation."

"Course he did," I spat, drawing my knees to my chest. "That's the only end to the story."

"Not quite," Wilder added. "We got all ten of those fuckers—hard. Levi's limp... he didn't have that a year ago."

"We beat his ass bloody," Rafael clarified. "Somehow, we think he figured out your sister warned us, because instead of getting us back, he went for her. Almost everyone hounded her last year, but Levi took it further. She saved our skins and becoming that fucker's next target was her reward."

The full story crushed me, but the end of it I knew. Levi did go after Winter with the harshness you expected of violent, vicious bastards. That's why he was the second person she named in her letter.

"We tried to help her," Lucien said, repeating Rafael. "I taught her to defend herself. And we told her all she had to do was give us a list—we'd take out everyone on it free of charge."

"But she said no," I whispered.

"She said no and asked us to stay out of it. Winter told us if we got involved, the situation would escalate and we'd make it worse for her. That's the last thing we wanted to do, so we backed off and only stepped in when they tried to pull something in front of us." Lucien tipped my chin. The shock of a stranger's touch faded as he stroked my cheek. "We were wrong, Luna. We shouldn't have listened. I'm so sorry... that we realized it too late."

Tears stained his fingers.

"That's why we'll do whatever you need," Rafael said, voice hard. "The Royals have it coming either from you or from us, so we might as well do it together. Between the five of us, we won't get caught, and we can't be stopped."

Clearing my throat, I swiped a hand across my face. "Again, thank you for what you tried to do for my sister. I truly appreciate that you were there for her, and I take back half the things I said about you just now. But none of this has anything to do with me. I'm not after revenge. Like I said, it was a prank. Harmless. I don't need your help or your tips." I stood up, staring Wilder down. "So, I'm going now, and I'll take my knife."

Rafael stepped between us, leveling me with his bare, painted chest. "Before you leave, consider what we bring to your plan—I know you have one," he said when I opened my mouth. "Thought out and planned to the last detail. You've got something picked out for each of them, you just don't have the skill to carry it out and not get caught. We do."

He pointed at Lucien. "He's mastered almost every martial art."

Lucien shrugged. "I've been around for one hundred and fifty-eight years. Had to do something to pass the time."

"Wilder is a hacker. He's also got a weapons collection that my father would give anything for."

Wilder glared at me harder.

"Cato is Cato."

I don't know what that was supposed to prove, but oddly, I didn't ask for more information. Deep down, I knew Cato wasn't someone you messed with.

"And I've made it my life's work to make the intentional look like an accident along with etcetera, etcetera, redacted, redacted. You'll find out the rest when you're one of us." He cuffed my chin. "So, stop playing hard to get. Become one of us. No one does it better than a Rogue."

I freed my switchblade from his grasp. "No, thank you," I said, sidestepping him. "Goodbye."

I made it five steps.

"Why not?" Rafael asked smoothly. "Out of curiosity."

Unbidden, my feet slowed, halting me in the grass. "Why?" Slowly, I turned. "For argument's sake, let's say I wasn't going to give Owen a haircut. Let's say I intended to... shave his beard. More than that, what if I want to shave the beards of everyone who hurt Winter? I'm supposed to believe you'll back me up? Hold them down while I pull out the shaving cream?"

"I'm loving this metaphor," Rafael hummed.

"You're not as deep in this as I am," I snapped. "I have nothing to lose. Yeah, my sister tipped you off about Levi, but guilt and regret don't come *close* to what I'm feeling. I don't want your help because you're not willing to take this as far as me. Know how I know? Because if you were, we wouldn't be standing here having this conversation right now. Owen, Levi, and all of them would be d—" I cut myself off, sense holding my tongue.

"They'd be bald and clean-shaven," I continued. "I was trapped in a Catholic boarding school across the ocean, then I spent the summer watching my mother night and day—terrified her cries that she wouldn't live without my sister, was more than the grief.

"*You four* didn't have those issues. You were here in Regalia, strolling around campus with them, going to their parties, and fending off their thrown panties. You could've done something—anything—to pay them back long before I enrolled here. Don't act like we're in this together. When it comes down to it, you won't risk yourselves for my sister. You won't take it all the way."

Turning away, I made for the tree line.

"You're right," Rafael called, stopping me in my tracks. "Partly. We didn't hunt down the shits over the summer because we couldn't. We had to wait until they all came back to campus where security is shockingly lax. Can't say the same about the guards, gates, and mansions they live in.

"When they did return to campus, you were here too, so I held off what we had planned since the one with the right to make them bleed is you, Luna." His voice, his footsteps, came closer. "But I can promise you, whether you were here or not, those guys wouldn't have gotten away with it. Would I have *shaved* their beards? No."

"Exactly, you—!"

"Because that's too good for them," he hissed, silencing me. "Winter Bowden was the only decent person in this gas station toilet of a school. She risked herself to save us, and she barely knew us. All they did to her and she didn't fight back, curse them, or give back the hell they deserved. She just kept hoping they'd find a shred of humanity in their rotted souls and leave her in peace."

I trembled, fists balling.

"What do you do to people like that? What do they deserve? I know this much, it's not a quick shave on a bench—drifting off fast and painless with no idea why or who brought them to justice. What I would do"—his arm encircled me, pressing me to his chilled chest—"is drag it out to the point of overkill. I'd make every waking second a nightmare, then slink into their sleep so it'd bring no relief. I'd put them through the pain Winter went through—helpless and alone, praying for it to stop and it never does."

His chill seeped into my skin, spreading ice through my veins.

"I'd strip away everything they loved out of their life. Destroy their reputations, drain their riches, and rid them of the easy lives and privilege that got them this far. Then when they can't take any more, I'd *strike*."

I jumped as he gripped me, fingers digging into my stomach.

"By then," Rafael said, tone lightening. "I wouldn't need to shave anybody, Sinclair. They'll put the blade to their throat themselves. That's what they did to Winter." A light kiss pressed to my temple. "Why shouldn't they go the same way?"

The guys surrounded us, their eyes holding a grim ferality I sensed was in Rafael's eyes.

"You would do all of that?" I rasped. "You'd hound and torture the Royals until they begged for you to end it?"

"Yes," Wilder, Rafael, and Lucien said.

"Then, prove it." I stepped out of Rafael's arms. "You say we're in this together and you'll go that far for a girl who barely knew you, then let me see a bit of your *plan* in action. If Owen Thasher doesn't have a limp to match Levi's by next Friday, I don't want to hear anything else from any of you. Stay the fuck out of my way."

Rafael bowed as they melted into the shadows. "As you wish, Cloud Girl. You don't make a move until we've delivered your present. Make sure you don't skip out on breakfast." His shiny smile disappeared into the trees. "First meal of the day is most important."

THE RIVER PULLED AT my feet, an invisible force around my ankles, yanking me from reach of shore.

My hands slapped the water—desperately clawing for purchase, my lungs abandoning the fight long before them. Suddenly, water swallowed me, rushing into my nose and mouth.

Mossy beds tinged a dark, growing color—spreading through the riverbed and clouding the clear blue water.

Red.

The river was bleeding red.

I kicked, thrashed, and swam—seeking air as my lungs withered away.

The surface broke. I burst up coughing and sputtering. Vision clearing, I fell upon the source of the river's new color, gazing into Winter's blue, bloated face.

I shot up in bed, throat raw and strangled midscream.

Sweat soaked my clothes and sheets, gluing them to my skin. Groaning, I fell against my headboard. A dull ache formed in my skull, set to grow throughout another sleepless night and pound my head throughout the day.

You'd think I'd be used to this by now. Nightmares were my one constant these days. My mother was slipping away. My stepfather was marrying me off to a guy who can't stand me. I was in a horrible new school with people who made it clear they planned to make me wish I was an actual dreg. Everything was shifting, except the nightmares. They followed me into my sleep almost every night, as if reminding me I didn't deserve rest while Winter lay unavenged.

Dragging myself up, I stripped my sheets and replaced them with fresh ones. I brought plenty of spares. That done, I peeled off my clothes and stepped into the shower, thankful again that rich schools like this gave everyone their own bathroom. Slinking out every night into a grotty public shower was a terrible addition to a rough night. It certainly made it harder to slink to the bottom of the tub and let the pounding streams wash down my tears.

I was going to do it. I was this close to ending the man who humiliated, harassed, and assaulted my sister—plastering her pain on the internet for the entire world to see. If Lucien hadn't grabbed my hand, Lindsay would've been the last woman Owen Thasher treated like dirt.

And he would not have known why.

Sliding down, I stretched out on the porcelain, surrendering to the steamy water. I could hardly process what Rafael, Wilder, and Lucien told me that night. My sister saved them, so they intended to get justice for her.

For so long I believed no one in Regalia University cared about Winter. Not only did they care, but they kept an eye on me—stopping me from making a mistake with Owen that would get me caught, and then offering to help me get it right.

What was I supposed to think?

They say they were cool with Winter, but Winter never mentioned the Rogues to me. A guy who thinks he's a vampire and another who wears a muzzle is the kind of thing you bring up in your weekly video chats with your sister.

What if they're lying? Rafael said he takes care of people's problems in exchange for favors and money. How did I know his girlfriend, Saylor, didn't put him up to the whole thing? Get close to me, lower my guard, and then destroy the Dreg she took a hatred to a second after she met me.

Couldn't they have turned me into the police if destroying me was the goal? a voice asked. *They grabbed you while standing over an unsuspecting victim, holding a knife.*

I flipped over, clapping my hands over my ears. I didn't know anything. Nothing made sense. Nothing felt right.

Four guys appearing out of nowhere, swearing they understood my agony and the lengths it drove me to. Not just understood, but were willing to help and protect me so I might get away with the unspeakable.

That wasn't real. Things like that didn't happen. Morally gray men didn't appear when you needed them. Help did not come when you called. And revenge did not serve itself up on a platter—ready-made and sprinkled with the final touches.

In the real world, there were no Rogues.

So, what did that make all of this but a trick? A cruel game like the many played on Winter. They heard Luna Sinclair was coming to campus, and connected a few dots of their own. What would I want more than making Winter's tormentors pay? All they had to do was tug that string and I'd eat their crap up.

I told them to prove themselves, but they didn't need to. I was on my own. No one could do for Winter what I had to do.

The Rogues can play their games with everyone else. If tonight was a scam, they'd end up on my list with the rest.

"WHAT'S YOUR PROBLEM?"

I lifted my eyes off my plate and wished I didn't. Victor was scarfing down his food like finishing his breakfast in five minutes was a squid game.

"Ugh. Want to slow down? You'll choke."

He replied around a mouthful of bacon. "Sooner I finish, the sooner I can leave."

"Screw you. You're the one who insisted we eat together, *fiancé*."

"Your point?"

Rolling my eyes, I drifted off him and toward the food line, searching out the Rogues. Monday morning, I rolled into the cafeteria at seven o'clock on the dot. This was a trick. They were probably going to cook something up with Owen, staging fake payback to get in good with me. All of this I knew. Still, something forced me out of bed—and it was only half my promise to Victor.

"Seriously," Victor said. "What's up with you?"

"I'm sitting here, eating my bacon and eggs panini, minding my own business. Why would something be up?"

Victor reached for his milk, fixed on me. "You blew off dinner Friday night, claiming you weren't feeling well. Then I heard you went to the ABC party."

I paused midchew. Wilder said the freshman Royals would know by morning. I'd give him credit. He was right.

"Yeah," I stalled. "So?"

"Why would you crash that party, Sinclair? What were you trying to prove?"

I frowned. "Trying to prove? I got dressed up and hit a fun party. I didn't mess with anyone, get wasted, make a fool of myself, or mess around with anyone's boyfriend. I was once again minding my own business, then Saylor got in my face. What exactly did I do wrong?"

"It was Royals only. You shouldn't have gone there without me."

My brows blew up my forehead. "Are you for real? Since when do I need you on my arm to leave my house? They don't clamp on the ball and chain until *after* the I dos, dear."

Victor shook his head. "You're trying to distract from the conversation by kicking off an argument. You always do this."

"No, I don't," I cried. "And you don't know me well enough to say what I *always* do."

"You shouldn't have gone to that party, Luna," Victor said, boring into me. "You crashed the party and punched Saylor Burkhardt. Do you know who she is?"

"She's a precious fucking Royal. I get it."

"No." Victor looked around, dropping his voice. "She's not just *a* Royal. She's one of *the* Royals."

I gave him a blank, slightly irritated look. It was his turn to roll his eyes at me. We really were a sweet couple.

"Look, it's like actual royalty. A duchess is a royal, but she doesn't out-rank the queen. There is a hierarchy among the Regalia Royals too—based on age, wealth, status, connections, and their standing in the community. The Burkhardts are at the very top."

"Why? Because her father is a senator? That beats you out over the families who own multimillion-dollar companies?"

"It's not about her father. It's her grandfather. William Burkhardt. He owns this town, Luna. The dirt everything is sitting on—it's all his. The houses, the businesses, the university," he said, "is leased. And the rent goes into his coffers. The deals to set up shops here were made with him. William Burkhardt giveth and he can taketh away. Especially if his falsely sweet favorite granddaughter drips her poison in his ear.

"Below her, are Saylor's ladies-in-waiting and the upperclassman Royals with the same net worth. A few people sitting on less are near their level too, but that's because they've been in Regalia for as long as the Burkhardts." He shook his hands. "Doesn't matter—the whole hierarchy is complicated. Lots of little things move you up or down. The point is, with-in the entire shifting, changing system, one thing remains the same: the Burkhardts are on top. If there's anyone in this town you don't mess with, it's Saylor."

I reclined in the booth, the picture of the party becoming clearer. "So, when Saylor Burkhardt announces a new addition to the shit list, the drones attack the stray bee, obeying their queen."

"That's a weird-ass way of putting it."

"But it's true, isn't it?" I squeezed his hand without thinking. "If she doesn't like someone, everyone trailing her on the list will shun them to stay on her good side. Tell me I'm wrong."

Victor hesitated, and that was all the answer I needed.

"I'm a class behind her," he finally said. "I don't know all the stuff they got up to. Just rumors. But... yes. If Saylor doesn't like someone—doesn't like you—life gets difficult pretty fast. It was a Burkhardt who started the whole Royal/Dreg thing. Separating the town and putting their family on top. Saylor's happy for it to stay that way."

I nodded. Yes, a lot of what he said fit into the things I'd seen in the mere week I've been at Regalia University.

"She could stop it too, couldn't she?" My voice was a low, thin rasp. "She can end the whole Dreg nonsense. She could take people off the shit list as easily as she put them on."

She could've helped Winter.

"No, she couldn't," Victor said.

"Why not?" I demanded, louder than intended.

"Because that requires— Oh, what do they call it? Kindness, empathy, a conscience." He tore off a strip of bacon. "You're asking a lot from the girl whose family carved out their own kingdom within the continental US. Because being rich as Midas and running the government wasn't enough."

I eyed him, picking up on his tone. "That's pretty harsh for a system you're a part of. Do you know how many people have shot daggers at me for bagging a Wilson? From what I hear, your family is high on the hierarchy."

"My parents are," he corrected. "Here, I'm just a freshman."

"Don't sell yourself short. No one is calling you a Dreg. No one is going to mess with you or get on your bad side, freshman or not. There's still hope you'll dump me and pick from the long line of eligible Royal bachelorettes. I bet Saylor and all the Royal girls have never been nicer to you."

Victor heaved a sigh. "If you've got a question, ask it."

"Are you really just a freshman?" I leaned over the table, looking him in the face. "How seriously do the Royals take this hierarchy thing? And if it matters so much, what does it mean that you're marrying me?"

"Like you said, it's a long way to the altar."

I stopped him picking up another slice of bacon. "Answer the question."

Victor lurched forward, snapping the food out of his captive hand. He grinned while he chewed—ridiculously handsome to the point it annoyed. No one should be that gorgeous and that infuriating at the same time.

"I really am just a freshman," he said, swallowing. "I'm higher on the food chain than some people, lower than others. But that doesn't make it smart to get in a senior Royal's face just because he's worth ten million instead of a hundred. He'll take over the family business and access his trust fund long before I do, and ten million is plenty to hire hit men, hackers, and fixers willing to fuck up my life to settle a score.

"Surviving in Regalia takes politics. Thinking five steps ahead. Making alliances with the right people. Circling the edge with your enemies—neither getting too close nor backing up too far that you fall over the cliff."

I nodded along with him. It wasn't lost on me that we were having our first civil conversation, and I was actually learning something from him. You couldn't take down an enemy you didn't understand. The world of the Royals was more complicated than I thought.

That could be why Katie hangs out with Saylor, Everleigh, Gabriella, and Piper.

She called them best friends, but there was real anger in her voice when she said they were bullying sociopaths. As unfiltered and awful as Katie is, she must understand there are people you drive off and people you keep close. What would the consequences be for her if she ended up on Saylor's bad side? And would she throw me off if I hugged her because Saylor is the queen bee, and Katie told her off anyway?

Katie would definitely shove me off her. She'd also follow my thank-you with a "fuck you."

"Some things move you up and some move you down," I repeated. "Our impending nuptials. Do I move you down the list?"

Victor flicked down to his plate. "It's not that simple."

"A yes or no will do."

"Yes."

I bobbed my head. This news didn't surprise me. "Because my mother used to be working class and I'm just the stepdaughter of a wealthy man?"

"Basically."

"Alright, here's my next question: if Saylor is number one, Gabriella and the rest are number two, where does that put your family on the food chain. Three? Four?"

I sensed he didn't want to answer. Victor stared at his empty plate, clearly wishing he had bacon to delay his reply.

"Victor?"

"Two, Luna. The Wilsons have been in Regalia since it was founded. There are Wilsons in the government, heading up most industries, running successful companies overseas, and then the family business, which extends to four continents. The only family above us are the Burkhardts."

"Wow." My voice was flat. "The questions just keep coming. Here's another one: Why the hell would your parents choose me of all people to wear your nana's ring? I'm now doubly sure you could've gotten a girl who would tie the knot early."

Victor shrugged. "I don't know all the details. It's only my fucking life. Why should I know? All my mother would say is they worked out an arrangement with your stepfather that'll be beneficial for both families."

"Did Jack tell them I've got a magical vagina and a genie comes out when it's rubbed? Because I don't know what else I'm supposed to give you when we tie the knot."

Victor snorted, cracking up. "Now that's an itty-bitty living space. I'd marry you for three wishes."

Giggling, I pictured him rubbing my clit furiously, demanding to never go bald.

Our eyes met and we clammed up. *What the hell? Did I just have a pleasant moment with Victor Wilson?*

"Anyway," I said, straightening. "Is that why you've been a jerk to me? 'Cause you're mad a Sinclair is dragging down the golden name of Wilson?"

"I'm a jerk to you? Are you kidding me? You start it every damn time."

"See? It's a jerk who rewrites history like that."

Victor dropped his head, sighing up at the ceiling. "It better be a magical vagina."

I cracked a smile, though I didn't let him see.

"No, Sinclair. Our problems are not because of your status or last name. I couldn't care less about that."

"Really? Why?"

Victor didn't look away from the patterned ceiling. "Because all that shit is poison. Look at what it's turned Regalia into? Look at what it's done to my family." The lines on his neck stood out, tightening with his fist. "First my brother, now me. I almost want you to take us down, Luna. Maybe then, we wouldn't have to care so much about what people think... and can just be."

I reached for him, and stopped myself. It was such a natural response—comfort someone who was upset. But this was me and Victor, and our mutual dislike was another constant. I needed a few things to remain the same.

"Thanks for the heads-up. I've already gotten one warning that I need to be smarter about how I deal with the Royals." Rafael and his leaves floated through my mind, leaving behind warm cheeks. "Two warnings and bruised knuckles are enough for me to take the hint."

"Did you get the hint?" He stood up with me, slinging his messenger bag up his shoulder. "I'm not going to hear you punched a Burkhardt again?"

I crossed my heart. "I swear that I shall not knock out a bitch, unless my sister's name gets in her mouth. So sayeth, so shall it be."

Victor wandered off, a mumbled "weirdo" floating over his shoulder.

I stayed behind for as long as I could. The Rogues didn't show up for breakfast, but Owen did—laughing and joking with a bunch of his friends. There wasn't a scratch on the asshole.

Standing up, I went to return my tray. A hard body slammed into me, knocking me to the floor.

"Oh no, I'm so sorry!" A girl with red hair and glasses helped me up, dusting off my back. "I didn't see you. Are you okay?"

"I'm fine."

Grabbing my fallen bag, I dumped my stuff and continued to class. Whispers and not-so-quiet murmurings followed me to the English building.

"...Sinclair..."

"...that girl's sister..."

"...heard she knocked out Saylor Burkhardt. Badass."

The last comment came from a guy leaning on the rail leading into the building. I caught his eye and he nodded at me, smirking. "It's about time someone made one of the Royals eat it. Nicely done, Sinclair."

I nodded back, though unease laced my smile. I've never seen that guy before in my life. He wasn't a Royal, in my dorm, or in any of my classes, but he knew exactly who I was and what went down the other night. If everyone knew who I was, they know about Winter. You didn't forget the girl who committed suicide on campus.

Thor forbid I credit the weirdos in muzzles and Victorian dress with being right, but if the people who publicly tortured Winter dropped dead, why wouldn't I be the first person they looked at? My hope of flying under the radar was blown. If I was going to see this through to the end, I couldn't let anyone stop me. There couldn't be proof even if there was suspicion. *Maybe I do need help—*

I cut the thought off at the knees.

I don't need the Rogues or anyone else. I have a plan. The other night I was raging and panicked about losing Owen. Next time, I'll pay attention to my surroundings—make sure no one sees me going after Owen, or follows me.

I do not need the Rogues, I repeated to myself. I can't trust those guys. This is too important to risk on guys who say they're not in with the Royals, but break off their engagements and trade their favors.

Professor Anthony stood at the whiteboard, writing the last letter in *ethos, pathos, and logos.* I lingered longer than needed as I headed to my seat.

The reason I blew off dinner was because I spent all of Thursday night rewriting his paper. Every time I thought it was good, I got in my head, wondering if my sentences read as airport advertisements. I crashed at three a.m. not able to type another word. That left Friday night and Saturday morning to perfect my outfit for the ill-fated party.

I wondered if Adonis showed and made up with his parents. I wonder if he read my paper. The big fat coward I was, I dropped it off outside of his office hours, leaving it with a teaching assistant who texted me later confirming it was in his hands.

"Hey, Luna. Luna."

Blinking, I turned, falling on three waving girls taking up the fifth row.

"Over here," one called. "Sit with us."

"Ah. No, it's okay," I replied, not slowing down. "I like sitting in the back."

"Come on, don't be like that. Sit with us. Dregs got to stick together."

The giggling girls from the week before passed by. "Yeah, because that's what everyone wants—the trash to clump together."

Her friend chimed in, "Like the nasty wad of slimy, dirty hair in the drain. Why don't you Dregs do everyone a real favor and get out of our school?"

"Why don't you shut your mouth before I make you eat that slimy hair wad," I snapped. "If you three don't have business, get some."

"Excuse me?" she screeched. "Who do you think you're talking to?"

I brushed by and pointedly sat down beside the "Dregs." "I don't have a clue who you are, so you can't be that important."

"Bitch."

"Common street trash."

They stormed off, cursing everything about me. I didn't care. They could say what they wanted. I've always had a tough skin. You developed it under the tutelage of nuns. Their tongues were sharper than the starched lines of their habits.

What I did care about was bullying. No one was going to call perfectly nice people a nasty hair wad in front of me and not get called on it. Who knows? Maybe speaking up and doing the right thing will catch on in Regalia, and other bullies won't spring up in place of Owen and Levi.

I dug my palm into my chest. *Crinkle, crinkle.*

Levi was next to go while Owen strutted around free and clear. Did I wait for the supposed proof from the Rogues or get on with it? The longer this went on, the longer those monsters breathed air they didn't deserve.

"—so cute. Isn't he, Luna?"

"What?"

"Oh, sorry. We haven't introduced ourselves." The girl directly next to me tapped her chest. "I'm Eva. This is Rose and Alice."

Eva had at least a foot on me, long hair, and braces. Rose was adorable in a floral dress, cardigan, and hair bows. Alice was their opposite—short, shaved head, and skulls on her dress.

"We were just saying how hot Professor Anthony is," Eva whispered. "Our other professors are pushing eighty and reeking of denture cream. Where did they find this guy?"

This guy bent over to pick up a dropped eraser, sending off a wave of bitten lips and raised pulses over his perfectly shaped ass. His outfit was standard—long-sleeve shirt, vest, black slacks, and polished shoes. Nothing about it said *trying to put the female student body into a coma.* But was the jerk doing it anyway? Absolutely.

The sleeves clung tight to his biceps—the fabric flowing over his dips and humps like a Slip 'N Slide. His pants molded around his butt leaving nothing to the imagination, and the chalk dust on his vest drew your eyes to his chest, forcing you to ask where the chalk came from when he's writing with a dry erase marker.

"He's cute," I said noncommittally.

"He's gorgeous," Alice corrected. "He can give me detention anytime."

Rose rolled her eyes. "This isn't high school, Alice. There is no detention. He'll bend you over his desk during office hours."

"I'll take it." They high-fived.

"All right, take your seats," Professor Anthony said. He dusted off his hands, rounding the desk to prop on the edge. "I'll assume everyone's done the reading, so let's jump into it. Mr. Branlon."

The guy sitting next to Victor jerked in his seat.

"Give examples of logos, ethos, and pathos in literature."

"Uh, but— The reading wasn't about that."

"No, the lessons on the three forms of persuasion were in the supplemental reading as outlined in the syllabus."

"But it said that was just suggested reading."

"Precisely. Suggested so you wouldn't end up in this position—unprepared." Professor Anthony moved on. "Miss Sinclair—"

"But, sir," Branlon cried. "It's not fair to list a reading as optional if it's not. I read what you told me to read, like I bet everyone else in the class did.

Right?" More than half the class nodded. "It's not our fault we're not pre-pared." *It's your fault,* went unsaid.

I turned big eyes on Professor Anthony, curious what he was going to say, and if Branlon distracted him enough he'd forget he called on me.

Professor Anthony crossed his legs at the ankles, stroking his chin. "In-teresting. What you just did was use an emotional argument, citing unfair-ness and ambiguity. Then you threw in a logical argument with the addi-tion of an informal class poll. Pathos and logos. If you threw quotes from the leading experts in syllabi structuring and the studies conducted show-ing how many students never read the supplemental reading, you'd have gone three for three and given us ethos too."

He grinned, holding out his hands. "Everyone get it or do you need an-other example?"

Laughing, the class clapped. I didn't stop myself joining in. That was the quickest, most effective lesson I'd gotten in my entire academic history. Quicker than the swimming instructor who threw me in the deep end to teach me to float.

I sank like a rock and my mother slapped him across the face with a pool noodle.

"Just in case, we'll go deeper into these terms and how they apply to lit-erature."

My notebook cracked open and my pen hit the page. We were silent and attentive taking notes.

For all his faults, Professor Anthony was a good teacher. Examples, demonstrations, visual aids. He made sure we understood the topic and didn't get huffy at a raised hand, taking time to answer questions patiently.

"Miss Sinclair."

My head snapped up, finding Professor Anthony staring at me. So much for him forgetting he called on me.

"Yes, Professor?"

"Some say fiction and storytelling are firmly in the realm of pathos. It's about no more or less than making the reader feel something. Can you think of a situation where ethos would apply in a fictional narrative?"

All eyes turned on me. One of the girls I told off followed it up by flip-ping me off behind her textbook.

"Yeah, ethos can apply in storytelling. The other day I read *Storm Cloud*. It's a story about an asexual Japanese woman who's heading toward an arranged marriage. The entire thing was fiction. The couple can't stand each other at first and the reader is cracking up over all the pranks they pull to drive the other away. Then they get caught in a typhoon and end up relying on each other to get home. It ends with the two of them happy they're marrying their best friend.

"All fiction," I said, "because the author isn't married and no one's lived through half the stuff in her book. But she is Japanese and asexual. There's credibility in her storytelling and portrayal of an asexual person because she is one too. The audience can trust her to write from a place that's authentic."

Adonis snapped his finger. "Excellent, Miss Sinclair. So good, it's going on the board."

Write from a place that's authentic.

"Everything we do this semester will boil down to this," he said, underlining my quote. "Authenticity. And start doing it now, because the essays you turned in on the first day were dismal."

People laughed like he was joking. Sadly, I knew he wasn't.

"Don't hand me sanitized, polite, uniform papers. This is literature class, not a résumé-writing class."

The corner of my mouth tugged up. Adonis didn't just say it, he lived it. I read passion on his face—felt it in his words.

"Be real, be honest. Mr. Branlon was pissed I called him unprepared, and he called me on it. Argued with emotion and logic, determined I acknowledge he's right and I'm wrong. Approach every day in this class the same way. With the determination to show the world your passion, logic, and authenticity."

The class applauded him. He waved it off. "All right, all right. Now, put everything away except your pencil." The corners of Adonis's mouth curved up too. "You have a quiz on the supplemental reading."

"What?" someone cried. "But, sir—"

"Supplemental is defined as in addition to what is present," he sliced in. "It's not defined as voluntary, which is what optional means. From here on, I'm sure you won't make the mistake of mixing those definitions up."

No one was clapping for him then. Grumbles filled the room, and Victor punched Branlon's shoulder. I guessed he mumbled something about his brother that wasn't too complimentary.

I took my quiz without a word. Unlike the rest of my classmates, I did the supplemental reading because my nightmares woke me up in the middle of the night and there was nothing else for me to do.

"You have twenty-five minutes," Adonis said. "No talking. Eyes on your own paper. Begin."

Bending over the desk, I scribbled my name across the top and read the first question. Silence blanketed the hall, broken only by the soft *scritch, scritch, scritch* of pencils.

"Psst." Eva tapped my thigh.

I glanced over as she slid a piece of paper across her desk.

Do you have an extra eraser? I read.

Nodding, I bent to grab my—

"Professor Anthony, she's copying off my paper!"

"What?!" I whirled to Adonis, whose shock melded into disappointment as he saw the scene through his eyes. Me hunched over and reading off Eva's desk.

I reeled back. "No, I didn't. I—"

"Quiet, Miss Sinclair. Hand in your paper."

"I didn't cheat!"

"Hand in your paper," he repeated, eyes hard. "We'll discuss this and the actions that'll be taken in my office this afternoon after classes."

My mouth hung open. Actions? I read the student code of conduct. Cheating was automatic academic probation. Cheating on a test, term paper, or final exam was expulsion.

I burned a hole in Eva's head, not missing for a second the smirks on Alice and Rose.

"What happened to Dregs stick together?" I hissed.

She shrugged imperceptibly. "What can I say? Someone dared me." Eva winked. "I win."

"Now, Miss Sinclair."

Stiffly, I got up and handed in my paper. My chest squeezed as he wrote a big, fat zero across the top.

I returned to my seat in the back where I'd stay for the rest of the semester. Snickers trailed me up.

Was the whole class waiting for her to pull that? Did the mean girl put on that routine to make me accept their invitation to sit down? They all looked pleased at my coming punishment, except for Victor who glanced between me and Eva in confusion.

He didn't know me well enough to say I wasn't a cheater, but for a second, I thought I saw his eyes narrow on her.

I spent the rest of class reading Winter's letter, reminding me of why I would not be expelled that day. I would get Professor Anthony to listen to me.

The clock struck nine thirty and the class filed out. I dragged my feet leaving, lingering behind to talk to Professor Anthony.

"I suggest you continue on to class," he said, attention pinned to the papers he was grading. "Anything you have to say will be said this afternoon."

I forced myself to leave. Ticking the guy off wouldn't help my case.

My next class was biology. Each two-person desk was filled up. Sitting alone wasn't an option, so I veered for the empty stool beside Branlon.

"Luna Sinclair," one of the Royal girls drew out. "Answer a question for us."

"No."

She and her three friends claimed the front two tables. The fourth seat was taken up by Victor.

She plowed on. "What do you call a Dreg who crashes a Royal party, causes a scene, and punches Saylor Burkhardt?"

"I'm sure you're about to tell me."

"And give it away? No," she said. "Come on, I'll give you a hint. It's the same name for a low-class dirty savage."

"Hey," Victor barked. "Cool it, Iris."

I was so surprised at him defending me, my comeback stuck between my teeth.

"I'm just kidding." Laughing, Iris rubbed his shoulder, and didn't pull away. "If she's going to fit in here, she can't be so sensitive."

Victor shrugged her off. My shock compounded as he got up, grabbed my hand, and led me to the back. "Get up."

Jason and Cory snatched up their stuff and cleared off quick. I squinted at Victor.

"You're being nice to me so I'll let you have your three wishes."

He snorted. "Shut up, Sinclair. What kind of weak-ass bitch would I be if I let people fuck with my fiancée right in front of me?" He motioned for me to sit down. "Shit."

"What?" I climbed on the stool, setting my bag down.

"Luna, put this on," he hissed. His jacket draped over my shoulders.

"No, thanks, I'm not cold. And we're good with the chivalry. Let's not get carried away."

He put it back on when I tried to shrug it off. "I'm serious. There's something on your back."

"On my back?" I whipped around, straining to see. "What is it?"

"An X. Unless that's some weird fashion statement, I'm guessing you didn't mark up a three-hundred-dollar shirt for fun."

"Four hundred!" I turned my shirt around, eyes widening at the glaring *X* stained in permanent marker. No wonder people whispered and laughed as I walked by. X marked the Sinclair-Bowden.

The incident in the café roared through my mind. Whoever that was knocked me down on purpose.

"Just wear my jacket," Victor said. "After class you can run back to the dorm and change."

"Thanks."

I hunched in my seat, eyes squeezing shut. The second day of the second week, and it was starting. How long until they tripped me walking down the stairs, stalked me around campus, and made my every waking second a nightmare to match my dreams?

Why are they doing this? Even before I got into it with Saylor at the party, tension started brewing. It can't just be because I'm a Dreg, because if every Dreg was treated the way they treated Winter, those fuckers would've realized they outnumbered the Royals and went *Lord of the Flies* on their asses a long time ago.

Rejecting a skeezy shit like Owen couldn't be the true reason the Royals turned everyone against her. And it couldn't be the reason they were turning on me now. What is wrong with this place? Who did Winter really piss off?

I was in a funk all through class, not paying a lick of attention. I stayed huddled in Victor's jacket, dizzy on his spicy-sweet cologne and trying not to cry imagining that Winter didn't even have this much support—someone to tell off a Royal jerk, take her away from the situation, and cover up their mean pranks.

She did have the Rogues. The stray thought whispered behind a door I closed two nights ago.

There were people who tried to help her. The same people who want to help me.

I peeked at the mark on my back. How long before I accepted one hundred against one weren't good odds?

PROFESSOR ANTHONY WAS in the same spot I left him that morning—reclined at his desk grading papers, except this time we were in his office.

"I didn't cheat. Don't know how tapped into student drama professors are, but I'm not well liked around here for being a Dreg, marrying a Royal, and bearing the last name Sinclair. Eva admitted someone dared her to get me in trouble."

"Is that right?" he asked mildly.

"Yes. I don't deserve a zero, Professor. I did nothing wrong."

"Why should I believe you? You'd say the same thing if you did cheat." He motioned for me to take the seat placed before his desk. I glanced around as I sat, getting a real look.

He wasn't finished moving in. Boxes of books stacked beside the window, waiting to fill the half-empty bookcases. On the walls, diplomas and awards boasted so many and so loud, you'd almost miss the small frame in the middle, protecting a photo of two young boys. Looking closer, I picked out a young Victor and Adonis. They were adorable cheesing at the camera with their missing teeth.

My sweep continued over the book titles, souvenirs from different countries, and the horrible asylum-white paint enclosing him in an office a quarter size of Katie's bedroom.

"I don't know how to prove it to you," I said. "I'm sure if you give it a few more weeks, Eva will prove she's a rotten person in a dozen other ways and I'll get my 'I told you so' moment."

I thought I glimpsed his mouth quirk up, but he was still head down and reading. I decided I imagined it.

"Right now I'm just hoping you'll let me make up the missed test and give me another chance. I can't be on academic probation."

"An emotional argument. Heads up, it's not swaying me. Want to try another tact?"

A muscle in my brow ticced. I was having a talk with John and Martha Wilson, and finding out what exactly they did to wind up with two first-class buttholes for sons.

"Okay," I forced through gritted teeth. "Before Eva started shouting her head off, I was breezing through my test, answering every question correctly. I didn't need to cheat."

"You could've gotten your correct answers from Eva's paper."

Leaning back, I folded my arms. "Easy enough to check. See if they're all the same. A cheater might change one or two of their answers, marking it wrong so the teacher can't say they match. But that doesn't make sense if they already know the correct answer."

"Hmm." Adonis finally raised his head, punching me in the gut with the full force of his sculpted cheekbones up close. The man was more hand-some than a mortal had a right to be. No wonder he was named for a myth. "That's a valid point, Miss Sinclair. If the tests were to mismatch, Eva would have the correct answer for the same question and you'd have the incorrect."

He slid two sheets across the table. "It's the other way around. All of your answers were correct. Most of hers were wrong. Eva clearly didn't do the reading and you clearly did. You'd be a fool to copy off her paper."

"So... you knew the whole time that I didn't cheat."

Professor Anthony lifted a shoulder, mimicking my recline. "I knew for the last two hours."

"What was all that about why you should believe me?"

"You were in the right. I was curious to see how hard you'd fight for yourself. The answer: not very. I had to prod you into trying another argument."

The muscle under my brow was thumping under control. "Ever the professor, you're always teaching."

A slow, irritatingly sinful grin spread across his lips. "That sounded a tad sarcastic."

"Did it? Let me try another tact: you're not a nice man."

Adonis laughed out loud. "I thought you were gearing up to say something harsher."

"I was, but it's not wise to insult your professor after he lets you off the hook for academic probation. If you're done torturing me, I have to get going."

"Hold on." He stopped me short of the door. "You're still receiving a zero for that paper."

"What? Why?"

Sighing, the self-satisfaction drained out of him. "Eva followed up with someone in administration, demanding to know what your punishment was for cheating."

"She did what? What the hell! What kind of shitbag takes it that far? I didn't do anything."

"I know that, and I informed Mrs. Lawson there was no evidence of cheating. Unfortunately, she did not see the two mismatched papers as proof. Regalia U had an incident with cheating last year and now all accusations are taken seriously. She agreed academic probation was off the table, but you have to get a zero for the test."

"Well, that's balls."

He chuckled. "You recognize that it's not appropriate to insult me, but balls and shitbag are okay?"

"I didn't say you were balls or a shitbag, so we're good."

His deep, rich laugh warmed my insides, then my face as it brought back the memory of that stupid kiss. It was just a quick, tipsy peck. Why couldn't I forget it?

"Still, I doubt you're this informal with your other professors."

"My other professors aren't my soon-to-be brothers-in-law."

Adonis's smile wiped off. "Of course."

Quiet spread like spilled tea. I said the wrong thing and I wasn't sure why. His problem was with his parents, not Victor. From the sound of it, Victor wanted to patch this up—keep his brother in his life. More evidence that they were cool—the picture of the two of them together was the only photo on his wall with another person. The rest were poses of him alone in the Alps, crowded marketplaces, and famous squares.

"Thanks for fighting for me," I spoke up. "I'll be more careful who I sit next to from now on."

"Don't run off yet." Adonis pushed himself up. "She said I had to fail you on that test. Mrs. Lawson didn't say I couldn't give you a makeup. Do you have time now?"

"Yes, of course." I ran up to him as he rounded the desk. "Thank you."

"I've graded my last paper for the day. We'll make it an oral test."

My eyes moved on their own power, drifting to his mouth at the word oral. The ghost of his soft, sweet lips brushed mine—rippling goose bumps down my arm.

"Miss Sinclair? Are you okay?"

"Fine," I cried—a little too loud. "I'm fine. Also fine with an oral test."

"Good." He pointed. "You start on those boxes, I'll start these. I arrange my books in alphabetical order by author last name."

I bounced from him to the boxes. "There is no Mrs. Lawson, is there? This was all a ploy for unpaid labor."

Adonis cracked up. My stomach fluttered like a stupid traitor.

I liked making him laugh the night we met. Apparently, I was still hooked on the drug.

Setting my stuff on the chair, I picked up a box and got to work.

"List three examples of an ethical appeal," he began.

"Three examples are..."

We went back and forth for twenty minutes, asking and answering back and forth, filling the shelves with his collections. Professor Anthony's taste spanned the genres. They even spanned languages—Latin, French, and Spanish.

How could his parents turn away such an impressive man? Goodness, he could be a drug-addled bum and I still wouldn't understand why they kicked him out of the family. Especially now that he needs them the most.

"Last question," Adonis said. "A celebrity endorsement in an ad is an example of which: ethos, logos, or pathos."

"Ethos. Their purpose is to add credibility to their product. Eva Longoria loves this stuff, you will too."

"Excellent. Well done, Miss Sinclair."

I puffed up like a peacock. After a week and a day of being treated, and feeling, like crap, it was nice to get a compliment.

Winter's letter crinkled under my palm. *I wish Adonis was here when you were. He would've fought for you.*

We stood side by side at the bookshelves, my quick glances in his direction going unnoticed.

"Professor Anthony," I began. "Can I ask you something?"

"That depends. Is it a personal question?"

I inclined my head. "That also depends. Do you consider the reason you go by Professor Anthony instead of Professor Wilson personal?"

"Yes," he clipped.

I waited a beat. "Does that mean you won't tell me?"

"It does."

"Then, can I ask why you won't tell me?"

He gave me a look, pulling a giggle out of me. "I exasperated the nuns too. Sister Mary got sick of me questioning biblical teachings and stopped calling on me in class."

Another quick quirk of the lips. I didn't imagine it that time, though it was over as soon as it started.

"I am your professor, Miss Sinclair. It's best we steer clear of personal questions."

I hummed. "Can I challenge that idea with a little logos?"

"Give it your best shot."

"Okay, first, I'm not just your student. I'm engaged to your brother. I'm the new guest at Friday night dinner. Professors and students don't trade personal questions, but sisters- and brothers-in-law do."

"In that case, it's still my choice how much of myself I wish to share. You're not marrying me."

"Which brings me to the final argument," I said, voice dropping to a whisper. "What else could there be to say that's more personal than the things we've shared already?"

The lines of his back went rigid.

"We bared our souls over a bottle. Explaining why you go by a different last name over a pile of books doesn't come close."

He gave me a long look. "I may be too good of a teacher."

I grinned lopsidedly. "Meaning you agree with me?"

"Meaning I will answer your question if you agree to never bring up that night again."

"That's not a fair trade."

"Excuse me?" Folding his arms, he leaned on the shelves. "A fair... trade?"

"You're bargaining for my silence. My mom used to ply me into the quiet game by promising me candy at the end of the car ride. I never lasted longer than five minutes." I mirrored his stance. "What if I agree and the secret, personal story behind your alias is you once had a pet hamster named Anthony?"

"Will you take my word that it's not?"

"Would you?"

Chuckling, he replied, "No, I'd stretch me over the barrel till I broke in half. But we've established that I'm not a nice man."

"I get to ask you five questions. You answer them all honestly and I'll never speak of that night to you, anyone else, or to my diary."

"Two questions," he shot back.

"Five."

"Three."

"Five."

"You're a stubborn one," he said, shaking his head. "Three is my final offer. Take it or leave it."

"I'll take it... and ask the final two another time."

Adonis looked to the ceiling for help. The nuns used to do that too.

"First one, why do you go by Professor Anthony?"

He shifted to the boxes, resuming our task. "I go by that because it's my last name. John Wilson is my stepfather."

My lips parted at the same time I realized I didn't know what to say. "I didn't know," I said simply.

"No reason you should." His back faced me. "My father died when I was three. Shortly after, Mom married John and he raised me as his own. Despite... recent events... John was a great father. He treated me no differently than Victor. Dad attended all my games. He gave me the talk when I hit puberty. Bought me a car on my sixteenth birthday. I was never without, but in his eyes, I didn't appreciate the honor of being a Wilson. Of being his son."

"Didn't appreciate the honor? What did he want you to do? Sign a pledge in blood every Father's Day?"

Adonis shot me an amused look over his shoulder. "No, but that might have helped. Actually, it was little things that grew into big things. I got closer to my biological father's family when I was in my teens. Spent summers with my grandparents, aunts, uncles, and cousins. More than once I begged to skip the Wilson family reunions for a vacation with the Anthonys."

"Strike one?"

"And two, and three, and four, and so on." Adonis blew out a breath. "When I was old enough, I changed my last name back to Anthony. My intent was only ever to honor him—keep his memory alive in me and... my future children."

I reached for him and stopped myself again. Adonis wanted me at arm's length. I had to blackmail him to get this far. Better not to clam him up by touching him.

"John was furious. He banged on about me rejecting him and the Wilson legacy. I deepened his disappointment by majoring in literature and declaring I had no intention of joining the family business. Refusing to give him grandchildren was the final straw. If I didn't want to be his son, he'd make it simple for me. I'm out of the family."

I hugged myself, so desperate to put my arms around him, I didn't know what else to do. "Adonis, I'm so sorry."

"Don't be." He shoved the books on the shelf with extra force. "There. That answers your question and the others, I'm sure. The whole tragic back-story. I assume we're done here."

I sensed his need for this discussion to be over. I'd give in—with one final word.

"I know you wanting to honor your father came from a pure place. I never knew my father. Only that my parents loved each other but their relationship was forbidden and doomed to fail."

"Forbidden?"

I shrugged. "Maybe he was her professor."

The look that comment bought me singed my eyebrows. "Do not make those kinds of jokes."

"Had to." I grinned. "Your angry face is better than the closed, emotionally blank one you like."

"So you made that up?"

"No," I replied, perching on the edge of his desk. "My sister and I really were the result of a forbidden romance. Mom won't confirm or deny, but the obvious conclusion is he's married. That's why she would never tell us his name. Your love children showing up on your doorstep eighteen years later tends to put a kink in the marriage."

"If that's true, I'm sorry too."

I dropped my head, not letting him see my expression. "The point is I understand why you wanted to feel close to the man you never truly knew. I apologize for dragging up sad memories."

"You have nothing to apologize for. I could've stopped at 'John's my stepfather.' I chose to tell you the whole story. I'm wondering why now," he muttered.

"I'm easy to talk to. Everyone says so."

"Does everyone include the mother who begged for your silence with sweets or the nuns who avoided you?"

"A very mean man indeed."

He laughed, and I internally kicked myself. I had to stop chasing that sound before it became an addiction.

"Can I still have my final four questions?"

"Two," Adonis said firmly. "Go ahead."

"Why literature?"

"Oh, well, that I would've given you for free. The real question is why not literature? Language and storytelling are what defines us as a species..."

I relaxed as he spoke, explaining the wonders of the voices on his shelves—passion lacing every word.

"This is what I was meant to do. I love literature, and it brings me joy to share it with my students," he finished. "What about you, Luna?"

My eyes popped at him using my first name.

"Why psychology? The real reason, not that damned-awful tripe scribbled on paper and handed to me."

I made a choked noise in my throat. "Jeez. I get it, my first paper was bad. The second one was better."

"The second was worse." The sentence dropped like an anvil on my good mood. "You loaded it with flowery metaphors and strangled prose to cover up the fact you weren't saying anything of substance. I'd rather you just tell me you're going into psychology for the money."

"That's not why," I blurted.

"Then why, Luna? You're not getting a third chance on this paper. Tell me something real or—"

"My sister committed suicide." The reply was a hard, rough string of letters. "Which you know because I told you the night of the party. Helping young men and women when they're in that dark, hopeless place. Showing them there's another way out. A light piercing the darkness if only they search in the right spot. *That* is and will always be what I'm meant to do with my life. There's nothing that matters more than making sure that one less family feels what I do now.

"Happy now?" I flung. "Was that what you were fishing for?"

Shoulders slumping, Adonis scrubbed his face. "Shit, Luna, I didn't— Fuck me, I'm sorry."

That was such an unprofessorly thing to say, it distracted me from calling bullshit.

"I was drunk that night. I remember telling you about Catalina, and I remember you..." He trailed off, not needing to finish that sentence. "Afterward, I felt like such a shit for doing that with my brother's soon-to-be wife, I snuck two bottles of wine out of the kitchen and finished them off.

I didn't remember our conversation—which confirms I'm a loathsome bastard. You told me something so difficult, and I forgot and threw it in your face.

"I'm sorry," he said softly. "Truly, I am. Please, forgive me."

Slowly, I shook my head. "It's okay. I'm a fraction less pissed now that I know you weren't baiting me. And you were right." Bitterness leeched into the admission. "I was holding back."

"You have every right to. Forgive me, if I'd known..."

Adonis drifted off, but I heard the regret loud and clear.

"Just a thought," I began. "Demanding authenticity of us is a great thing, and I agree the best work comes from a real place, but Harper Lee and Gabriel García Márquez didn't turn their novels in for a grade. I couldn't face telling you the truth about Winter, only to receive a mark that said 'good effort, next time more imagery. C-plus,'" I mocked.

He cracked a smile. "I would've plumbed my depths for more sensitivity, but your point is taken."

"I'm not telling you how to teach, but I don't know how much honesty you're going to get from us when we're judged for it. I'd never put the pain of losing Winter into a school paper—even if I get straight Ds."

Sighing, Adonis straightened up. "No, that's a valid point. Who wants to be honest and then told it's not good enough? You've given me a lot to think about."

I got up too, moving back to the bookshelf. For a while, neither of us spoke.

"Your final question." Adonis broke down his last box. "Do you still want it?"

"I'll save it for another time. Terms apply till then. I won't bring up the engagement party."

Adonis gave me a smile reminiscent of that night. Something close to regret pulsed between my ribs. "I appreciate that."

"Of course."

Smile fading, he squinted at me.

"What? Is there something on my face?"

"You've got an eyelash." I swiped my cheeks. "Here. I'll get it."

His thumb caressed my cheekbone, rippling a strange sensation through me. He pulled away.

"Wait." I grasped his wrist unthinkingly. "I have to make a wish. Girl like me needs all the luck she can get."

Closing my eyes, I plumbed my own depth, and came away with another truth that would never be shared—certainly not with Professor Anthony. Opening them, I blew gently on his finger, sending the lash soaring.

I tried to follow its path and met his eyes. Our eyes locked, my lips puckered, his pulse jumping beneath my fingertips. We stepped toward each other.

Adonis roughly cleared his throat, tugging his wrist free. "Thank you for your help, Miss Sinclair. You've received an A on the test. You may go now."

"Oh, um, right."

I made for the door, doubled back for my backpack, and then went again to get my phone off the windowsill. I was more turned around than the time I got lost at the carnival. Adonis's attention on me just left me more flustered. Did he think I was going in for another kiss? I don't know what the hell I was doing, but trying to kiss my professor and fiancé's brother couldn't be it.

"Bye, Professor Anthony."

I booked it out of the office and didn't slow down until I was in my dorm room, shutting and locking the door behind me.

Victor and I have a no-hookup rule. The administration had a little no-hookup rule between professors and students too. Whatever flash of emotion I felt between us, I imagined. That's what I'd tell myself until my mission was complete and whatever was left of me went away to never come back.

Engagements do end every day. Ours would and Victor would go on to a wife, family, and running the company with his brother by his side. Neither one would remember the angry, broken Sinclair girl, so desperate to feel something other than sadness for a moment, she chased the wrong guy down the risky path.

"That was nothing. Nothing happened and nothing was going to happen."

I kept repeating it until I believed it.

Chapter Six

Tuesday morning, I repacked my bag for the new day of classes. The best part about having only Psychology Intro and anthropology that day was that neither of them was English. I still couldn't think about the day before in his office without kicking myself. Why didn't I listen to the man when he said we needed to keep it professional? I was determined to make a fool of myself in front of him, and I had no idea why.

Glancing at the clock, I read six a.m. and picked up the pace. Anthropology wasn't until ten, but I missed the Rogues the day before and didn't want to miss them again. As much as I didn't trust them, I couldn't resist the urge driving me on to see what they were going to pull to convince me.

Rafael gave a big speech about draining the will to live out of Winter's tormentors, but the fact remained they had futures and freedom to lose and they weren't going to risk it over a girl they didn't know, to help another strange girl who wasn't going to pay them. Even if they weren't working for the Royals, the small-time prank they pull will seal the deal.

Only I would go as far as it takes.

I walked out of the dorm as Katie walked up the stairs, sipping her latte. "Hey, were you coming to see me?"

"You are so full of yourself. How do you support that big head on those bony shoulders?"

"Good morning to you too, Katie. See you around."

I strode off. Katie fell in step with me, proving for as long as I lived, I'd never understand this woman.

It was a perfect autumn day. Leaves danced with the wind, kicking up rainbow swirls everywhere I looked.

"I heard what happened at the party. You busted in with the biggest damn ladle you could find, and stirred the shit right up."

I chuckled at the image. "I want to disagree, but it pretty much went down exactly like that. You can say I told you—"

"I told you so, dumbass." Katie whirled me around and I finally saw the concern written on her face. "Do you have any idea what you've done? It wasn't enough that you crashed, you had to go and *punch* her! Saylor told every Royal in the university that you're public enemy number one. Why didn't you listen to me?"

"I didn't want any of that to happen," I cried. "I just wanted to see the people who hurt Winter. To know who they are and if they felt an ounce of remorse. Yay," I mocked, "I've got my answer."

Katie blew out a breath. "There's no choice now. You have to transfer out of Regalia University."

"I'm not going anywhere."

"There you go again, ignoring the wise advice coming out of my mouth. Can I just ask, what the hell is wrong with you?" She planted her hands on her hips. "Did you come here looking for punishment as some kind of disturbing penance? Did you want to get the Royals riled up, so that when they strike, you have an excuse to strike back hard?"

"No, and no. I told you why I'm here and what I want, Katie. My answer won't change no matter how many times you ask. But you feel free to answer some questions for me."

"What are you talking about?"

"What does it mean that Saylor made me public enemy number one? Is that all it takes for people to write on my back, knock me around, and try to get me expelled for cheating? She snaps her fingers, then Royals and Dregs attack the straggler bringing up the pack?"

"Don't be ridiculous. Saylor may be a Burkhardt, but people aren't about to fight her battles for her just because she says to. Don't get me wrong, you just pissed away your chance at making any friends at this school—no one is trying to be on her enemy list with you. But ignoring you and trying to get you expelled are two different things."

"Obviously, it's not. People are coming after me because of her."

Katie shook her head. "Open your eyes, Sinclair. Saylor hates that the school isn't Royals only. If she had the power to drive out everyone she can't stand, the student body would be cut in half right now. I'm telling you, punching Saylor will have consequences, but she'll dole those out personally. For the whole school to turn on you, there'd have to be something in it for them. They..."

She trailed off, brows furrowing.

"They?" I prompted. "They what?"

She mumbled something, turning away and gazing over her shoulder. I followed her line of sight but saw nothing other than the library and gym.

"Katie?"

Shaking herself, she faced me. "They won't bully you on her orders." Katie pushed out her lips. "Well, Piper, Gabriella, and Everleigh are going to make your life hell, but you'd expect no less. Girlfriends stick together."

"Um, actually I do expect more."

"If someone's grilling up some other kind of beef, Ima guess you served it." She peered at me through her lashes. "Someone tried to get you expelled?"

"Yeah. A girl named Eva lied and said I cheated off her paper. I've never spoken to her before, so no, I didn't serve her beef."

"Not on purpose, but remember I warned you more than a few women aren't pleased you're marrying Victor Wilson?"

My mind suddenly flashed to Iris's nasty smirk, and her possessive hand on my fiancé.

"He dipped his bag in a lot of steaming mugs, my friend. Make sure you separate out the people who are after you, and who are after your man. The latter will be twice as vicious."

Unease curdled my stomach. Dear Thor, was I the target of all of Victor's ex-girlfriends? The guy couldn't keep it in his pants during a meet-and-greet with his potential wife. Who knew how many girls were secretly glaring daggers at me for taking the hot, rich jock off the market?

"Thanks for the heads-up."

"No problem. It's important you understand just how many people you've ticked off in your short time here. I, for example, am raging that you blew off my advice and made yourself Saylor's target."

"I was already her target, if that helps."

"No the fuck it doesn't. She hated you as much as any Dreg before, but now that you've punched her in front of everyone who matters, she's got something to prove. She'll do whatever it takes to make your life hell, and you've stuck me in the middle." Fury flashed in her eyes. "I told you I wanted one year of no drama. Dammit, I would've taken one month!"

"Katie, I'm sorry, but—"

"You should be." Snatching my belt loop, she tugged open my pants, and dumped her iced latte inside. My scream made two people walking by trip over their feet.

"Katie!"

She sniffed, brushing off her hands. "That'll teach you to ignore what I say, you selfish ass. I'll work on Saylor to see if I can get her to calm down, but we're not going to hang out for a few days. I need time to cool off."

Katie marched off, nose in the air—heels clacking on the sidewalk. Bugged out and ice running down my legs, I gaped after her, brain trying to comprehend what just happened and stop me from chasing after her and tackling Katie into the grass. How in the hell does she offer to help me, scold me like I'm a bad friend, and then make me look like I soiled myself all in the space of three seconds?

Fuming, I spun around and beat it into the dorm and my shower. "Still waiting for my dislike to turn into love!"

I WAS LATE TO BREAKFAST that morning. It didn't even matter. Nothing was going on in there—the Rogues were nowhere to be seen.

The next day, I didn't expect to see Katie waiting on the steps and I was right, she wasn't there. I set out early, rolling out of the building at six a.m. It was Wednesday. I was due a breakfast with Victor, and there were three more mornings left for the Rogues to prove something to me. Neither one of them said I had to be there that early.

Unfortunately, nightmares invaded my dreams. I woke at four a.m. with a sore throat and split lip from where I bit through it. There was no sleeping after that, so the cafeteria was as good a place as any.

I pushed inside, my click-clacking mid-heels echoing through the short hallway.

"Hello?!"

The shout stiffened my spine.

"Is someone there? Help me! Get me down!"

Picking up the pace, I skidded onto the café floor. My bag slipped off my shoulder and hit the tile, spilling its contents.

Suspended from the ceiling, shouting himself red, was Owen Thasher.

Strips of white tissue paper covered his bent body. They'd hogtied and lashed the ropes around his chest and thighs, hanging him stomach down. A red rubber wattle stuck to his crown, matching the chicken's beak on his face.

A piñata.

The Rogues turned Owen into a chicken piñata, but the tissue paper did absolutely nothing to cover the fact he was naked. His unimpressive cock swung down for the world to see. The guys weren't generous enough to cover it in tissue paper.

"Don't just stand there! Fucking do something," he barked. "Now, you stupid bitch!"

It barely registered that he spoke. Dropping my gaze, I fell on the bucket placed innocently beneath him. Paintball guns filled it. On its side, they placed a sign:

Hit Me If I've Ever Hurt You or Didn't Stop When You Said No

"Hello? Are you listening to me?" he shrieked.

My fingers closed over the handle. Voices filtered into the cafeteria as students with early morning classes came in for their breakfast.

"Hold on— It's you. Luna Bowden." Hatred poured out of his mouth. "You did this, didn't you? Didn't you! Because of your useless fucking whore of a—!"

The pellet struck him dead in the mouth. Owen retched, gagging on the paint. Witnesses rushed me as I let loose.

"Whoa. What the hell?"

"What's going on?"

"Is that Owen?"

"Someone get him down!"

A pellet struck his stomach, tearing a cry out of him. It didn't come from me.

Lindsay moved me aside, leveling the paintball lower. She smiled at her horrified friends. "What's the panic? Someone will get him down eventually. In the meantime..."

The two girls looked from her, to the bucket, to Owen, and then at each other. They both picked up guns.

An hour later, Owen Thasher was a mess of paint, welts, and soggy paper.

"P-please," he sobbed. "Let me down. Help... me."

I leaned against the back booth, grim satisfaction tugging the corners of my mouth up, though I repeatedly forced it neutral. I couldn't stop myself. Almost everyone who found Owen in this state responded in one of three ways: they picked up a paintball gun, took out their phones to record his misery, or called their friends to join in. Seven a.m. on a Wednesday and the cafeteria was packed with nearly every Dreg in the school and most of the Royal girls.

No one tried to help him until one of his friends burst in, shouting for someone to get security and snatching guns out of the girls' hands. Soon his other friends were there backing him up, keeping people away from him, though they couldn't get him down. All they were doing was giving an unobstructed view to the complete wreck that was once the great and popular Owen Thasher.

"—move. Excuse me. Out of the way this instant."

A man in a sharp, tailored black suit and wire-rimmed spectacles pushed through the crowd. I recognized him immediately.

Dean Simmons.

He took one look at Owen and surprise blew apart his professional mask. "Heavens, what on earth— Out," he cried. "Everyone, out. The café is closed for the rest of the day."

A paintball splattered across Owen's cheek.

"Miss Donahue! Put that down right now," the dean snapped. "Out!"

I peeled off the booth, following the crowd trudging outside. Security blew past us as we escaped the café, two of them carrying a ladder.

Movement out of the corner of my eye turned my head toward the side of the building. Rafael posted up against the wall, head bobbing to music only he could hear. He saw me and winked.

The handsome figure in leather and jeans was gone by the time I escaped the crowd's clutches and rounded the rail. That didn't matter. I knew where he went.

I ran all the way to the archeology building. Bursting around the corner, I found all four Rogues exactly where I left them the night of the party. They said nothing as I caught my breath.

"Who?" I rasped. "Which one of you came up with that?"

"I'd like to take the credit," Rafael said, "but Wilder was the mastermind on this one. Some of his best work."

I ran to Wilder, arms out. Throwing myself at him, strong hands seized my arms and suddenly the world spun. I stumbled in the grass, facing the opposite direction. I rounded on Wilder crouched with his hands up, readying for my second attack.

"I was trying to hug you, weirdo. And I'm going to try again." Pushing his fists firmly down, I slid my arms around his broad shoulders, burying my face in his neck. For a paranoid, angry conspiracy theorist, he smelled like apples and rain. I hugged him tighter.

"Thank you," I whispered. "I thought— Man, I don't know what I thought. That all of this was a trick, or maybe you were secretly working with the Royals and getting close to me was step one in destroying another Sinclair-Bowden. But there's absolutely no way—"

Wilder untangled and shot out of my hold. "Your thanks is noted and unnecessary. Especially in the form of physical affection. I don't know your decontamination routine. You could've exposed me to countless pathogens."

I blinked. "Did you just say you don't know if I shower?"

"Sounds like it," Lucien said lightly. The out-of-place outfit of the day was a paisley ascot, matching vest, high-waisted pants, and polished black boots. His unnaturally sharp canines gleamed as he grinned. "But no. Wilder's referring to a CDC-level decontamination that no one in the world puts themselves through on a daily basis... except for him."

"Right." I lurched forward like I was going to hug him again, and his hands flew up to defend himself from one hundred and twelve pounds of me. I giggled. "Like I was saying, I was so twisted up about you guys coming out of nowhere, for a second I thought you could be working for Owen,

Levi, and those other shitholes. But there's no way on earth Owen agreed to that humiliation to get you guys in with me. That was amazing."

I held up my hands. "Look at me, I'm still shaking. Hearing him scream and beg like that, I pray he felt even a fraction of the pain, fear, and humiliation Winter felt the night he and his friends assaulted her and posted it for all the world to see."

"All the world is going to see this, darling." Rafael held up his phone, flashing a video of Chicken Owen dangling from the ceiling. "Two thousand views in an hour."

I laughed—a cruel, evil, delicious sound. *I hope you're watching this where you are, Winter, and that the angels are giggling with you, pointing out his minuscule package.*

"I'm going to watch this every night before I go to bed and drift off into blissful, peaceful dreams." I squealed, half jumping out of my skin. I took back everything I said about the Rogues out loud and in my head. They were the best men I ever have or ever will meet. "Is that why you guys do this? Getting paid to make bastards like Owen pay? Does it feel like this every time?"

Rafael smiled right back. "Feels even better, love. We went easy on him the first round. It only gets worse from here."

A literal shiver went up my spine. That was the most incredible thing a man had ever said to me.

"Yes, yes, and yes." I grasped Rafael's hands. "Your whole plan. Your weapons, your resources, your strength needed to hang a muscled jock from the ceiling—I want all of it. Let's do it."

"Slow down, Cloud Girl." Rafael snaked around my waist, holding me to him like the night we danced. "If you want to be one of the Rogues, you've got to play by our rules."

My smile faded. "What does that mean?"

"It means Thasher doesn't have a clue who put him up there or how. There's not a single camera that recorded us, or a person who can say we had beef with the guy. We weren't even there while they pelted the sobbing piñata. We don't get caught, act recklessly, or make a move that hasn't been planned out from every angle.

"That's easy when it's all about the money. Keeping your feelings out of it is impossible for you."

I swallowed tightly. Of course it was impossible. My rage was the only thing getting me out of bed in the morning. Without it, I'd slowly lose myself on the pillow beside Mom.

"We're not asking you to approach this unemotionally," Lucien spoke up. "And we're not telling you that we're in charge. You are, Luna. We'll follow your lead on this one—"

"—but you have to let us do what we do," Wilder continued. "You looking to get caught?"

I shook my head.

"Then trust us. When we say we have to pull back or something won't work, swear that you'll listen."

"I will," I said easily.

"Don't say it if you don't mean it." Rafael probed me through hooded eyes. "If we stumble on Thasher, chilling alone on another park bench, and I say right then isn't the time for a... shave... will you be able to control yourself?"

"I can do it." Saying it out loud, I knew I could. "This isn't about me. It's about Winter. I won't do anything if it risks me not finishing what I came here to do."

Rafael straightened. "That's all we need to hear. Swing by the Gallery after classes. Behind Grayson Hall. Five o'clock."

They filed off.

"Wait, that's it? But I have forty-five minutes until class. That's more than enough time to hear what else you've thought up for Owen."

Rafael snorted. "Trust me, it's not. Even if it was, domination is best discussed behind closed doors."

"But—"

He switched on his music, strutting off with a sway in his step. Wilder sidestepped me with slitted eyes. Lucien bowed and kissed my fingers. Cato snapped and pressed his muzzle to my cheek. I wasn't certain if that was a kiss goodbye, or a fond wish to bite the flesh on my face.

I hung around for a while, as if hoping they'd come back. I wasn't too sure what to do with myself. Of all the things I imagined doing to Owen, they all included a secluded spot and a baseball bat. I never considered making his pain public. Letting the whole world see him for the small, mewling crap bag he was.

I didn't consider it because I didn't know how. The only things I had to my name were a monitored, and nearly depleted, bank account from my stepfather. A backpack with some self-defense gear. A Royal fiancé who couldn't stand me. A Royal friend? who dumped a latte down my pants for refusing to end the fight, and a letter that spurred me on despite everything.

Just a taste of what the Royals could do, and the undercurrent of help-lessness and loneliness was fading. I wasn't alone, outnumbered, or out-gunned. I was taking the fight to the Royals, and for the first time since I set foot on campus, I knew without a doubt, they'd lose.

ADONIS WAS STRAIGHTENING papers on his desk when I walked into class. My skin heated and I tore off him, landing on Victor sitting in the front row beside Branlon. On his other side, sat Iris.

She leaned over his seat, looking straight at me as she whispered in his ear. They laughed.

"He dipped his bag in a lot of steaming mugs, my friend. Make sure you separate out the people who are after you, and who are after your man. The lat-ter will be twice as vicious."

Irritation tightened the grip on my bag. If I was fighting a war for a man I didn't want whether I liked it or not, I wasn't about to lose.

"Victor, sweetie." I sidled up to them, running my fingers through his hair. "Let's sit in the back."

Victor stared at me like I grew a third arm out of my forehead. "What the hell are you talking about?"

"In the back," I said through my teeth. "You and me. Come on."

He must've picked up the forcefulness in my tone because he got his stuff and followed me up. Iris glared daggers at me, stomping over to sit with her friends now that her toy boy was gone.

"What was that?" he asked as we sat down.

"I should be asking you that. Why were you letting her paw you like the last piece of shrimp on the buffet table?"

"Why?" Victor grinned wolfishly. "Were you jealous? Disgusting."

"Asshole. I'm not jealous. It looks bad if you let people walk all over your fiancée, and it looks bad if I do nothing while women flirt with mine. Although, I've got to say, it would help if you didn't flash that 'get naked in the closet with me' grin at everything that moves."

He shrugged. "What can I say? I'm a slut. The grin comes automatic now."

I rolled my eyes so hard, it hurt.

"But we made a deal—no hooking up. I'll keep up my end no matter how many women tempt me." He gave me a look. "So from now on, hands to yourself. And don't ever call me sweetie."

"Honey pie it is."

We grumbled to ourselves, slapping our binders and pens on the desk. What did Victor have to be mad about? He was getting everything he wanted. I was giving up everything I needed.

"Good morning, class."

"Good morning, Professor Anthony," we chorused.

"Before we begin, I'm announcing a change to the syllabus." He held up his hand. "For which you can thank Miss Sinclair."

All eyes turned on me, frozen like deer facing oncoming death.

"She pointed out to me that true, raw honesty doesn't flourish in an environment of judgment. First and foremost, my job is to prepare you for the world ahead. Not all of you will become great authors, but if I've taught you well, it'll be because you lack the desire, not the ability. With that in mind, your papers will be marked on a pass/fail scale. A pass for turning in your best work that meets the standard requirements. A fail if you can't be bothered to turn in anything at all.

"I will mark down my impressions and suggestions to elevate your writing, but as long as you're turning in honest, authentic papers, you should have no fear of failing this class."

"Yeah!" Branlon whooped. "Thank you, Sinclair."

Half the class erupted into cheers, clapping and carrying on. The same people who a day ago were hissing nasty comments at my back. I guess malice takes a day off when you grant your entire class an easy A.

"Settle down, settle down." Professor Anthony adopted his cross-ankle stance against the desk. "Naturally, this doesn't apply to tests, quizzes, and exams where you're required to know the material. Speaking of, I assume everyone went over the supplemental reading." He held a sheaf of papers over his head. "Pop quiz."

The groans started up right on cue.

I bent to get my eraser and noticed Victor watching me.

"What?"

"When did you have this chat with my brother?"

My brows snapped together. "What do you mean?"

"You know what I meant. What did you say to him that convinced the guy to throw out his entire lesson plan? Why are you even talking to him?"

"Okay, hold up. I had to see him in his office after one of your possible mugs tried to get me expelled. Adonis gave me a makeup test and— What's your problem now? Why are you looking at me like that?"

"Adonis? Who said you could call him that? Did he?"

"So what if he did? He's going to be my brother-in-law."

If I thought I was getting a narrow-eyed glare before, I could hardly see his irises now. "Don't even think about it, Sinclair."

"Think about what?" I whisper-shouted.

"I've seen that look before. You're into him."

"I am not—"

"Save it." Victor leaned in close, making sure I heard him clearly. "Even if we lifted the no-hookup rule, my brother is off-limits. He's got too much shit to worry about for a coed to toss her 'let's get naked in the closet' grin and ruin his career. I'm serious, Luna. You try something with him and our engagement is over."

My grip squeezed to break my pencil. Flashes of the drunken kiss and moment in Adonis's office tormented me, pissing me off more. "Who exactly is it that you don't trust, Wilson? Me or your own brother? He wouldn't have anything to do with me even if I was interested. Which I'm *not*. Wake up. This is not the nonstop sex, booze, and spending cruise you've been on your whole life. In the real world, there are consequences. I stay on the right side of the line."

He wasn't moved. "You wake up, honey pie. That's my ring on your finger—the all-access pass to the sex, spending, booze cruise. You're one of us now, and I've been checking my back for the knife ever since you slipped that on your finger."

I STOPPED ON THE SIDEWALK, gazing up at the house. I was sure I was in the right place, though I wouldn't call it a gallery.

Behind Grayson Hall, Rafael said. The only building behind Grayson Hall was a single three-story structure that appeared as if it were plucked from Greek Row and dropped on the lawn. It was the only building back here, tucked away like a secret.

It was nondescript for a secret. Three levels of brick, windows covered with blackout curtains, a heavy wooden door, and a metal box under the doorbell.

Walking up, I hitched my bag up higher and knocked on the wood.

"Who is it?" Wilder poured out of the intercom, making me jump. "What do you want?"

I pressed the button to speak. "You know who it is. You told me to come here."

"Look into the camera."

I whipped around. "What camera?"

"It's Sinclair," I heard him say. "She's alone. Come in."

A buzz cut through the afternoon. Swinging the door in, I stepped inside a short hallway with not much to say for itself other than a shoe organizer with nine cubbies.

"Take off your shoes. Remove your listening and recording devices."

Where is his voice coming from now?

"Do you mean my phone?"

"Yes. Unless you're packing something else."

I put my hands up for the unseen camera. "Not packing anything. Off my shoes go." I toed them off, stuck them in a cubby, and put my phone in after it. That done, I continued down the hall, coming out—

A nozzle stuck in my face.

Pssssssstt!

A harsh, astringent smell overpowered my nose, and face, and chest, and legs, and back. Wilder sprayed me all over, uncaring of my shrieks.

"What are you doing?! Stop!"

He dropped the can. "Disinfectant."

"More like acid!" I wheezed, coughing and hacking the cloying stuff out of my lungs. "What was that for?"

"The SB3A virus was developed in government labs three years ago and made to mimic the common cold. If contracted, you die a slow death, bleeding through all orifices. SB3A was stolen and unleashed two years ago."

Psst!

"For all we know, it's spreading through campus as we speak."

Psst!

"Stop that!" I made a swipe for the can. It was swiftly lifted out of my reach.

Wilder held out both hands. "Now, you may hug me for a duration of five seconds. Your hands are not to move lower or higher than my forearms. If you wrap them around my neck, I will perceive this as an attack and respond accordingly."

I gaped at him. Five seconds. That's how long it took me to regret this.

"Wilder, my friend, what are you doing to the lovely Luna?" Lucien came out from behind him, dressed in different, but equally ridiculous, Victorian clothes. "Forgive us for the welcome. You can see why the Gallery doesn't get many visitors."

Grasping my fingers, Lucien trapped my gaze as he brushed his lips over my knuckles. A ripple raised the hairs on my arms. "Come with me, my dear." He threaded my arm through his, leading me away. "I'll give you the grand tour."

"Uh, okay." I'd let him take me away if it meant my disinfectant bath was over. "Rogues' Gallery. I get it. Cute."

"Cato thought so. He's got a unique sense of humor."

"Wow," I breathed as the hallway opened up, letting us out into the living room. "And you all have a unique sense of style."

The entire room was a bachelor pad paradise. Black covered the walls, which should've made it dark and depressing—if not for the neon-green lamps and the backlights scattered about the room—behind the big-screen television, and shining from the ceiling. A row of guitars lined both sides of the TV. Placed in front of it were two green and black gamer chairs, and a black leather sectional. It was as though I stepped into the world's first nightclub/movie theater.

"This is the living room."

"Yeah, it is," I cried. My socked feet sank into the plush carpet. "This is sweet. What do you have to do to get a place like this on campus?"

"My descendants own and operate a string of hospitals across the country. What it takes is a sizable endowment."

"By descendants you mean..."

"My great-great-grandson and his wife."

"Naturally."

Lucien led me on. "This way to the kitchen." Moving ahead, he held open the door and waved me through. "After you."

"Such a gentleman for a vampire. Shouldn't you be feasting on my sweet life nectar right about now?"

He winked. "I learned to control my bloodlust decades ago. It was also decades ago that I learned the way a gentleman is supposed to treat a lady. There have been many advancements in the last century, but not in manners."

Laughing, I said, "Can't argue with that."

It was weird how comfortable I was starting to feel around them.

Except for paranoid Wilder.

And growling Cato.

And strangely flirty and enigmatic Rafael.

Okay, so it was just weird.

The two of us entered the same hall through another door and moved into the kitchen. Rafael stood with his back to us. A young guy sat at the table, scarfing down a bowl of oatmeal and watching the small television parked on the kitchen counter.

My heart thumped an extra out-of-sync beat.

He was beautiful. The heavens literally opened up, and set this sable-haired, pine green–eyed masterpiece among us to see how quickly we'd tear ourselves apart trying to have him. A broad, pointed nose hung over his wide, soft lips.

"Holy hell. Cato, is that you?"

The guy looked at me, saying and doing nothing. I came closer, drawn like a moth to flame. He was so damn gorgeous. How could anyone so handsome be dangerous? He wouldn't—

Cato's face crumpled. His lips curled in a snarl, growl ripping out of his throat. He jumped up, both feet planted on the stool, and crouched like he was ready to leap over the table and bring me down like a pack of wolves. I tripped over my feet running back to Lucien.

My well-mannered friend laughed his ass off. "It's okay, Lady Luna. He won't hurt you."

"Really?" My voice came out a high-pitched squeak. "Then why does he growl and snap at me all the time!"

"You get too close," Lucien breezed. "Cato's had a rough history of nurses, doctors, and orderlies grabbing and holding him down. Injecting him with things and restraining him when he fought back. He doesn't take kindly to anyone getting too close to him or Rafael."

As if to underscore his response, Cato settled and went back to his oatmeal and television show like nothing happened.

"All right, so he just wants people to keep their distance. I can understand that. But what's with the muzzle? If he chills out when people respect his space, it's harsh and demeaning making him wear that thing."

Cato bobbed his head—whether it was at what I said or what the television said, I had no idea.

"He has to wear it on campus when he's out of the Gallery."

"Why?"

Wilder blew inside, heading for the fridge. "Because he bites."

"Whether you respect his space or not," Lucien continued. "He's liable to tear a chunk out of you for looking at him wrong." He caught my look and shrugged. "I said he had a hard time in those psychiatric hospitals. I didn't say he wasn't there for a good reason."

"So you lied when you said he wouldn't hurt me."

"I didn't lie. Cato likes you. He won't do anything to hurt you."

I eyed him, my stomach fluttering traitorously at how stinking handsome he was. "How do you know?"

"He's had many opportunities to do that, and he hasn't taken them. That's a good sign. Means you're most likely safe."

"Uh, most likely?"

"I cannot say enough that he's a frequent mental hospital patient. If his behavior was that easy to predict, they wouldn't have locked him up."

"Okay," I said, pushing down unease. "Let's just stop talking about him like he's not in the room. It's not nice."

Cato flicked to me, slipping under my defense and dragging me into lily pad–covered pools. I read so many things within his depths, but madness wasn't one of them. I got the sense he wanted...

"I'm sorry," I said. "Can I sit with you?"

Once again, no move or response. Slowly, I pulled out a stool and sat down. Cato let me without growl or curled lip.

Maybe he does like me.

"Hey, Rafael," I called.

Wilder spoke up. "He can't hear you. His plugs are in."

"Plugs?"

"Rafael was caught in an explosion when he was young," Lucien explained. "Affected his hearing and gave him a hypersensitivity to certain sounds and frequencies. A hearing aid and carefully curated playlist outside, and earplugs inside. It helps give him peace."

"Oh."

Wilder tapped Rafael's shoulder. The guy turned and his expression lit up when he saw me. I blushed like a silly little girl.

"Cloud Girl." Pulling out his earplugs, Rafael replaced them with earbuds. He moved aside and I saw what he was doing—counting out pills. He placed the handful beside his brother with a glass of water and slid up next to me.

Behind his back, Cato grimaced at the lot. He picked two pills out of the fifteen, swallowed them, and tossed the rest in the trash while everyone was looking at me.

That doesn't bode well.

"Sooo," I drew out, looking between Rafael, Cato, Lucien, and Wilder. "You've successfully lured me into your lair. What happens now?"

Rafael chuckled. "You tell us. You're in charge, Sinclair."

I straightened my spine. That's right. I was in charge. "Okay, then, first, I'd like to get to know you guys better. How did you end up doing what you do? How far are you willing to go, and what else had you planned before I showed up? If it's anything like what you did in the café today, you better keep that disinfectant handy, Wilder, because the hugs will be nonstop."

He moved back like I was next to leap over the table.

"What else is there to know?" Rafael asked.

"How did you all become friends?"

"The three of us went to the same school," he replied, pointing out Wilder and Lucien.

I almost asked where Cato was. Obviously, he was in the hospital Rafael broke him out of.

"Lucien, did you dress like this in high school too?"

"Of course."

"When did you get the veneers?"

Lucien cocked his head, frowning. "Veneers?"

I tapped my canine. "They look super sharp. Don't you ever hurt yourself biting your tongue?"

"They're not veneers. And what kind of self-respecting nightwalker would I be if I savaged my own tongue?"

"True, but for real, Lucien. What got you into vampire culture?"

"Ah, yes. I was turned in 1864 by a shopkeeper who—"

"—whose lonely ass had a little crush on you. I've got the official story," I broke in. "Seriously, I researched vampire subculture online the other night. It's a whole thing with underground clubs, dress, blood play, and all that. Pretty cool."

He scoffed. "Those fools mock and exaggerate the torment of true nightstalkers. Their silly little games are nothing more than foreplay for slightly taboo, but still bland, sex. If you want to know the truth, I'm your source."

"The truth about what?"

"The life of a real vampire."

"Um... but you're not a real vampire."

Lucien held out his hands. "I'm sitting in front of you. You don't believe your eyes?"

Soft, warm lips pressed to my ear. "This is the part where you give up," Rafael whispered.

I jumped, then quickly covered with a cough. A grin was a permanent fixture on his face, so I couldn't tell if I got away with it.

"If you're a real vampire, how can you go out in the sunlight?"

Lucien tugged a chain from beneath his ascot, flashing me a beautiful, intricate golden pendant. The dragon's body weaved through a symphony of flames, crowning it with his open, roaring maw.

"Eighty years ago, I stumbled on a shaman who blessed this for me. Now I walk in the light with you mortals."

"A shaman?" Disbelief scrunched my face. Was this guy committed to the role, or was he truly delusional? "Are you shitting me?"

"I am, in fact, not shitting you."

"What about crosses, garlic, and holy water?"

"All myths made up by the phonies you wasted your precious time researching."

"By any chance, are your great-great-grandson and his wife under the delusion that they gave birth to you? Could they possibly have photos of a squalling infant that looks like you?"

"Yes," he said smoothly, "we doctored those to keep up the ruse."

Rafael tickled my ear again. "You're stubborn. I kinda like it."

My cheeks heated, so did my fervor. "Photos," I cried. "If you lived for over a hundred years, you should have photos of yourself through the many decades." I smiled broadly. "Let's see them."

"I would love to show them to you, Lady Luna, but unfortunately, they were all lost in the fire set by Levi and his friends."

"Oops," Rafael crowed as I pinched the bridge of my nose. "He got you there."

Lucien laced his fingers through mine, placing his palm over our clasped hands. A strangled noise escaped my throat. "I would never lie to you," Lucien whispered. "This is who I am. It's hard to understand—harder to accept. But all that matters is I would never hurt or turn you." Trapping my gaze, he kissed my palm—slow, deliberate, sensuous. "I promise."

My knees pressed together tight, heat pulsing in an entirely new place as his lips traveled down, pressing to the jumping vein in my wrist. I internally screamed at my body to stop, knowing I had less of a chance of winning that battle than my failed attempt to argue with Lucien.

Three of my prime hormonal years were spent in an all-girls Catholic school. Despite Katie's quips, I never dipped in my roommate's honeypot. All the time I was supposed to spend building an immunity to hot, seductive guys was spent wishing there was a single hot, seductive guy around.

"You're cheating," I rasped.

Lucien's lips curved in a wicked twist, revealing those deadly fangs. "I could play fair, if you want me to."

I was saved thinking of an answer as he placed my hand back where he found it. He was saved too, because I don't think I'd question him ever again. Not unless we were alone... and I wasn't engaged.

I found my voice, facing away from him. "So, Wilder, what about you?"

"What about me?" He leaned against the fridge, sipping from his water bottle and watching me with an unflinching stare. I leaned a little side to side and his blue orbs tracked me like a lightning rod.

"What do your parents do?"

"Why?"

"Just wondering. Making friendly conversation and all that."

"Huh."

I waited for more and none came. "Okay, then, what about you? What are you studying? What do you like to do? How did you get into hacking?"

"What are you, writing a book?"

"What are you," I burst out, "playing some game to see which one of you drives me nuts first? Just answer one question."

Wilder bobbed his head, lips pursed in thought. "No."

"Okay," I said, throwing up my hands. "Now I give up."

Rafael cracked up. "But you haven't gotten to me and Cato yet."

"I don't have the strength. Let's get to the point of why I'm here." Climbing off the stool, I leaned against the kitchen counter to look at all of them at once. "How did you get into this? Why?"

"Don't you know already?" Rafael plopped in my vacant seat. "Because it's fun."

"You said you came up with a plan. Give it to me. Whatever makes those bastards cry, we keep. Whatever doesn't, we fix."

The guys exchanged looks.

"We'd prefer to hear your plan first," Rafael said. "No metaphors. No double-talk. What did you want to do to them?"

"I was going to slit Owen Thasher's throat." I dropped it as easily as Cato dipped a spoon in his oatmeal. "Let him bleed to death scared and alone in the dark. As for Levi, his death I'll make look like an accident. He's got a limp—people will believe he fell down the stairs. Two down, three to go.

"That's when my engagement to Victor Wilson comes in handy. I'll throw a party and use his name on the invitation to get all the Royals to come. I'll seduce one of them—which doesn't matter. Once we're alone, he meets with another accident. If I can get away with that once, I hope to get away with it again, luring number four away either with sex or threats—whatever works.

"By then, the final shit stain should be suspicious. He's the only one left of their torture campaign against my sister. He'll probably hire security, watch his back, and warn people I'm the one with the motive if anything happens to him. I'll pay one of his guards to drown him in the river my sister died in."

Rafael nodded along, his face as expressionless as the guys around him. "And then, you break into an NSA facility, erase yourself from every database, and go on the run because you'll be the prime suspect in their deaths for the rest of your life." Shaking his head, he blew out a breath. "Damn, darling, you need us bad."

I peered at them through my lashes. "No comment on my plan to kill them? Because the end result won't change."

Lucien tucked his shaman's gift under his clothes. "One of them tried to burn us to ash—a method that would've ended my living death too. All five of them bullied, assaulted, and tormented the girl who saved us just because they could."

"Did you think we were going to cry, wail, and beg for their eternal souls?" Rafael said. "Do whatever you want to them. Just don't get caught."

I scanned their faces, neither one seemed to disagree with Rafael. "Your turn," I finally said. "What did you have in mind?"

"Buckle up, princess. You're about to throw yourself in my arms."

Rafael explained what they planned to do to each one of them—with Lucien and Wilder throwing in details. My eyes widened in places. Three times I gasped. Four I laughed. Once I confirmed it: there wasn't a soul left in me to care about right and wrong.

He grinned at the expression on my face. "What do you—?"

I took a running leap, jumping Rafael. He almost fell off the stool catching me. "Yes," I stated. "Yours is better. Your plan is *way* better. We start now—tonight. Owen doesn't get another good night's sleep."

I shook him, wicked glee spilling through my pores. "You're right. Once we're done with them, I won't have to lift a finger. They'll slit their own throats."

"You're terrifying, Cloud Girl." Rafael slipped around my arm, perfectly happy to have me in his lap. "I'm finding it very sexy."

"Behave," I said with a laugh. "This is a business arrangement."

Rafael flicked to my finger. "Is that a business arrangement too?"

I covered my ring. "This is... what it is."

"A nonanswer. You've been around Wilder too long."

Time to end the hug. I hopped off, tucking my ring hand under my arm. "Victor isn't important to what we're doing."

"He could be," Lucien replied. "If he takes issue with you moving into a house with four men."

"Excuse me? Why would he take issue with that?" I asked slowly. "I'm not moving into a house with four men."

"This doesn't work if you don't," Wilder added. "How can we be your alibi, saying you were with us the whole time, if you're not with us even half the time? Plus, the dorm security is a joke. This house is the safest place on campus. People who start wars don't live behind paper walls."

"I'm not moving in here." My reply was firm. "You're sweet to worry about me, but I can take care of myself."

"Is that the reason?" Rafael asked. "Or do you not trust us? Despite everything we're about to do together."

"It's because of everything we're about to do together that you know I trust you enough. We're not actually having this conversation, guys. I'm not moving in here." I made for the door. "Are we set for tonight?"

"Depends on if Owen spends the night in the infirmary or if he goes home to Mommy. We can't get to him in the Thasher Estate."

"Okay. Keep me updated."

I left them to it, heading back to my dorm. I had mountains of homework to do and two texts from Katie saying she was willing to gift me her presence again if I took her out for an expensive makeup dinner and shopping that night. At this point, I assumed saying no would get me another latte down the pants, so I texted back yes as I crossed campus. Maybe she'd tell me she made progress getting Saylor and her friends to back off.

If I'm not friends with Katie, how exactly do I keep getting sucked into her orbit? The question taunted me while I climbed the steps and entered my building.

A couple of students hung out in the common area, studying or talking over a bowl of popcorn. Both activities ceased when I walked in. One after the other, they stared at me, eyes blank.

My neck hairs stood on end. Curled lips and shining eyes were wrong, but at least they expressed an emotion. This dead-eyed look as though they were seeing through me. As if I were a dust ball that blew in through the window, reminding them the floating specks of nothing they dismissed, were once living.

Shivers crawled up my skin. I hid it, defiantly staring back. They could call me a Dreg as often as they wanted. I would never let them forget that I matter—that Winter mattered. I rounded the corner, feeling the exact moment their gazes fell away.

My makeup dinner for Katie was more an order than a suggestion. Her text said she was picking me up in twenty minutes and to wear something that wasn't shit embarrassing. I had a feeling the only ones of my outfits dubbed perfect in Katie's eyes were those she picked out for me. They were exactly what I would not wear.

I was still pissed after my unwanted coffee shower on the quad. Let her hide behind her menu, cursing me in the ugliest, mismatched outfit I could dig up.

"I might even wear clogs."

That got a laugh out of me easier than in months. It wasn't a laugh borne of happiness. That emotion was gone from me like an ex who cheated, wrecked my credit, drained my bank account, and gave my name to his angry bookies before skipping town. It was over between us, and I didn't want that bitch back. Being happy without Winter in my life was the final betrayal against my sister.

No, my laugh returned for one reason only: the fact that I'd take the happiness from Winter's murderers permanently.

I turned the key in my lock, pushing open the door. *Please let Owen have opted for the infirmary instead of running home to Mommy. Rafael promised the next place they hung him from, it won't be so easy to get him down.*

Giggling, I flicked on the lights.

Six figures pressed on my vision, defying the empty space I meant to walk into. Wrongness jarred me, paralyzing my feet for the few precious seconds it took for my mind to scream, *Run!*

Whipping around, I sprinted for the door.

"Get her!"

A wall of flesh slammed into my spine, dropping and pinning me down.

"Get off!"

I struck wildly, glancing off a hip bone. I yanked up cloth and dug my nails in the flesh, ripping out a yell that pummeled my eardrum.

"Stop standing there! Help me," he shouted. "Grab her hands."

That was the cue.

They piled on me. Sitting on my hands and legs, kneeing my head into the carpet. My door slammed shut as the last of my cries bounced down the hall, calling for the students eating their popcorn in the common room.

Thunderous footfalls did not return to me, letting me know who was coming to help.

No one.

"Get her up."

They hauled me to my knees—a hand fisting my hair, wrenching my neck back to face the one guy who didn't move or join in.

Owen's sneer was terrible on his red, splotchy face. Welts covered every bit of exposed flesh. At his feet was a single black duffel bag. Between the fading red paint and the bruises, he looked like one massive, bleeding sore. To even sit on my bed, he perched on the end of it—his arms held out to avoid touching anything or himself.

And I smiled.

Fury twisted his features unrecognizable. "Think this is funny, bitch?"

Taking my eyes off him, I twisted as far as the vise on my scalp would allow me, scanning the faces of my captors.

Darren Johnson. Caleb Madden. Silas Brown. Emmett Jones. Levi Thompkins.

My skin burned looking into his hate-filled eyes. The worst part was I wasn't surprised to feel Levi's nails pierce my scalp. I wasn't shocked that he was Owen's first call when he decided to break into another girl's dorm and assault her. Soulless bastards stick together.

"Yes," I hissed, looking Owen right in the eyes. "I think this is hilarious."

Owen didn't react the way I expected. He didn't react at all.

The silence spread down my back, stiffening my spine.

Moving gingerly, Owen picked himself up off my bed. Slight winces shattered the cool mask he clung to. "Luna... Bowden... Sinclair."

"Just Luna Sinclair." I was proud of my voice for holding steady. "I didn't take my stepfather's last name."

"And I bet you thought that would hide who you were? Stupid," he spat. "Your brain-dead sister tried to do the same thing, going around calling herself Winter Bowden, so everyone would think she was the tire king's daughter. A potential Royal." He barked a laugh, and cut it short—grimacing.

"As if she could be one of us," he forced. "In Regalia, we can find out a person's lineage faster than that slut could find a dick looking for a free blow."

I lunged. "Don't talk about her that—!"

Levi hauled me back, muffling my shouts.

Owen continued on like I hadn't spoken. "She had no right to come in our town, in our school, and pretend like she was one of us. She got exactly what she fucking deserved. Which is why I won't bother to ask why you did what you did to me this morning. We both know why we're here."

Grim understanding dawned. Owen thought I turned him into a human piñata, and why wouldn't he? No one on this campus could possibly hate him more than Winter's sister.

"I could tell you that you're in way over your head." Owen paced the length of my rug, so desperate to act the cool, powerful menace even though he was a walking Rorschach test. "You're playing a game where you don't know the rules, the players, or how to make it end."

My chest heaved, breathing hard against the clamp stemming my curses.

"I could tell you that whole thing with your sister wasn't personal," he mused. "The bitch had to be put in her place, and if we didn't do it, someone else would've. Bowden could've made it stop at any time, but as we both know, she was stupid."

Mentally screaming, I ordered my heart to slow and racing mind to halt. *Stop and think, Luna. You can get out of this. You can make Owen eat those insults!*

"It could've ended, Sinclair, but then you had to come to this school." He shook his head like he was disappointed in me. "You had to come for me and start this shit all over again, like I don't have better things to do than waste my time on another worthless Dreg. I wish I could say we were even. I showed the world the truth about your sister, and you got me back."

Owen stuck his face in mine, swallowing me in hostile depths. "But it doesn't work that way, bitch." He headbutted me, making us both cry out. "The Royals do what they *fucking like* and you Dregs don't get to do shit about it! Your sister had to learn that lesson the hard way, and looks like you will too. Strip her!"

I thrashed—bucking and wrenching my limbs from their grip. Darren, Levi, and Emmett held me fast, crowing and laughing as Silas tore off my shirt in one vicious move.

"Hmmm!"

The door flew open. "Lu-Lu, I told you to—"

Katie stood in the entrance, jaw dropping faster than her phone hit the floor. She took in the scene, eyes huge.

Katie was right. She said the day was coming quick that I'd be happy to see her. Relieved tears coated Levi and my cheeks. I screamed for her, shaking over the tatters of my shirt.

"Owen? Levi?" she rasped. "What the fuck are you doing?!"

"Get out of here, Katie." Owen slashed a hand at her. "This has got nothing to do with you."

"Nothing to— Let her go!" She charged my captors and was caught by Silas and Caleb. They handled her a lot less roughly than they did me, but from her bucking and cursing, their grips were iron. "Get the fuck off me, Madden, or your dad's company is going to know what it's like to be fucked up the ass too. Oops—was the Dom that ties him up and fucks him in the House of Pain supposed to be a secret?"

Caleb paled. Seems it was a secret to him.

"Let her go, you rapist cunts!"

"Calm down, Katie," Levi snapped. "It's not what you think."

"No one is going to rape her," Owen said. "We're just teaching her a lesson. Payback for what she did to me in the cafeteria."

"In the cafeteria? Are you insane?" Katie got free and smacked Caleb across the face. He stumbled into my desk, looking dazed from more than the slap. I guess he really did not have a clue about his dad or the House of Pain.

Silas was left to wrangle her arms behind her back. "How is she supposed to have strung you to the ceiling, Owen? That skinny bitch can barely lift a potato chip to her mouth."

She was trying to help me. In her mean Katie way, she fought to make them question how I could've pulled off something so masterful. And she was right. I couldn't pull that off if I had ten years to plan my revenge. I weaved my vengeance on a keyboard. The Rogues trumpeted his humiliation with a fifty-member orchestra.

"No one else would dare," Owen replied. "The Dregs—"

Katie scoffed, rolling her eyes like him, we, and all of this was an annoyance out of her day. "You can look further than the Dregs, honey. Girls talk, Owen. By now, every Royal with a vagina knows you're a sleezy bastard. After Lindsay, you pissed off the last one willing to have anything to do with you. Trust me, there are dozens of people on this campus that ache for you to get yours." She stuck out her lips, fake pouting. "Or did you think all those women pelting you with paintballs were trying to help you down?"

Owen's mouth turned down as she landed the first blow in his self-assured armor. Oh no, maybe there were other people who hated his rapey, women-hating ass.

"So let her go," Katie ordered. "Going after some random Dreg to prove you're the big Royal on campus is too little, too late. We've already seen your little winkie."

I snorted—a short, muffled sound. But it whirled Owen to me, him flushing a deeper shade of red at me on my knees, exposed... and laughing at him.

"Shut up!" He snatched Katie's throat, wiping the smirk off her lips. "That's always been your problem, Langford, you've never known when to shut the hell up. You say the girls talk? They talk about you too. So do the guys.

"Literally everyone thinks you're a bitchy slut who's so in love with yourself, you'd fall down a manhole while walking down the street, admiring yourself in the shop windows. None of the Royals *like* you. And here's a perfect reason why: if Sinclair is just a random Dreg, what are you doing knocking on her door and going against us to protect her?"

Katie kicked him in the shin. He howled, releasing her to grab his leg and then letting go as his grip hurt his welts. Owen fell on his ass, bleeding shouts through his teeth.

"Enough!" Levi twisted my hair, springing tears to my eyes. "I don't know what you're doing here, Katie, and I don't care. She attacked one of us. What comes next has to happen and you know that. She's a Dreg and we're Royals. If you're one of us, you'll turn around and walk out. If you don't, we don't care who your parents are—you can say goodbye to your Royal status, and end up on your knees next to her.

"Please, pick choice number two." I heard the leer in his voice. "It's been so long since I've seen those yummy tits."

Just like that, Silas let her go. Katie stumbled over her high heels.

"What's it going to be, Katie?" Owen pushed himself up, and drew something out of the duffel bag. He aimed the paintball gun at her head. "You joining the party?"

Katie looked from him to my bulging eyes. I saw the second she made up her mind.

"*No!*" I shouted through his hand. "*Katie, please. Don't leave me here with them!*"

She backed away, reaching behind her for the doorknob. Katie opened her mouth to say something.

Caleb yanked the knob from her grasp. "Get out!"

Turning tail, she ran.

My cries stopped. I stared in disbelief as the door slammed against the frame. *She left me. Katie just... left me.*

"All right, boys." Owen's grin returned as he dumped out the contents of the duffel bag. "Where were we?"

It was Levi who tore off my bra, whipping and waving it over his head, hooting as Darren held his phone on me. Emmett tore off my pants and underwear. He stuffed my boy shorts in my open, wailing mouth. Levi was too busy tying my hands behind my back to act as my muzzle.

My tears flowed hot and free. Humiliation sank into my pores, tightening my skin tauter than a bowstring. I curled into myself—praying I'd disappear as Levi handed paintball guns to everyone.

I didn't know Caleb, Darren, Silas, or Emmett apart from the fact they were also in my sister's class. Whatever part they did or didn't play in my sister's death, I couldn't say. But they sure as hell didn't know me nor did they have a shred of proof that I hung Owen from the ceiling. None of that tamed the enjoyment on their faces as they took their guns and aimed.

"All right, boys," Owen crowed. "Let's see how she likes it."

They let loose.

Paintballs splattered and broke on my tender skin. This would hurt if I was wearing the right gear. Naked and helpless—the strikes were agony.

I shrieked, curling myself as tight as possible and pressing my face into the carpet. The shots were vicious cruelty on my skin, marking their domination over me in the bruises that would last for days, giving warning to all the Dregs who dreamed about standing up for themselves.

A ball struck my temple, knocking me back. They fired wildly at my soft lips, blemished cheeks, and tender eyes—seeking to cause real damage.

My face soaked in paint and salty wetness, and I called out, for Winter.

I bawled for the brokenhearted betrayal of watching her friends turn their backs on her. I screamed for the agony of her alone and unprotected in the brutal hands of Owen and Levi. I cried because I finally understood why she gave up.

"Stop," Owen ordered.

The paintballs ceased flying. I flopped limp on the floor, my entire body an exposed nerve ending doused in pain. My toes sang for mercy. My hair cried hanging on to my aching scalp.

I wanted to be cool and calm. To laugh in their faces and prove nothing they did could get to me.

I wanted to be a bear.

But on that floor with my own panties in my mouth and my punishment filmed on his phone, I was nothing more than a rabbit.

"What do we think, guys?" Owen asked. "Has the message sunk in?"

Caleb's laugh was a nasty, hard sound. "Yeah, I think she's learned her lesson. Next time she sees a Royal, she'll bow her head and curtsey." He shook Darren's phone at me. "Or the whole world sees this, Sinclair. Got it?"

"No," Levi sliced in before my brain sent the command to nod. "What kind of pussies are you, letting her get off this easily? She stunned Owen till he passed out in a puddle of piss. She turned him into a chicken piñata and hung him from the ceiling, and he didn't get the option of not going viral.

"Everyone saw what she did to him." Levi brandished a knife. "Everyone's going to see what we do to her."

"Hmm!" Panic flooded my mind. I rolled away, banging against the desk.

Emmett lurched away. "What the fuck, man?! Why do you have that?"

"No. No way," Silas cried. "I'm not a part of this. I don't even know this chick. I'm not going to prison for killing her!"

"Relax, idiot." Levi closed the distance, limping slightly on his bad leg. "We're not killing her. We're giving her a gift."

"Gift?" Owen repeated. He didn't appear pleased at the knife in Levi's hand, but he wasn't shouting in my defense either. "What gift?"

"Sinclair will have a permanent reminder of what she is and"—he hauled me across the carpet and straddled me—"who she belongs to. Right here." Levi tapped my forehead with the hilt. "*Property of the Royals* carved into that hard little head."

I bucked, fighting harder than ever. My fear emboldened Levi, feeding the burning malice in his eyes to flames. At that moment, I didn't question that he would set fire to a building with people inside. These were the eyes of a man raised by privilege, fed wealth, nurtured by lack of consequences, and turned on by power. He truly believed he could do whatever he wanted to anyone without punishment. Seeing as he was still strutting around Regalia after what he did to the Rogues and my sister, maybe he was right.

"What's wrong, Owen?" Levi's glare pinned him through. "You can't do this? Too *chicken*shit?"

Owen jerked like his taunt was a physical blow. His red face shuttered closed. "Hold her still." The other guys were slow to move. Owen barked at them again. "You four rank too low to be questioning us. Remember that. And then think about how many places you'll move up after tonight if you put this Dreg in her place. Even Saylor Burkhardt will look at you with respect."

"Hphmf!" I shouted at them—smothered cries appealing to their sense of humanity. Those cries fell on deaf ears as one after the other, they grabbed my legs, arms, and head—pinning me to the floor.

Levi positioned the blade above my forehead. Leaning in, he whispered against my mouth. "Your sister whined and cried like a little bitch too. Guess it runs in the family."

Breaking free, I smashed my forehead into his nose. Levi flew back, howling.

"Fuck's sake!" Owen shoved him off me. "I'll do it."

Grabbing the knife off the floor, Owen climbed on top of me as Darren and Silas wrestled my head back down.

"Apparently, I don't listen when someone says no." Owen's wrist shook as he pressed the tip to my forehead. "So I'm listening. Say no and I'll stop, Sinclair."

Smothered shouts poured through the fabric.

"What was that? Hmm. Didn't sound like a no to me. Oh well."

Owen pressed, splitting my skin. My blood coated the tip.

The door blew off the hinges, crashing onto my desk and taking Emmett out on the way. Over Owen's head, they filled the entrance—avenging angels of fury.

Caleb ran at them—to attack or get away, I had no idea—but Cato leaped out of the pack, his muzzle nowhere to be seen. He tackled Caleb to the floor, his teeth sinking in his shoulder.

"Ahh! Help! Get him off!"

No one was in a position to help him.

Wilder ripped Owen off me and sank a fist in his gut. The mottled red dick doubled over on the carpet, the knife clattering to the floor.

Levi sprang up. In one fluid move that could've been the first step in a dance, Rafael kicked him in the face. Levi clutched his ruined nose, blood pouring through his fingers as a sob ripped unbidden from his lips.

Emmett, Darren, and Silas abandoned me on the floor to help their friends. Lucien was on me in an instant.

Ripping off that long, ridiculous, old-fashioned coat, he covered me head to toe, his touch impossibly gentle. He lifted me up, carrying me through the fray into the bathroom.

"It's okay, Luna." Lucien pulled the panties out and threw them at the tub. "You're safe now."

I sobbed—lung-shredding cries that made it impossible to breathe. Of all the things this was, okay was not one of them.

"Stay here." Lucien stroked my tangled, paint-splattered hair. "I'll be back in two minutes."

Lucien joined the fight, standing there as the thin, pale extra who wandered off the set of Sweeney Todd. Emmett threw a punch at his jaw, and Lucien caught it in midair.

Twisting his fist, he dropped Emmett screeching to his knees. Bending his arm back, he struck him once, twice, four times in the face. Emmett dropped unconscious on my rug.

Darren broke away, racing for the door. Cato shot out, sweeping his legs. He was on the fallen man before his head bounced off the carpet. I winced as Cato's teeth closed on his ear, and the screams followed.

Everywhere I looked, the Rogues were fighting, punching, throwing, biting, dancing around my room, reducing my attackers to the bleeding mess on the carpet that I was.

They came for me.

I slumped against the bathroom cabinet, black crowding my vision.

My heart raced out of control. Pain and adrenaline battled to overtake my senses. All I wanted was to not feel.

Oblivion opened its arms. Willingly, I sank. The last thing I recalled was a beautiful, heavenly sound rising above the shouting, lulling me to sleep.

Chapter Seven

"**...I**s she okay..."

"...got there as fast..."

"...bastards will regret..."

Noises pressed on my ears, peeling an eye open. A blurred, shiny shape stood over me. Objects bobbed around its head.

"Luna?" the shape called to me. "Are you awake?"

Darkness crept back in, stealing me away.

THE NEXT TIME I WOKE, it was the arms of sleep that willingly set me free. No voices, lights, or figures helping me along.

I blinked up at the pale-pink ceiling, slowly taking stock.

A deep-seated ache burrowed into my skin. I didn't need to see my arms to know they were covered in bruises.

Owen, Levi, and the Royals attacked me. They held me down and...

...the Rogues saved me.

I turned my head, almost expecting to see Rafael in my bed. Instead my gaze fell on a bay window. A very familiar bay window.

I knew where I was. Turning my head the other way, my nose tickled the hair spilling onto my pillow.

And I wasn't alone.

I reached under the sheets, shaking her.

"Luna?" Sliding across the pillow, Katie flicked on the lamp. "You're awake. Are you— Whoa, that's a look."

A head-melting glare more like. If the thought of moving didn't make me want to cry, I'd fly across and rake my nails down her face.

"What am I doing here?" The thin, wispy rasp grated out of my throat. "Why am I in your room?"

"Because no matter how much those weirdos argued with me, it wasn't a good idea for you to wake up alone in a house with a bunch of strange men after you were just assaulted."

The Rogues.

"Doesn't explain why I'm here with you." I tried to snap it, and croaked it instead.

"I would've taken you home, but I didn't want your folks to see you like this after... Winter. Thought it might bring up some difficult stuff."

Put in the simplest terms, but still the truest thing she ever said. If my mother and stepfather opened the door to me naked, unconscious, and covered in bruises, it wouldn't matter if I married the prince of Monaco, they'd never let me set foot in Regalia University again.

"I know what you're thinking, Lu-Lu. You're thinking it was exactly how it looked. I ran off and abandoned you."

"You did!"

Katie was calm. "I ran to get campus security. It was five against two, and no one else in the dorm was coming to help us. I left you to get someone to stop them, but none of the guards would come."

None of the guards would come.

The horror of that sentence tried to sink in, but there was too much pain for it to penetrate and add any more.

"I wasted so much time screaming at that bald-headed, impotent shithead to come with me, after he walked off, I didn't know what to do. I shook off my personal security to pick you up for dinner. It would've taken even longer for them to get to campus." Katie rested her pillow against the headboard, then herself after it. "So, I called a number I never dialed before, bringing down the only people on campus who aren't afraid of the Royals."

Katie drew the covers to my chin—the nicest thing she'd ever done for me. Or it seemed, the second nicest.

"Rafael and his boys came right away. They didn't ask for anything in exchange, and I was told their prices are steep. I bet they're into you," Katie added for no good reason. "Heaven knows why."

"Another unneeded comment," I muttered. "So you called the freaks and weirdos… to save a Dreg. Then you let me sleep in your bed, protecting me."

"Joseph Collins, woman, don't get all weepy about it."

I was getting weepy. Wetness collected on my lids, but for so many reasons than just Katie.

"I'm not going through round two of this," Katie stated. "I will have my fun fucking year—partying, shopping, drinking with my friends. You insist on being one of them, so that includes you too. A couple of rapist pricks I can't stand don't get to mess with that any more than you do.

"Owen rounded up his friends and attacked you because he's too lazy to remember how many women want to cut off his dick. You were the last person to piss him off, so he came after you and went way too far. After last night, he won't make that mistake again. A Royal is a bad enemy to have. A Rogue is even worse. You're safe now."

I wished that were true.

"Thank you for calling them, Katie. For a second I thought— I thought they would—" I touched the bandage on my tender forehead. "I was really scared."

"I'm sorry I left you." She made like she was going to touch me. Hovering over my body, Katie finally patted my hip and pulled away. Giving comfort was definitely not in her top-five skills. "Even though I had a good reason, it was a shitty thing to do. I'm just glad I forgave you in time. I don't want to think about what would've happened if I didn't walk through your door last night."

"The dorm security is a joke. This house is the safest place on campus. People who start wars don't live behind paper walls."

I shivered. Levi and that chickenshit Owen proved Wilder right too quickly. With all the personal safety gear I keep on me at all times, none of it was enough to protect me from the gang of monsters casually waiting in my room to jump me. How would I ever feel safe in my dorm again? Especially now that Katie proved campus security wouldn't rush to help me.

"It's late," I whispered. "We should get some sleep."

"You can stay here until your bruises fade. And after, if you need more time. When you're better, you should probably think about moving back home."

"Don't worry, I'm not going back to that dorm."

THREE DAYS LATER, MY pain scale drifted down to a three, leaving me enough strength to pack and clear out my dorm.

I climbed the steps of my new place. Faint specks of paint covered my nails like a fashion statement as I rang the bell.

Wilder opened the door, his brow arching at my bags.

"Which room is mine?"

He didn't say anything. Reaching down, he picked up my stuff and jerked his head for me to go inside. I stepped over the threshold, nerves slapping me full in the face. I couldn't stay with Katie forever. This was my only idea, but that didn't necessarily mean it was a good one.

"This way." Wilder brushed past me. "It's already done up for you."

I nodded, accepting this. "You knew I'd change my mind."

"I knew you wouldn't want to sleep somewhere you didn't feel safe. Basic human instinct that years of advancement can't drive away. Neanderthals headed for the nearest cave for a reason. We hate feeling exposed."

I accepted this too. "I won't be any trouble. I'm neat, clean, and I don't blast music like an asshole. Also, I'll buy my own food and stay out of yours. I don't know what the payment situation is here, but I'm paid till the end of the semester for Abbott Hall. If you need me to pay for staying here, I can. I truly appreciate everything you've done for me. Let me know how I can repay you."

"Don't be ridiculous, Sinclair."

Warmth spread in my chest.

Wilder finished, "You wouldn't be here if I thought you were trouble."

Said warmth vanished. Of course Wilder covered his bases, checking up on the second Sinclair sister about to invade his cave.

I reached out to touch him and my fingers fell short. I returned them to my side. Wilder couldn't be clearer on his feelings about disinfectant-free groping. I could give him the respect of heeding his boundaries, after he pummeled six guys who disrespected mine.

Wilder took me through the kitchen where three pairs of spoons paused in their cereal bowls. We headed for the stairs to the sound of chairs scraping back and footsteps trailing us.

"Lady Luna, you're here."

Why did such a harmless nickname make me want to duck my head?

"Yeah," I replied uselessly.

Cato pushed through them, getting uncomfortably close to my face. Apparently, that's only cool when he does it.

"Are you okay?"

I tripped and grabbed the railing to catch myself. I didn't spare much thought to what Cato's voice sounded like, but a deep, silvery trill that snuck in my head and burrowed inside to stay for the rest of my life, was not it.

"Yes," I said softly. "I'm okay."

"Did Langford take care of you?" Rafael demanded.

The first reply that sprang to my lips was I didn't need to be taken care of. Then I remembered I said close to the same thing to him before I marched into my dorm and was attacked by Owen and Levi. The men I blew off for protection, had to burst in and protect me. My blustering didn't hold water with these guys.

"Katie's not really the nurturing type," I amended. "She did let me sleep and eat chef-prepared meals in her bed. That was more than I could ask for from a girl who barely knows me, and it was what I needed."

"Owen, Levi, and his buddies slept on itchy, piss-stained cotton and ate hospital food. That's also what you needed."

I covered my chest, skin prickling recalling the state they found me in.

"You have nothing to be embarrassed about." Lucien rested a barely there hand on the small of my back, guiding me on. "It's those guys and the parents who failed them who should feel ashamed. When we're through with them, mortification is the kindest emotion they'll feel."

"You say the nicest things to me, Lucien."

"Then you can't have met many nice men, for I am just getting started."

I did duck my head then, hiding behind my curtain of hair. I didn't know many nice men. The only man I had regular contact with while living in the boarding school, was the priest who performed Sunday mass. It was optional for us to attend, but I went most weekends because Father John was a cool dude who chuckled at my endless questions and brought news of the outside world.

I didn't come to Regalia expecting to meet more kind, pious men. I knew here be monsters. And they shocked me with their cruelty all the same.

Only a monster could think to carve his ownership into someone's skin.

"Did you tell your fiancé what happened?"

Rafael's expression gave nothing away, though I thought I sensed an edge when he said fiancé.

"Victor doesn't know. No one does thanks to you guys breaking their phones. I'd like to keep it that way."

"We won't tell a soul," Lucien said, "and this isn't me suggesting that you should, but in our quest to make these men pay, Victor Wilson could be a valuable ally. The only thing that matters more than money in Regalia is status. Losing it would splinter their armor before we strike the first blow, ensuring devastation. If anyone has the power to drag those guys as low as a Dreg, it's a Wilson."

Owen's promises to his reluctant friends came back to me. "But Victor said no one listens to a freshman—Wilson or not."

"That's true," Rafael added, "but we're not talking about who hosts the summer bonfire. They hurt the fiancé of someone who's years away from becoming one of the most powerful men in Regalia, and the country. If Victor demands the older Royals punish them, they're not about to ignore the guy. One day, he'll be an enemy you don't want to have. And if you two do get married, you'll both remember who didn't help you."

I paused on the steps, two things hitting me at once: all the power I would have as Victor Wilson's wife, and that Rafael said *if* we get married.

"Want the quick tour before you see your room?" Lucien asked.

Shaking off my thoughts, I said, "Sure."

Lucien and I broke off at the top of the stairs, heading in the direction of a black door. The hallway we were in was a long one. Five doors on each side, giving no clue to what lay behind them. The final sixth room was open and Wilder ducked in with my bags, Cato and Rafael going in with him. At the opposite end of the hall was a boarded-over window.

Lucien pushed open the door, waving me in. I didn't ask whose room this was.

Bloodred damask wallpaper wrapped around the space, providing the only color breaking up the black on black on black. Black-framed mirrors. Black wardrobe. Black bed. Black rug, and resting on top of it, a shiny black coffin.

I stepped in, a low whistle leaking out at his commitment to the life and style. Everything in here was screamingly expensive. It was hard to call something kitschy when it was twice the national average salary.

"I like what you've done with the place."

"You assume this is my room. You believe you have me all figured out, do you not, Lady Luna?"

I almost smiled. Almost. I was done with those for a while. "Sorry, my mistake. Whose room is this?"

"Ah, well. As it happens, this one is mine. But my point still stands."

Another tugging smile drew on my lips. I fought it off.

"You shouldn't have started with this room. The others can't top it."

"Don't be so sure." His handprint burned another mark on my dress. "There's something I want to show you." Lucien led me out of his room to the door opposite. "I've had decades' worth of living and too much time on my hands. Any style of fighting you can think of, I've mastered."

Lucien let me go in first. My toes sank into the padded floor, enjoying the coolness of the plastic spreading through my heels. Wall-to-wall mats met my attention, and the attention of all the Lunas bouncing off the mirrors. They turned the room into a dojo.

"If you ever want to benefit from my experience, it'd be an honor to teach you. I can turn you into a lethal weapon, my dear. No fangs, stun guns, or pepper stray required."

I swept the place, a clear vision filling my mind of forcing Owen Thasher to his knees and punching his teeth in.

I smiled. "Oh, Lucien, you really do say all the right things."

Flicking off the lights, Lucien led me to the room beside him.

"Actually," I began, resting a hand on his wrist. "Can we pick up the tour later? I woke up at three a.m. this morning to clear out my dorm before anyone got up. All I want to do right now is crash."

"Of course. After you."

I drew ahead of him, anticipation quickening my steps. Wilder said they did my room up for me. This entire place was a quirky artist's paradise. I couldn't wait to see what they did in there.

Rounding the corner, my excitement crashed into the rocks and sank beneath the shoals.

White walls, white dresser, white-painted wooden bed with a gray comforter, and not much else. This was the plainest room in the Americas.

Rafael reclined in the white leather armchair pushed against the wall. You'd think it was positioned to face a television, except the only thing across from it was paint and plaster. Cato stretched out on my bed and Wilder leaned against the dresser.

"Not much to look at," Rafael acknowledged, "but you can do it up however you want. The Gallery used to be a frat house, so we each took two rooms to do with them what we want." He gestured around. "None of us needed three, so this has been sitting here empty."

"Thank you for doing this, guys. I've felt safer since I heard the security system rearm itself."

Wilder inclined his head. "Best security system not on the market. The government wishes they could get their hands on it."

"How did you get your hands on it?" I asked.

Wilder's eyes narrowed to slits. "Why?"

"Kind of a natural question in response to a statement like that."

"You ask a lot of questions."

"You say a lot of things that need questioning."

Scoffing, he slipped one of my bags off his shoulder, unzipped it, and unceremoniously dumped out the contents.

"What are you doing?!"

"Checking for trackers and listening devices." Wilder riffled through my underwear without a break in conversation. "Triad-owned garment shops sew them right into the lining," Wilder said. A knife appearing in his hand out of nowhere. He picked up a dress. "I'll have to destroy half of these to check. You'll be reimbursed."

I rushed him. "No!"

"No need to cut up her delicates," Rafael smoothly broke in. "I'll have them checked out, x-rayed, the whole thing."

"Fine." My pulse restarted as he dropped my sixteenth birthday present from Winter on the pile. "Hold out your arms."

"Why—"

Wilder lifted them for me, commencing the pat-down.

"I'm starting to rethink this."

Rafael laughed. "You didn't think living with rogues was like a summer in Barbie's Malibu playhouse, did you?"

Wilder's hands slid down my leg, firm and gentle. Molding to my calf, he ran down my body like a steamy, sudsy shower—warm, clinging, and laying my goose bumps down flat.

I felt the callouses on his fingers and palm, promising a life of work and toil, so unlike the soft, pampered hands I shook at my engagement party.

What gave you those callouses, Wilder O'Rourke? And do other women get to feel them skating their bodies?

Starting, I caught the stray thought and shoved it deep into my subconscious. I was not going there. Us five had a job to do and nothing was more important. Winter would not go unavenged because I got into a messy relationship that grief was destined to kill. Bitter exes tend to rethink their stance on risking prison for you.

Also, I had a fiancé. Couldn't forget that asshole.

Wilder stepped back and a stupid part of me missed the loss. Sidestepping me, he walked out. I thought that was the end of my pre-move-in check, until he came back with a metal detector wand.

"You've got to be kidding me."

"Hold still. The tracker would be at the base of your skull."

"What tracker?" I cried as he spun me around.

"A covert division of the government has been implanting trackers in unsuspecting citizens for decades. You'd have no idea it happened. Their MO is to pump knockout gas through the vents and operate while the household is sleeping." He waved the thing all around my head without a beep. "You're clean."

"Of course, I'm clean. No one is breaking into anyone's house and—"

Looking me dead in the eye, Wilder moved the wand over his head, positioning it behind—

Beep. Beep. Beep. Beep.

Jaw working, I croaked, "You made it do that."

"I'm afraid not. Don't worry." He held out my arms again. "Mine is dead. Hit it with an electromagnetic pulse."

Wilder waved it down.

Beep. Beep. Beep.

Then back up, stopping the noisy machine over my chest. "Is there underwire in your bra? Remove it."

"Get out."

The wand bobbed up and down. "Unless your nipples are pierced. Remove your bra to confirm."

"I said out. Now."

Shaking his head like I was the problem, Wilder tromped out, Lucien, Cato, and a sniggering Rafael following behind.

I made to slam my door and my hand closed on air. Eyes bugging, I patted the wall where my door should be leaning.

"There's no door," I said. "Why isn't there a door?"

Wilder looked the hinges up and down, and then me. "I took the door off last night."

"Why?"

"Because you were moving in."

The first straight answer he gave me, and it made no damn sense.

"What the hell does that mean? Why would you take off my door?"

The calm, cool, collected façade shattered all over the hardwood. "Because you're not going to be in there plotting, planning, and getting up to who knows what kinds of shit behind closed doors," he growled. "You may be Winter's little sister, but who says we can trust you? Who knows who you're working for? The Russians, the Chinese—"

"I'm not working for anyone!"

"—the North Koreans! That's a real nice American accent, by the way. How long you been working on it? Or should I say, gosaenghaesseoyo!"

Huge eyes beheld that reddening, handsome face. "What is happening?"

"Winter said you were away at boarding school, but everyone knows foreign governments pay headmasters to float them a few kids for covert training while giving false reports to their parents overseas. We don't know where you really were."

"France," I said slowly. "I was in France. St. Thomas's Academy."

"That's what they told you to say."

"Who is they?!"

Wilder leaned in, overwhelming my senses with citrus, mint gum, and psycho. "I'll find out. Until then, I see you and what you're doing at all times. You've got a problem with that, then I'll know you have something to hide."

Steaming, I scrambled for a reply.

"You can't watch me all the time," I blurted. "I could lock myself in the bathroom, run the water, and do all my plotting and planning in there. How would you know?"

Wilder froze.

Behind him, Rafael slapped a hand over his face. "Oh, darling. How did that make sense to say out loud?"

"What—?

Whipping around, Wilder stormed down the hall. He returned with a power drill.

An hour later, I was wide awake, rumpled, and sitting on my bed glaring at the doorless bathroom across the hall.

Round One: Two points to Wilder.

THAT NIGHT, I WENT into the kitchen, my wanderings ending in there. Regalia University was filled with opulent offices, decked-out cafeterias, and the fancy dorm rooms that million-dollar endowments could buy, but I was certain there wasn't a building that matched the Rogues' Gallery.

Rafael said the four of them claimed two rooms. I stuck my head in them, feeling zero ounces of guilt about invading their privacy after two particular doors came off the wall. I wandered inside them all, barring two rooms that were bolted with half a dozen locks each. I didn't ask whose rooms those were.

Lucien was the owner of the dojo and death den. For Cato, I swung the door in, heard him growl on the other side and closed it shut quickly. Padding across the hall, I walked into a reader's paradise, or their nightmare.

Books on books stacked as high as the ceiling with no discernible system, and no bookshelves to create one. A mound of hardbacks in the corner. Paperbacks lining a path to a squishy armchair in the middle of the room. Hundreds of books of all genres, sizes, authors, and centuries covered the carpet.

Cato.

I couldn't say why I knew this space was his. I just knew.

My tour took me to the room next door. Rafael's.

Band posters covered almost every inch of wall. He built a workbench connecting his nightstand to his desk, stretching the length of the back wall and sticking his messy queen-size bed next to the door. I tiptoed inside, checking out the bands, and raising a brow at all the weird stuff on his desk/ bench.

Rafael was in the kitchen, standing over a bubbling pot of something that smelled delicious. It was almost dinnertime. His headphones were in, but the lovely sound spreading through the room was coming from him.

"Surrender to me," he sang, catching my breath.

Beautiful. His voice was just... beautiful.

I squeezed his shoulder, ending his song and hating myself for it.

"Luna." Rafael tapped his phone, shutting off the music. I waited as he switched out the headphones for his hearing aids. During the one day we lived together, I noticed he alternated between the aids, headphones, and earplugs. The world's noise did not touch him freely.

"You hungry?" he asked, shutting off the stove. "I made chicken chili soup."

"Oooh. Sounds yum. I'll get the bowls."

Checking the cabinets, I found what I was looking for over the sink. Rafael's fingers brushed mine as he took them from me.

"Enjoy your snoop?" he asked.

"Yep. Is the library Cato's?"

He smiled at me, making my cheeks heat for no good reason again. "You're cute calling it a library."

The "cute" compliment didn't go down easy either.

"Yeah, it's Cato's. My bro likes to read."

"There are multitudes hidden in his head, aren't there?"

"Personalities? Nah, that's not his diagnosis."

I poked him. "That's not what I meant, and you know it."

Rafael chuckled. "Yes, there are. People don't see past the muzzle, and the growling, and the biting, and the pyromania, and... I had a point when I started that sentence."

A giggle escaped me—over as quickly as it started, and a miracle all the same. Just an hour before, I was convinced I wouldn't laugh again for a lifetime.

"Cato is more than people think he is," Rafael finished. "I won't let anyone stigmatize and put my brother in a box, because they can't bother looking past the face he shows the world. We all wear a mask, and we all get a chance to show what's behind it. Cato should get that chance too."

I laid my hand on his forearm, looking at him, but seeing her. Winter said she wasn't a bear, but it wasn't me who broke Billy Canton's nose for pushing me off my bike and making me skin my knee. I was busy crying on the sidewalk while she chased him around the yard—four feet tall, pink bows in her hair, and beating the crap out of him.

My vision swam. That was something I would truly never stop doing. "Big siblings. You never stop taking care of us."

"Didn't know it was an option." Rafael caught a tear chasing the other down my cheek. "But you're right, I wouldn't take it if it was."

Rafael carried our bowls to the table. Wiping my face, I hopped on the stool, facing him.

"I popped into your room too," I said, changing the subject back. "I'm in love with almost every band on your walls."

"Then you have excellent taste, Luna Sinclair. Just when I think I couldn't like you more."

I arched a brow. "Do you flirt with every girl like this?"

"Only the beautiful, smart, badass ones."

"You are on a roll."

He laughed. "I can stop, if you want. This is your place now. Wouldn't want to make you uncomfortable here."

I flicked down, suddenly interested in my soup. "You're not... making me uncomfortable."

"Good to know."

Oh yeah, that was definitely the wrong thing to say.

"But all that stuff on your bench," I said, steering the conversation again. "The wires, and tubes, and fake packages with explosive warnings. What's that about?"

Rafael didn't pause dipping his spoon in his soup. "Those aren't fake, Cloud Girl. They're bombs. Very real bombs."

I stared at him, the sentence going in my ears, penetrating my brain, and evaporating in the space. "Excuse me?"

"They're bombs."

"No, they're not."

"But they are."

"They're not."

Amused, Rafael tossed his head. "They are."

"They're not," I pushed through gritted teeth, "because no one in their right mind would plop half a dozen bombs next to their bed. What happens if you flip over and smack that *alarm clock*?"

He barked a laugh. "Nothing good."

"Rafael! Tell me you aren't keeping a stash of explosives in your bedroom."

"Well, I'm not going to leave them lying around the house. How irresponsible do you think I am?"

"Get rid of them. Right now. You want to talk about making me uncomfortable? A pile of bombs right down the hall does that!"

"Relax," he breezed. "I haven't put the triggers in any of them. They're harmless."

"I doubt that. If you won't get rid of them, I will."

Rafael arched a brow. "Oh, you will? You know how to safely dispose of explosive material?"

My mouth opened and nothing came out. Dispose of it? I wouldn't make it out of the house with that stuff without crapping my pants at the first person to give me a weird look.

I snatched up my spoon. "I hate you."

"Damn." The bastard was far from put out. "And we had such a good mood going."

"This isn't over."

Pulling my bowl to me, I focused on my food to give me something to do.

One swallow of his soup and I moaned, eyes rolling up in my head. I promptly ignored why I was pissed at him.

"Oh my damn, this is amazing." I scooped three more swallows in my mouth, moaning louder. "Shit on a stick, Rafael. Where did you learn how to cook like this?"

"My mother taught me. She was an assassin, specializing in poisons. Want to get your target to swallow it? Sprinkle it on the best thing they've ever tasted. They'll lick the plate clean before they're choking on it."

He dropped these electric-chair confessions so easily, it was impossible to know when the man was serious.

"Tell me something normal about her, so I can believe it."

Rafael grinned at me across his soup. "She loved Shakespeare, as you can tell from Cato's name. Purple was her favorite color. Purple walls, purple furniture, and on Christmas, purple food. Sometimes she took me with her on jobs, leaving me in the car with music blasting. I heard the best off her playlists."

My face fell with every word. "Was?" I whispered.

His grin melted away. "Yeah... she died."

"I'm so sorry."

Rafael leaned back on the stool, bracing his palms on the table edge, and fixing darkening eyes on a spot on the wall. I knew this move. He was distancing himself from me, this conversation, and the pain that went with it.

I didn't try to draw him back. I didn't say anything. For a long time, we sat in silence, eating our soup and listening to the guys shuffling upstairs.

"It was an explosion."

I slowly set down my bowl.

"Same one that fucked with my hearing," Rafael said, almost too low for me to hear. "I was nine."

"I'm sorry, Rafael." My hand found his, lacing our fingers together across the table. The question pulled out of me. "Was it an accident or...?"

"Or."

I squeezed my eyes shut, my heart shrinking in my chest. Losing your mother that young was devastating enough. But finding out she wasn't lost, but was taken—that smashed you into dust.

"Did they find the person who did it?"

He shook his head. "Ten years later, we still don't know who rigged our house or who hired them to do it. Mom and Dad had enemies spanning six continents. Too many to name."

"So." My head tilted to the ceiling. "All those *devices* in your room. How can you stand to be near a bomb when one took your mom?"

Twin, swirling pools captured me. "How can you stand to be on this campus when it took your sister?"

I stiffened, my grip strangling his fingers.

"You don't have to answer, because I know." Rafael placed a light kiss on my knuckles. "This place isn't a reminder, it's an enemy. You have to destroy it in her place. Prove it wasn't stronger than her, or you.

"Like I have to study, pick apart, and examine everything on this planet with a trigger until I understand them and the man creating them. They'll lead me to him, then give him the death he chose for my mother."

Gazing at our clasped hands, I stopped questioning why Rafael was willing to go so far to help me.

"You'll find him." I didn't recognize the hard, empty voice that came out of me. "Give him a death *worse* than the one he gave your mother."

"Yes." Rafael trailed his lips over my knuckles—soft and tickling, kissing each one. "I like you a lot."

Alarm bells started to sound, but I didn't pull away. "Can I ask you something?"

"You can ask me anything." He was moving down, kissing my trembling pointer finger.

"What does your world sound like?"

"Hmm. How about I show you?"

The question was no sooner out of his mouth than Rafael was on his feet and pulling me up with him. He drew me close, pressing me squeaking to his chest.

"Close your eyes."

"Why?"

His smile made me feel like I was cheating. "Trust me."

Breathing deep, my eyes fluttered shut.

"Every sound. Every song." His words whispered around us. "Has a feel, a color, a scent."

My eyes popped open. "A color?"

"Close 'em," he said amusedly, "and listen...

"*Happy birthday to you...*"

My brows popped as that angel's voice crooned the *Happy Birthday* song. My confusion grew as he went, wondering when he'd let me open my eyes. A memory floated up, almost tugging a smile.

"There," Rafael said. "What did you just think about?"

"It was nothing. I was just— Well, most people don't sing that version, but one year, Winter sang it to me. She had the *worst* voice, and she loved it. She'd practically scream at the top of her high-pitched, off-key lungs. I finally gave her the biggest piece of cake to make her stop."

Rafael traced my smile, catching the laugh off my lips. "So what's that song feel like?"

"Happy," I murmured.

"Feels like happiness. Tastes like buttercream frosting and sprinkles. Sounds like the soundtrack to a great day and perfect memory. We experience sound with all five senses, but most don't notice. At least they don't unless it's important.

"Hearing your father's voice when he comes home is joy, hugs, and gratitude if he just returned from war. It's fear, trauma, and a desperate place to hide if he's an evil, vicious bastard who just returned from the bar."

I found myself nodding. Explained in that way, how could it not be true?

"When they dug me out of the rubble—unconscious and bleeding out of my ears—that's when sound stopped being one sense, and became them all. Every minute of every day. All the time. I feel loud, clanging construction like a nail going through my brain. It bangs in my skull, clenches my teeth, overloads me till I want to take a real drill and finish what the explosion started."

"Oh, Rafael."

"But it's okay." And he was grinning, so maybe it was. "Because of Mom."

"Your mom?"

"She gave me all the beautiful noise I need, Cloud Girl." Rafael brushed the shells of my ears, tipping my head back as he put in his headphones. "Close your eyes."

They closed before he finished the sentence.

"What does this feel like?"

Surrender poured out of the speakers. A haunting, sweet melody of first love like the real fairy tales. Of mermaids that transform into sea-foam, carnivorous doves, and poisoned apples. It was feverish kisses, bitter fights, and passionate makeups.

Love in its raw, messy form demanding that you give it everything. That you surrender.

"What does it feel like?" I whispered—to Rafael, I wasn't sure.

I've never felt love like this. Never seen it in the polite, mature love between my mother and stepfather. Couldn't place it with my friends from school, swearing they loved the guy they were sexting with that week, and the next deleting his number and sexting someone else.

Memories. Bittersweet longing. Giggling under the pillows. Crying watching A Walk to Remember. *Hope.*

This is what his world sounds like.

An arm circled my waist. Resting my head on his shoulder, I kept my eyes closed as we danced, lost in this new place with him. I sighed as the last notes faded.

"...beautiful noise keeps me company, bringing back the sound of Mom's voice. And it holds me under the grip of yours. You were meant to be heard in all five senses, Luna Sinclair."

I flushed to my toes, face pressed against his rock-hard pecs. Was I supposed to hear that, or did he think the music was still playing?

"What's going on in here?"

I sprang away from him. Lucien strolled into the kitchen, smirk twice as unsettling with his fangs peeking through. "Don't mind me. Just getting my dinner."

Lucien reached into the fridge and got out a sports bottle filled with crimson liquid. He bowed his way out of the room, lips rimmed red.

"On that note, it's time for me to go to bed." I turned and stopped, twisting back to squeeze Rafael's arm. "Thank you for telling me."

"I'll tell you anything, Luna."

"Will you tell me Wilder's middle name?"

"Except for that."

Smiling crookedly, I gave him one last "watch yourself" poke and went up to bed.

I slept fitfully that night, tossing and turning over odd dreams. I ran through an endless library, books stacked stories high and falling down around me. Unseen missiles bit into my skin—opening cuts, painting my fleeing footsteps red with blood. I skidded around a book tower and tripped, falling headfirst into the water. Winter waited for me at the bottom.

Gasping, I shot out of bed, sheets soaked in sweat. Panic gripped me.

It's okay. I'm in the Rogue House. I'm safe, it's okay.

Over and over I repeated it until the remains of the dream leaked out, leaving the exhausted empty shell behind.

The house is quiet. At least I didn't wake anybody.

Dragging myself out of bed, I tiptoed to Cato's reading room, chose a book at random, and settled into my bland armchair, in my bland room to read. In between I thought of little things I'd do to brighten up the place—pictures of me and Winter, a new bedspread, some of that wallpaper Lucien put up. It'd make a decent accent wall.

The clock ticked down, bringing the sun up. Around six thirty, I called it and headed for the shower with my sheets. I hung them up, covering the gaping entrance and cursing Wilder O'Rourke the whole time.

The bathroom was bigger, and cleaner, than I expected. Double sinks, double vanities, and black memory foam bathmats warming my toes. I took my time under the heated spray, letting it wash the remains of the nightmare down the drain.

Climbing out, I wrapped up tight in my robe and padded across the hall, where I hung another sheet and carried my change of clothes into the closet. Wilder's plan to stop me plotting wasn't working. I thought up half a dozen ways to kill him while hopping into my underwear, banging my head on the hanger rod.

That morning, I chose a skater dress and black tights—close to what I wore that birthday Winter sang to me. Out of the closet, I finished my routine, dabbing on a touch of makeup and spangly earrings.

None of the guys were up, so this was my chance to whip up breakfast, thanking them for letting me move in and beating the shit out of the boys that made it necessary. The plan was on hold for Levi and Owen at the moment—until they got out of the hospital.

Grabbing my phone, I headed out.

"Ahh!" Jumping back, I banged into the doorframe. "Joseph Collins, what the hell are you doing?!"

Cato crouched on the floor, concealed by the wall where scaring the shit out of me is made simple.

"Don't bother staring at me with those moon eyes, refusing to speak. I know you've got no problem talking and I've checked out your reading collection. Spill."

Cato raised his head, and said, "Everyone expects you up there." He pointed, making me look up automatically. "But no one expects you down here."

"Both accurate and incredibly creepy, Dumont." That got a chuckle out of him. "From now on, can you be where I expect you at all times?"

"No."

I tossed up my hands. "Well, at least you gave it some real thought."

Another chuckle. "You're funny. How do you do that?"

Getting to his feet, Cato straightened to his full height—no crouching, hunching, growling, or snapping. Just all five foot eleven of every gorgeous inch of him.

I swallowed hard. Looking at him then—clear, enigmatic eyes; soft lips; shining raven hair; it was easy to forget I saw those lips rimmed with blood as they tore into human flesh.

"How am I funny?" I asked, voice a touch raspy.

"How do you make jokes when you're sad?"

I froze. "Wha— I'm not. I'm not sad."

Cato cocked his head. "You're so sad, day can't contain it. So in your dreams, you cry."

A statement both simple and lyrical, and it punched the air out of my lungs. He heard me. During the night, Cato listened to me whimper and cry under grip of my nightmares.

Shame slicked my palms. "I'm sorry, Cato."

"Why?"

"Because my nightmare woke you up. I don't mean to make that much noise."

His brows crowded together. "It's not for you to be sorry when you're sad. It's for me to make you happy."

My lips parted as my mind processed that. "You don't have to make me happy," I squeaked.

"I do. You're kind. Beautiful. Smell like peaches. And you're Winter's," he said, light and matter of fact. "Now you're ours."

Dizzy, my legs tried to dump me, dropping me on the doorframe. So many things said in such short sentences, and I couldn't handle a single one. "I— Yours?"

Looping around my waist, Cato drew me in, molding me to his chest. My breath stopped as his cheek pressed to mine—smooth and warm—caressing as he did that day.

"I'll make you happy again, Luna. Guard your dreams, steal your tears. Around your neck you'll wear them, and they'll never hurt you again."

"I'm not sure what that means," I whispered, resting my head on his shoulder as my arms moved on their own power, wrapping around him. "But I think I'd love that."

"A present. I have one for you."

I'd have to get used to Cato's way of communicating, but it wouldn't take me long. It was then wholly clear to me that I'd devote a significant portion of my life getting closer to Cato Dumont.

Dropping his arm, Cato got something out of his pocket and presented it to me. My eyes bugged out of my head and rolled down the hallway.

"Cato," I breathed.

A diamond choker necklace glittered on his palm. Rows on rows of diamonds meeting in the center and cradled a teardrop-shaped emerald pendant.

"Oh my gosh— How can that be for me?"

"It's beautiful. You're beautiful. It's for you."

I flushed down to my toes. "You Dumont boys are versed in flattery."

He grinned, worsening my dizziness. "Take it."

My fingers twitched for it. "No, I can't. It's too expensive."

"Wasn't expensive."

"Cato, those are real diamonds and that emerald is bigger than my nose. This must have cost you thousands."

"No," he said simply.

Opening my hand, he handed over the necklace. My jaw went slack as I got a closer look.

Is that...?

Strands of blonde hair tangled in the clasp. There was a spot of color on one of the diamonds. It looked like... blood.

"Cato," I said slowly. "Where did you get this necklace?"

"Found it."

"Did you happen to find it around someone's neck?"

He said nothing.

"It concerns me that you're not answering."

Cato laughed—a deep, smoky sound that had a powerful effect when paired with his hand still holding mine.

"It belongs to you," he said, closing my hand over the gift. "Take it."

"Morning, all." Rafael came out of his room, dressed in nothing but boxers slung low on his hips. The sight distracted me, swiveling my head around and following him until he disappeared down the stairs. When I turned back, the door was closing on Cato's room.

I tucked the suspicious necklace in my drawer, then went to intercept Rafael. I plucked the pan from his hand. "Ah ah. I'm making breakfast this morning. As a thank-you."

"Nice of you, but you'd only be making it for me and Cato. Lucien's on a special diet and Wilder doesn't eat anything he hasn't made himself."

"Course not," I muttered. "But wait, I've seen him in the café."

"He has a theory the cafeteria ladies spike the coffee with various mood- and brain-altering serums. It's why no one's normal around here," he said. "Every now and then he pops in to try and catch them in the act."

There was nothing to say to that, so I didn't try. Steering him back, I made Rafael sit and began breakfast domination. "Eggs, toast, and oatmeal okay?"

"Oh, yes. Vast improvement over the French toast, maple bacon, and veggie omelets I was about to make."

I gave him a look. "That sounds like sass, sir."

Rafael popped his foot on the stool, stretching over the table and resting on his elbow. The effortless pose of a bare-chested supermodel, I was half certain he wasn't aware of the sharp tightening that struck my core. "I'm all sass in the morning, darling.

"And all sex at night."

The pan almost slipped out of my hand. Recovering quickly, I cleared my throat, forcing myself to turn my back on him under the pretense of getting the eggs.

I forced my voice to remain even. "What are you in the afternoon?"

"All mischief."

"So, how does Mr. Sex, Sass, and Mischief end up friends with a vampire and government conspiracy theorist?"

"Same way most people do. We sat down at the same table in the cafeteria, and figured if we're going to watch each other eat, might as well be friends."

"You said you went to the same school." Our conversation washed over me while I prepared our food.

"Middle and high with Wilder. Lucien transferred in junior year of high school. My vamp boy's fight skills are sick. We got into it one day after school and he nearly put me on my ass."

"Brotherhood forged in violence. It'd hurt less if you guys did it like girls do it, and bonded over the mutual hatred of the same person."

He laughed. "We all despise the Royals, so you could say we did. Plus, Wilder figured out how to hack the school's database from day one. We had five extra early-release days, pick of our teachers, access to all the school's cameras, and the answers to every exam. Fools didn't know a thing."

"Um, that's terrible."

Rafael let out a gusty sigh. "I'm a bad boy, Cloud Girl. I hope you can accept me for who I am."

Why does everything he says sound like a come-on? It's that voice. It has to be.

"I'm still learning who you are. Katie said you're not Royals, but you're not Dregs either. Were you always apart from this weird-ass caste system, or did they give you another title when they learned you weren't people to mess with?"

"Are you asking if we have the money, status, and influence to be Royals if we wanted?"

I shrugged, whisking the bowl. "I guess I am."

"No, Luna. That weird-ass caste system wasn't made for us. There's a reason we're in a category all our own. Our legacies are formidable in ways that have nothing to do with money. Though, we have a lot of that, if you were also wondering."

"Formidable how? Lucien said his family owns hospitals."

"His family owns underground hospitals, my dear. A concierge medical practice to the mob, criminal syndicates, crime families, and gangs of America. Giving new faces, plucking out bullets, and keeping no records. Every psychopath in the country knows the name Calais."

I dropped my whisk, gaping at him.

"Good news," Rafael said, beaming. "He's got access to all the black-market blood he wants."

My stomach twisted. "And Wilder?"

"In a world full of locks, the man with the key reigns supreme. The guy can get into any system, through every passcode, and behind any firewall. The shit he's seen made him paranoid enough to stockpile an armory that'll scare you worse than a few bombs on my bed." He clicked his tongue. "So as crazy as I know you think he is, I wouldn't dismiss him so quickly."

"You mean there really is a man-made virus that makes you bleed from all orifices?"

It was his turn to shrug.

"Okay," I cried. "Let's end the conversation here while I still have an appetite and a chance for a good night's sleep."

I got on with breakfast, whipping up scrambled eggs, avocado toast, and oatmeal with brown sugar and apple bits. Competing with Rafael's breakfast pushed me to up my game.

"Aha!" I set out the plates before Rafael and Cato who wandered down while I was halfway done. Wilder leaned on the counter, clocking my twitches, and Lucien stood by the other end of the table, drinking that red drink. "Sass that, Rafael."

"Looks delicious," he said, giving me that crooked smile. Goose bumps rippled down my back as he grasped my hand, kissing my knuckles. Memory transported me to the night before—his lingering kisses and the feel of him holding me as we danced. "If moving you in grants me this kind of gratitude, what do I get for walking you to and from class, guarding that lovely person?"

I have a deal with my fiancé. I have a deal with my fiancé. I have a deal with my fiancé.

"You get absolutely nothing."

"Ah." He jerked his chin. "Then Cato can do it." Rafael reached for his fork.

"You're not seriously going to eat that," Wilder said. "Did you watch her the whole time? Who knows what she put in that?"

"Salt and pepper," I spoke up.

"Like you'd admit it if you slipped in something else."

Thus kicked off an argument about micro-cyanide packets, and how I'd never heard of such a thing, so how could I have snuck it in the food? At one point, Wilder gave me another pat-down, running his hands down my ass for an early morning groping. It was hard to call it sexual, since he berated me the entire time, swearing he was onto me.

Eventually, I escaped upstairs, grabbed my backpack, and headed out to my first class.

Morning dew sprinkled the blades, collecting on the soles of my wedges and giving my toes wet kisses. I inhaled a deep, steady breath—buoying on the fresh, clean air. Wilder informed me the air in the Gallery was filtered and recycled, so any attempt on my part to pump knockout gas through the vents would fail.

"Again, so much crazy in one handsome package."

Footsteps sounded behind me. I caught Cato as he loped out of the house, a black rose muzzle riding his face.

"Wait. You guys were serious about stalking me?"

He dipped his head.

"I don't need guarding. Owen and the bastard brigade ambushed me. It won't happen again, and it definitely won't happen in broad daylight in the middle of the atrium. You can go back inside."

Cato didn't move an inch.

Stifling a groan, I tried a deep breath instead. "What will it take to convince you?"

"You're mine." His voice was muffled and those words still came through loud and clear. "I'm going with you."

"We really need to discuss the definition of 'mine' and how it does not apply in our relationship?"

Cato scooped me shrieking over his shoulder and strode off.

"Cato, put me down! Put me down right now."

He could've been carrying a sack of books for all the attention he gave my squawking. Lucien warned his behavior was unpredictable. Was that the word for gifting a necklace I was ninety-eight percent certain he ripped off a neck, and carting me around campus like a sack of flour?

My demands fell on unbothered ears as we joined the bustle of early morning campus, gathering stares the farther we went. I didn't know if Cato was paying attention to the remarks following us, but I was.

"Isn't she engaged to Victor Wilson?"

"Dipping that gold-digger's shovel in the Dumont fortune too."

"Good luck," a nasty voice replied. "The insane don't inherit."

I tapped Cato's back. "Please, put me down. I've accepted my fate."

He set me on my feet, letting me fix my dress, and give those girls a lethal glare. Once again, I'd never seen them before in my life, yet they were comfortable running their mouth.

"Those mouths are going to run straight into my fist," I snapped. "You gossipy harpies will have heard what I did to Saylor Burkhardt, so am I bluffing?"

I charged them, fist raised. They took off running, screaming and flinging curses back at me.

Dusting off my hands, I fell in step with Cato. "On to English."

The building came into sight as four shadows fell over us.

"Luna Sinclair. Daughter of Elise Sinclair. Father unnamed."

Saylor, Everleigh, Piper, and Gabriella stepped in front of me, pulling me up short. A piece of paper clutched in one of Saylor's hands and an iced latte in the other. It brought me an unkind amount of joy seeing the make-up she caked on to conceal her bruised, swollen lip.

Her glee faded when she noticed Cato. "Ugh, what are you doing here— Wait." Suddenly, she perked up, lifting her cleavage and fussing with her hair. The other girls did the same. "Is your brother here?"

"No," I said. "Rafael is off having sex with anyone who isn't the four of you. He's not that picky. I hear that's his only requirement."

Everleigh snorted. "Jealousy looks as good on you as that hideous rayon disaster. But what can you expect from the illiterate daughter of a house-keeper?"

I rolled my eyes. "If I'm illiterate, what does it say that we got into the same school? Think your insults through, Barbie doll. See? That works because you're pretty, fake, and empty-headed."

Cato laughed out loud as Everleigh's cheeks stained red. "Watch your mouth, bitch! I could ruin your stepfather with one phone call."

I shrugged. "I barely like the guy. Go for it."

I didn't mean that of course, but in my experience, people who were actually going to carry out a threat, didn't waste time shouting about it.

Saylor held up a hand, cutting off Everleigh's reply. "All this fighting is a distraction when—"

I got a look at what was in her hand. "Is that my birth certificate?"

"That it is," Saylor said, beaming. "You were born right here in good ole Regalia, so it was no sweat getting my hands on it. A shame Mommy didn't know who your dad was, but she was illiterate, a housekeeper, and trash dumped off a fishing boat. We've established she didn't have much going for her. Sleeping with anything that moves to numb the pain was her best option."

My knuckles cracked. "You really want a black eye to match that lip."

"You're going to hit me? Go ahead." Saylor slid off me, glancing to our right. I followed her line of sight to the campus security guard hovering near a bench, and looking right at us. "Get yourself expelled and make my year."

"Not today, Burkhardt." I forced my fist to unclench. "You'll have to masturbate to someone else's pain today. May I suggest visiting a terminally ill ward or watching a vet put down puppies? That oughta get you going."

"Aww, how sweet, but I think I'll let Rafael take care of my needs tonight... again."

Something must've flashed on my face because her grin widened.

"I'm late for class." I tried sidestepping them, but they moved with me.

"Not so fast," Piper said. "We walked all over campus looking for you. Don't you want to know why?"

"Not particularly."

"It's about your status," Gabriella said.

"And about your fiancé," added Everleigh.

That stopped me. "What about Victor?"

Saylor opened her mouth. "If you've learned anything, you know— Cato, go away. You're freaking me out."

Growling, he advanced on them, moving the Royals back quicker than I did.

"Fine, stay," Saylor snapped. "Like I was saying, if you've been paying attention, you'll know how the rules and rank work around here—and who decides it."

"No, but I can guess: you."

"So you can be taught." Saylor tucked my birth certificate in her Fendi bag, pink lips wrapping around her straw. She drew a long, needlessly drawn-out sip, proving she could demand my attention.

"Victor Wilson is ranked almost as high as it gets—status that passes to you if you get married."

Why does everyone keep saying if?

"I say if," Saylor continued, speaking to my unspoken question, "because my father had a talk with his parents the other night, urging them to rethink this ill-suited match."

A thick sludge coated my mouth, sticking my tongue to the roof. *What did she just say?*

"Obviously, there's some reason why the Wilsons need to marry their son off this soon. Probably because the stepson is a dud— I don't give a shit. What I do care about is a respected, important family in our community forced to add a maid's bastard to their family to get out of whatever trouble they're in."

It was almost impressive Saylor's ability to say the most horrible, bitchy things with a smile and sweet, charming twang.

"Katie banged on and on about how *you're not that bad* and *the Dreg can be wrung out of you.* She thinks you should be allowed to stay here and I may be persuaded to let you off—granted you do a few things for me. But first things first, Victor Wilson is not for the likes of you. So, here's what's going to happen: you're going to dump Victor publicly and brutally."

"No, I'm—"

"I'm not finished talking." She looked around at her friends. "Did it seem like I was finished talking?"

"Nope."

"Nah."

"Not to me."

Saylor shook her head. "This girl has no manners. Further proof she has no business becoming a Wilson."

I swung to the guard, tempted to kick his ass too for not coming the night Owen and his friends attacked me, but eagle-eyeing me now that Saylor Burkhardt was in my face.

"You are going to dump Victor"—Saylor grasped my chin, swinging me back to her—"and you won't tell him why. As far as the Wilsons will know, you backed out because you got cold feet."

I shook her off. "Why in the world would I do that?"

"To clear the way for Everleigh and Victor. They're ranked the same and the match will benefit both families, expanding their businesses."

"Plus, he's cute and great in bed," Everleigh threw in. "My parents will start talking engagements in a few years anyway, why not lock down the most eligible bachelor in Regalia now while he's looking?"

"Because he's not looking," I replied. "Victor is marrying me. I am marrying him. Is that clear enough for you?"

"Don't be so hasty. You haven't heard what you'll get in exchange," Saylor said. "No doubt the tire king was thinking he could advance himself by marrying off the ready-made kid his wife brought into the marriage. Not a bad plan, but a change in your status and the protection that comes with it, doesn't kick in until you say *I do*.

"Life will get horrible around here for you, Luna Sinclair. In fact... it already started."

Right then I knew. Saylor knew what Owen, Levi, and the others did to me.

"The wedding won't be held until next year, but can you hold out that long?" she asked, tone soft and mock sympathetic. "Winter couldn't."

A growl broke the morning. It came from me. "Say her name one more fucking time and find out how much I care about that security guard."

"Whoa, easy," she said exaggeratedly. "There's no need for that. Believe it or not, I'm trying to help you, Sinclair. Regalia will be hell for you until you walk down that aisle, and honestly, afterward the strikes will be more subtle but they won't really stop. Is all of that worth it for a guy you don't belong with?

"You're better off matched to— Well, someone like him." She flapped her hand at Cato. "It's no wonder you two are so comfortable with each other. This is the guy for Luna Sinclair. If you accept that within the next few days, and dump Victor so harshly, his parents will never think of the name Sinclair-Bowden again, I will give you and your family what you want."

"What is that exactly?"

"Power. Position. Money. Respect. And for you, Luna, protection." She held out her hand like she wanted me to take it. "The Bowden name moves up in Regalia and the stain on the Sinclair name is forgotten. My father rips up the lease for the land Bowden Manor is sitting on and sells it to him outright. He'll become the official tire supplier to the Burkhardt company cars. And for the next four years and beyond, no one will touch, taunt, disrespect, or bother you again, Luna."

"It's a good deal," Piper tossed in.

"It's the *best* deal," Saylor corrected, "that anyone has ever gotten from me, and it's the only one you're going to get. What do you say?" Her hand inched closer, demanding to be shaken. "Do we have a—?"

"No."

Saylor blinked. "Excuse me?"

"No deal. I'm not breaking off my engagement. End of. So, thanks for making me late to class, but if that's all, I need to get going."

Anger lit in her eyes. "Did you hear a word I said? I'm giving you better than you'll get if you marry the guy. What is your problem? Take the deal."

"And again, no. Your *best deal* stinks worse than shit."

Saylor scoffed at my crudeness.

"Why would you track down the girl who punched you in the face, just to make my life easier? You don't give two craps in a bucket about me. What you do care about is this little system that puts you on top."

"That's why I'm doing this," she gritted. "This isn't a double play. I'm being very clear that the only reason I'm making this offer is to keep you away from Victor Wilson. Royals marry Dregs they knock up every now and then, but not Royals like him. You're not even good enough to carry his mistake, let alone be his wife. Do the right thing and release him from whatever you've got hanging over his head."

"Hmm, nope," I sang. "Victor chose me. This match makes sense, and if it pisses you off, that makes it all the more sweeter."

Her lips peeled back from her teeth. "You're messing with the wrong one, Sinclair. I can just as easily make my dad renege on the lease. You'll be shaking a can of nickels outside the homeless shelter in a week."

"Oooh. How quickly we skidded over to threats. You really don't want me to marry Victor and now I have to find out the real reason why. Maybe my future hubby will have some ideas." I pulled out my phone. "I'll ask him now."

"Don't!" She made a grab for my phone and smacked Cato's palm. His hand shot out, blocking her. "This isn't funny, Sinclair."

"You're telling me. I'm tired of you four getting in my face. Back off and stay out of my business, or Mrs. Wilson hears about this conversation too."

Stiffly, Saylor lifted her chin, staring down her nose at me. I didn't have to be a mind reader to know the thoughts running through her head weren't pleasant.

"Never let it be said I'm a vindictive person," Saylor said, swiping her hair over her shoulder. "I'll give you to the end of the week to make your decision. By then, you should have a better understanding of the consequences for refusing me." She put her mouth to my ear, dropping her voice. "If you thought the last couple of weeks were bad, you have no idea the hell you're in for."

Stepping back, Saylor turned to leave and— "Whoops."

Her latte launched out of her grip, flying at my face. I opened my mouth to scream as Cato flashed out of the corner of my eye.

Whacking the cup, he sent the latte spiraling, spilling its treat on everyone in a two-foot radius—including Saylor, Piper, Gabriella, and Everleigh.

"Ahh!" Saylor flipped out, smacking her hopelessly ruined white lace top. "You freak! Look what you did!"

"Hey," the guard shouted, running toward us. "What's going on over there?"

Cato grabbed my hand and we sprinted off. I was laughing so hard, he had to tug me wheezing behind him. The guard shouted for us to come back. We didn't stop till we arrived inside the English building.

I doubled over, grabbing my knees and laughing myself breathless. "Cato, that was amazing. I take back what I said. If your daily stalking means I get to see that look on Saylor's face again, you can come with me anywhere I go."

"Yes." Cato tipped my chin up, silencing my giggles. I sobered under the intensity in the only part of his face I needed to see. "Mine."

With that, he crouched down and took off growling and snapping at two guys from my class, standing near the entrance to the hall. I left them to their fate, stumbling inside.

Professor Anthony stopped mid-lecture. "Nice of you to join us, Miss Sinclair."

"Sorry I'm late."

"You're in college now. You can show up late and throw away this expensive education all you want."

I gritted my teeth as not-so-hushed snickers echoed his reply. Once again, the nice, understanding guy I spoke to when we were alone, was replaced with the asshole that showed up in public.

"It won't happen again," I said.

Humming, he lifted a paper off his desk. "Take this. We're going over the common issues I found in last week's writing assignment and discussing how to improve."

I reached for my paper—glad mine wasn't one of the assignments with issues. Professor Anthony gave us the paper before Owen attacked me. I did it while I was recovering at Katie's house, because a prompt discussing how a writer's pain transforms into deep, relatable storytelling was spot-on. I had a lot to say about pain. With the weekly papers now graded pass/fail, I was open, honest, and more vulnerable than I ever was in an essay I turned in to a teacher.

Excited, I grabbed my sheet, flipping it over. My hopes burst like a blimp.

Average. You've moved past empty, overused metaphors to make way for saccharine tales of trauma making you stronger. A message we've heard many times and in every way. If you don't have something new to say, don't bother putting pen to paper.

"Take your seat, Miss Sinclair." My head snapped up, paper crinkling in my fist. "We were just about to get into communicating a message in a way that feels new to the reader. In other words, originality."

I trudged to the top row. The *pass* written across the top of my page was hollow when compared to the words beneath it. I couldn't look any deeper into why. I wasn't failing the class—that's all that should matter. I wasn't upset about falling over in Professor Anthony's estimation.

Of course not. I threw my bag at the chair next to me. *This paper was good and he knows it. The man has ridiculous expectations. I bet he shredded everyone's assignment. That's why we're devoting an entire class to reviewing it. He's incapable of giving anyone a break.*

I clenched my teeth all through class, feeling each comment on "originality," "tired similes," and "shallow as a spoonful of milk" like a dart through the chest. By the time the clock ticked nine thirty, I was bursting to tell him what I thought too.

Victor hung back again to talk to his brother. "—this Friday. Luna will be there."

"What? I'll be where?"

"Dinner with my parents this Friday," Victor replied to me, but spoke to Adonis. "She'll be there too."

Adonis flicked to me and looked away just as quick. "Why would her presence tempt me into going?"

"Because we'll have a guest. Mom and Dad will be on their best behavior. You know it's *uncouth to air your dirty laundry before an audience*," Victor said in a high, snooty voice.

Adonis and I snorted. If that was an impression of his mother, it was perfect.

"Come on, Don. At least come to get to know my fiancée." Victor snaked an arm around me, snapping me to his side. "In a year, we'll all be family. No matter what anyone says."

"Well, Miss Sinclair?" Dark curls hung over unreadable eyes. "Would you like me to attend, so we can get to know each other?"

Why does this feel like a trap?

"Yes," I finally said. "That would be nice."

"Then, I'll be there—provided we can all be civil."

"Good." Victor dropped his arm, my usefulness over. "I'll tell Cook to make your favorite."

He left, leaving me and Professor Anthony alone. As soon as the door swung shut, I slapped my paper on his desk. "Professor, I'd like to discuss your comments on my paper."

"Of course, you would," he breezed. "Because the wise thing to do is stroll in ten minutes late, then hold me back ten minutes to argue you know more than me."

"Exactly."

He flashed me a look through his lashes, though I could almost swear amusement played on his lips. "I can save you the trouble: my comments stand. Prove me wrong by doing better on this week's paper."

"How can I? You say you want open, so I give you open. You ask for vulnerability, I rip open the deepest wounds of my childhood and spill them on the page. I talked about the pain of not knowing my father and the other half of me, but that it's taught me to cherish the family I've got."

He pulled a face, gazing up at the ceiling. "Now, where have I heard that— Oh, yes. In every greeting card ever made."

"See, this is the *not nice* thing we were talking about."

I didn't mistake his expression that time. He was definitely amused with me.

"It's not my job to be nice, likable, or everybody's buddy, Miss Sinclair. It's my job to push you to your highest potential. This"—he dangled my paper in front of me—"is not it. Don't argue with all this passion. Write it. Prove you've got something real to say." He snapped his briefcase shut and headed for the door. "See you Friday. Oh, heads up, my mother prefers semiformal attire at dinner."

"I know what she prefers," I snapped at the closing door. "Ugh. Great comeback, Sinclair."

Snatching up my paper, I stuffed it in my bag, mind turning to that week's assignment.

Discuss a book, essay, or work of fiction that's had a significant effect on society.

Seemed like an easy, researchable question, but I knew whatever book or essay I picked would tell more about me than it did about the effect on society. I could choose *Uncle Tom's Cabin*, *Beloved*, or *The Grapes of Wrath*, and is there a single thing I could say about any of them that he wouldn't call unoriginal? Especially since literature PhDs have been talking about these books for decades.

I have to come up with something else. Something he won't expect. Even better, a book he's never heard of.

I left the classroom, walking out of the building into the clear, cool morning. Cato waited for me at the bottom of the steps, flipping and clicking a lighter on and off. He took pages out of his backpack and set them on fire, watching them curl, crinkle, and burn.

Gazing past him, I spotted a security guard talking fast into his walkie, fixed on Cato.

"Nothing about this can be good," I muttered. "Hey, Cato. We should get going right—"

A missile struck the side of my head, exploding ice-cold wetness in my hair, ear, and down my shirt. Shrieking, I whipped around as the shutter click went off. Hanson, one of the guys in my class, howled as he snapped pictures.

"Your fucking face! That was—" His eyes bugged. Turning tail, he booked it as Cato chased him, the two of them disappearing around the building—the security guard hoofing it after them.

The three of them were gone, but the people hanging around, laughing their asses off were not. Iris took over taking pictures in Hanson's place.

I glanced at the thing he threw at me, blood curdling.

An iced latte.

Chapter Eight

"Where are we going?"

The next morning, I strolled by Rafael's side, growing more confused as he led me around a part of campus that was new to me. His headphones were on, playing a hummable song going by the soft, pleasing sounds coming from his throat. But I knew he could hear me. It wasn't that he didn't hear enough, it was he heard too much.

"Ever wonder why the Royals go into the café, grab their food, and walk out with their trays?"

"I don't question why Royals aren't around—except to hope they don't come back."

He chuckled. "There's a spot behind the music hall where they hang out, eat, and congratulate themselves on being young and rich."

"Let me guess, we're going there so I can get another coffee bath?"

"I'm sorry, Luna." Rafael's pinky hooked through mine. "We should've been there to stop it."

"No," I said, releasing him quickly. "Don't apologize when it wasn't your fault. If Cato wasn't there, it would've been much worse."

As it was, they got me with a latte in the face four times. That's right. Four.

I don't know what impressed me more. How quickly Saylor mobilized her minions, or how creatively they got around my silent, aggressive bodyguard.

When Cato was next to me, no one looked in my direction, but he couldn't be with me all the time. I stepped inside biology and Eva nailed me with a mocha vanilla. I had to rush to the Gallery to change. On the way back, I rounded the corner and was hit with pumpkin spice. That was three before lunch.

It looked like I was going to make it through the rest of the day, until I left calculus class to go to the bathroom and someone gifted me a face full of hazelnut.

I avoided telling the guys because it wasn't their job to follow me everywhere, fighting my battles. Unfortunately, news in Regalia travels as fast as a thrown cold drink.

"This way."

Rafael helped himself to my pinky again, leading me off the path onto the grass. The music hall, a grand building of blue spires, red brick, and an ornate clock tower. Inside, plush red seats gazed down on a grand stage, used to host world-class orchestras in the summer. During the school year, the reception room doubled as a venue for alumni dinners and charity events. Seeing as it was built to show off the wealth of Regalia University, it was locked, bolted, and off-limits to students unless they were practicing for a concert.

I never had a reason to come this far on the other side of campus. No one did.

Which makes a great spot for the Royals to enjoy life away from the Dregs.

Enjoying life was exactly what Saylor, Piper, Katie, Gabriella, Everleigh, and fucking Victor looked to be doing.

Rafael and I hung out under the shade of a weeping willow, gazing up at the pretty, young, rich people on the balcony.

Benches and tables were set out for some. The others hung their legs over the ledge, laughing back and forth. Victor opted for the table—alongside Saylor, her crew, and Katie. Everleigh sat on his right, giggling over something he said and touching his arm five times in the single minute I'd been standing there.

Sliding away from them, I fell on the guys sitting a few tables over. I automatically reached for the note, and stopped myself. My sister's letter was safe in the Gallery, sporting a coffee stain. I wouldn't risk these jerks ruining it further.

"Rafael, can I ask you something?"

"Anything." His finger was still curled around mine.

"When I told you the names of the guys I'm after, why didn't you ask what they did?"

"They drove Winter to kill herself. What else do I need to know?"

"Is that it or... does everyone know what they did to her?" I held my hand over my heart anyway, sensing Winter even though her letter wasn't with me. "I thought no one knew the worst of it. That if they did, people like Saylor wouldn't think of throwing her death in my face. None of them could make jokes or say she was weak, if they knew the truth of how they destroyed her.

"But yesterday, she didn't outright say it, but I got the feeling she knew what Owen, Levi, Darren, and the rest did to me in my dorm that night. After Cato hit her with the latte, the news spread and someone carried out her revenge less than two hours later. Is it not even a secret what th-those shits did to Winter?" My hand trembled in his hold. "They're sitting up there—happy and carefree, and no one cares that they're eating with monsters."

"Luna." He lifted both our hands, stroking my cheeks. "No one on this campus knows more than me. I heard about that piece of garbage Giovanni, and that Owen and his friends harassed her. I saw the video they made the night they attacked. What else happened, Winter didn't talk about it and neither did anyone else. I'm pretty sure no one up there knows who they're sitting next to.

"But that doesn't mean they'd act any differently if they did. Dregs are nothing to them, Luna. It's in the name."

The pain in my chest eased slightly. The Royals were all complicit in my sister's death for standing by and doing nothing in face of her torture.

"But Owen Thasher, Levi Thompkins, Wesley Hill, and Giovanni Natale went far and beyond." I narrowed on the handsome Giovanni, his long black hair piled in a bun on his head. It should look stupid, but instead the guy appeared as if he rolled off the pages of Italian *Vogue*. "You were kind not to ask, but I want you to know, Rafael. Understand why I have to do this, and won't stop until it's done."

Nails clutching, then piercing my shirt, I lifted the words directly off Winter's letter. "Giovanni Natale seduced her. Spinning pretty, sweet lines. Telling her she was smart and beautiful while everyone was calling her a filthy slut. Saying he wanted to love and protect her while Royals made her life hell.

"Winter didn't buy it at first. She said she wasn't interested and rejected him over and over. Giovanni could've gold-medaled in persistence. For two months, he pursued her. He cursed out the Royals and defended her. He wore her down with the nice-guy routine, playing it to perfection," I said roughly. "His final performance—the grand gesture. He dressed up as one of her favorite characters, Cyrano, and serenaded her in the café while the school's band played."

Rafael nodded along. He knew this part.

"He was so sweet and... Winter was so lonely, she relented and started dating him." I opened and closed my mouth, fighting to get the rest out. "I could go into the whole thing, but all that matters is how it ended. With Giovanni dumping her in the middle of a party, his true girlfriend under his arm. He told her, and everyone there, that he never loved Winter and only got involved with her on a dare to see if she was really as dirty in bed as everyone said.

"The rotted, maggot-infested carcass of a human being spilled the details of their sex life to everyone in the room. He was still yukking it up for his friends when she ran out crying."

Rafael let out a low, furious hiss.

"I wish it ended there," I said, tone as dead as my soul. "What Levi did to you, and what you did to him in return, didn't teach that guy a damn thing. He set your place on fire to force you guys out into a brutal beating. For Winter, he paid the security guards to ignore calls for help like he did the other night with me.

"Winter was walking back to the dorm late one night when a girl ran up to her, bawling that her friend crashed her bike and messed up her leg. She begged Winter to help carry her friend to the infirmary. And the good person that Winter still was, she rushed to help without a thought, and ran straight at the eight girls Levi paid to beat her black and blue while he watched."

"Fucking hell," Rafael breathed, dropping his head on the bark. "Dammit, Winter. Why didn't you say?"

"I've asked myself that so many times. She had me, Mom, Jack, and now I know she had you guys too. But Winter didn't feel that way. I was in France. Mom and Jack were off traveling, island-hopping, and enjoying married life with the kids out of the house. Maybe she thought we were happy, and she couldn't make us all come rushing home to fight her battles. Whatever she thought, she was fucking wrong!"

I gasped, tossing my head. "I'm sorry. I shouldn't have—"

"Don't," Rafael sliced in, squeezing my hand. "Be angry at her, Luna. Scream and curse and cry. She told you everything... when it was far too late. Of course it makes you mad."

"I can't be mad at her. She was hurting. In pain. She—"

"You can list all the reasons you shouldn't be angry, but emotions don't listen to reason. You're feeling it anyway, so let it in, so you can get it out."

I didn't say anything for a long time. "I do want to let it out," I whispered, "but not toward her. My rage is solely reserved for those three, and their two friends waiting for me in the hospital. I will get it out—leech the poison, so they can choke on it."

"That's always been my way."

"Why did you bring me here?"

"Because it's day one, darling." Rafael straightened, laying his arm around my shoulder. It didn't cross my mind to move it. "The fun begins."

"With who?"

"Wesley Hill."

I nodded, grim satisfaction taking hold of me as the sandy-haired guy across from Giovanni typed on his phone. "The beast who arranged for Winter to get into *accidents*. Sabotaging her bike brakes, messing with her food, fucking with her car. Her car skidded into a ditch and she broke her arm because of him."

Rafael met my eyes. "I always understood why you wanted them dead. What I didn't expect, was how badly I'd want it too. They're going to pay for Winter. If you didn't believe this promise before, believe it now. I won't stop."

Something fluttered in my chest, awakening a part of me long dead. My hand skimmed his cheek, cupping his smooth, strong jaw. "Ask me again what I'll give you for being there for me?"

Eyes darkening, Rafael moved as I did.

"Hey, man, you okay? Wesley? Wesley!"

Our necks snapped to the side. Wesley shot up from his chair, gasping and clutching his neck. He gestured wildly at his mouth, miming to Giovanni.

"In your research, did you find out that Wesley is severely allergic to peanuts?"

"No," I drew out, grin stretching my mouth.

"It's very bad, darling. If he doesn't get a hit from his EpiPen soon, his throat could close up and—lights out."

Half the Royals were in a frenzy. Piper got on her phone calling for help while Giovanni tore Wesley's backpack open.

"They better find it soon unless—" Rafael took the injector out of his pocket, tossing it up in the air. "Whoops. Looks like I've got it."

Laughing, I jumped up and down, restraining myself from throwing my arms around him. I lost the fight and did it—hugging him tight.

"You are incredible, Rafael Dumont. You planned this morning's surprise for me. To cheer me up after yesterday."

"Did it work?"

Wesley—the guy who almost killed my sister by messing with her brakes, and then did kill her when his cruelty added to the weight pushing her down—dropped to his knees, his desperate wheezing heard clearly from our spot.

"Yes," I said. "It worked. The next time you sing *Happy Birthday* to me, this'll be one of the memories that come up. It's the best gift I've ever gotten. But I want to be a part of it from here on. The five of us—a team."

"The five of us." Rafael tucked me under his arm again. "Rogues."

"ARE YOU GOING TO TELL me why he's staring at us?"

I snapped out of the memory playing on repeat. Over and over, Wesley collapsing on the concrete as Giovanni bellowed for help. The scene ended when a Royal joined the balcony crew with his breakfast and saw what was going on. His EpiPen was safely in his backpack, and he administered it in time for Wesley to wake up and wave away the paramedics.

"Luna, what's with that guy?"

Victor stared across to Lucien sitting two booths down. The gentleman he was, he offered to give me and Victor privacy. That might've worked if he didn't stand and glare away everyone that came near me holding a drink. He was drawing attention—Victor's most of all.

"Nothing," I said. "Lucien heard about the new game everyone's playing and that I was chosen for target practice. He offered to look out for me."

My explanation didn't appear to satisfy him. On the contrary, his handsome features screwed up further. "Why is he looking out for you? How do you know him?"

"We met the first week of school."

"Luna, did you...?" He checked around, lowering his voice. "Did you hire the Rogues to protect you?"

I blinked. "Hire them? You know what they do?"

"Everyone in Regalia knows what they do," he hissed. "Are you insane? Do you have any idea what people will think if they see you getting chummy with those guys?"

"Victor, how long have you known me? Do you seriously believe I give a shit what anyone around here thinks about me?"

"It's more than that. Calais dresses like a lunatic, pretending he's another harmless nutjob—"

"All the words you're using are insensitive."

"—but it's an act," Victor said forcefully. "It's plausible deniability in case the cops ever pick him up, demanding to know about his folks' mob connections. Prosecutors can't put a guy who thinks he's a *vampire* on the stand."

I bobbed my head, lips pushed out. "Not a bad plan."

"Don't get me started on Dumont's old man."

"But I have a feeling you will anyway."

"He's dangerous." Victor grabbed my hand. "He does the kind of jobs for people that gets his name whispered in the back of a bar. Word is Rafael helps him. And O'Rourke? The guy is a paranoid delusional."

"Is that a noun?"

"He thinks everyone's out to get him whether it's true or not. He's destroyed people and their reputations because he thought they were poisoning his food or spying on him. When we were in high school, I heard he refused to go on a field trip because he was convinced the bus was taking them to a secret government testing facility. He made the bus lady cry."

I inclined my head. "Now that, I believe."

"And Cato..." Victor gave me a look like that's all that needed to be said about the youngest Dumont. "These aren't the kind of guys you hang out with, Sinclair. You wouldn't kick back with Al Capone and Jack the Ripper, but you would expect everyone to keep their distance if you did."

"Hmm. Then this will be super awkward," I began. "We're not just kicking back. I'm living with them. I moved into their place over the weekend."

"What? Why!"

Shrugging, I flicked down to the hand curled around mine. "Because when I'm around them, everyone keeps their distance."

Victor quieted, brows drawing together. "This about the lattes?"

My shoulders stiffened in a hard line. "You saw Iris drench me in the middle of class."

"And I gave her hell for it after you left."

"You did?" That was news to me. Everyone was sitting quietly, working on their bio assignments when I returned to class. The smirk Iris shot me wasn't from someone who got bitched out.

"So you're paying those guys to watch your back and let you live with them because people are messing with you? No."

"I'm sorry, did you just say no?"

"No. That's ridiculous, Sinclair. You don't need them, you have me."

My brows were halfway to my hairline. "I have you to do what?"

"I'll watch your back. And if you need someplace to stay, you can move into the mansion. There are over fifty rooms."

I pushed aside my half-eaten omelet. "Let me get this straight. You're going to protect me from the same people you were getting chummy with behind the music hall? Your best friends Saylor and *Everleigh* told people to nail me with drinks after their attempt failed. You going to give them hell too?"

"Yes."

"I'll believe that when I see it."

His face crumpled in a scowl. "You're so damn annoying. I'm offering to help you. Why can't you say thanks like a normal person?"

"Ah, there's the jerk I know and love." I smiled sweetly. "The macho protective act you were putting on was starting to freak me out."

Inexplicably, he mirrored my grin. "Then your skin's about to be crawling, wifey, because it's not getting around that my fiancée needs the Rogues to do what I can. We'll walk to and from class together, and the invitation to move into the manor still stands."

"But—"

Victor pulled me up by my captive hand, slipping a protective arm around my waist. I goggled at him as he snapped at Lucien, "Your services are no longer required, Calais." He marched us out of the café.

"We don't even have the same classes together today," I said, wiggling free outside on the steps. "I have psych."

"I'll pick you up and drop you off."

"Are you noticing that you're *telling* me instead of *asking* me?"

"I did notice that." The ass tossed his amber crown, winking. "Glad you did too."

"Ugh." I stormed off. Victor just jogged after me, falling in step beside and brimming with joy at irritating me so early in the morning. Glancing over my shoulder, I spotted Lucien tailing a fair distance behind. "What's with you lately? Is this really about showing off that you're a good fiancé? Because that feels less like you care, and more like an advertisement to ladies like *Everleigh* that you'd be a great pick after you dump me."

Victor's expression didn't twitch. "Why do you keep saying her name like that? Actually, why do you keep bringing Everleigh up at all? What does she have to do with anything?"

"She seems to think she's a better match for you than I am."

His brows popped. "No shit? Damn, when did she say this?"

"Why?" I flung, rounding on him. "Are you interested?"

"Whoa." Laughing, he threw up his hands. "Why am I in trouble? I'm hearing all this for the first time."

"Yeah, right. I saw her flirting and pawing you yesterday."

"You did? When?"

Sense seized control of my tongue, snapping my mouth shut. *You almost admitted you were lurking in the shadows while Wesley was choking on his swollen tongue.*

"Doesn't matter when. The point is she was doing it and you know she was coming on to you. That's why you're not denying it."

He lifted his shoulders. "Everyone comes on to me. Look at me." Victor did a little spin. "I'm fucking hot."

"I hate you."

Cracking up, he said, "I don't notice when girls flirt with me anymore. It's as common as saying hello."

"I hate you more."

"I'm not trying to get with Everleigh," he said, humor lacing his tone. "Or advertise to other women that I'd make a good husband—or whatever crazy shit you just said. If I'm advertising to anyone, it's you, dumbass."

"Wait, what?"

"I'm trying to show you that even if we don't fall head over heels in love with each other, we can still have a good marriage. Even, heaven forbid, be friends."

I screwed up my face. "Again, what?"

"I've been thinking since the other day when you got jealous over Iris and tried to flirt with my brother."

Irritation blazed into an inferno. "Neither of those things happened."

"Keep telling yourself that," he scoffed. "Anyway, we've been fighting, arguing, and digging at each other since we met, and it's already getting old. I'm not trying to spend the next sixty-plus years sleeping next to a woman who hates me, checking for the knife in my back every morning when I wake up.

"I grew up in Regalia. I've seen the arranged marriages that went sour quick. They can't stand to be in the same room as each other. They're cold, bitter, and hiding an army of mistresses, escorts, and boyfriends to get what they're missing. Is that what you want?"

"I..."

I fell quiet, considering it for the first time. I didn't really think past the proposal that would secure my spot in Regalia University and seal my deal with Jack. Honestly, I stopped thinking about my life after avenging Winter. What did any of that matter? Winter wasn't here.

"What do you want?" I asked softly, closing the distance.

"To be friends, at least. Partners. Equals. Our kids can see an example of two people who respect each other, instead of Mommy drinking herself to death on the couch and Dad pretending he works late every night. I want us to go on family vacations and have inside jokes about how much we used to despise each other."

My eyes glazed, staring off into a distant future so different from the one I dreamed of when my world was a happy one. Different, but... not bad.

"That sounds nice," I muttered.

"I also want sex."

The sweet, family picture imploded.

"Lots of it. All the time. Hot, nasty, and willing," he dropped. "I've got the sex drive of a Lamborghini with an unlimited gas tank, and your boy's not interested in a life of celibacy."

"Annnnd you're back." Spinning around, I walked off. "Nice chatting with you, Victor."

He jogged out in front of me, pulling me up short. "I'm serious."

"Trust me, I know."

"Is there a chance of any of that happening between us, if I sit on my ass in a corner, keeping my mouth shut while people bully you? Could you ever respect a coward like that? Let alone touch, sleep with, or pop out his kids?"

Meeting his eyes, I spoke honestly. "No, I couldn't. I would never forget that you did nothing."

I looked past him at the Royals and Dregs happily going on with their lives. *Like I'll never forget that you all did.*

"There you go. I'm trying to show you I'm not the guy you think I am, Sinclair. I can be there for you. I can protect you. I can make you— You fucking throw that drink, Juan, and you'll lick every drop off the concrete!"

I twisted to find a random guy behind us, latte raised suspiciously over his head. Near him, two guys hurriedly put away their phones. "I wasn't doing anything," he rushed out. "Chill out."

He took off in the opposite direction, where Lucien trailed him.

"—happy," Victor finished like nothing happened. "Would it be so terrible to let your fiancé prove he can be a good husband?"

My face warmed. When he said it like that, I sounded like the asshole.

"No." My voice was hardly more than a grumble. "Not terrible."

Triumphant, Victor threw an arm around my waist again, getting real comfortable with the touching. "Good. And in the meantime, you should start working on how you'll make me happy. So far, I'm doing all the work in this relationship."

I rolled my eyes. "Oh yes, hubby dear, please, tell me how I may please you?"

"I mentioned the hot, dirty sex, right?"

I shoved him, giggle almost slipping through my lips. Dear Thor, since when did Victor Wilson make me giggle?

A stray, wild thought popped in my head. "Can I ask you something? Now that we're talking about what comes after."

"Shoot."

We ambled toward anthropology, taking our time.

"What if we never feel *it*?" I asked. "The 'head over heels in love' stuff. One day, I could get past the fact you're conceited, snobbish, and prone to sticking your dick in anything that moves—"

"Put that on my tombstone. Sums me up perfectly."

"—and become your friend," I finished. "Maybe even your friend with benefits. But what if we never get past that, Victor, and feel something deeper. Could we really be happy?"

"A different kind of happiness, but yeah. There are people who marry for love and are divorced in a year. They hate each other. Is that better than a relationship built on friendship and respect?"

"Better than that example, definitely. But better than friendship, respect, *and* love...?"

He observed me out of the corner of his eye. "What are you saying, Sinclair? You don't want to do this?"

"I'm not saying that." Amazingly, I wasn't. "It's just that I know I'm not your first choice. I was the *only* choice willing to marry you now, and the banshee brigade is looking to change that—snatch my paws off Regalia's most eligible bachelor. What if that doesn't stop after we're married and you take notice of one of the women throwing themselves at you? What if you fall for her because she gives you what our relationship is missing?"

Annoyance flashed across his face. "I wouldn't cheat on my wife, Luna. What kind of guy do you think I am?"

"No, I— That's not what I'm saying," I cried, massaging my temples. "Okay, I'm not explaining this right. What I mean is, there are all kinds of marriages... and I'm open to... discussing." The face reflected in Victor's eyes was turning neon red. "The right kind... for us."

"Are you clumsily proposing an open marriage?" he asked, blunt as a truck.

Yes, for sure neon red.

"Why? Is there some guy you're hoping to slip in our bed after we tie the knot?"

Rafael floated through my head. "No!"

"Would that mean I can fool around with Everleigh Starling?"

"I mentioned that I hated you, right? Forget I said anything."

"Hold up." Victor grasped my elbow, stopping my escape. "Five years."

"Excuse me?"

"We give our marriage a real shot for five years. The love stuff. The romantic shit. Getting to know each other. Counseling. Communication. All that crap," he rattled off. "Five years of just the two of us, and when time's up, if both of us don't feel we'll ever be more than friends, we can do the open-marriage thing. Discreetly."

"Both of us?" I repeated, turning over what he said. "What if only one wants the open marriage?"

"Then, we'd have to split, wouldn't we? If you were in love with me, could you stand to wave me out the door when I dash off to bang my lady on the side? You bare your teeth when I say Everleigh's name, and you barely like me right now."

"I don't," I said quickly, but that wasn't the point. "Okay, you're right. That would have to be something we both wanted. But why five instead of three or one? Would it take us five years to figure out if we love each other?"

"Five years in, we should have a kid. And I don't need to be wondering if the bugger is mine."

"Can you please stop bringing up children so casually?" I hissed. "You know we're getting married next year. Are you trying to be a dad before twenty-five?"

"I'm trying to be a husband at nineteen and a CEO by twenty-one. Why not a dad before twenty-five? We can afford a fleet of nannies, Sinclair. You wouldn't be choosing between your career."

"You concern me."

He barked a laugh. "You're concerned because I've thought about your future, and you haven't. It's a personal problem."

Got the bull's-eye with one arrow.

"So, five years," he said. "We good with that?"

"It does sound reasonable." I shuffled on the grass, glancing toward the anthropology building and away. "But what about now? Giving our marriage a real chance makes sense, but right now, we're basically strangers coming off half a dozen terrible first impressions. I know we made a deal, but what if we treated our engagement like"—I cast about for the word—"dating? Feeling each other out. We can come up with new rules for it."

"Like what? That we can hook up with other people?"

His bluntness was going to be a real problem. "Maybe," I hedged. "I know I said no hooking up because your mistresses would throw it in my face, but they're doing that anyway. I say we start over, take the pressure off, and do this the normal way. Ignore the rings on our fingers. We can talk exclusivity when I can look at you and see a man I want to be committed to, and vice versa."

Humming, he pushed out his lips. "Start over?"

"Yes."

"Act like we just met and are about to have our first date?"

"Yes."

"Nonexclusive?"

Lifting my chin, I said, "Yes."

"Okay, then I have one question."

"What is it?"

"Are you going to be cool with me fucking Everleigh, because she is so damn—"

"Stop bringing up that bitch!"

Guffawing, Victor clapped me on the shoulder. "That answers that. Exclusive it is." Victor set off without a look back. "Let's go. We're late for class."

I stood there fuming for a full ten seconds, and shockingly, my anger wasn't directed at Victor. I was pissed at myself. When did he become the reasonable, forward-thinking, accommodating one in this engagement, and I became the jealous, possessive jerk?

I was not liking this shift in our dynamic.

KATIE SUMMONED ME AFTER my final class of the day let out. I wish I had another word for the text she sent me—instructing me of the place and time I was supposed to meet her, so I could treat her to dinner. But a summons was the only word for it.

Victor, and Lucien, escorted me to the fountain where she waited, and not alone. She and Dean were making out hardcore. They nearly tipped over the rim twice since I laid eyes on them.

"You good?" Victor asked. "Want me to hang around campus till you come back?"

"No, go home. I'll be fine."

He didn't move. "Where are you staying? I should've asked this earlier, but why did you move in with the Rogues? Did something happen in the dorm?"

I studied him. "You really don't know, do you?"

His forehead crumpled. "Know what?"

Victor didn't hear what they tried to do to me that night. He's not in the same class and they're not friends, but it looks like the Royals aren't as tight knit as I thought.

"You heard I got into it with Owen and shocked him," I finally said. "Well, it didn't teach him a lesson. He's gotten twice as loud, threatening, and abusive since."

"What?" He ate the distance, fists balled. "Did he do something to you? Is that how you got those bruises?"

I crossed my arms, hugging myself tight. How did he know? Most of them faded, and for those that didn't, I covered in heavy makeup. I thought I did a good job—until then.

"That's how *he* ended up in the hospital."

"Luna—"

"Please," I whispered, voice trembling. "I don't want to talk about it, Victor. He's never going to mess with me again. That's what's important."

"You're fucking right he's never going to mess with you again." I leaned back at the fury on his face. "Levi's in the hospital too. And Darren, Caleb, Silas, and Emmett. Were they all in on it?"

My silence spoke volumes.

Victor breathed hard, nostrils flaring. "I'll take care of it."

"What?" I said to his back. "What does that mean? What are you going to do?" He strode away without a reply.

Putting aside my unease, I went to peel Katie off Dean. She extracted herself with extreme reluctance. "We won't be long," she told him. "Come over around eleven."

"Better be naked when I get there."

"Really?" I tugged her away. "'Cause I was thinking I'd wear whipped cream and two cherries."

"I take it back. Wear that."

"Or maybe—"

I picked up the pace, dragging her too far to continue the conversation.

"You're so repressed, Lu-Lu." Katie slipped free of me and led the way to her car. "I have so much work to do to fix you."

My phone buzzed with a text. Reading it, I grinned.

"No, thank you," I replied, "but there is something you can do for me."

"Which is?"

"Since it's my treat, let me pick the restaurant."

"And where do you want to eat? Hometown Country Fried?"

"No." I said that with more patience than I knew I possessed. "Let's go to Toussaint's."

"Huh. That's actually a decent restaurant. I see a few weeks back in civilization has scraped some of the Dreg off your tongue. You're ready to eat, behave, and dress like the rest of us." She wrinkled her nose. "Well, not so much the dress part. We'll stop by my place first and change into something decent."

"I'm just going to say yes if it gets food in my belly faster."

Not arguing with Katie was the quick way to an easy life. She drove me back to her house, dressed me like one of her mannequins, then we set off for Toussaint's.

The French bistro nestled in the richest part of town, excluding the street with all the mega-mansions. Despite the modern chandeliers, marble floors, upholstered booths, and the cocktail dresses and heels we had to wear to get in, Toussaint's was considered *informal* dining for the Royal crowd. Here they had five-course menus instead of the traditional seven, and one of the sides was black truffle oil French fries—therefore, informal.

"Good evening, mesdames." The host bowed. "Party of two?"

"Yes," said Katie. "We'd prefer seats near the back."

"Of course. Please, follow me."

I whispered in her ear when he was out of earshot. "Are you trying to hide me?"

"On the contrary, my clingy, insecure hanger-on." We rounded the bar, coming into full view of Saylor, Gabriella, Piper, Everleigh, Iris, Branlon, Giovanni, and the horde of Royals taking up the back room of Toussaint's.

"I'm showing you off," Katie announced.

I STUDIED MY MENU LIKE there'd be a test, skin prickling under the half a dozen pairs of eyes boring a hole in my skull.

Chancing a peek, I peered over my menu at Giovanni and his date, Annika. Annika Mitchell, to be exact, the girl he was really dating while seducing my sister. The same girl who gave him the green light to sleep with her—all in the name of humiliation.

Victor was wrong. I bared my teeth at the thought of Annika Mitchell, not Everleigh.

It wasn't a coincidence the two of them were here. Rafael and the guys told me this was the Royal equivalent of a local dive bar. The waiters never carded them, and since nothing on the menu was less than two hundred dollars, Dregs didn't eat here. Giovanni and Annika ate at Toussaint's almost every night.

My gaze slid to the right. *Apparently so do Her Royal Highnesses.*

"Why are you showing me off?"

Katie half shrugged while buttering her bread. "You picked this place, not me. Saylor always eats here on Tuesday night. This is her folks' weekly sex night and the other side of town isn't far enough away."

"And now I know that."

"If we're going to be here and she's going to be here, I might as well teach her a lesson."

"The lesson being?"

"I've been trying to convince her that you're only half the loser you seem to be, but she's not buying it. Yeah, your mother was a housekeeper, but she snagged a decent catch while no one was looking, raised one cool daughter, and the other isn't so bad when we get you out of the disgusting clothes and ignore the Virgin Mary thing."

"Well, did you say it in such a sweet, loving way?" I mocked. "Gee, wonder why that didn't work."

"And the sarcasm," she shot back. "But Saylor said you suck a dog's anal glands—her words, not mine—and until you accept her offer, she doesn't want to hear your name or for me to have anything to do with you." Katie bit off a dainty bite. "Sometimes I have to remind her that even though the lemmings treat her like a queen, no bitch rules Katie Langford."

"I admire your confidence, Katie."

She rolled her eyes, flipping her hair. "You more than admire me. You love me, and it's dull. Enough with the fawning and order me a glass of champagne, and fig and goat cheese tartlets."

The waiter came by and I ordered two whiskeys with smoked salmon dill canapés, and I beamed at her while doing it. Katie hated whiskey, salmon, and dill.

She laughed. "Touché, but you're eating all that by yourself."

A rough throat-clearing broke into my reply. Saylor pushed away from her table, bearing down on us fast.

"Katie," she said, lips so tight they barely moved as she spoke. Saylor turned her back on me, her ass in my face. "What are you doing?"

"What does it look like, Saylor?"

"We didn't know you were coming to Toussaint's tonight too. We've got room at our table. I'll have Maurice set another place."

Katie blinked rapidly at her, smiling away. "The invitation to join you guys for dinner should've come hours ago when you made the plans. As it is, Luna is treating me and it'd be rude to ditch her."

"Since when do you care about manners? You weren't worried about being *rude* when you fucked Piper's boyfriend in that toolshed the weekend she went away to Aspen."

"What?!"

Katie leaped to her feet. "I was wasted and he told me they were broken up! Dammit, Saylor, you promised!"

"What do you mean she promised?" Piper cried. "Saylor, you knew she slept with Ahmed and didn't tell me?"

Eyes big, I leaned back in my seat, reaching for a roll. I was doubly glad I came.

Saylor threw a hand up at Piper. "This is not about you, Piper!"

Katie and Saylor squared off, the air sparking between them.

"What about your promises?" Saylor flung. "Some friend you are, clinking glasses with the bitch who punched me in the face."

"Everyone wants to punch you in the face, Saylor. If I avoided all the people who hate you, my only friend would be your mother."

Damn. One point to Katie.

"At least people bother to fake it for me, Katie. Your only friend isn't even your mother. It's whoever you're banging at the time." Saylor dropped to an exaggerated whisper. "Just so you know, the I love yous don't count if he only says them when you're sucking his dick."

"He also says it when he's fucking me up the butt. Do those count?"

I choked on my bread. We had the attention of everyone in the restaurant now.

"Ugh," Saylor screeched. "You're filthier than the pube wad you spit up after every blow job."

"And you're a stuck-up bitch with delusions of grandeur, so I guess we've all got problems."

"Ladies," a waiter called. "Ladies, please."

"Oooh," Saylor crowed. "Grandeur? Where'd you learn that one? Is there a dictionary at the end of Dean's cock?"

"Your frigid ass will never find out."

Grinning, Saylor cocked her hip, planting her hands on them. "My frigid ass found out three times the night of the ABC party."

Katie, Everleigh, Annika, and I gasped.

"Bitch," Katie shrieked.

"Slut!"

"Cunt!"

"Whore!"

"Ladies!" I shot to my feet, slamming my fist on the table. "It's flattering that you're both fighting over me, but maybe we should take it down."

"As if. No one gives a shit about you," Saylor snapped. She snatched my ice water and tossed it in my face. Freezing cold penetrated my pores. Water rushed down my cleavage, chilling my flesh in an instant. "There. Now you're five for five. Cross your fingers you hit the high score.

"Katie, are you coming or not?" Saylor demanded.

"Not."

She stormed back to her table.

Wow. Katie calls her a friendless cunt and still gets an invitation to eat with her. I stand there breathing and I'm put through the mini ice bucket challenge.

Katie threw herself in her seat, angry-buttering another roll. I excused myself to the bathroom to stick my head under the hand dryer. When I came back, Katie had two bottles of champagne, a plate of cheese tartlets and the scandalous steak frites on the way. She and Saylor glared at each other across the room.

That would've been a great time to leave, but I wasn't there for Saylor, and I also wasn't there for Katie. Giovanni was still at his table, tracing designs on his girlfriend's palm. I wasn't leaving until they did.

"Can't believe her," Katie hissed. "Hooking up with Dean? And she calls me a bad friend."

"Mmm-hhm."

Giovanni raised a hand, signaling for the waiter. I sat up straighter.

"She just will not get it through that bleached head that she doesn't get to tell me what to do with my life."

"Yep, she sucks," I said absentmindedly.

"She was always like that, you know. Since preschool." The waiter came to us first, carrying those bottles. Katie downed a glass before he got to Giovanni's table. "She had to be the queen, or the boss, or the princess, or fairy. She made the rules, and if we tried to go off and play without the tyrant, we didn't get invited to her super summer slumber party."

"Princess fairy queen of the tyrants."

"Here, Maurice." Giovanni handed over his credit card. "We'll also take some chocolate-covered strawberries to go."

Annika giggled, delighting in how hot, rich, and privileged she was. How did I know? I just fucking did.

Acid burned my throat watching them. Giovanni was everything women fooled themselves into believing they wanted. Long, luscious hair. Strong nose. Olive sun-kissed skin. Full, smirking lips. And his demon mistress, Annika, was so pretty it hurt to look at her. Waves and waves of chestnut hair fell around her shoulders, framing a heart-shaped face and flinty eyes.

Maurice returned. "I'm sorry, sir. Your card was declined. Do you have another form of payment?"

"Declined?" Giovanni repeated. "You made a mistake. Run it again."

Maurice remained where he was. "There was no mistake, sir. I must ask for another form of payment."

"Fine, whatever." He pulled another from his wallet. "Use this."

"—acts like we're so lucky to be in her presence." Katie's rant was going full steam. "I wasn't kidding when I said no one likes her. You should hear the stuff Everleigh, Piper, and Gabriella say behind her back."

My ears perked up. I *should* hear what they say.

"But I would never tell you," Katie continued, "because *when I promise to keep a secret, I don't go back on my word like a frigid bitch!*"

"Get over it," Saylor threw back. "Ahmed bragged about it to the entire football team. Everyone but Piper knew, and it's about time she figured out you're nothing but a slut!"

"You're calling me a slut when you slept with my boyfriend."

"Guys," Piper spoke up, eyes suspiciously bright. I don't think she was quite as prepared for the news as Saylor believed.

"Now he's your boyfriend? What happened to slumming it with the Dreg for a few *O* cocktails?"

"Sir, I regret to inform you this card was declined too."

My attention snapped back to Giovanni.

"There is a one-hundred-thousand-dollar limit on that card," Giovanni forced through gritted teeth. "It can't be declined. Run. It. Again."

Maurice dipped his head, ever the polite employee. "Of course, sir."

Off to the register and then back again. This was my favorite game of ping-pong ever.

"Declined again. Do you have another—?"

"It can't be declined. If it's not going through, there's something wrong with your machine."

Katie paused the war and turned to see what I was looking at. Saylor and her crew did too, then the entire back room of Toussaint's stopped talking, watching the show.

"I'm afraid not, sir," Maurice said patiently. "We've had no issues with the card reader tonight. It is only yours that have been declined."

"Excuse me? What are you trying to say, you minimum-wage, cheap-cologne-stinkin' moron?"

Annika flapped her hands, trying to get Giovanni back in his seat.

"I've got more money tucked in my sock than you see in a year. If I say your machine is broken, it's fucking broken."

A man with thinning hair and a three-piece gray suit hurried out from the direction of the kitchen. I pegged him as the manager.

"Hello, my name is Mr. Shaw. I'm the manager."

Bingo.

"Whatever the problem is, I'm sure we can resolve it."

Giovanni shoved Maurice. "This fool said I can't pay my bills."

Shaw jumped in front of his employee. "There's no need for that. Maurice did not intend—"

"Everyone heard it. I come here almost every night. He knows who I am and that I can cover my bills, but instead of admitting the card reader's broken, he tried to embarrass me in front of my friends and girlfriend."

Maurice spoke up. "I apologize for any offense."

"I want him fired," Giovanni said without sparing him a look. "Get rid of him, or none of us will eat here again."

I cleared my throat, swiveling the spotlight to me. "Before an innocent man loses his livelihood, why don't we make sure the card reader is broken, and this is not a tantrum thrown by some broke loser who thinks kicking up enough of a fuss will get his meal comped."

"What the fuck did you just say?" Giovanni sputtered. "Stay out of this, Dreg! Who even let you in here?"

Flashing him a smile, I mimed zipping my lips.

"Gio, this is stupid." Annika ripped her wallet out of her bag. "Just try my card."

Maurice accepted it and left.

"Everything is under control, ladies and gentlemen," Mr. Shaw called. "Please, enjoy your meals."

Maurice came back with a card, receipt, and a self-satisfied smile. "Thank you, madam, the bill is paid. I apologize for the trouble. Please, allow me to gift you those chocolate strawberries free of charge."

I, and everyone in the restaurant, noted Maurice's graciousness in the face of the reddening jackass.

"Oops," I said under my breath. "Next time put a dead bug on your plate."

Katie heard me and snorted a laugh.

"Thank you, Maurice." Annika wasn't too impressed with her boyfriend either. She pushed him firmly back into his seat. "What is wrong with you?" I heard her hiss. "You humiliated me, and for what? This isn't the first time you've overdrawn your account."

"I didn't overdraw shit. Look." Giovanni jabbed on his phone. "There's enough in there to buy this dump. I'm telling you... the reader is... broken..." He trailed off, olive skin flushed sickly yellow under the fluorescent lights.

"What?"

"My money," he rasped. "Where's my money?"

"I see, I knew you—"

"Shut up for a fucking minute! It's gone!" Giovanni snagged the tablecloth jumping up. It ripped off, showering the floor in smashed china, crystal, and butter rolls. "A quarter of a million dollars! Where the hell is my money?"

"Gio, calm down."

He didn't hear or he didn't care. Giovanni stormed out of the restaurant, barking into the phone before he hit the door. Annika ran to catch up to him.

"Mom? Mom! What's going on!"

Reclining in my seat, I poured myself a glass of champagne, raising it in the air. "Maurice, let's get a round of champagne for the house—make up for that appetite-ruining scene."

"Right away, ma'am."

"Except for that table," I said, pointing to Saylor's. "They're underage."

An hour later, I stumbled into the Gallery, giggling on too much bubbly juice. Every time I tried to think sober thoughts, Giovanni's face as he read triple zeros on his screen flashed in my mind and set me off.

The house was quiet. I stuck my head in the living room.

No one.

My next stop was the kitchen.

Wilder looked up from a plate of chicken and roasted veggies. His neutral expression washed away in an instant.

"What do you want?"

"Your disinfectant spray, friend. Because you're about to get hugged."

Wilder dropped his attention to his food, spearing a carrot. "I take it you got my text."

"Got your text and then went to Toussaint's where I got to see the beautiful moment live in 3D. The look on his face was priceless. Wilder, you're amazing."

He grunted. "I do not require praise or physical affection. Emptying their bank accounts was part of the plan. I held up my end."

"You're still getting a hug." I hopped up on the stool beside him. "When there aren't two of you."

"Here." His long, built arm reached the fridge from his seat. He plopped a water bottle in front of me. "Drink."

"Thank you." We fell silent while I downed half the bottle. That's the only reason there was silence, because I had plenty to say. "It's only Tuesday, and it's the best week I've had since I stepped inside this hellmouth they call a college campus. I'll replay Giovanni's crying for his mommy over and over again in my dreams. Now that's the making of an *O* cocktail."

"*O* cocktail," Wilder repeated slowly. He picked up his plate, edging off the stool. "Good night, Sinclair. Don't touch anything. I'll know."

"Wait." I leaped over the table and snagged his sleeve. "On the drive, I was thinking about the SB3A virus. Why would the government create something so horrifying?"

Wilder stilled.

"Made to appear like the common cold. Did they do it so people would snuggle up in bed, convinced all they need is rest and tea, giving the virus all the time it needs to rip through their system?"

"Yes," he replied, eyes big. "Exactly."

"It's as genius as it is evil. Which is why the person who created it gets the title. But why wasn't that guy locked up instead of given millions in funding?"

"Biological warfare." Wilder reclaimed his seat, propping his forearms on the table. "There's an underground facility with hundreds of man-made viruses like SB3A. Each one deadlier than the last."

"But SB3A got out."

"It was stolen," Wilder corrected. "I suspect by a disloyal employee looking to sell the virus to an overseas enemy government. I have two monitors devoted to tracking him down, but the guy's a ghost. He had an expert erase his online presence."

I wasn't counting, but I was pretty sure this conversation topped the most words Wilder said to me combined, and that included his rant that I was a North Korean sleeper agent.

"The US government's been on red alert for two years, illegally tracking hospital records for patients bleeding from the eyes, mouth, and ass."

"But wait? If they've been on red alert, preparing for a pandemic, why were they so woefully underprepared when the last one hit?"

Wilder threw up his hands. "That's what I'm saying! It doesn't make sense. It's not logical," he burst out. "They have warehouses full of vaccines and scientists on standby for new variants. Protocols were put in place.

Aid stockpiled. The government wasn't underprepared. They released the hounds, closed the gates, and let us fend for ourselves."

"Why would they do that? Put all that money and effort into protecting us from one disaster, only to intentionally unleash another?"

"Oh, it's simple, Sinclair. SB3A is a plague. It's the decimation of three-quarters of the population and the end to the country as we know it. But that bastard they let loose, that's control. That's one million people wiped out. Thousands of businesses collapsed. Jobs lost. Homes lost. And everyone looking to the government to make it better.

"They hit the big reset button on wages, healthcare, and education, and now we're not asking for more. We're begging for the little we can get. They're in our heads. They're in your head." He grasped my skull, giving it a little shake to prove it. "And you don't even know you're behaving exactly the way they want you to."

Passion laced his tone, transforming his entire face... into Tom Hiddleston's Loki laughing over his short-lived triumph. Undeniably handsome, and undeniably loony toons.

I smiled just listening to him, enjoying the peek into the mind of Wilder O'Rourke. Talking to Rafael about him made me realize why the guy wasn't taking to me. Every time he talked, I looked at him like he popped his head off his shoulders and juggled with it. What if I just sat down and listened to him?

The answer was we'd talk for so long, I'd start the conversation drunk and wind up sober in the middle.

"You really think there's a captured alien aircraft in Area 51?"

"It's almost a certainty." Wilder popped off the chocolate chip ice cream lid and handed me a spoon. Our fingers brushed as I took it, and he didn't reach for the hand sanitizer. "The advancements we've made in technology over the last few decades is a direct result of studying that aircraft. Steve Jobs, my ass."

Chuckling, I held out my spoon.

Wilder cocked a brow at me, getting his own. Ours crossed dipping into the carton. "Everything I've dug up on the site supports the evidence, but they've been smart. There are no cameras in or allowed into the facility, so I can't hack them for the proof the world really needs: photographs."

"If aliens visited once, they might again," I offered. "Maybe next time, they'll make too big of a splash for the world governments to cover up. Like crashing into Big Ben."

He grinned—the curve of his lips catching the light and casting a tiny shadow beneath his mouth, drawing me to his hard, stubbly jaw. Every inch of him was strong from the ropey muscles to his name: Wilder O'Rourke. It evoked visions of hot, sweaty days and a hot, sweaty Wilder—his shoulders rippling as he swung the axe, cleaving firewood in two.

"Nice reference," he said, tugging me out of the fantasy.

"You watch *Doctor Who*?"

"Religiously. There's nothing fictional about sci-fi, Sinclair."

"Really? All of it's true?"

He nodded. "Yep."

"Superintelligent robots?"

"We've already got them."

"Intergalactic space wars?"

"There's life out there, Luna. Odds are, they're fighting over something that belongs to neither of them but they all want."

I shivered at the way his lips formed my name. "Dragons?"

"That's fantasy," he said with a chuckle.

"Oh, right. Okay, how about... one of the first science fiction stories ever made? The creation of life cobbled together with dead body parts and a little bit of genius."

"Ah, Frankenstein's monster," he mused. "Nah, that shit's totally fake."

We busted up.

"That really was impressive what you did," I said after we calmed. "Even though you don't need praise. Giovanni Natale played my sister like a violin, then he snapped her over his leg and threw Winter in the trash. Even though his millionaire parents are going to drop double what he lost in his bank account tomorrow, it felt great to see him lose something he cared about. He for fuck sure didn't care about losing Winter."

Wilder turned his head toward the stairs. "Come with me. There's something I need to show you."

He took my hand, leading me up. Surprise quickened my steps when I realized where we were going.

Wilder spent five minutes unlocking his door. Standing aside, he waved me in—to be a gentleman or because he didn't want me at his back, I didn't ruin the mood by asking.

I ducked my head in, lips parting as I swept the room. "Oh my goodness, where am I?"

Computers.

Computers on computers, next to more computers everywhere I looked, and all of them running at once, casting a cool, blue light that pierced the gloom. He didn't have posters on the wall or a coffin next to the dresser, but little peeks into Wilder teased me in the ornate snow globe on his nightstand, the stack of science fiction novels, and blue. Blue comforter, blue carpet, and blue desk chair.

I filed it all away, but none of it was the sight to see. A full-size pillow-top bed lay in the middle of the room, enclosed in a metal cage.

"A Faraday cage."

"It's for—"

"—blocking electromagnetic fields."

I saw his pleased grin out of the corner of my eyes.

"Exactly."

"Wow, I didn't know they made these bed-sized." I went in and hissed, rubbing my arms. Cool wasn't the word. "It's below freezing in here."

"With all the processors going, it's got to be cold so they don't over-heat."

Wilder opened the cage and grabbed a fleece off his bed. Draping it over my shoulders, he drew me in, and my breath out. I froze as he rubbed my arms, popping goose bumps down my body that had nothing to do with the temperature.

"Better?"

"M-much better." I cleared my throat. "So, what did you want to show me?"

"That screen behind you."

His warmth, and touch, disappeared. Wilder grabbed his desk chair and moved it in front of a screen nestled between three bigger ones. He gestured for me to sit.

"Let's see. It looks like a banking website."

"It's Giovanni's account." Wilder traced a line down the withdrawals. "That's the last hour. He, or his parents, or the bank employees they're cursing out right now, have tried six times to disturb that zero balance. Every time they do, the money automatically transfers into a separate account. So no, Luna. He's not going to feel the loss for a night. It'll be weeks before they sort this mess out."

"Wilder, you're kidding me," I cried. "What's the separate account?"

"A charity fund for a women's shelter."

"Oh man, that hug is coming and it'll be way longer than five seconds."

He chuckled. "Then I shouldn't tell you that I've got this program running for all five of them, draining the money out of every account in their name. They can still use Daddy's credit cards, of course, but now they know."

"That someone is watching, waiting... and coming."

"Did Natale see you at the restaurant?"

"Yes," I admitted. "Saylor and Katie got into a knock-down, drag-out, and I ended up with ice water to the face. I had zero chance of flying under the radar."

"You can't be anywhere near these guys for the next couple of days, Sinclair. They can think you're behind this all they want, but they can't prove it. Not if you're never around when shit goes down."

"I know the plan and I agree with it. I just couldn't resist checking to see if one of them would be at Toussaint's tonight. Katie demanded I take her to dinner and it felt like fate." I glimpsed a name on the screen to my left. "Hey, did that say Branlon?"

"Most likely." Wilder turned it for me to see. "This program monitors the communications of the group calling themselves the Royals."

"Monitors their communications? You're spying on the Royals?"

"Surveilling."

"Another way of saying spying." I squinted at the string of information. "How long have you been doing this?"

"I started it recently. I have a theory that the Royals are also members of a secret underground society that's controlling the student body. They know more than they're saying."

"I bet they do, but what's the secret part?" I asked, lips twisting. "From what I see, they do their worst right out in the open."

Sighing, Wilder shut off the monitor. "I'm sorry, Luna. I should've said that sooner."

I gave him a smile that didn't reach my eyes. "I know you're sorry about Winter's death. You guys did care. You've proven that—"

"No." Something in his tone silenced me. "I'm sorry for... not seeing how lost she was. I'm sorry I didn't stop her."

"Wilder, why would you say that?"

"Because," he burst out. "All these programs, subroutines, and feeds monitoring every inch of this campus, and I couldn't see that she needed help." Wilder balled his fists, glancing away. "I, more than anyone, owe you and your family a debt. I don't want your thanks or praise, Luna, because I don't deserve it."

I shook, lids welling. "Winter didn't just save you from the fire, did she? You two were friends."

Wilder dropped his head, the shadows lengthening across his face. "She was like you," he rasped, breaking something inside me. "She never called me crazy."

My palm warmed his wrist, traveling up his arm, turning his gaze to my touch, then to me. I slid around him, molding to Wilder's body, burying my face in his sweet-scented neck—my tears dampening his skin.

For a full beat, he didn't move. When the slight pressure graced my hip, I almost didn't connect it to him. Then he threw his arms around me, holding me as tight as I did him.

For a long time we embraced, mourning the loss of the best person we ever knew.

Much longer than five seconds.

Chapter Nine

Water surged into my nose and mouth—a ruthless assailant grabbing and whisking me into the dark. I thrashed, clawing for the surface as the reeds tangled my legs. I wasn't going anywhere, ever again. Through the inky darkness, a face appeared, peaceful in the permanent sleep that would be mine.

I gasped awake, heart rocketing into my throat and choking me. Dizzy and wheezing, my stomach flipped—burning with bile and fighting to eject from my system.

Shhh, you're safe. A soft crooning whispered through my mind. Sweet and gentle, it soothed as warmth surrounded me, calming my overloaded system.

My lids fell heavily, shutting out my spinning room, drawing me back into sleep. I laid my head on my pillow, sinking into the depths.

I DON'T KNOW WHAT IT was that woke me. One moment, I knew nothing, then consciousness flicked on like a light switch, peeling my eyes open. A fact became clear to me immediately: there was someone in my bed.

Not just on my sheets, but on me. His legs weaved through mine. His arm draped over my waist and my arm over his. Face pressed to my neck, his breaths were warm puffs on my skin, bringing me back to the reality of what was happening as my mind went blank with shock.

Someone is in my bed!

Screaming, I threw out my limbs, trying to throw them off.

A grunt, then a warm hand covered my head, stroking my temple. "Shh," he whispered. "You're safe."

"Cato?!"

Whipping around, I fell on the handsome face sharing my pillow.

"What— How— You can't just—!" Words deserted me, leaving behind unintelligible shrieks. In the haze, the night before came back to me. A horrible nightmare and then something—*someone*—easing me back to sleep. "What the hell are you doing here!"

Footsteps thundered down the hall. "Luna? What's wrong?"

Rafael skidded into my doorway wearing nothing but a pair of boxers and concern that flashed away when he took in the scene. "Ah, so it wasn't that kind of scream. Whoops, I'll leave you to it."

Fire licked my cheeks. "You're not leaving us to anything. Nothing happened." I scrambled free of Cato, climbing off the bed. "Cato, I don't even— What were you doing?"

"You were having bad dreams. I helped," Cato said simply.

"Guarding my dreams was not literal. You can't just get in bed with me!"

Sitting up, he cocked his head. "Why?"

"Yeah, why not?" Rafael echoed.

"You can go," I barked at Rafael.

His reply was to grin and fold his arms, leaning against the frame. "Nah, I want to see how this plays out."

The feel of Cato was all over me. His impressions left in my skin, hair, and in the knowledge that was the best sleep I've had in months. It made it even worse.

"Because spooning is something couples discuss before it happens. At least so they can decide who's the little spoon!"

Cato turned this over. "Okay. Discuss."

"What are you talking about?"

He gestured between us. "Let's talk about spoons, so we can sleep."

My jaw worked. "I said couples discuss this."

"We're a couple."

Thor, help me. What is happening?

"No, we're not."

"Yes," Cato said slowly. "You're mine. I am yours. You are one. I am one. One-one makes two. Two is a couple. We are a couple."

My mind spun following his logic. Once again, both simple and impossible to comprehend.

"I told you, Cato, you can't call me... yours."

"Why?"

"Yeah, why?" Rafael threw in. The bastard was enjoying this.

"Because we're two people, but we're not two people who make... a couple."

"That doesn't make sense," Cato replied.

"No sense at all," added Rafael.

"Both of you, out."

Laughter bouncing through the halls, Rafael strode back to his bedroom with a headshaking Cato on his heels. Somehow, I lost that round and I was the one who had no idea why.

A COUPLE OF HOURS LATER, I banged the pots around making breakfast, and not a morsel of it was for the Dumont Menaces. I didn't know what knocked me further off-balance—that I spent the night tangled in a guy's arms and had no clue, or that said guy was so committed to my peaceful sleep, he climbed out of his bed to comfort me. It was both the sweetest and most disturbing thing anyone had ever done for me.

Wilder entered the kitchen midbite of bacon.

"Morning," I said around a mouthful of meat.

"Morning."

"Would you like some bacon and eggs?"

"No, thanks." He took down a box of cereal and a bowl.

I watched the muscles in his back ripple as he fixed his food.

"Thank you for last night."

Wilder halted.

"Even though I bawled all over you, it was nice to just... you know."

"My shirts are yours to ruin any time."

"Thanks," I said with a laugh. "I'm glad we're friends now, Wilder. There's a lot of exploring I plan to do in your mind."

He chuckled. "Little chance of that happening. We're not friends."

The bacon hung out in my mouth midchew. "What? What do you mean? What about last night?"

"Last night was great, but there's every chance you feigned interest in topics I like for the sole purpose of getting me to open up. A tactic you'd have been taught if my suspicions are correct and you didn't spend the last four years in a French Catholic school and instead were trained in covert ops."

My mouth fell at each word.

"I can't locate most of your records, half of your family history is unknown, and you only butter half a slice of toast when making a sandwich. I don't know what that last thing proves, but it's weird."

"What's weird about buttering half a slice of toast?" I cried. Of all the nonsense he said, that offended me. "And if you still don't trust me, why did you let me into your room, share those things with me, and—and— Why, Wilder?"

"Why?" He faced me, an expression on his face that I'd never seen before—heat. "Because you were wearing that dress and talking sci-fi. I didn't stand a chance." He shrugged. "I've got a weakness for beautiful women. Especially when they're looking so sad, I have to do something about it."

Wilder headed for the stairs. "I'll be ready in ten minutes. Again, don't touch anything that's not yours. I'll know."

He left me frozen in his wake. *"I've got a weakness for beautiful women."*

If I thought waking up to a Cato-sized body pillow was my biggest shock of the day, I could thank O'Rourke for fixing that.

"Lady Luna?" Lucien appeared in the hall between the kitchen and living room. "Your eggs are burning."

"Shit." I switched off the stove and scraped the charred remains of my breakfast in the trash.

I guess I am eating with Victor.

Our morning meetings still stood, but with access to a stove, I planned to eat beforehand, so we could keep it short. I was mixed up over our talk the other day.

He was mature and serious about our future, even going so far as to say he'd give me a divorce if we couldn't make it work, or an open marriage if I wanted that instead. While I was over here sleeping with the very guys he asked me to stay away from, and having fantasies of those guys that were very nonexclusive.

Was I into Rafael, Cato, Lucien, or Wilder? Could I be?

They were gorgeous, but handsome and flirty weren't two characteristics to risk an unhappy marriage on.

And Victor. Are we doomed from the start? The question of if I'm attracted to him isn't a question at all. Victor could cause a pileup even if he rolled out of bed with ratty hair, sleep in his eyes, and holes in his boxers. The conceited jackass became that way honestly. His mother should've dubbed him a god of beauty too.

Maybe I should give him a real chance. Why can't we—?

Victor in the closet getting his dick sucked, and Everleigh's hands running all over him behind the music hall crashed into my head.

Oh yeah, that's why he pisses me off.

"Luna." Lucien cupped the small of my back, tugging me out of my thoughts. My chest fluttered as he turned me, hands on my waist. "You don't have class between one and three. Is then a good time?"

My speech took a second to catch up. Lucien wore his usual wrong-century getup. I'd never tell him the fitted black pants and maroon velvet coat looked darkly sexy on him—like the mysterious prince living in the manor on the hill came down to see how hard I'd blush under his touch.

"A good time?"

"You said you wanted to be a part of it."

Understanding dawned. "Yes, I do. Are you sure I can help you? Wilder reminded me last night how important it is that no one can point the finger at me."

"They're not going to see me, so they won't see you."

"Then one o'clock. Let's do it."

I went upstairs, finished getting ready, and met Wilder on the front steps. Together we crossed campus for the café, talking our favorite sci-fi shows.

"None of these titles double as my passwords, by the way. Those are a series of random numbers and letters that change daily."

"I'm not spying on you, O'Rourke. What can I do to prove it to you?"

He hummed, turning his head to the sun and capturing golden light in his locks. I jumped when he spoke, realizing I was staring.

"You'd have to do something to compromise your mission. Then I'd know where your loyalties lie."

"But I don't have a mission, apart from the obvious one, and I won't be compromising that."

"Compromise your mission to infiltrate this upper-class community for the purposes of recovering trade, government, or family secrets that'll destabilize the country."

"Huh." We reached the steps to the cafeteria. "You mean like you are?"

Wilder stopped dead. "What?"

Grinning, I spun on the steps, facing him. "By your own admission, you're surveilling members of this upper-class society. You refuse to share details about your background. You're going to extreme lengths to conceal the information stashed away in your room. You conduct who knows what kind of business in the only room in the house I haven't been inside, and you've expressed anti-government sentiment on more than one occasion. If there's anyone suspicious around here, it's you, Wilder O'Rourke."

I flicked his nose and his jaw slackened like it was the lever. "But... I didn't..."

"You're not getting anything out of me until I know you can be trusted."

He nodded, teeth grinding. "Well played, Sinclair. Very well played."

I winked. "I know."

Spinning around, I made to leave.

"But just so you know, as sexy as that was, making me fall for you won't distract me from revealing your true purpose."

I tripped over my feet. Wilder strolled off as my stuttered reply was still making it through my head. I forced my feet to continue forward, heading inside the café and joining the line. Victor appeared at my side in a blink.

"Sinclair."

"Wilson."

We slowly moved up the line, me stealing glances at him when he wasn't looking. "So, we're just not going to talk about it," I blurted.

"Talk about what?"

"Owen, Levi, and those other guys. You said you were going to take care of it, then you walked off all tough. What did you do?"

"It's ongoing," Victor replied, stepping up to grab a tray. "I'll tell you when it's done."

"Why are you being mysterious? Just tell me."

"Why are you being impatient? Just wait."

I groaned. "I don't need you to fight my battles."

"No, you'll just think I'm a sexless coward if I don't."

My eyes popped. *Is this guy for real?* "Hey, you were the one who—!"

Victor sweetly cut in. "We don't fight in public, remember, honey pie?"

Huffing, I snatched up my tray and made a beeline for the cinnamon buns drizzled in chocolate hazelnut sauce. I could list a million awful things about this school, but their food wouldn't be on it.

Victor met back up with me at the drink station. He poured coffee while I opted for milk and shooting him dirty looks. And to think there was half a millisecond where I thought he might not be that bad.

Settling down at our table, we ate our breakfast in silence.

I should've given the eggs and bacon another try.

Victor smothered a laugh.

"What are you laughing at?"

He chuckled, silver pools shining with mirth. "I'm laughing at you."

"Me?" My hand flew to my face, checking if there was something on it. "For what?"

"Did you know you make this kind of moany, snorty sound when you eat something good?"

"I do not," I cried.

"Oh yeah, you do." He snorted, mimicking me, and nearly toppled his chair cracking up. "Like a happy little piggy."

Embarrassment melted me into a puddle on the leather. "I will take you down in this café in front of all your friends."

Breathless, he threw up his hands in surrender. "Hey, I didn't say it wasn't cute. You can be my happy piggy all you want, Luna Sinclair."

And then the puddle evaporated and reduced to vapors escaping in any direction as fast as they could. If there's something to say in response to that, I didn't know it.

"You going to let me try one of those cinnamon buns?"

His grin was doing weird things to my body temperature. Let him try it? I was about to have them checked for tampering. Wilder may have had a point about eating in this place.

"I'm not sure," I replied, forcing an even tone. "I'm still considering choosing violence."

"It's inevitable that I'll grow on you." Victor helped himself to my bun, painting his lips with icing and chocolate, then swiping his tongue over the treat as my legs clenched under the table. "As annoying, arrogant, and spoiled as you think I am, it won't change a thing. You falling for me is going to happen. But I'm still curious how you plan to win my heart, honey pie. I'm not a cheap date."

This is our game, Luna. Play it. Keep a cool head in, and your feelings out.

"Pretty sure I don't have to do much," I breezed. "Just flashing you my boobs will get you in a closet with your pants down."

He held up his hand. "I say we test that theory."

Biting my lip, I penned in a laugh. "I get it. I should put in as much effort as you to make this work." *Despite being blackmailed into this engagement in the first place.*

"Does Friday night dinner count for sixty percent of the effort? Because your mother has perfected making a person feel small in five words or less."

"That's her superpower," Victor said, chuckling. "While Dad has perfected carrying on a conversation without listening to a word you're saying. It's almost frightening how well he maintains eye contact and nods in the right places. But in his head, he's calculating stock prices and planning his next fishing trip. I've gotten him to agree to give me three cars, a ski trip to Aspen, and a wet bar in my room. The last one was an overreach and Mom lost her shit... in five words or less."

I couldn't stop that laugh. We went back and forth, trading funny parent stories until the clock reminded us we had class.

Adonis was where I expected to find him on a Wednesday morning, setting up the PowerPoint for that day's lecture. I placed my paper in his tray with a smirk he noticed and raised a brow at.

"You seem confident, Miss Sinclair."

"I am, Professor Anthony. I put a lot of thought into this paper."

"I'm abuzz with excitement," he said, rounding his desk and the obstruction between us. "Can't wait to read it."

"Even though you're not grading these anymore, when you read mine, you'll be forced to give me an A."

A deep, rolling laugh emerged from his chest. "Is it a good idea to build it up so highly?"

"That's how confident I am. You—"

An arm hooked me around my waist, carrying me off. "I'll catch you after class, Don," Victor called over his shoulder. "Honey pie." Said in that tone, it couldn't be mistaken for a term of endearment. "I thought we discussed you flirting with my brother."

I gave him a crazy look. "That depends on if you define having a normal, human conversation with him as flirting."

"You made him laugh. Don doesn't get chuckly and chummy when he's got his tie on, proving to the world he's not too young and pampered to be taken seriously in his field."

Despite his accusations, Victor plopped down next to my usual seat.

"I don't know what to tell you. We were talking about the paper. That's it," I said. "Also, I have to remind you again that he'll be my brother-in-law. We should be chummy."

He grunted, making me roll my eyes.

Victor dropped it, so I did too. We listened and took notes for the rest of class, then packed up and headed for the next one. After biology, I had a nice gap until my calculus class. A gap where Lucien and I would move forward with my only mission—secret or otherwise: destroying Owen, Levi, Wesley, and Giovanni.

Our bio professor was usually among the last to arrive—flying inside minutes before the clock called time, and mumbling like he just left behind important work, and was continuing it in his head until he was done wasting time with a college freshman class.

Walking inside to find him seated at his desk with a stack of papers wasn't good news. It meant he pulled himself out of the experiment or academic paper to plan something we weren't going to like.

"Everyone get settled in," Professor Rhinebeck called. "Today I'm assigning our first group project."

I stifled a groan, trudging to my stool in the back with Victor. If the group was bigger than one and I couldn't be paired with Victor, this project would be a disaster. My classmates had not warmed to me. The Royals kept coming on to my fiancé. The Dregs tried to get me expelled. Both groups used me for target practice. I didn't want to think of the new ways they'd mess with me if I was forced to interact with them and they had my grade in their hands.

Setting my bag down, I hopped on my stool, already thinking of a way to make the project less of a disaster.

Eeeeeee

A crack sounded in my ear, and my seat pitched to the side. I screamed, scrabbling for the tabletop as the legs gave way—dropping me on a pile of splintered wood. Momentum tossed me feet over head, bouncing my skull off the tile. The world washed in pain, crowding in blinding, dizzying light to block it out. One sound brought me out of the haze: laughter.

"Luna? Luna!" Victor toppled off his chair, pushing my skirt and legs down, and helping me sit up.

Dazed, my senses delayed—leaving me limp in his arms as my classmates crowded in, laughing their asses off as people stuck cameras in my face.

"That's enough! Back to your seats now." This was the first I heard Professor Rhinebeck's bellow. "Anyone who is not in their seat in five seconds receives a zero on this project!"

Victor was holding me, asking if I was okay and checking me for injury. I didn't respond as he and Rhinebeck lifted me up and I saw the remains of my chair.

Clean cuts.

This was no accident. Someone sawed the legs so they would snap.

Acid eroded my chest as I passed through the smirking, laughing faces. Victor and the Rogues stopped them messing with me outside of class. Leave it to the best and brightest of the American education system to find a way around that.

I WAITED ON THE BENCH, dialing and redialing my mom. The calls rang out, beeping in my ear, and then cut out to a cheery message asking me to leave my name and number, so she could call me back.

Maybe that's the real reason I kept calling though she never answered her phone these days. I liked remembering the time she was happy.

"Luna."

I looked up as Lucien descended the hill, a lion-headed cane gripped in his hand. He met me in my cool, tree-shaded secluded spot.

"I heard what happened."

My lips pressed tight together. "Course you did," I forced out. "This was texted to me, and I assume the entire school, thirty minutes after it happened."

Flipping the phone around, I showed him the cameraman's lucky shot. Someone got me just as I hit the floor and my skirt flew up, flashing my blue boy shorts covered in little ducks. The photo even came with a caption: Rubber Duck Butt.

"We can do this tomorrow if you—"

"No," I broke in. "Trust me, Lucien, this is exactly what I need to be doing right now."

He sat next to me, taking the phone. "Who sent this to you?"

"Iris."

"Iris Dalton. Daughter of James and Gemma Dalton. Granddaughter of Richard Dalton." Leaning back, Lucien crossed his ankle over his knee and draped an arm over my back. He thought nothing of tugging me close and laying my head on his shoulder, and I thought nothing of snuggling in close. "I knew her grandfather when he was a young, brash twenty-three-year-old looking to make his fortune any way he could. Including building it on the backs of unpaid, undocumented labor who he shuffled from warehouse to warehouse. The one where he made them work, and the one where they were locked in at night."

"Oh my gosh, are you saying he trafficked people into slave labor?"

"That's exactly what I'm saying, Lady Luna."

"But, how do you know this? Does everyone know?"

Lucien absentmindedly stroked his pendant. "I found out when he brought a woman in labor into my great-grandson's clinic. The kid was his, and I guess he felt something in his dead heart for her or the baby, because he brought her in after hours of pushing and the kid not coming.

"It was obvious she wasn't well. Dirty, underfed, jumping at sudden moves. I did some digging and found out about his sick operation."

"What did you do?" I asked. Not for a second did I believe these events happened to him, but if Lucien was claiming the memories of his grandfather as his own, I still wanted to know how this story ends. "I got the police involved—discretely. What he was doing was illegal, but so were the clinics I was running. The cops couldn't know how we got involved."

Lucien sighed. "Not that my efforts mattered. The cops took my tip, and then they took his bribe—looking the other way."

"Are you serious? They didn't do anything?"

"Oh, they did plenty to cover his tracks and make reports disappear in exchange for a nice cut. But actually do their fucking jobs? No." Lucien stroked my temple, fingers skating along my ear and caressing the nape of my neck.

My eyes fluttered shut against my will. His touch was doing more for my pounding headache than the two pain pills and an ice pack.

"It was a different time, Luna. A couple of white men exploiting unprotected people of color were just continuing the tradition of their forefathers. No one cared about them," he said, "so I broke into Richard Dalton's house one night and beat him until he bled and I was fed. I told him to free the people working for him and send them off with enough money to start over. If I ever got wind he shorted a single paycheck, I'd be back for his children and his children's children. I didn't have to come back. He got the message."

"Wow," I breathed. Even replacing vampire Lucien with his human grandfather, that was an amazing thing that man did for those people—fighting for them when no one else would. And Victor said it was the Rogues with the shady legacies in Regalia. "That's incredible, Lucien, but what's it have to do with Iris?"

"No one cared then, lovely, but now..." He whistled. "Imagine the headlines: *Dalton's Luxury Legacy Built on the Back of Slave Labor*. It's a PR nightmare and it won't get better when the illegitimate son that he cast out, comes to light. Their money is tainted. Their reputations and standing in the community—tainted.

"Iris doesn't care about kindness, decency, or other people in general. But she's a Royal, and they *all* care about their reputation in Regalia. The story breaks and so do the ties to her family. Everyone will distance themselves from them, and her status drops to barely above Dreg." He tipped my chin, gaze piercing me. "Say the word and the whole world knows by morning."

I considered for half a second. "Do it. This isn't about if she messed with my chair, it's about the truth. If her shit bucket of a grandfather built his business on human trafficking and police corruption, the world should know. That's why none of this stops, Lucien. Because their evil lives in the dark."

"Not anymore." He threaded his fingers through mine, rubbing slow circles between my thumb and finger. My head started pounding for a different reason. "Owen, Levi, Giovanni, and Wesley are coming out of the dark."

I stared at our linked hands, and the ring on my finger. "Lucien, I'm engaged," I blurted.

"I was aware, my lady, but it's nice to hear it from your lips."

I blew out a breath. "You've been around long enough to watch the Royals arrange marriages and then break those engagements off. I don't know what's going to happen between me and Victor, but he's been trying and..." I pulled my hand away. "I have to try too. Us sitting on a bench, cuddling and holding hands, would not make him happy."

"What would make you happy?"

Holding up my end of the deal with Jack, so Winter is avenged. I can sacrifice a lot, but not my sister. I won't let her down again.

"If Levi, Giovanni, Owen, Wesley, and that disgusting shit sack of a man were dead."

The corner of his mouth curled. "On that note, let's start making their graves look more attractive."

Lucien helped me up and off we went, slipping through the trees and approaching Lyon Hall from the back. Five stories of brick, arched windows, single-person dorms, full-size common kitchen, and a theater room complete with reclining leather chairs, big screen, and popcorn maker. Lyon Hall was dubbed the best and most coveted dorm for a reason. Outside of the frat and sorority houses where they lavished even more luxury on you, everyone who applied to Regalia University wanted to be assigned Lyon Hall.

Which is why it was exclusively Royal, and the dorm of Giovanni and Wesley.

"What about the cameras?" Two hung over the back door, pointed smack at the doorknob.

"The cameras turn on and off based on who is paying Eugene the most at the time. If it's the university, they're on. If it's me, they're down for maintenance." Lucien strode up bold as ever and swung open the door. "After you."

Excitement building, I hurried to catch up, sticking my head in the entrance. There was no one in the sweet-smelling, red-carpeted hallway. Voices and music floated under the door cracks.

"What if someone sees us? Your outfit is pretty distinctive, Calais."

He chuckled. "Trust me, those guys aren't going to ask if anyone saw a vampire in the halls the day this all went down. They'll have bigger problems to worry about." Lucien gestured with his chin. "This way."

Silent as death, Lucien climbed the back staircase to the third floor. I was not as quiet—my footsteps bouncing off the concrete and my breaths basically gusts of wind, they sounded so loud in my ears. We stopped on the landing, chancing another check for anyone loitering in the halls.

It was clear.

"Wesley is 309 and Giovanni is 314," Lucien said. "Want to split up?"

"Are you sure they're not in there?"

"We're in the same class. We've got physics this hour and I made sure they were both there before I slipped out the back."

I considered it, then shook my head. "I want to see you in action."

"Then follow me," he said with a laugh.

"How are we going to—?"

Lucien plucked a leather case from the folds of his tailcoat. I marveled watching him pick the lock. Fifteen seconds and I heard the click.

"Will you teach me how to do that?"

"I'll teach you anything you like."

I warmed under the collar. A harmless response, but my traitorous imagination summoned dozens of dirty examples of the things a man with a long life, no consequences, and decades of experience could teach me. Lucien wasn't a vampire, but doesn't every girl have an Edward Cullen fantasy?

Again Lucien gestured for me to go in first. Wesley's room was cleaner than I expected—very clean. Shelves built in a staircase design went up and down his four walls, displaying a high-end sneaker collection. Thousands of dollars' worth of product hanging out in a dorm room, and there wasn't a speck of dust on a lace.

His four-poster queen-size bed was neatly made. The rug vacuumed. The pencils on his desk lined in a row, and a look in the bathroom proved it was immaculate.

"I guess if a guy can plan all those accidents injuring and nearly killing my sister," I said, lips curled, "he can figure out a vacuum and dust rag."

"He'll also notice if something is out of place," Lucien replied. "We have to put everything back exactly the way it was."

Lucien was so serious about this, he had me take pictures of everything before we moved it. I didn't argue with him. They had this all planned for the guys to suffer at the highest possible pain for the maximum amount of time. Thor forbid I do anything to rob them of that gift.

Lucien lifted the desk chair and placed it in the middle of the room. "Now comes the easy part."

He climbed on, his cane clutched in his hand. Carefully, he lifted a ceiling panel, pulled a small, round object from his coat, and—

Thunk.

The speaker landed somewhere above me.

"I've got five more for him and another six for Giovanni," Lucien said. "Spread them around."

I claimed my three, going straight for the closet. Speaker number two found its place behind a shoebox. "What about Levi and Owen? They're still in the hospital, but when they get out, we're doing this to them too, right?"

"When they get out from the hospital, my dear, they'll pray we send them back."

"Perfect."

Lucien and I hid his speakers all over Wesley's and Giovanni's rooms. Some in obvious hiding places and others in spots they wouldn't think to look.

We shut the door on Giovanni's.

"From here, Wilder does what he does," Lucien said. "I hope you don't have plans tonight. I'd be honored if you attended a movie with me."

Lucien offered me his elbow which I happily slid an arm through. "It'd be my pleasure."

"SNUGGLE UP WITH ME, darling." Rafael patted the spot beside him on the couch. "I've got your caramel popcorn right here."

I laughed, running and bouncing down next to him. "Luring me in with caramel popcorn. Effective."

"I'll keep that in mind."

I nudged him. "Am I going to have to give you the same speech? I can't fall prey to your spinning web of flirtiness while this ring is on my finger."

"Hmm." Rafael leaned back in his seat, dropping it faster than normal.

"Hmm what?"

"You said *can't* fall prey to me instead of *won't*. Word choice is everything, Sinclair."

"I meant won't," I said quickly.

Rafael sang back, "But it's not what you said."

"I'm about to take my popcorn and go."

"And you'd come back," he said, "because I've got this too."

Rafael reached down beside the couch and revealed two cans of my favorite peach soda. I swiped at one and he tipped out of the way, making me fall across his lap and spill half the popcorn. We cracked up—me so light and happy like I could only be before I brought pain to Royals.

Lucien and Cato were set up in their seats. A sandwich and a bowl of pills for Cato. Lucien's snack of choice was that glass of red liquid. I hadn't yet found the courage to ask what it was.

Moving back and forth behind the television, Wilder connected wires, fiddled with technical stuff, and hooked up two laptops to the big screen.

"It's up," Wilder announced.

On cue, the television turned on, displaying split-screen video of two darkened figures on a mattress, lit up by moonlight.

Wilder dropped next to me, passing over a laptop.

"Ready?"

"I'm ready."

He pointed. "That key for Wesley. That one for Giovanni."

I bashed them both. Viking metal blared out of the speakers—ear-pounding in our living room, even worse in theirs.

"Fuck!"

"What the—!"

The lumps shot out of bed, one of them tipping off and crashing to the floor. I lifted my fingers just as Wesley and Giovanni snapped on their lights. Wesley whipped around, chest heaving as he struggled to figure out what caused that sound. His pajama bottoms were half up his ass from the wedgie he gave himself falling out of the bed.

Giovanni was having the same reaction, except he was butt-ass naked and his bedmate Annika was freaking out along with him.

"I didn't know she'd be there," I said around a mouthful of popcorn, "but it's a lovely bonus."

Rafael adopted a deep, announcer's voice. "It's the look of confusion on Giovanni's stupid face that gets me. *What was that noise? What is noise? Wow, is that what I look like with bed head?*

"What are your thoughts, Luce?"

"It's Wesley that concerns me, Rafa," Lucien replied, the both of them teasing giggles out of me. "He ran back and forth from the bed to the door five times now. I believe he's literally had the sense scared out of him."

I jabbed the buttons again, making all three of them clap their hands over their heads—mouths open in shouts I didn't hear over the music. My laugh rang out through the Gallery. "This is amazing. Wilder, how does it work? How'd you even come up with it?"

"This was a joint collaboration, Sinclair," Wilder said. "Rafael thought it up."

Rafael swept out his arms. "No one knows the misery of relentless, discordant sounds more than me."

"Cato chased the guy out of the store, so Lucien could steal the speakers." Lucien bowed in his seat. Cato went on with his meal, fixed on the show. "I hacked into their computers, turned on their webcams, and linked with the Bluetooth speakers hidden in their rooms. Oh, and Cato did one more thing that should be obvi— Ah, there he goes."

Wesley made his choice, racing to the door. He twisted the knob, and nothing. Yanking, pulling, and throwing his weight back, Wesley strained to get out. The door didn't budge.

"Cato, you locked them in," I said, grinning wide. "I love you."

"Love you too," he replied without skipping a beat—taking a needle to my happy balloon and a flush down my neck. Did a guy just tell me he loved me for the first time and I had no idea if he meant it seriously or jokingly?

Yes, that's exactly what happened to this milestone in my life.

And this is the part where I move on like nothing happened, and obsess about it later.

I didn't sleep that night, and to my delight, neither did Annika, Wesley, or Giovanni. For about half an hour, they pounded and hollered at the door, calling for help. They did try calling on their phones, of course, but unfortunately for them, Wilder rerouted them to a number that rang endlessly and never picked up.

After both these attempts failed, they tried getting some sleep. I blared the music again until Giovanni lost it and threw his chair at the door.

He had no one but himself to blame for so many reasons. Just because he was a lying sack of duplicitous scum, but also because he had to have the best dorm on campus, and Lyon Hall rooms were soundproofed.

The boys all passed out long before me—Rafael's leg pressed against mine, and my untrusting Wilder's head on my shoulder.

I stared at my captives—tiredness pressed at the back of my eyes and film layered my mouth from too much soda and popcorn. Over and over I pressed the buttons, my smile huge and curled into aching cheeks.

TWO HOURS LATER, THEIR banging got the attention of someone passing in the hallway. I figured this out when the door flew open and three guards poured in.

It's the only reason I let Rafael drag me away, promising that if I liked the night before, I'd love what he planned for Giovanni that night.

After grabbing a quick shower and bite to eat, I floated to my first class of the day—Cato by my side. For weeks and months, I thought of nothing but making the five men on the top of my list suffer till they begged for death. That my soul was warped beyond saving wasn't lost on me. I didn't miss the girl I was before. I just missed her big sister.

Fingers probed my skull. I hissed as he brushed over the bump.

"Fuckers got me good." I gently drew his hand away, letting ours swing between us. "I am fine. The nurse checked me for signs of concussion. What really gets me is I don't know for sure who it was. Saylor said I had the week to reconsider tossing Victor back into the Royal dating pool. If I didn't, life would become twice as miserable for me here.

"I can believe sad little Royals would torment me to suck up to her, but I don't get why the Dregs would join in. It's not just Royals throwing drinks in my face, and it wasn't a Royal who almost got me expelled. A Dreg could've messed with my chair too, but again why? I've seen the way Saylor treats other Royals, let alone the Dregs.

"Saylor and her friends are awful to them, so what's the upside to bullying someone else to make your bully happy?"

"Because maybe then they stop bullying you."

Said so simply and matter of fact, the statement stopped me in my tracks. "Do you really think that's it?" I breathed. "Like how the Royals play this stupid game of status? Life gets easier for a Dreg if they do their bidding."

My gut churned. "So that's why *none* of them helped Winter. Fuck, that's why they participated! Better some random former housekeeper's daughter than one of them."

Cato's fingers glided down my cheek. "You're crying."

I hadn't noticed I was until he said.

"Here." Opening my hand, Cato placed something on my palm. My brows popped at the lighter. "They make you sad. Make you cry." He closed my fingers tight. "They can't do that if they're burning."

A shiver skittered up my spine. Cato Dumont was so many things behind his muzzle, but his stays in psychiatric hospitals were no accident.

I tasted the darkness in him. Watched it grow as a black-and-white movie on my mental screen. A young, handsome boy raised in money, amorality, and violence. An explosion rips his mother out of his life and not one, but two brothers are forever changed. Both driven to conquer pain and flames. Both courting brutality at the end of their marionette strings. Neither one of them subscribing to society's sense of morals or sanity.

I don't know when exactly our life scripts intersected, but I knew it was long before we met.

I slipped the lighter in my bag. "Thank you, Cato."

He walked me to the door of the anthropology classroom, us arriving seconds after Victor. Wilson's usual *I'm God's gift to the world* grin faltered at the sight of my silent shadow in the muzzle. I waved bye to Cato, waiting for it to come.

"What happened to staying away from the Rogues?"

"I never agreed to that, Victor."

He threw an irritated look at the spot Cato was standing. "Why would you even want to hang around them? You're still giving me dirty looks for hooking up with someone after knowing you for three whole hours? Those guys sell their services to the highest bidder, but they're cool? Are you going to keep up this twisted logic after we're married?"

"Most likely."

Victor pinched the bridge of his nose, turning up to the ceiling for help.

Cupping his cheeks, I brought him back down, making him meet my eyes. "Have you considered that maybe the reason I won't dump the Rogues is because if I do, I won't have a single friend on this campus? Besides Katie," I added. "Who only half counts since she bullies me in other ways.

"You may not get this because you fit in wherever you go, but it's hard to get sneered at in every room you walk into. They're nice to me, okay?" I dropped my hands. "So I'm not shaking them loose—even if it causes problems between us. If it does, that's not a great sign. A good fiancé would care more about me being surrounded by good friends. Not how those friends affect his reputation."

Something flashed across his face, too quick for me to pick it up. "Ever think it's your reputation I'm worried about?"

I smiled to ease the tension. "I have considered that, and if it is the reason, I might have to call you the *s*-word. Which would be weird for me to say and you to hear."

"What's the *s*-word? Shithead? Because you've called me worse."

"No, it's sweet," I cried, swatting his arm. "I would think it was sweet if you were looking out for me. Come on, Victor. I'm not that bad. I can give you credit when it's due."

He screwed up his face. "Uhhhh..."

"I can! Look, I gave you a hard time before, but it's been nice you walking me to and from class, getting your demon friends off my back. And yesterday when I fell off the chair, you were all gallant rushing me to the infirmary and waiting while Nurse Gale checked me out. It was *sweet*," I drew out, "and I appreciate it."

"This is the end, isn't it? This is the sign of the apocalypse."

"Oh my goodness, you're such an ass," I groaned.

Victor breathed a sigh, face smoothing out. "Whew, good. You're back."

"Get out of the way."

A hard shove propelled me at Victor. He caught me, arms encircling instinctively and pulling me in rather than back on my feet.

"Iris, what is your problem? Were you always like this, or did I miss your transformation into Saylor?"

I faced her as she sniffed. Two of her friends flanked her, readying for the showdown outside anthropology that nobody asked for today. "You wish you were a Burkhardt, then you wouldn't worry about your mother forcing a bottom-barrel fiancée on you eight years early to wipe away the stink of getting a girl pregnant."

A roaring sounded in my ears. *Pregnant?*

"—not true! I didn't get anyone pregnant. June left to study abroad, not to have my kid, and she's as fucking tired of those rumors as I am. Someone started it to take the Wilsons down, but that's not going to happen, neither is it getting between me and my fiancée."

"Aww, you sure about that? Because she looks upset."

I swallowed hard, struggling to smooth out my expression.

"Did you not know about the youngest Wilson, or do you not even know what's happening right now? You've got a blank, stupid expression on your face. Are you still messed up from that hit to the head, Rubber Duck Butt?"

I found my voice. "I am a little achy, thank you for asking. But luckily, I didn't have as bad a fall as the one that fucked up your face, so I'll recover."

Iris's friend snorted. She cut it off quick, slapping a hand over her mouth, but from the red-hot rage on Iris's face, she wasn't pleased.

"You're not very smart, Sinclair. How many ways do we have to say it? We're over our limit of gold-digging Dregs latching on to the first Royal dick they find to save them from the double-wide trailer in Duck Butt, Nebraska. You don't belong here, so leave," she gritted, erasing the distance. "Sooner or later, we'll stop asking nicely."

Victor moved between us. "Back off, Iris, and that is me asking nice. Find out from Thompkins, Thasher, Johnson, Madden, Brown, and Jones what happens if I ask again."

"Victor, it's okay." I grasped his arm and draped it over my shoulder, smirking at the spark of anger in her eyes. "Iris is lashing out because her family is today's headline, and the photo they used is not her best angle."

"What are you talking about?"

Shrugging, I led Victor off. Without talking about it, we grabbed seats together in the third row, far from where I usually sat. I didn't know when we landed on sitting together in every class.

"Cute panties, Sinclair." Chester—a tall, dark-haired Dreg who was among the first to snap pictures of my underwear—twisted in the seat in front of me to show them off. "Are the ducks wearing little rain boots? Can I see—?"

Victor flung his phone at the wall, raining bits on two shrieking girls. "Say one more fucking word to her, and it's your face in that wall next!"

Not another word was said.

No, I didn't know when we decided to sit together every time, but I was starting not to mind.

"This isn't true!" Iris sounded from the hall. "My grandfather would never do these things. Illegitimate son?!"

I relaxed in my seat—content.

Let them bang on about rubber duck underwear. Wesley, Annika, and Giovanni had a terrible night and Iris was in for a bad day. Everything was turning up roses for me.

I WAS IN MY LAST CLASS of the day, taking up a row in the back by myself. Victor didn't have Intro to Psych, though he did walk me to class and say goodbye by asking if my rubber duck underwear was a sample of my taste in lingerie, because if it was, he knew what he was gifting me the night of our wedding. I tapped into my inner Cato, chasing him out the door.

It boggled my mind that the guy who defended me one minute could become such a rubber duck butthead the next.

My psych class was smaller and filled with less irritating people. No Eva, Iris, Alice, or Rose. Just fifteen students and one teacher coming in, focusing on the lesson, and behaving like this was a professional environment and not every bad high school clique movie ever made. It was no wonder this was my favorite class.

Silence blanketed the room, broken only by the occasional cough or Professor Burgess's squeaky marker as she wrote on the board. I breezed through my quiz, marking the answers on functionalism and structuralism, while my mind wandered back to Iris shrieking that her human sewer rat of a grandfather was an honorable, upstanding man who laid the bricks in the foundation of Regalia and the country.

All right, she didn't say the last part, but with how thick she was laying it on with their family's charity work, how generously their company treats their employees, the lack of proof, and what a friend Grandpa Dalton has been to everyone in the community. By the end of her speech, *we* were the jerks for believing the horrible lies in the news.

In between replaying her splotchy, furious face, I pictured her smirk over Victor's secret love child.

That can't be true, can it? Just a vicious rumor like Victor said—thought up by someone trying to smear his reputation.

His reputation as a rich, handsome playboy who drops his pants for any pair of tits walking by, a harsh voice reminded. *Knocking a girl up would fit in with that reputation, not ruin it.*

I shook my head, refocusing to answer the last question and flip my paper over. Staring at the blank page, my thoughts flooded back.

Is that the real reason his parents got on board with marrying off their eighteen-year-old son to the tire king's stepdaughter—the kindest title I was given. It wasn't about his father's health or proving he was responsible enough to run a company.

But how would marrying me help him? I'm not the one carrying his kid. A shiny new stepmom wouldn't make him less of an irresponsible dick who didn't step up for his child.

If there is a child. Rumors about pregnancies tend to prove themselves in approximately nine months. From the conversation, *June* took her studies to another country. If she came back with an auburn-haired, gray-eyed bundle of chub, then there's something to talk about. But if not, I wasted precious time out of my life worrying about something that came out of Iris's poisonous mouth.

How do I know what's true?

My hands clenched beneath the desk, fists pressing to my stomach to force the deep breath I sucked in to release. A sick heaviness was pressing on my gut, making the room spin.

So many people in so many ways—one of those people being myself—have questioned why on earth a family with such high standing would arrange this match. What if there was more to this than what Victor told me? What if I could find out the real reason?

"No one on this campus knows more than me."

The heavy feeling lifted and a new, worse one crept in. I was living with four men who made it their business to know everything going on in Regalia. Wilder drained bank accounts without breaking a sweat. He tracked everything the Royals did.

What has he dug up on the Wilsons?

It'd be so simple just to ask. To have Wilder hack into their phone and computers, or take a peek through their security cameras. What if there was a record of the deal his parents made with Jack? A contract stating he becomes the tire supplier to NASCAR seconds after the I dos, then stated on the bottom, what the Wilsons get in return.

It's not like men and women don't check up on their other half all the time. People run background checks. They do their due diligence before marrying a complete stranger.

Someone came in the room and spoke to Professor Burgess in low tones.

"Miss Sinclair?"

Torn out of my thoughts, I heeded her gesture for me to come up to the front.

"The financial office closes in an hour," she said. "It seems there's an issue with your dorm refund and one of the staff is asking you to come in and resolve it. Have you finished your quiz?"

"Yes, I'm done."

"Then you're free to go. The notes on the rest of the lecture will be available on the portal tonight."

"Thank you, Professor Burgess."

The messenger was a tall, sturdy girl in a button-down top and black pants. I grabbed my stuff and followed her out into the hall.

"Did they say what the issue was?"

"No, but my guess is Florence is going to tell you in person that you can't get a refund," she tossed over her shoulder. "The cutoff for that passed."

I sighed. "Yeah, I'd guess that too."

My attention wandered back to Victor, and my hand wandered to my phone. Pulling it out of my backpack, I pulled up Rafael's name and hovered over the message button.

I shouldn't think of it like I'm breaking Victor's trust. What I'm doing is proving I can trust him. Proving that he's worth the commitment he's asking of me. Proving I'll find something to love within those five years. When put like that, I have to ask Rafael to spy on my fiancé.

We left the building, strolling down the wide concrete path to administration. I hit *message*, started to type, and then closed out.

What good would come of digging up the Wilsons' secrets? Even if there is a mini-Victor floating around, knowing about them wouldn't change a thing. Jack won't pay for Regalia U unless I walk down that aisle.

The plan is finally moving forward. The Royal Bastards are facing their punishment one after the other. Now isn't the time to find out something that makes it impossible to look Victor in the face. The time for that is after the five of them are dead.

Worrying my lip, I pulled up Rafael again. *Maybe just a quick check to make sure there are no Robert Dalton-sized skeletons in his—*

"On your left."

A hard force struck me in the back. I fell smack on the concrete, face bouncing off the ground and phone flying out of my hand. Vision blurred, I didn't see the gray mass coming until it was on top of me.

Bike wheels ran over my wrist.

"Ahh!"

"Oops," a voice said. "Sorry, Dreg, but when you lie on the ground like that, it's easy to mistake you for trash."

"Oh, no."

"Is she okay?"

Pain racked my body, stealing air from my lungs faster than I breathed it in. I strained to move—lift myself as figures surrounded me.

"Let me help you," cried the financial aid office messenger. She ran to me, tore my bag off my arm, and dumped the contents on my head.

"Stop!" They snatched my binder, textbooks, folders, and papers off me—ripping and shredding them apart. "Stop it!"

Iris, Eva, Alice, Rose, girls from the sophomore class, and girls I didn't know piled on—screaming, cursing, showering me in glossy paper confetti.

"Slutbag Dreg!"

"Stealing our guys!"

"Get the fuck out of our school!"

Iris tangled in my hair, wrenching my neck around to glare in her hate-filled eyes. "It was supposed to be me and Victor." Spittle showered my cheek. "Our engagement's been unofficial since we were five. I waited while he fucked all those other sluts! Then *you* came out of nowhere and now he hates me!"

Swinging blind, I struck her across the temple. Iris reared back and kicked me in the stomach. The hit reverberated through my system, twisting me in on myself and stunning my lungs.

"No one had to dare me to kick your ass," Iris spat. "It's my pleasure." She snatched my last surviving page of calculus homework, ripped it up and threw it on my face. "Stay away from Victor."

They walked off without sparing me another glance. I lay there—wheezing, wrist throbbing, wetness pressing behind my eyes. In the distance, four girls, each prettier than the last, watched me from the steps of the psych building.

I could do nothing as Piper, Gabriella, Everleigh, and Saylor approached, crushing my things beneath their Prada shoes.

"Hmm, she doesn't look so tough now," Gabriella mused.

"Tell me, Sinclair," Everleigh said, "is Victor worth this?"

Saylor crouched beside me. I cried out as she snatched my bad hand, forcing the engagement ring off my finger. "This is for you." Something dropped next to my head. "Be punctual."

"Y-you..." I rasped. "You'll... pay—"

"There's one more thing I was supposed to do," Saylor said. "Piper, what was it—? Oh yeah, this."

Saylor punched me in the face. My skull bounced on the concrete, black spots dancing in my vision.

"We're done here, ladies. Let's go. Douglas is waiting with the car."

I lay there long after they left. Dozens of students passed by, but no one helped.

Chapter Ten

"**A**re you sure you're up for this?"

Rafael helped me off the bed. Despite the question, he held up my jacket for me to put my arms through. "I'm watching the whole thing from a distance. You can too from the comfort of your sheets."

"No," I mumbled. Every word out of me stumbled over my busted, swollen lip. "I want to come."

"You have a broken wrist."

"Bruised." I shuffled across the carpet, wedging my feet in a pair of flats. "Ice, rest, and a few days in the brace and I'll be fine. Let's just go, Rafael. I've been waiting for this all day. I won't..."

I trailed off as a warm hand caressed the back of my head. "We should've been there."

"They planned it so you guys and Victor *wouldn't* be there. Lured me right out of class into their ambush. Saylor said it'd only get worse for me." My eyes fluttered shut under his touch. "It'll take me all night to redo those assignments. And the textbooks. The shopping spree emptied my bank account. My stepfather won't give me more money until the end of the semester. If I tell him I need more because the Burberry Bitches attacked and shredded my books, he'll stop paying my tuition—deal or no deal."

"You have a deal so he'll pay your tuition? Because they didn't want you coming here after Winter," Rafael said, getting it in one. "Neither of those things is a problem. I'll pay to replace your textbooks."

"You don't have to—"

"I wasn't there to protect you, Luna." The hard edge in his tone smothered my denial. "I do have to. At the very least, let me keep you here, so I can protect you always."

I held my hand over my heart, and Winter's letter. It wasn't safe to have it on me these days, but then more than ever, I needed my sister with me.

"You guys have taken me in like a little wounded bird," I whispered. "Why do you care so much about me?"

"Don't ask me why we're not like those shits who walked past you like you weren't there."

I winced. "I'm sorry, I just— I want to go, Rafael. Turn this into a good day. Please."

"That I can do." A kiss pressed to my temple. "Give me ten minutes. I'll be back."

Ten minutes turned into thirty. A knock sounded on my frame as I sat at my new desk, redoing my homework. A glance at the clock read eleven.

Rafael was a figure cloaked in shadows. They disappeared into his midnight-blue shirt and black pants, and formed a halo around his headphones, a dark crown for a dark prince.

"Is it time?"

"It's time."

Rafael helped me up, encircling my waist and taking my hand in his. I let him hold me. Be kind to me. Comfort me. I needed it after crawling across the concrete, a certainty settling in my bones that the world had none of either left.

Rafael helped me downstairs and across campus to his car. I would've whistled at the black Grand Sport Bugatti taking up two spaces, preventing anyone from parking too close, but my lip hurt at the thought.

We didn't say much as he turned down the unlit road, putting Regalia University in our rearview. It didn't occur to me to fill the silence. Rafael's whole world was noise. I'd let him have quiet and he'd give me my revenge.

I rested my forehead against the cool glass, a soft sigh fogging my sight. A lot could be said about the town of Regalia. It's exclusive, snobbish, unwelcoming. But no one would ever say it wasn't beautiful.

The trees were losing their green and gifting the seaside town a blanket of reds, oranges, and burnished golds as their final farewell to autumn. Mansions towered in the horizon, but it wasn't just the soaring spires, rising columns, and dancing topiaries on their grand estates that lent Regalia its beauty.

It was the willow trees stretching their branches across the road, their limbs entwining like laced fingers, hiding where one began and the other ended. It was the rolling hills, historic structures, cobblestone streets, and a memory of a time I was happy here with my two favorite people—giggling as Mom chased me and Winter through the park.

Rafael laid his hand over mine, bringing me out of my musing. "The letter," he said. "What does it say?"

My jaw clenched. Removing Saylor's parting gift from my pocket, I read the swirly name written on the embossed envelope: Luna Sinclair.

"I don't know," I replied. "I haven't opened it yet. Maybe it's my transfer papers—prefilled."

"Only one way to find out."

Why not? What's it matter now?

Sliding my finger under, I broke the seal and pulled out the note. I frowned, reading it once, twice, three times.

"Luna Sinclair," I read, "you are cordially invited to the home of Saylor Burkhardt on the night of Saturday, September Twenty-Ninth at eight thirty p.m. This invitation grants you admittance, present it to the guard at the gate. Yours, Saylor Burkhardt."

I flipped it over, looking for the "gotcha!" written on the back. "What the hell is this? She gets me jumped, punches me in the face, and then *cordially* invites me to her place for tea? Is this a trick? A trap?"

"Traps don't usually come with an invitation." Rafael's attention broke from the road. He stared at the invite with the same expression. "But yeah, that's weird as hell. Why would she ask you there? No one gets an invite to Burkhardt Manor."

"They don't?"

"If you're Alvar, Starling, or the other one," Rafael said, waving off Saylor's gorgeous friends who hit on him every chance they got. "Sure, they're on the guest list. Otherwise, that's not the place you stop by when you're in the neighborhood. Every party they host is in the country club. Business meetings in the office.

"My dad's done five jobs for the senator and he's never been inside— Correction, my father's never been *invited* inside. As it is, Dad hasn't visited the place in daylight."

My brain latched on to his last comment. "Senator Burkhardt hired your father five times? Your father the supposed hit man?"

"You can drop the supposed. And yes."

"Why?" I sat up straighter and cringed, instantly regretting jostling my wrist. "Are you telling me our elected representative of this United States has paid for five people to be murdered?"

"I'm not saying that, even though it's likely, because my dad honors client confidentiality. He carries out many jobs for people and not all of them require killing. For a senator, it works as well to destroy an opponent's reputation. The risk of a life sentence isn't necessary. But again, I can't say for sure," he admitted. "I don't know the details of those five jobs."

"Who am I to talk?" I asked, pushing down my unease. "There are five men I plan to murder too."

"Is it still five, Luna? After today?"

I gazed down at my bad arm, emotions swelling. Hurting Iris, Eva, Saylor, and the rest of them was the single thing I could want as much as seeing Owen, Levi, Giovanni, and the others ruined beyond saving. But—

"It's still five. Those five took a life. Saylor and the Bitch Crew didn't. I'm not that far gone yet, Rafael. Why?" I heard myself ask. "What would you do if you were me?"

Rafael turned off the paved road, shutting off the headlights. "I'll show you."

Moonlight lit our path, leading us down a single stretch of road. I recognized where we were without asking.

The Bluffs.

Small, rising cliffs lined a private stretch of beach on the north side. Part-time summer Regalians built their beach homes overlooking the bluffs, walking out on their balconies to watch sea-foam sprinkle the shore as they sipped imported coffee and cheered their lives. The night before I crashed the yacht and bought myself a one-way ticket to France, my friends and I partied in one of these beach houses.

I looked back on that night almost every day, wondering what would've changed if I hadn't been so drunk, stupid, and determined to impress my new rich friends. Maybe I wouldn't have been sent away. Maybe I would've been here for Winter.

Rafael reached the end of the road and kept driving, rumbling up the hill and cutting the engine right before the cliff gave way.

"Wait here," he said.

"Why?"

He climbed out, leaving me twisting in my seat, tracking him. Rafael popped the trunk and disappeared behind it. My confusion grew as he thumped and shuffled around back there.

After ten minutes, I popped open my door, sticking my head out. "Rafael? Is everything okay?"

"Fantastic, Cloud Girl. You can come out."

I did so—inching around to the back of the car. "Oh my goodness," I breathed. "What's all this?"

"Part one of cheering you up."

Two foldable chairs planted in the grass. A blanket took up one. Rafael draped it over my shoulders, using it to tug me forward and onto my seat. Between the chairs sat a small table carrying drinks—one of them a can of peach soda.

"Part two." Rafael opened the cooler tucked inside the trunk and lifted out two covered plates. My stomach growled just smelling the scents wafting under the tinfoil. "Empanadas, fried plantains, cilantro lime rice, chips and salsa."

"Yes, please." I wasted no time tearing the foil off and stuffing an empanada in my mouth. One bite and I melted in my seat. "How do you do this?"

He chuckled. "Cooking's easy, darling. It's the only time in your life you can do everything right and it turns out exactly the way you expect. No surprises. No mistakes. No wrong turns."

"Hmm. I never thought of it that way."

Rafael dropped next to me and picked up his beer. He was only a year older than me, but it was a little silly to expect him to obey drinking laws when he played fast and loose with all the others.

I gazed at our setup, drifting back to him each time I tried to look away. From an outside view, this wasn't romantic. We weren't lying on a picnic blanket under the stars, surrounded by candles, or singing along to love songs played on his car radio. There was nothing here that a fiancé could object to.

So why are my palms sweating as I hold this delicious meal made for me? Why does my chest pang at the sight of that peach soda?

Why is he resting his hand on my knee? I bit my lip as he squeezed me, thumb stroking my tender skin. *Why aren't I stopping him?*

"Look," Rafael whispered. "Part three is here."

I sat up, following his line of sight down the hill. A car rumbled down the same road and turned off, heading for the nearest beach house. We were far enough away we couldn't make out the two people who climbed out and went inside. But I wasn't so far that I didn't recognize the car as Giovanni's.

"Are we sure that's her?" I asked. "You said Giovanni steals away with his side girl on Thursdays because that's the night Annika stays late practicing with her acting coach, but what if this is the night she blows off to bang her boyfriend at the beach?"

"She bangs him in her dorm, his dorm, his car, his house, and the men's room in Toussaint's. They don't need to make a special trip of it to get naked." Rafael motioned with his beer. "Giovanni saves that for girlfriend number two. Neither his parents nor Annika have a reason to come out here. The two of them have gotten away with this for over a year."

"So Giovanni cheated on my sister with two women. Both of whom knew what he was doing, but couldn't find a shred of decency in their souls to warn her." The food turned rancid on my tongue. Rafael stopped me while setting it down.

"All three of them pay for that tonight." His hand was warm cupping mine. "That's part four."

He got to his feet. "Speaking of, shall we?"

My burgeoning good mood returned. "Yes, we shall."

Together we crept down the hill, staying low of anyone glancing out the window and spotting two approaching shadows. Something that wouldn't be too hard to do since Giovanni's beach bachelor pad was all windows.

We crouched beside his car, watching the lights flick on and him stumble into the living room—pants around his ankles. My eyes bugged when his companion ran inside after him, pouncing him onto the couch.

"Gabriella?" I blurted. "That's who he's cheating with?"

"You should read the texts between those two. Creative stuff," he said, sounding impressed. "He's got a second phone so Annika doesn't find out, it's all dirty stuff they have, will, or want to get up to—complete with pictures."

I scoffed. "Is it also complete with declarations of love and promises to leave his girlfriend?"

"Got a few of those in there too, but they both know it can't happen." Together we made a dash for the porch, ducking behind an oversize planter as Giovanni's pants finally came off and Gabriella swallowed a mouthful of dick.

"Why can't it happen?"

"The Montanas and the Natales are rival families. The invention that made Grandpa Montana a billionaire, Giovanni's grandfather swears it was stolen from him. Lorenzo Natale eventually had another great idea and got rich anyway, but neither side can forgive the thieves or the lying bastards calling them thieves. If their families find out they're together, they'll probably be disowned."

"Aww, how Romeo and Juliet," I simpered. "So are you taking the pictures or am I?"

Grinning, Rafael handed me his phone. "You, of course. You open the presents when it's your party."

I went wild snapping photos, pressing the button so fast I filled his gallery with half a dozen burst shots. "I'll call this collection: The Many Shapes, Bends, and Positions of Payback."

Rafael bobbed his head, pushing out his lips. "I like it. Simple, but evocative."

I clapped a hand over my mouth, smothering a laugh. Now was not the time to get caught. Although, from the bouncing-on-his-lap, head-thrown-back-in-ecstasy thing they were doing, I'm pretty sure all they were hearing were their grunts and moans.

"Romeo and Juliet," I said as I swiped through the photos. "Think their story will end as tragically when these photos come out?"

He let out a low whistle. "Worse. Their grandfathers ran into each other at a gala last year." Rafael grabbed my hand and escaped with me back up the hill. "They got into a fight. Pushing seventy years old and Natale shoves him over the appetizer table. The hatred is very much alive."

"That's all I need to know." I typed a message on his phone. "Wilder said there's a way to send a text and mask the number. Can we do that now?"

We reclaimed our seats and our dinner. "Sure thing. What's the message?"

I showed him.

Your boyfriend and Gabriella Montana are banging in his beach house. If you want to catch them at it, you better hurry.

"I won't send her the pictures," I said. "I want her to rush down here, anvil pressing harder on her chest the closer she gets—the whole time praying it's not true and this is all some cheap trick. She arrives, sees the car, asks herself why Giovanni came out here without telling her, but still not letting herself believe that's the reason.

"Then, Annika bangs on the door, demanding he open up. They try to run before she darts around and spots them naked and sweaty on the couch, but it's too late. The sweet, loving relationship she thought she was in crashes into the bluffs and explodes in her face. The same sentence she and that limp-dick granted my sister."

I grinned at Rafael over my peach soda. "It's all in the buildup. You taught me that."

"I am... very turned on right now."

"Rafael!"

"What?" The devil fell to shame before that trickster's smirk. "I don't see a ring on that finger."

"I can't believe you'd make that joke. Just give me the phone."

He did as I asked, passing the phone back to me for the honor of hitting *send*.

Relaxed, I kicked back to eat and enjoy the starry night with a chance of oncoming storms. I tried to fight it, but my eyes kept drifting to my bare finger.

"Do you think Saylor took my ring to force me to go to her house and get it?"

"I'm sure the thought crossed her mind. Hold on a sec." Rafael took off his headphones and replaced them with his hearing aids. Scooting in closer, he rested his hand on my chair arm, leaning in. "Okay, we're good."

"I'm sorry." I traced his ear's blue companion. "Is my voice bothering you? We don't have to talk—"

"Your voice is the most beautiful music I've ever heard." I swallowed hard, wishing I could look somewhere else, and powerless as he trapped my gaze. "It's not you, darling. It's the cicadas. Night ambience to everyone else, Chinese water torture to me.

"It's a noise-canceling hearing aid. Let's me tune out the background noise and hear you. Only you."

I pushed him back a little bit, if only to steady my heartbeat. "Got it," I said, voice wavering. "What were we— Oh yeah, Saylor. I have to go. There's something she owes me... and something I owe her."

"If you go, you go in alone. That invitation admits one."

"I'm not afraid of her. Saylor hides behind her money and her accident of birth. She doesn't know what it is to fight for something real. Her quest for social domination is shallow. My fight for Winter is the sole purpose of my life. That's why no matter what happens, I'll never stop."

Rafael's phone lit up, interrupting his reply.

Annika: Who is this?

Annika: You're lying. Giovanni would never do that to me.

Nothing for ten minutes, then a flood rained down, kicking up a buzzing worse than the singing cicadas.

Annika: It's you, Rikva. Bitch! I warned you what would happen if you didn't back off. Giovanni doesn't want you. Your lies won't get between us.

Annika: Who is this?!

Annika: If you have the balls to send that text, you should have the balls to reveal yourself.

"I hope she's not texting and driving," I said mildly. "Very dangerous."

Laughing, we clinked can and glass.

Rafael counted it down. Exactly twenty-six minutes from the time we sent the text, headlights came barreling down the dirt road. I dropped my soda as Annika's car Tokyo-drifted alongside Giovanni's, skidding into the drive and falling out before the car was even off.

The small, dark figure that was her flew at the front door, playing out the scene as perfectly as I pictured.

Annika followed our path, running around the side of the house and—

"Ahhh!"

"There goes part five," Rafael cheered. "There's something to be said for taking charge of your own happiness."

I giggled. "I just wish we had—"

He lifted something out of the trunk, beaming wide. "Binoculars?"

I barely stopped myself from saying I loved him. I learned my lesson from the last Dumont brother I said that to.

Taking mine, I pointed them at the scene, swinging the spotlight at them just as Giovanni stumbled out the door with his pants unbuttoned and shirt in the corner where Gabriella threw it. The first string of panicked bullshit dropped from his mouth—his hands up as I read the pleading in his expression.

Annika slapped him across the face, pulling "oohs" out of both of us. She darted inside while his head was busy snapping around and hitting the doorframe.

"Her acting coach taught that girl to hit with feeling," Rafael said.

"At least those lessons aren't a waste of money. That's one thing she has going for her because an honest relationship isn't it."

Giovanni ran inside after Annika, who no doubt blew in there to fuck up Gabriella too. From our angle, we couldn't see inside, and risking another jaunt to the house would let them know exactly who set them up. An unseen enemy couldn't be stopped. A seen enemy is lured out of class and beaten, kicked, and spat on in broad daylight. These guys would not know it was me for as long as possible, then they'd have no chance of stopping me.

"Thank you, Rafael." I dropped my binoculars to gift him a smile. "You really know how to cheer a girl up."

He winked. "I'm not done yet."

"You're not? But we've got the pictures. Annika is kicking Gabriella's ass right now. What else is there to do?"

Rafael wasn't done pulling surprises out of the trunk. My eyes popped seeing the small device in his hand.

"Watch the fireworks."

My fingers twitched for the trigger. "But you said it wasn't time yet."

"This isn't to kill them. It's to keep the fun going longer." He shrugged, flashing that lopsided grin. "Plus, it's been a while. A guy likes to keep his skills sharp."

"Okay," I said, "but what's it for?"

I pressed the button on the end of my sentence. An explosion ripped through the blissful beach night, blowing me back in my chair. Flames billowed out from the ruin of Giovanni's car, catching its neighbor alight. Both cars engulfed in fire.

"Giovanni loves that car," Rafael said, "and we both know he's a bit skint at the moment. Can't afford to buy himself another one. The three of them can mourn that fact together. It's a long walk back."

I laughed—loud and riddled with dark delight. Forget keeping my head around the Rogues. "Rafael, you're amazing."

"This is true— Oh, look. They're coming back out."

My binoculars flew up to position. Giovanni tripped running out of the house. He dropped to his knees before the Lamborghini—half a million dollars becoming charred scrap parts before his eyes. He didn't notice, or didn't care, as Annika wrenched Gabriella out by her hair.

Bending her head back, Annika ripped a cry out of the half-naked Gabriella that we heard from the hill. Gabriella kneed her in the stomach, doubling Annika over and freeing herself. She took off running.

Annika was far from beaten. Picking herself up, she ignored her burning car and worthless boyfriend, chasing after Gabriella. She tackled her within feet of the bluffs.

"Ouch," Rafael remarked as Annika rained punches on her captive. "I'm starting to think she's taken more than just acting lessons."

"She's really whaling on her." I winced as Annika grabbed a hank of her hair and ripped. "She's fucking this girl up."

Giovanni finally noticed what was going on. He abandoned his car, running at them. I swung off him back to his girlfriends. Gabriella kicked Annika off her. She rolled and landed smack on the edge of the cliff.

"Wait," I said.

The girls clambered to their feet, hatred etched in their snarling lips and bleeding cuts. They launched at each other.

"Stop," Giovanni shouted. "Annika! Gabby!"

Annika struck Gabriella across the cheek. She snapped back and grabbed her wrists.

"Wait, stop." My grip strangled the binoculars. "Fuck's sake, stop!"

Gabriella forced her back, running her at the edge. Annika broke free at the last moment, just as Giovanni reached them, and Gabriella shoved.

Annika flew as my binoculars did, pitching off the cliff. My scream trapped in my throat as Annika's echoed all the way down, then stopped.

Chapter Eleven

"Holy shit!"

"Rafael! She killed her. Oh my gosh, she wasn't supposed to kill her!"

"Calm down." Shooting up, Rafael started tossing our things in the trunk. "We don't know that she's dead."

"Don't know— She pushed her off a fucking cliff!"

I fell off my chair, clutching my head. I hated Annika. I wanted her to hurt for giving Giovanni the green light to fuck over my sister, but I didn't want her dead. It was Giovanni who lied, manipulated, humiliated, and broke Winter's heart. It was him who should go over a cliff!

"What now?" I cried. "What— Wait, what are they doing?"

I snatched up the binoculars. Giovanni and Gabriella stood at the edge of the bluff—still. Neither one was running for the metal staircase built into the rocks, leading down to the beach.

"What are they doing?" Rafael in my ear made me look up.

"They're... arguing. Gabriella is pointing down and waving her hands. I can't see Giovanni's face, but he's just standing there. Why isn't either one of them going to help her? See if she's okay— No, hold on. He's running for the stairs."

I watched Giovanni take off and Gabriella run after him. She hauled him back, said something that involved a lot of shoving and fingers in his face, then she spun and stormed toward the house. Ice chilled my veins as Giovanni cast one last look at the bluffs, and followed her.

"I can't believe it," I breathed. "They're leaving her. Giovanni's dated her for over a year. Gabriella's gone to school with her their whole life. The two of them are just abandoning her in the cold and dark."

"Those shits can do what they want. Come on." Rafael picked me up and steered me toward the car. "There's another way down to the beach."

That snapped me out of it.

We took off in his car, driving to the other set of stairs. Killing the engine, we tumbled out, taking the steps two at a time.

A still figure lay at the base of the bluffs. Rafael ran ahead of me, skidding to a stop next to her, falling by her side.

Her eyes were closed as if in sleep. You could almost mistake her rest for peaceful, if not for her leg twisted at an unnatural angle and the growing dark pool beneath her head.

"Rafael, is she…?"

"No," he said, checking her pulse. "But it's faint. She needs help and I have a feeling those two didn't run inside to call an ambulance."

"I'll do it."

"Stop," Rafael broke in. "Use my phone. Mask the number. I'm not trying to cover my ass, but a Dumont at the scene of an explosion and attempted murder won't go well. The cops won't believe I wasn't involved."

He *was* involved. Rafael was roped into my revenge scheme, doing all of this to leech a fraction of the hatred consuming me. But it was me who lured Annika here. It was me who wanted a brutal confrontation. I wouldn't give Giovanni and Gabriella the perfect scapegoat to pin this on.

"Rafael, leave."

"What? I'm not—"

"I'm serious, go! Someone has to stay with her until the ambulance comes and we both know that can't be you."

"It can't be either of us. They'll question why you're here too."

"Do you have a better idea?"

His idea wasn't better, but it was the only one we could come up with that didn't end with the wrong people sitting in a jail cell awaiting questioning.

Rafael and I ducked behind a rock as voices approached, letting go of Annika's hand at the last possible second. Her pulse was still fluttering beneath my finger. She was alive, and in the ten minutes we waited with her, neither Giovanni nor Gabriella descended the staircase.

The two of us stayed low, hands covering the other's mouth as the para-medics strapped Annika to a backboard and took off. Rafael was correct in pointing out they wouldn't waste time searching the rocks for us when there was a girl bleeding out in the sand.

"We have to go," Rafael said as their voices faded in the distance. "The police will be right behind."

It was a long drive back to campus. My mind twisted in circles, recon-ciling the dark turn my revenge had taken. One text message and Annika ended up in the back of an ambulance speeding to the hospital.

When we made it back to the top, it was clear Gabriella and Giovanni were long gone. The lights were off in the beach house, and a stillness settled over the property that unsettled me to the bone.

Did they get their stories straight as they walked a fair distance down the road to the car they called to pick them up? Would Giovanni say he and Annika were minding their own business when some masked stranger blew up their cars and tossed his girlfriend off a cliff? What would he say to any-one, including himself, about the horror of leaving Annika there alone?

He was scared. He was in shock. But he was innocent of all except for cheating while Rafael and I committed serious crimes. So why was he the one to leave, and we were the ones who stayed?

Not to mention the coldness on Gabriella's face...

"I finally understand."

My whisper stopped Rafael on the steps of the Gallery.

"I finally understand who I'm dealing with. That's why you and the Rogues had to stop me that night with Owen. I came to this campus think-ing I was dealing with normal schoolyard bullies, but the kids on this play-ground are like no one I've ever met."

Rafael turned his head, face cloaked in shadows.

"I understand," I said again, "and I know what to do. We're scrapping you guys' plan. From here on, I'm taking over."

"Luna." That was all he needed to say. I heard the warning loud and clear.

"It's okay." I gazed down at my hands, palms stained with Annika's blood. "It's the perfect recipe. Everything will be done right and it will turn out exactly the way we expect. No surprises. No mistakes. No wrong turns.

"No Annikas," I stated. "Let's go inside. We've got to wake up the boys."

THE NEXT MORNING, WILDER and I headed to the campus bookstore. We spoke in low tones as I searched the shelves for replacement textbooks.

"She's in the hospital," he said under his breath. "Unconscious, but in stable condition."

"That's something at least. She'll pull through this, right?"

Wilder glared at a guy coming down our aisle. He caught the look and turned back around.

"Regalia General Hospital has a good record. Below average number of malpractice-related deaths in the country. There's an underground organ-harvesting ring operating out of three nearby hospitals. Far as I can dig up, RGH has kept out of it. I'd go there if I was hurt," he said. "That should tell you something."

"It does," I admitted. "If you trust those doctors, everyone can. But what about Giovanni?"

"The police roped off the beach house and closed down the bluffs. It's officially a crime scene."

I nodded, chewing my lip. "They can't ignore that both of their cars were there, burning side by side."

"They haven't ignored it. I hacked the RPD server this morning." Wilder lifted my English book off a high shelf and handed it to me. "They pulled Giovanni's file. Next stop is bringing him in for questioning."

"He won't go down for this." We drifted along the stacks, me lazily scanning for *Introduction to Psychology*. "Between the high-priced lawyers and the fact he didn't touch her, Giovanni will find a way out of this. The only question is will he throw Gabriella under the bus."

"Whether he does or doesn't, once Annika wakes up and tells her side of the story, Gabriella is screwed. I'm more interested in the lengths she'll go to cover her ass. She's got a lot more to lose."

I inclined my head. That was a good point. "Do you think there's any chance he'll do the right thing and tell the truth about what happened at the beach house?"

"That someone lured Annika out there to catch him in the act, blew up his car, and caused the circumstances that led to his girlfriend thrown off a cliff? This after his bank account got drained and he was trapped in his room and tormented all night." Wilder dropped that without inflection. "I don't know if he'll tell the cops all that, but he'll tell someone. His next step is personal security tailing him whenever he leaves the house."

Nodding, I replied, "Then, it is good that I changed the plan. Less full-frontal assault, and more underhanded tricks. They won't know what's happening until it's done."

Wilder walked back, picked up the psych book that I passed, and added it to my pile. My eagle-eye companion missed nothing. "Your plan is good, but Owen and Levi are out of the hospital. I still say the two of them along with Giovanni, Wesley, and bastard number five would benefit from a swing on the ceiling."

"I say that too, but we have to do this another way now. I wanted Annika to see that Giovanni gives as much a shit about her as he did Winter, but I didn't want her to find out by way of accidental homicide and abandoning the scene of the crime. No collateral damage from here on."

"I need to tell you"—Wilder slipped around my waist, spinning me to face him—"you're showing more restraint for the Royals than they would show toward you. Girls you didn't know attacked you on the quad. You said you understand the game now. Start playing," he tossed over his shoulder, walking off.

I was quick behind him, falling in step. "This is a phrase you hear a lot and ignore every time, but this time fight your natural urge and *trust me*. Just because I don't want to hold another girl's hand while she bleeds out in the sand, doesn't mean I'm going soft. If you guys do exactly what I say, we can take out all five of Winter's killers in one move—and only them.

"As for Saylor, Iris, and others who jumped me, they won't get away with it. Most importantly, they won't put their hands on me again. A fact I intend to make clear to Saylor tomorrow night."

"I could tell you *again* why accepting that invitation is worse than a terrible mistake, but you weren't listening last night and I doubt you will now."

"Thank you for handling both sides of that argument. Now we can move past it."

He narrowed on me as I stepped to the checkout counter. I paid for my stuff and headed out, expecting my muscled companion to follow.

We made it to the English building twenty minutes before class. "All right, thanks, Wilder. Text me if you hear anything else about... you know."

Wilder shot in front of me as I reached for the knob. "What are you doing?"

"Um, going to class?"

His frown deepened. "Is this what you always do? Skip inside every closed room? You don't know who the hell is waiting in there for you. No wonder Saylor and her crew made an easy target of you."

"Okay, ouch," I replied. "No need for that last shot. And I'm not skipping into ambushes, I'm going inside my classroom."

"Not like that you're fucking not. From now on, you make sure the entrance is clear. Like this." Wilder spun and kicked the door in.

Bang!

"Agh! Fuck!" A body thudded to the floor.

"See?" Wilder said to my bug-eyed horror. "What did I tell you? Some sneaky fuck was lurking in there waiting for his chance." Wilder went in and glanced down at the sneaky fuck. "Hmm. I'd put some ice on that.

"The room is clear, Sinclair." He blew out the door and took off. "See you in an hour and a half."

"What the—Wilder!"

Running inside, I nearly tripped over Wilder's victim flat on his back, clutching his dented head.

"Professor Anthony?" I dropped beside him, cursing handsome blond conspiracy nuts.

"What the fuck happened! Luna?" Groaning, he tried to get up and ended up half in my lap. "Did you throw the door open like that? The fuck?! Who shitting does that?!"

Adonis devolved into a string of profanity that wouldn't get points for creativity, but would get him an A-plus and star sticker for passion. I grasped his head, keeping him still.

"Professor, it wasn't me, I swear. Here, let me help you." Getting an arm under his shoulder, I helped him up and guided him onto his desk chair. I hissed at the golf ball growing on his forehead. "That's not good."

"I'm fine, Luna." He took hold of my wrists like he was going to push me away. "Wait. Someone else was with you. Who was it? Did they do this?"

"Uh." I turned my back on him, riffling around in my bag. "I can neither confirm nor deny that person or persons unknown opened the door with too much force."

"What the fuck are you talking about?"

I bit hard on my lip, penning in a laugh. It was hilarious listening to my serious, no-nonsense professor cursing like a drunk postgrad who just broke up with his fiancée. You didn't have to ask me which version of him I liked more.

"Here, this will help. The nurse gave me extra for my wrist." Cupping the back of his head, I gently tilted him back and placed the instant cold pack on his temple.

A soft sigh of relief cut into his rant, making his lids heavy. "Who was that?" he asked in a more even tone.

"He's long gone, Prof. You'll never catch him."

"Don't be so sure—" Adonis's eyes popped open and locked on mine... over my breasts... which were in his face... as I stood between his legs... leaning so close over him I could erase the distance between our lips in an inch.

His gaze drifted down to my mouth. Beads of sweat prickled beneath my collar under his attention.

"Are you sure you're okay, Professor?" His hair was soft against my palm. My fingers curled in his strands unthinkingly.

"I'll be better," he said softly, "when I give your friend a busted head to match."

I giggled. "Schools tend to frown on professors bashing students over the head."

"He's a student? At least we've narrowed it down."

Adonis was still looking at my lips. And I was still standing too close.

He rose, closing the distance between us.

"Did you do the reading last night?"

We sprung apart like colliding ball bearings, Adonis tripping over his chair legs, shooting away. I was on the other side of the desk as Alice and Eva walked in—the two of them threw me smirks on the way to their seats, but there was nothing else behind their looks to suggest they thought something weird was going on between Sinclair and the professor.

There is nothing weird going on! Adonis was not about to kiss me. The man has a head wound. He confused up and down, and didn't know what he was doing.

Adonis roughly cleared his throat. "Thank you for this, Miss Sinclair." He dropped the ice pack on his desk. "I'm fine now. That'll be all."

I crooked a brow at his send-off. That'll be all? What was I? His secretary?

"All right." I took up my ice pack. "Are you sure there isn't anything I can do to help? Pass out papers? Set up your lecture—?"

"No," he said too quickly. "I mean, no. I can handle it from here, Luna. Please, take your seat."

It was the first name that got to me. I made for my seat, ignoring the hissed insults from Alice. Victor soon arrived and dropped next to me. I quickly hid my hand and missing ring under the desk. There was no hiding my brace.

"What happened?" Victor asked.

"Bike accident," I said simply. "It could've been worse."

"Is that how you hurt your lip?"

I nodded.

"Do I need to review basic bicycle safety with you, Sinclair? Do you need a helmet, kneepads, braces, and lingerie as my marriage gift?"

I would've flipped him off, but neither hand was up to the task. "Wait till you see what I give you," I muttered.

"Ready for tonight?"

"You mean the family dinner you invited me to so I could distract from the family drama? Yep," I said, popping the last letter. "I've got my dress picked out."

"Good. Mom wants to talk floral arrangements and food allergies on your side of the family. She says she tried calling your mom and no one answers."

My chest tightened. Swallowing hard, I replied, "From now on, she should call me. It is my sham of a wedding after all."

"Hmm. Maybe we don't put that on the save-the-dates."

I almost cracked a smile.

"Hey." He nudged me, dropping his voice. "Did you hear about last night?"

"No, what?"

"Giovanni Natale and Annika Mitchell were attacked," he whispered. His cinnamon soap fogged my mind, trying to distract from my growing dread. "It was some real *Friday the 13th* shit. He said two guys busted into his place. They set fire to their cars so they couldn't get away and then whaled on them."

As in Annika kicked his ass, and then Annika and Gabriella kicked each other's.

"They ran out the back door. Giovanni thought she was behind him, but they got separated in the woods. He looked for her all night." He shook his head. "It was too late. One of those cowardly masked fucks grabbed and threw her off the bluffs."

I cringed remembering the scene. "That's awful," I said, and meant it. "Is Annika going to be okay?"

"She hasn't woken up yet, but she will." Victor squeezed my hand. "Be careful, okay? Gio couldn't identify those guys and they got away. I just can't believe something like this would happen in Regalia."

"You can't believe tragedy would strike in this picturesque little town? It already did, Victor. Long before Annika." I slid free of his touch. "Nowhere is paradise. Regalia least of all."

Victor looked away, a muscle jumping in his jaw. "I keep doing that with you."

"Doing what?"

"Saying the wrong thing." He sighed. "I know you hate it here, Luna, and you have every reason to."

"Do you? You never mention Winter. Nothing more than the flowers and condolence card sent to the memorial, and I figured your mom was behind that."

"I sent it, Luna. I wanted to say more, do more, but it kinda seemed like..." He trailed off.

"What, Victor?"

"Seemed like the only time you didn't look so broken that you could fold in on yourself like a dying star, was when you were yelling at me. The spark would light your eyes again," he said. "I guess I thought if I mentioned Winter and what happened to her, it'd bring it all back. And now that I'm saying it, it sounds so stupid. Pissing you off isn't better than being there for you during the worst time in your life. Damn, you were right all those times you called me an insensitive ass."

Smiling, I grasped his chin between my fingers, making him look at me. "It's not stupid. The truth is, the only times this summer that I wasn't curled in a ball on my bed, crying my eyes out, was when I was telling you exactly what I thought of you, Wilson.

"I'm not buying that you were that obnoxious on purpose." We chuckled. "But it is sweet that you noticed then and there wasn't the time to remind me my life was a festering pit of grief. It's sweet. Dang, you got me to say the *s*-word."

"You didn't say shithead, but I'm going to take it anyway."

I shoved his shoulder, the both of us grinning.

"All right, class." Professor Anthony drew our attention to the front.

"Professor Anthony, are you okay? What happened?" Eva asked.

"A mishap," he said simply. "I'm fine. To start, each of you come down one at a time and collect your papers. Review the comments over the weekend and consider how you'll use the suggestions to improve next week's assignment. Today, we're going over the reading, then you'll write a short essay on the themes. After you complete your essays, you're free to leave early."

Everyone was plenty happy for that news, even though the early release was likely because the golf ball was growing into a grapefruit. I was last to go down and get my paper. My eyes went round at the red *FAIL* written across the top. They grew wider as I read his comments.

"But, Prof—"

"Sit down, Miss Sinclair." His voice was hard. "Now is not the time or place."

Fuming, I stormed upstairs, seriously considering that the man had multiple personalities and the asshole alter emerged whenever he had a pen in his hand. *Give me the swearing and ranting Adonis any day. Even better, give me the maudlin drunk who sat with me and shared our problems.*

I bore a hole in his swollen head all through class. Professor Anthony must've noticed because his gaze didn't travel higher than the seventh row. After review time where I reflected on the comments *"this was a waste of my time and your talent"* and *"if you're not going to take this seriously, you're better off handing me a blank paper,"* he handed out the essay tests.

I finished quickly and waited, and waited, while the other students finished up and left.

"Miss Sinclair." I jumped, snapping up to Adonis climbing the stairs. "Are you finished?"

"Yes, but—"

"Give me your paper. You can go."

I hesitated. "I was hoping to speak with you at the end of class."

"I'm sure you were, but I was hoping to swallow a handful of ibuprofen and save getting told off by my student for when I don't have a splitting headache." He slipped the essay out from under me and swept out a hand. "Goodbye, Miss Sinclair."

Gritting my teeth, I reminded myself he did get hit over the head because of me. "See you tonight, Professor." I hoped it sounded like a warning, because it was. He was not getting out of this conversation.

My classes passed quickly. The last few weeks taught me the lesson of checking my chair before I sat down, ignoring sudden calls pulling me out of class, avoiding my classmates and their camera phones, sitting next to no one other than Victor, and not traveling between classes alone. It felt I was attending school in a war-torn nation rather than the top private university in the country.

Despite all my precautions, no one messed with me other than tossing me triumphant, self-satisfied smiles. They thought they neutered me there on the concrete, bruised and buried under textbooks. Why wouldn't they?

My ring was gone. It looked like they got everything they wanted and I tossed *their* man back.

That evening, I padded upstairs to shower and get dressed for dinner. Heading for my room, I halted in the middle of the hallway, slowly turning my head. Rafael paused with his hands in his hair, achieving that windswept tousled look I thought was effortless.

Steam billowed out of the shower from his bath and clung to his naked chest. Water droplets slip-slid down his pecs like happy sluts that then got the privilege of soaking the towel wrapped low on his waist. Many things hit me at once as we stared at each other, but they were all summed up by two facts: Rafael was standing half naked in front of me, and I could see this because the sheet acting as my door was in a pile on the mat.

"What's up?" Rafael asked. He pointed down. "Want me to drop the towel?"

Fire burned through my skin and veins, reducing me to a pile of Luna ash on the carpet. "What the—! I don't— What kind of person asks something like that!"

He shrugged, grinning away. "What kind of person thinks about saying yes?"

Rafael worked his hips, thrusting and grinding to douse the Luna ash with gasoline and set it ablaze again. "Oops, it's slipping. About to come off by itself."

"Rafael, I swear!"

Laughing, he stopped. I tried very hard not to notice the towel did slip down, revealing more of that *V* and a patch of raven hair.

This guy is an explosive. Destroying monogamy wherever he goes. But he's not getting to me. If I expect Victor to keep it in his pants, I have to hold myself to the same standard. Victor wanted to see other people but be discrete about it. It was me who brought up the no-hooking-up rule in the first place.

I had to go and open my fucking mouth the first time. Then I did it again at the mention of Everleigh. This is one of those times when I truly have no one else to blame.

"What are you doing in my shower anyway?" I called, ducking into my room to lay out my dress. "You have one in your room."

"Cato's in mine."

"He has a shower in his room too."

"There was an accident. A little fire damage. No big deal."

"This is the point where I stop asking questions."

"You're learning, Sinclair."

"Can I also learn when I get my doors back?"

Rafael resumed fixing his hair, and not his towel. I kept flicking down to the loosening thing, sliding lower down his waist. "Gotta ask Wilder that one."

"You guys know you can trust me by now. We—"

The towel gave up, pooling around his feet.

"We'll talk later," I cried, racing across the hall. Rafael's laughter taunted me as I ran into Lucien's room and bolted the door. My chest heaved like I ran farther than six feet. I dropped my head on the wood, resolving then and there to get my doors back, even if it meant kicking Wilder's ass. The guy was twice my size, but I was highly motivated.

"Lady Luna?"

I spun around and got my second shot through the chest. Lucien spread out on his bed, divested of every dark, fitted layer of those Victorian clothes, wearing nothing but white, thin undergarments and the fine black hairs on his ropey bare chest. His underwear was so white and thin... I could see right through it.

"Holy hell, Lucien! Where are your clothes?"

Calm as ever, he pointed to the corner. "In that hamper over there. Everything okay?"

"Cover up, please." I didn't give him the choice. Snatching a throw off the coffin, I tossed it over his bits. Lucien just eyed me through the exchange, forehead wrinkled like there was something wrong with me. I did burst into his room, freak out, and throw things at him, so he may have a point.

"I'm fine," I said, willing myself to relax. It helped to firmly put the image of Lucien's and Rafael's *manhood* in a box, lock it, and mentally blow it up. "But while I'm here, there is something I need to ask you."

Lucien and I talked. The whole time, he didn't see the need to cover up his chest, or stop posing like a damn vampire supermodel basking under the full moon. I thanked my fortune that his bottom half stayed under the blanket.

After we were done, I was clear to take a shower and get ready for dinner with Victor and his parents. I borrowed Rafael's car and left for the mansion on the hill. It would've been easier to have Victor pick me up and drop me off—except that wouldn't be easy at all. The guys conveniently forgot I was engaged whenever it suited them. I didn't want to find out how they'd act around Victor.

"Evening, Miss Bowden," the guard greeted.

I didn't bother correcting him. "Evening."

"Please, drive up to the second garage and park inside. Mabel is waiting to receive you."

"Thank you."

The gate rumbled open, unveiling a sight more magnificent than the last time I'd seen it. Technically, the life of the young and wealthy was mine. Regalians cracked jokes about the Tire King, but His Royal Highness was sitting on a seven-figure business. Before we lost Winter, my folks sat down and explained that they would take care of us for as long as we needed, and when they passed, Jack's fortune would go to us.

This life was mine now, and no matter how many times I repeated that, it wouldn't sink in. I was out of place among these Royals—separating people into categories, fighting over status, playing chess with real lives, sacrificing families, fortunes, and reputations as pawns.

I didn't fit in among crowds buying two homes twenty minutes from each other just because one was closer to the beach. I wasn't the one tossing my coat at the butler, demanding the chef bring me breakfast in bed, or vacationing in the tropics. This was my world, but it wasn't my life.

Mabel welcomed me with a bow and a tray carrying refreshments. I thanked her, helping myself to a pink lemonade, and followed her inside to the sitting room. Mr. and Mrs. Wilson rose at my entrance. Her pink, long-sleeved gown and his tux proved I made the right choice with my red satin empire-waist dress.

"Luna." She homed in on my hand like a heat-seeking missile. "Where's my grandmother's ring?"

"It's being cleaned."

"Cleaned? What have you been doing that it's gotten dirty?"

"Nothing," I said, standing taller under her shrewd look. "But it's recommended to clean your engagement ring once a week, and it's important to me to take care of such a beautiful family heirloom."

"Hmm. All right." Martha grasped my hands, kissing me on both cheeks. She drew back and held out my arms to take me in. "Oh, dear. Red is not your color."

My polite smile burned up. *Red is not your color.* See? I said she only needed five words or less.

"Isn't it?" I said tightly. "I've always loved this dress. It flatters my figure."

"Figure?" She laughed. "My dear, you're a thin little rake of a girl, and I'm jealous. I remember when I was that thin. Two sons saw the end of that."

I wasn't sure if that was a compliment or insult. Maybe a little of both.

"Anyway, I didn't know how to accentuate my shape back then either. But don't you worry." She flicked my nose. "Now that you're about to become my daughter, I'm here for a shopping trip whenever we're both free."

Insult. Definitely insult.

"Thank you so much, Mrs. Wilson. I can't wait." *To not do that ever.*

She clicked her tongue. "None of that. I told you to call me Martha."

"Of course, Martha, and may I say, you look beautiful."

She beamed. "Yes, you may."

Martha Wilson truly was a beautiful woman. Middle age and two kids did nothing to dismiss the youthful color in her cheeks; soft, shining red crown; piercing gray eyes; and the perfect symmetry of her upturned nose and heavy lower lip.

Her husband, Mr. Wilson, was a handsome man too, in that classic-good-looks, distinguished-older-gentleman way. The result was they made children more beautiful than anyone had a right to be, and it struck me as Adonis and Victor came into the room.

It also struck me that the temperature dropped twenty degrees and I forgot to bring a sweater. I slid out of the way as Adonis approached Martha.

"Hello, Mother." He kissed her cheeks. "You're looking well."

"Hmm. Now I look well? Luna says I look beautiful. I've gone down in my son's estimation."

"Don't be ridiculous," he said smoothly. "You're a vision, Mother."

"Thank you, my darling. Say hello to your father." It was an order, not a request.

"Hello, Father."

Mr. Wilson cut a look over his scotch. "Father? Are you speaking to me? It's my understanding that fathers and sons share the same last name."

"That's because you understand very little."

John puffed up fast. "Excuse me? Who do you think you're—?"

"That's enough." Martha sharply cut through the argument. "We have a guest."

Gotta give it to Victor. He said I'd make the perfect social buffer and he was right.

"Adonis, Victor, Luna, sit." Martha gestured to the couch, retaking her place on the loveseat with her husband. She gripped his thigh—a warning if I'd ever seen one. "Help yourself to refreshments. Should be ready in thirty minutes."

Thirty minutes? What the hell, Victor? Why did you tell me to come so early?

The guy must've read my mind because he flashed a knowing grin at the wide-eyed expression on my face. This was going to be a problem. I couldn't marry a man sneakier than me.

Adonis claimed the far side of the couch, putting distance between him and his father. Victor, ever the peacemaker, claimed the spot closest. Which left the middle for me.

Gingerly, I wedged between them—my skin heating up where Victor's leg pressed against mine, and Adonis's and my shoulder bumped.

The coffee table was loaded down with appetizers, much more than five people needed. I inched forward out of their orbit, helping myself to smoked salmon crostini, French onion cups, coconut shrimp, and chips with feta dip.

Victor leaned over me to grab a shrimp. "Stuffing your face now so you can beg off early from dinner, saying you're too full to eat another bite—that won't work."

"I despise you and I want a divorce."

He barked a laugh. "Gotta get married first, sweetheart."

"It's such a treat having all of us together for dinner," Martha said. "Your father and I were just saying we hope this becomes a weekly tradition."

I wiggled back in, nibbling on my appetizers.

"Especially after you kids are married," John added. "Stopping by with our grandchildren. Eating and spending time together, seeing you happy with your families, that's all we want."

I felt Adonis tensing up next to me.

"Let's not get ahead of ourselves," I blurted. "Victor and I are only eighteen. Kids are way down the line."

Martha winked at me. "Don't be so sure. I had Don when I was nineteen. His father and I had a whirlwind romance, got married months after we met in college, and then our Don came along. I wouldn't be surprised if the same happens between you two, and we have little Wilson feet running around the manor again."

There was so much frightening about that reply, I didn't know where to begin. How exactly does an arranged marriage with a dash of blackmail add up to a whirlwind romance? And more importantly, did Mrs. Wilson think we were going to live here in the manor after we were married?

Stop talking about kids. Steer the conversation away, Sinclair.

"How did you and John meet?"

The couple shared a smile. "John and I met at a fundraising gala here in Regalia. It was fate," she said. "I had my bags packed and plans to move to New York with Don. After losing his father, the memories here were too painful to bear. Then, John and I bumped into each other—literally. We spent the whole night talking and I knew as the sun rose that I wasn't going anywhere."

I dropped my head—a feeling both sweet and sad taking me out of the moment. I couldn't imagine a night like that. Meeting someone and connecting with them so instantly. It was something out of a fairy tale, and my life would never be one of those.

"—do, Luna?"

Blinking, I refocused on John Wilson. "Sorry, what did you say?"

"You're studying psychology. What do you hope to do with that?"

"Clinical psychology. The plan is to specialize in young adult mental health and start off working in schools, but one day I hope to open a private practice."

"A noble goal." He gave me a kind smile, proving he knew why I chose this career path. "I have no doubt you'll succeed."

"Thank you."

"Yes, I always hoped my eldest son would have such ambitions."

Oh, no.

"Taking over Wilson Industries, advancing the nation, doing right by thousands of employees. Don was destined to do great things," John said, his smile twisting. "But he chose... books."

"I chose literature, Father. I chose to study the works of minds who've advanced this nation through prose with the hope I could one day write something even half as great."

"Half as great? Your grand goal in life is to fall short?"

Victor spoke up. "Dad, you know that's not what he meant."

"It's what he said. He wants to read dusty old tomes while he toils away at his magnum opus, praying it could one day rise to the level of mediocre."

"That is my dream, Father," Adonis replied. "Given the choice, I will always pick mediocre writer over your corporate stooge."

John slammed his glass on the side table. "Do you hear this boy, Martha? He has no respect for the man who raised him. Daring to sit there so superior when he is neither a writer nor a businessman, he's a college freshman English *teacher*."

Adonis shot forward. "It's a job, Dad. That I earned. On my own. Without your money, connections, or support—all which you made clear I lost the day I stopped letting you run my life."

"John," Martha cried. "Adonis, that's enough."

"Earned without my connections?" John barked a laugh eerily similar to Victor. "Is that what you think? This is Regalia. Whatever name you call yourself, you're a Wilson, and a Wilson opens doors in this town. You can thank me for your position as you can for everything I've sacrificed to get you where you are."

"You did not get me this job."

"No?"

"No," Don said firmly. "The dean hates you. He made of point of saying so during the interview. Something about a bet you reneged on twenty years ago." John was flushing an angry, concerning red. "It's more accurate to say I got this position despite everything you've done."

"That grudge-holding officious twit. I owe that man nothing."

"Of course you don't, sweetheart." Martha had a strangle grip on her husband's knee. "And of course you earned your job, Don. I bet you're a wonderful teacher. Luna, isn't he a wonderful teacher?"

I froze with the shrimp half in my mouth. So much for eating saving me from talking. "Uh, yes," I said. "He's one of the best teachers I've ever had. Most of my professors read off PowerPoints like they're boring themselves, but not Professor Anthony. He makes us a part of the lecture—a part of the literature. He takes a book written over a hundred years ago and makes it relevant to us today.

"We think we've come so far with feminism, sexuality, and equality since the day *The Scarlet Letter* was written, but I was called a slut yesterday for talking to a guy fully clothed on the quad in broad daylight. My point is," I said quickly at their bemused expression. "I used to think English class was about reading ancient books written by dead men who wouldn't have understood my life if I lived in their time, and definitely wouldn't understand it now.

"Because of Professor Anthony, I see writing isn't about that. It's about seeing the world the way it truly is—stripped of the bullshit, the niceties, and the lies—and reflecting it through the language all cultures have shared since we came out of our caves: storytelling."

My cheeks were heating up fast under their stares. Turning and looking at Adonis would make this twice as impossible to say. "I know I sound intense, but that's because of his class. He's so passionate, he forces you to care. To try harder and find the truth in yourself. I can honestly say I didn't work this hard on writing assignments before I took his class. If only he wasn't impossible to please." Yes, I had to add that last comment.

"I'm not impossible to please," Adonis replied. "You said it yourself. I expect my students to care as much as I do. That last paper you handed me was a joke."

I whirled on him. "It wasn't a joke."

"I said a book, essay, or work of fiction that had an impact on society. You wrote about the movie *Mean Girls*."

"That was based on a book," I cried. "The book led to the movie. The movie had an impact."

"On what? October third?"

"On young women," I forced through gritted teeth. "On the way they relate to each other, and how the creation of cliques and outcasts reinforces the same hierarchical systems we fight to shed in every equal society. We don't see that we're undermining the very feminist goals we hope to achieve when we shun a girl for wearing the wrong sweater.

"That book and the movie it led to does exactly what I said, Adonis. Exactly what you taught me. It shows life in Regalia University as it truly is—stripped of the bullshit. I explained all of this in the paper. Did you even read it?"

He hummed, helping himself to a crostini. "I did, but once again, you deliver a much better speech than you do a paper."

"You are such a—" I cut off, suddenly remembering where I was, and the three pairs of eyes staring at me.

Smiling at Victor and his parents, I cleared my throat, and said in an even tone, "Excuse me, Adonis, what I meant to say is, this is why people kick doors at your head."

Victor, Martha, and Adonis choked—Adonis on a guffaw. He busted up, smiling for the first time since he entered the room.

"All right, Luna," he said between chuckles. "You've made your point. I'll give your paper another look."

"Thank you."

"See?" Martha said. "That's kind of you, dear. Proof you're a fair-handed, inspiring teacher. Although, Luna, I wouldn't be so quick to dismiss Adonis's comments. Claiming Regalia University is anything like that silly movie is preposterous. It's a wonderful school filled with strong, supportive women who accept everyone as they are."

Oh yes, one of those strong, supportive, inclusive women kicked me in the stomach for stealing your son, and the other stole Grandmammy's ring. Lovely people.

Martha stood up. "I'm going to check on dinner. You four behave while I'm gone."

Thank the lucky stars, dinner was in the middle of being placed on the table when she stuck her head inside. We moved the party into the dining room, sitting down to a meal of tomato farro salad, lemon sole, and baked apple tart.

John kept a steady flow of scotch going throughout the meal, holding up his glass for the servers to pour more before he finished the last drop. We tried to stick to polite, surface topics of conversation, but John managed to wrangle out a dig at Adonis every time.

"The wedding will be here, of course," Martha said. "A venue lovelier than our home does not exist."

"Fine with me," I replied. "I told Victor we can do whatever he wants. Honestly, I'm cool with a couple petals on the grass, a simple dais, and a priest, but Victor said no." My hand cut through the air. "It's custom cake toppers, a photo booth, herb centerpieces, and a wedding dais shaped like a heart, or he's not showing up.

"He's gone full groomzilla on the whole thing, Mother Martha, but it's just so sweet how much he cares about our wedding."

"You do, dear?"

"Oh yes," I said, speaking over Victor. "Don't let him fool you. He wants to be a part of every decision. Every meeting with the wedding planner, florist, the photographer, the videographer, the caterer."

Martha laid a hand over her heart. "Aw, that's so sweet."

"Now I want a divorce," Victor hissed under his breath. "Yes, Mom, I was saying to Luna that I wanted to be involved, but today I realized that you've got everything under control. I wouldn't want to get in your way."

"My sweet boy." She patted his cheeks. "It's just as well you do leave this to me. Herb centerpieces? Over my dead body."

"Yes, son," John chimed in. "Let your mother do this. She was already robbed of planning her eldest son's wedding. Don't break her heart a second time."

Adonis threw down his fork, opening his mouth to let loose.

"That's not true," Victor said. "When I marry my second wife, Mom can be all over that wedding."

"Victor!" his parents cried at the same time. I cracked up.

"Don't say things like that," Martha scolded. "You two will have a happy, loving marriage."

I was still laughing.

"Course, Mom. It was just a joke. Good thing my future bride thinks I'm funny."

Our eyes met, shining with mirth. Victor could make me laugh even when he was pissing me off. The guy had a quick wit. Damn, he always smells good too. Like sunshine after it rains and that first steamy whiff of hot cinnamon cocoa. He's been so sweet watching my back, threatening violence against everyone who looks at me wrong. And the other day when he—

"See," Martha drew out. "I knew you two were a perfect match. Sensed it from the moment I met you, Luna."

We reeled back—faces bleached sallow. How long had I sat there gazing into his moon eyes? How long was he looking into mine!

"You're the one for my boy." Martha winked at me. "You kids say the word and we can move up the wedding."

No words were said. Not from me or Victor for the rest of the meal.

After dinner, Martha snatched me and Victor up, taking us into her office to show us her plans for the wedding. In true Wilson fashion, she did a lot of *telling* me what we were going to do instead of asking me.

Twenty minutes in, I begged off, saying I needed to use the restroom. I made it as far as the library.

Padding inside, I curled up on the seat under the bay window, resting my forehead against the glass. My thoughts calmed as I breathed slow, and in that calm place was Winter and her murderers.

"Had to get out of there too?"

Adonis stepped out from the stacks. Picking up my feet, he made room for himself, joining me before the window. For a while, we didn't speak.

"Sorry about tonight," I said. "I didn't do a very good job being your buffer."

The corner of his mouth tugged up. "It wasn't your job to be my buffer, Luna. If it was, you're owed a substantial fee. No one silences my father. Even so, I noticed you and Victor trying. I appreciated it."

"It's just so silly," I burst out. "John Wilson has a successful, hardworking, independent *living* son and all he cares about is that he can't control every aspect of your life. The time we have with the people we love is short. Why do we waste it on stupid, petty drama that's never worth it in the end?"

"We're human, Luna. We learn every lesson when it's far too late."

I gazed at him, noticing the moonlight reflected in his eyes, though I knew I shouldn't. "Did you really think my paper was terrible?"

"I did," he admitted. "I don't now."

"Why do you pretend you don't know me?"

"Excuse me?"

"The paper." I drew my knees to my chest, resting my chin on them. "You say you forgot the first time we talked about Winter, but now you know what happened. You know that essay about Mean Girls was really written for her, but you pretend you don't understand me, so you can call me shallow and demand more than I have to give. Why do you do that?"

Adonis sighed, looking away. "I don't know you, Luna. Not in any special, particular way. You're not separate from my other students who I grade with impartiality. Can't you see the issue? I can't grade you based on drunken talks and inappropriate games of ask-me-anything in my office. We've crossed enough lines, Luna. I'm not the professor you praised downstairs if I let myself cross any more."

"That's why you have to be so rigid and serious whenever I walk into a room? We can't be the first student and professor to have a friendly relationship. Sure, we won't go out and get our nails done together. But we can talk about things—real things," I whispered. "The stuff that only people who know true loss can say to each other."

Adonis's smile didn't reach his eyes. "No, Luna. We can't."

Hurt and anger flared in my chest. "What are you so afraid of?"

He gave me a long look. "Is that your final question?"

For a second I didn't know what he meant. "No," I said. "My question isn't a question. It's a request. Read me something you've written, Adonis. From the magnum opus. I want to know what the world looks like to you when it's stripped of lies."

"Hmm. I'll never know what to expect from you, will I?"

Adonis turned to face me, pulling out his phone. I held my breath as he scrolled through the screen, not daring to believe this was really happening. He was going to read to me. Share his work for my comment and judgment.

"I saw you through the window this morning," he began. "Flowers in your hair, your shoes sprinkled with dew. I saw you through the window and I was there. Transported to damp sheets and a wheezing fan, I counted the strands curling around my fingers, marveling that each one got to be with you every day. They got to kiss your shoulders and tickle your cheeks.

"My gift was to hold you that one night, spending our time together in envy at the sun who'd steal you away and the sheets that'd remember your smell longer than me.

"My boss waves his hand in front of my face. Spittle dotting his desk as he yells my distraction is further proof I'm slipping. My work isn't what it was. I can't concentrate. I'm ruining everything that I've worked for. He orders me to pull myself together or consider this the end. I should care, but I can't.

"Because I looked out the window, and there was you."

My lips parted and fate stole the words off my tongue, leaving me speechless. What could I say in response? I didn't have the right to comment or judgment. I didn't have the right to question his marks on my papers. Nothing I would ever write would be worthy of him.

"That was beautiful," I whispered. "Did you write it for Catalina?"

"No, Luna." Trapping my gaze, he tucked his phone away. "I didn't."

My heart pounded loud in my ears. I should leave, walk away, go back to Victor. There was nothing more Adonis and I needed to say to each other in a darkened room, sitting alone. He was right. It was because we would one day be brother- and sister-in-law that right now all we should be is teacher and student.

At that moment, I took my silly, impossible crush on Professor Anthony and locked it away where it would reside with my useless thoughts about Rafael, the vision of Lucien on his bed, the feel of Cato wrapped around me, and Wilder holding me as I cried. There was nothing that mattered more than making it work with Victor, because there was nothing that mattered more than Winter. As long as there were men on my list, I needed to be at Regalia University, which meant I needed to be his fiancée.

Dropping my feet, I leaned in. "Do I get my final two questions?"

"I agreed to three."

"How about this? I ask them, but you have the right to refuse to answer."

His smile started to return. "I always had that right, but okay. I'll play along. Two more questions."

"Can you teach me how to curse like you? Because once you get going, there's no stopping you."

Adonis tossed his head back laughing. I giggled as the tension broke.

"I'm afraid only years of practice can get you to my level. Plus, four years of rugby. Collect enough injuries, you'll teach the paramedics to carry earplugs."

"Sorry again about your..." I gestured to his bandage.

"You can admit now that you did this."

I threw up my hands. "I swear it wasn't me. I was the one who came running to your rescue with a bag full of medical supplies. When you tell this story in the future, name me as the hero, not the suspect."

"That I can do."

"And my last question." My smile faded. "Can you forgive me for kissing you and making everything so awkward?"

Adonis slid his fingers under mine. "I—"

"Kissing?"

We jerked, whirling around as Victor stepped out from behind the stacks. Storm clouds cloaked his expression.

"What the fuck, Luna? You kissed my brother?"

I shot up, slipping out from Adonis's touch. "Victor, wait. Let me explain—"

"Explain what? That you kissed Don and didn't tell me? When did it happen?" He threw himself back when I tried to get close, keeping the distance between us. "How long has this been going on?"

"Nothing's been going on," Adonis said. "Vic, it's not like that. Just calm down and listen."

"Don't fucking tell me to calm down! My brother and my fiancée are sneaking off together, messing around behind my back!"

"We didn't!" I seized his arm, trying to make him look at me. "It was one time and before we agreed to be exclusive. Victor, I was drunk!"

"And that makes it okay!" He threw me off. "If it was that long ago, why didn't either of you tell me?"

"Because I—"

"Save it," he growled. "I don't give a shit. I didn't want to marry you anyway. Get out, Sinclair."

I reeled like he slapped me. "What?"

"You heard me. Get the fuck out. We're done."

He stormed off, slamming the door hard enough to rattle the windows.

"Luna..."

I couldn't look at Adonis, even if I wanted to. Tears blurred my vision, strangling my throat as I raced out.

"Luna, wait!"

His footfalls followed me down the steps, through the dining room, and into the garage. I threw open the door, throwing myself on the driver's seat as Adonis stumbled out.

"Luna, don't leave like this! Just let me talk to him. Let me—"

The rest was smothered by the squeal of tires. I sped away from Wilson Manor, wetness soaking my face and neck as *Surrender to Me* crooned through the speakers.

I PEELED MY EYES OPEN the next morning, sleep and crusty tears gluing them together. My reason for waking stroked my hair, their soothing touch easing the headache that chased me into sleep.

"Cato," I croaked. "You have to go back to your room."

"Who's Cato?" asked a very feminine, and very not-Cato voice.

"Mom?" I lifted my head from the pillow, looking into my mom's gentle smile.

The night before came back to me. Running from Victor's house, taking off in the car, racing back to campus, doing a U-turn, and going home. I burst in on Mom and Jack eating dinner in bed, and kicked my stepfather out. Mom held me for hours, whispering comforting things until I fell into an exhausted sleep.

"How are you, my baby?" She kissed my temple. "Are you feeling any better?"

"No," I muttered.

Pushing up, I got a proper look at my mother. I fell asleep with my head on her lap, leaving her to spend the night propped up against the headboard. She appeared as tired and uncomfortable as you'd expect from spending hours in that position, but... that was all I saw looking at her.

Her hair was clean and tied with a single ribbon. The robe that had become her second skin lay on the chaise, and the pajamas she had on were new. I knew this because I'd seen every one of my mother's pajamas since I returned home. She stopped wearing anything else.

"Mom, are you feeling better?"

Smiling, she stroked my cheek. "No, Luna. I do not feel better, but I do feel different."

"That's good, Mom." I hugged her tight. "Different is good."

"My baby needs me, and this time, I'm here for you. We're going to get you out of that horrible place, Luna. Mommy and Jack will take care of everything."

"What? Mom, no," I said, releasing her. "It's not that. I didn't come here because of problems at school. I came because I did something stupid."

She frowned. "What do you mean? What could you have done?"

"This time it really was all me. I... got drunk and kissed Victor's older brother. It was over in a second and he didn't kiss me back," I rushed out. "But I didn't tell Victor about it and he found out in the worst way."

"I see."

I waited for more. None came. "That's it? Mom, what do I do? Victor was raging. He threw me out of his house."

"The only thing you can do now is let him cool off." She guided me back onto the pillow, running her hands through my hair like she did when I was a little girl. "Things are said in the heat of the moment that become regrets in the cold of the morning."

My arms curled around her, as if maybe if I squeezed her tight enough, I could keep her here to stay. It's been so long since the mom I knew comforted me, gave me advice, told me everything would be okay. I had come to accept that the day my sister died, I lost two people.

"How could he forgive me? It didn't feel like I was keeping secrets from him. It was only recently I got used to the idea of being around him without fantasizing about strapping him to railroad tracks and kicking back to watch the show.

"There's nothing going on between me and his brother. There can't be for so many reasons. What was the point of bringing up a kiss both of us had to forget?"

"You made a mistake, baby. You're young. We just lost W-Winter." Her voice cracked. "This is a terrible time for our family, and you're due a moment or two of bad judgment as long as it comes with remorse. When Victor's ready, he'll realize that and listen to your apology. One day, this will be one of those bumps in the road that you'll look back on—thankful that it made you stronger as a couple."

I sniffed. "Thanks, Mom."

"Of course, baby. That's why I'm here."

"I missed you so much," I said, eyes welling. "I thought I lost you too."

Her voice was barely a whisper. "For a while, you did. Jack brought almost a dozen psychiatrists into our home, and I finally let the last one speak to me. She made me see that I have another child that needs me, and I do not honor Winter's memory by letting you slip away too."

"I'm not slipping away. Mom, I'm fine." That would've sounded more convincing if I wasn't bawling on her lap like a little girl.

"You're not fine. I took my eye off you, Luna. I let you enroll in that horrible, disgusting place. Then, I let Jack talk me into this ludicrous arranged marriage. I hope you and Victor make up, but even if you do, you're both much too young to be thinking of marriage.

"I let too much go on while I hid in this bedroom, Luna, but no more. We're withdrawing you from that school and putting an end to this marriage nonsense."

"B-but, Mom," I stammered. "I can't drop out of Regalia U. The semester already started. Jack paid all that money, and I made friends. I can't just—"

"Shhh." Mom kissed my temple. "Don't argue with me, Luna. My mind is made up. That place will not take another one of my girls. Now up," she said. "Winter's garden is starting to wilt. We'll spend the morning weeding and planting new flowers. For your sister. How does that sound?"

"Okay," I replied, voice small.

I was helpless to stop her gathering me up and taking me down to the kitchen where Jack was in the process of burning our breakfast. I stood silent as she told him my marriage to Victor Wilson was off and I was withdrawing from Regalia U.

It struck me as I kneeled in the dirt that Saylor, Everleigh, Iris, and the others didn't need to harass, taunt, bully, and beat me to get me out of the university and away from Victor.

All they had to do was wait.

I BOUNCED ON THE BALLS of my feet, keeping my hands up.

"I don't have a choice, Lucien. There's nothing I can say that'll convince her to let me stay in Regalia and I can't blame her. I hate this place as much as she does. I mean, she's finally out of her room. There... There was a time right after we lost Winter that Mom was on suicide watch." My lips trembled. "We found her in the bathroom just sitting there, holding a razor.

"I'm afraid that if I dig my heels in on this, she'll sink back into that depression and *I* will be the reason my mother can't get out of bed." I stopped, clutching my head. "How can I do that to her? What am I supposed to—?"

Lucien swept my legs out from under me, dropping me flat on my back. He stood over me—shirtless and wearing one of those white pantaloons like a Victorian bare-knuckle boxer. His canines gleamed in the dojo's harsh lighting. "Never lose focus, Lady Luna. An opponent won't take a break for you to cry."

He kneeled beside me. "As for your mother, I can't imagine how hard this is for both of you. She's trying to protect you, you're trying to protect her. After I was turned, I walked away from my family. My bloodlust was out of control, and though I knew deep down I'd never hurt them, I was afraid of looking in their eyes and seeing a monster.

"I thought it was better for everyone that I disappear, but all I did was abandon my wife and leave my son without a father. I've regretted it for over a hundred years." Lucien caught my tear on his knuckle. "I'll never know what could've happened if I told them the truth. You still have time, Luna. Tell your mother why you need to be here."

I tossed my head. "Tell my mom I walked into the hellmouth to get revenge on the devils? She'll pull me out of here so fast, my bags will be left on the sidewalk. I can't do that."

"Then, you have to go."

I quieted, the hopelessness of my situation sinking in. She was my mother, I couldn't be the reason she had another breakdown. But I also can't tell her the truth about why I enrolled in Regalia U and let Jack push me into an arranged marriage to do it.

So how many options does that leave me but one?

"I can't think about this right now," I said, pushing myself up. "You said you'd teach me self-defense. I need to learn no matter where I go to school next semester."

"I'm more concerned about tonight. Are you still accepting that invitation to Saylor's?"

Bitterness slicked my tongue. "I have to, Lucien. She has the ring. It belonged to Martha's grandmother. I can't let that harpy keep it."

"That's what she's counting on."

I was saved from replying by hands on my hips. Lucien turned me toward the mirror, fingers pressing into my waist as he squared my stance. "Feet firmly planted for stability."

Heat, and his breath, traveled up my neck. His middle molded to my backside, putting me in proper alignment with a thrust. My knees nearly gave out.

"Luna, are you okay?"

"Fine," I rasped. "It's just been a long night."

He patted my thigh. "Okay, this time when you throw your punch, pivot on this leg and keep the other still. The power is in your stance."

"Power's in my stance." His hair was tickling my cheek. The warmth coming off him penetrated my skin, making me highly aware of his moves, sounds, and honey soap. "Got it."

I threw a punch, watching Mirror Luna's fist come at me.

"That's good." He grasped my hand, popping goose bumps down my arm. "Next time, hold your thumb over your middle finger like this."

"Okay, so do I—" I turned and my thigh pushed in on his middle, brushing up against the distinct bulge that took a peek at me the day before. I shot away. "Oh my gosh, I'm sorry!"

"Luna, it's okay—"

"I didn't mean to—" My feet tangled. "Ahh!"

"Luna!"

Lucien tried to grab me and we both went down, crumpling into a heap on the mat, Lucien landing on me hard.

"Shit! Luna, are you okay?" He cupped the back of my head, raising me to meet the concern written across his face. "I'm sorry. Did I hurt you?"

Wind knocked out of me, my chest heaved with rough pants, brushing my breasts against Lucien's arm. His leg hooked over mine—toes tickling the arch of my foot. His body lay over me like the Thor-blessed blanket that got to cover him the day before—touching all of my interesting bits.

Our gazes locked. "I'm okay," I whispered, fighting everything in me not to look at his lips. Or think about him stroking the nape of my neck. Or wonder what I'd do if he stood up, taking it all away.

"Good." Lucien tangled in my hair, bringing me closer. Did he know he was doing it? His eyes glazed as if the lust had taken over. "I'd hate it if I hurt you."

"You couldn't hurt me." Visions of the night before flashed in my mind. Victor tossing me out like trash without giving me a chance to explain. "You wouldn't."

"All that matters is protecting you, Luna." His mouth glanced against mine and pulled back, stealing a taste. "You're the one I won't run away from."

We moved at the same time, lips connecting in a shower of sparks. I fell back on the mat, running my hands in his hair, bringing him closer. We devoured each other—a torrent of pent-up emotions unleashing as Lucien's tongue broke the seal, tangling with mine.

My experience with men was limited in the extreme. Genital-less Barbie and Ken saw more action than I have in my lifetime. The first time I was truly with a guy, I was destined to bonk his nose, flail around freaking about where to put my hands, bite him, or use too much tongue. My inexperience left me clueless to the fact that none of that could happen with Lucien Calais.

Our mouths fit together like puzzle pieces, moving in perfect sync. He had no problem moving down to my hips—holding me close and firm. I didn't pause a breath draping my arms around his shoulders, moaning as he teased and tasted me, setting off the fuse in my core that zinged up and exploded in my mind. I could kiss Lucien all—

Pain pricked my lip. "Ow."

"Oh, my apologies." Lucien pulled back, a drop of my blood glistening on his fang. "Let me."

Peering into my eyes, he descended, licking the blood off my lips. My legs clenched, lower belly tightening.

His pupils dilated to saucers. "That's the end of the lesson for today. I'm afraid if I continue, I'll do something very ungentlemanly."

"You promise?"

Lucien traced my lips. "I can promise to let the other side of me take over, if you promise this isn't about getting back at your ex."

Reality doused a cold bucket of water in my face. I pushed Lucien off. "Victor isn't my ex. The marriage was arranged. It was forced on me in exchange for tuition. If anything, I'm celebrating getting to throw that damn ring in his face. It made me ashamed to have feelings for other men, even though the man it tied me to didn't give a shit about me."

"Forgive me. I was wrong."

"You were wrong," I flung, shoving to my feet. "Except for one thing, we are done for today."

I left him on the mat, storming to my room. For thirty seconds, I got to forget about the terrible decision hanging over me, the humiliation of the night before, and the uncertainty of the night to come. Thirty damn seconds to just be a girl with a boy I liked, and Lucien had to bring it all back.

"And to call Victor my ex?" I slammed around in my room, snatching the wall decals I ordered out from my desk drawer and slapping them up.

In no universe was that man my ex-anything other than my ex-impending disaster. We never even got to the point where we liked each other as people, let alone a couple with an ended relationship worth mourning.

I was wrong for not telling him about the kiss, but it happened before we agreed to be exclusive. While on the other side of the double standard, he fucked other girls before we became exclusive, and I didn't throw his ass out of my house.

There was nothing between me and Victor. And if I ever felt like there was, my neglected lady bits are to blame. He's hot and my body responded to it. There wasn't anything else.

"Sinclair." Wilder leaned against my doorframe. "When you're done banging on the wall, come upstairs. There's something I have to show you."

"Show me what?" I asked, though I set down the decals and trailed behind him.

"Since you insist on going tonight, there are a few things you should take with you."

I followed Wilder up to the third floor. My interest piqued as he made for the locked door on the end—the only room in the house I hadn't seen inside.

The locks opened with a symphony of clicks, bangs, and clangs. Finally he stepped to the side, letting it swing open. "After you."

"Wilder, how..." The rest faded off my tongue.

There was no other word for the place I was standing in other than armory. Weapons of all kinds, shapes, and sizes claimed the walls, tables, floor, and two locked display cases. I bumped against the butt of a rifle and freaked. Running back to Wilder, I put him between me and the room full of weapons.

"Wilder, are you insane?! If campus security raids this place, you'll end up in jail for forever. For *two* forevers," I cried. "This is the stockpile of an Armageddon nutjob who filters his pee for drinking water!"

"I still drink regular spring water, thank you," Wilder breezed. "Relax, Sinclair. Ninety-nine point nine percent of the time, this stuff remains under lock and key. A digital weapon gets the job done better than steel the majority of the time. This is so I'm prepared for anything." He held up a case with a biohazard sign. "Chemical warfare. SB3A could be aerosolized and dropped on our heads as gas bombs any day now. I've got four suits, but yours is ordered and on the way."

He crossed the room. "Over here are the weapons for a hostile alien attack. Over there is the stuff for a non-hostile alien encounter. In case they just want to meet and get to know us, we'll need gloves and specialized masks. Who knows what kind of foreign pathogens they're bringing from their home world?

"This." He gestured to the entire wall of guns. "Is for when the government initiates the program to separate the masses by gender, lock up the women, and use them for breeding stock. Shoot the bastards, Luna. Don't let them take you alive."

"Goodness, Wilder." I winced at a pair of deadly throwing stars. "Where are the barbwire-wrapped baseball bats for the zombie apocalypse?"

"Zombies aren't real, Sinclair. What you're worried about is a toxin called tetrodotoxin that shuts down the nervous system and makes it appear that you're dead when you're not. Actual rotting corpses aren't going to take over the world." He shook his head. "You've got to stop it with those fantasy books. They're warping your sense of reality."

I flipped him off and got a laugh in response.

"Over here." Wilder circled my wrist, tugging me to the far wall. "Are the concealed weapons. I like the stuff you bought, but you can do a lot better. Some of these might be taken away by Burkhardt's security, but they won't get them all."

Okay, my interest was definitely piqued now. I wasn't afraid of Saylor, but the girl got me jumped and punched me in the face. Only a dummy wouldn't be prepared when her opponent has already chosen violence.

"Try this." Wilder took down a pen and placed it on my palm. "Looks like a regular pen. Take off the cap and its pepper spray."

"Genius," I muttered. "Where was this when I was buying?"

"And this. It looks like a cell phone, but it's actually a stun gun. You already got a stun gun flashlight, but if they get it off you, they won't expect you to have another one."

I nodded, sticking them in my pocket as fast as he was giving them to me. If any of this ever ended up saving me, I'd never question Wilder again.

"Now we've got your key chain strikers, knuckle strikers, and self-defense keys." He handed them all to me. "There are also GPS apps. You can set them to alert us and send your location. That night in your room... If Katie wasn't there..." Wilder clenched his jaw, knuckles cracking. "That's never going to happen again."

Holding the gear to my chest, I said, "Thank you, Wilder. No matter how suspicious you are of me, I feel safe with you. It makes me happy that I can say that after everything that's happened. There are men in this world that I can trust."

Wilder roughly cleared his throat, looking anywhere but at me. "Yeah, well... I may be coming around to you, Sinclair. They did all kinds of stuff to you in France, but you're Winter's little sister. From DNA alone, you've gotta be alright."

I laughed. "No kinds of stuff were done to me, but thank you." I ran my finger along the key chain's tip. "I'm done fucking around."

I SLOWED THE CAR BEFORE the gate, straining over the wheel to see the manor.

Hedge upon tree, upon topiary, upon hedge were put up, blocking any view of the mansion. The Burkhardts didn't want people seeing the inside of their home. They weren't too keen on people seeing the outside either.

A guard stepped out of the booth, clipboard in hand. I rolled down my window.

"Name."

"Luna Sinclair."

"License and invitation."

I passed it to him, waiting patiently as he studied me like I was about to see the pope instead of a mean socialite thief.

"Pop your trunk, step out of the car, and hold out your hands."

"Excuse me? I didn't sign up to be groped or searched. Saylor has something of mine. Tell her to toss it through the gate and I'll be on my way."

His blank expression didn't shift. "I understand this is an inconvenience, ma'am. I assure you these precautions are for your safety as well as the Burkhardts'. Please, open the trunk and step out of the car."

I weighed my chances of talking him out of doing his job—which he was likely paid well for. Giving in, I popped Lucien's trunk and climbed out. Driving his car onto their property was the safest option. He claimed he didn't like the modern contraption, so he was rarely in it and did not keep things inside it. There was nothing for a handsy guard to find.

"Hey," I cried, twisting away as his hands traveled up the inside of my thigh. I wore a tight peplum dress and wedges. "There's nothing for you in there, my friend."

"I apologize," he said, tone blank. "One moment."

The guard scanned my front seat, back seat, and stuck his head in the trunk. I went to climb in when he stopped me.

"Open your bag."

Swallowing my irritation, I opened my purse for him to look inside. One by one, he pulled out my self-defense key chain, the flashlight, my phone, and since he was already suspicious by then, he uncapped my pens and lipsticks, and found the pepper spray. He crooked a brow, eyeing me over the fake stun phone. "I will have to take these, ma'am. They will be returned to you when you leave."

"Sure thing." I slid back onto the driver's seat. "You're very good at your job, security man. I hope they pay you well."

He didn't reply, but I could've sworn I caught a flash of amusement as he returned to the box and buzzed me in. Finally, I set through the maze, riding down the winding path till the trees and hedges cleared.

Burkhardt Manor appeared in all its glory.

Their home was fit for the royalty they called themselves. If you put photos of Saylor's house and the Palace of Versailles together, you'd point at Saylor's and go "ooh, look at that fountain of Greek gods, columns shaped like palm trees, and are those windows lined with gold? I want to go there."

I'd never seen any place so glamorous in my entire life—and I've been inside Wilson Manor. It suddenly made sense how the Burkhardts found themselves on the top of this food chain. They weren't obscenely rich, they were insanely, Thor-damned offensively rich.

As I pulled up to the steps, three men in suits came out of the house. One came down to meet me while the others waited at the top.

"Good evening, Miss Sinclair." The staffer boasted a pleasant face, neat haircut, and a smile. "If I may, I'll park your car in the guest lot."

"There's a parking lot for guests?"

Why if they never have anyone over?

Stupid rich, Sinclair, a voice reminded. *They have one because they can.*

"Sure," I said. He bowed, taking my hand to help me out of the car. "But park it close, I won't be long."

He drove off with Lucien's car, leaving me well and truly with no means of escape other than my two feet.

"Good evening, Miss Sinclair." The gentleman on the right bowed. "My name is Campbell. This is Sanders."

Sanders bowed as well. Since everyone was doing it, I grasped my hem, dipping into a curtsey. "Nice to meet you, Campbell. Sanders."

"If you would follow me," Campbell said. "Miss Saylor is expecting you."

It wasn't a surprise the inside of the mansion was twice as magnificent as outside. Everywhere I looked there was gold trim, gleaming marble, intricate mosaics, stained glass, and golden chandeliers. Sanders bent for me to take my shoes off *in his hands.*

"Here you are, Miss Sinclair." He claimed a pair of slippers from an antique wardrobe and placed my wedges inside. A priceless piece, and it was being used as a shoe rack.

"May I get you anything to eat or drink?" Sanders asked.

"Uh, no. Thank you, I'm fine." My stomach gurgled traitorously.

Sanders didn't move. "Please, it's no trouble. Miss Saylor asked the chef to prepare shrimp tartlets, lamb skewers, oysters, stuffed garlic mushrooms, as well as mojitos and sangria for her guests. What would you like?"

I hesitated. They've taken my car and my shoes. The next step was a laced drink and I'm waking up in the maze, stumbling around praying I don't spring a deadly trap.

"The stuffed mushrooms and lamb sounds delicious," I said. "No alcohol, but I'd love a glass of water, please."

"Right away." Another bow, then he headed down a long hallway. Campbell led me through another opening at the back of the grand room. Stopping before massive double doors, he bowed again as he opened it for me.

"Miss Saylor, may I present Miss Sinclair."

"Thank you, Campbell. That'll be all."

I slowly stepped over the threshold, taking in the scene. Saylor was the only person Campbell addressed, but she wasn't the only one in the sitting room. Saylor, Everleigh, Piper, Gabriella, and Katie stretched out on the chairs, couches, and chaise, watching four women parade across the carpet like a runway—showing off their dresses, skirts, tops, and jewelry.

Saylor sat in the middle of it all, nodding or flapping a hand at the outfits and accessories. Seeing them, the image took hold. *A princess with her ladies-in-waiting.*

"Lu-Lu." Katie ran up, air-kissing my cheeks. "What the hell are you doing here? Why would you actually show up?"

"Really?" I hissed. "Because I was wondering what the hell you were doing here. You and Saylor were fit to rip each other's heads off the other night."

Katie rolled her eyes. "Grow up. Saylor and I have been friends since preschool. We fight, we make up. That's how it goes."

"It *goes* like that even after she sleeps with your boyfriend and calls you a whore?"

That got me another eye roll. "Dean isn't my boyfriend. And I called her plenty of shit too. Aww, Lu-Lu, what kind of shallow, pointless friendships do you have that you can't understand forgiveness?"

The vein between my brows twitched. "Well, you're the only shallow, pointless friend that I've got, but now that you mention it, there's plenty I don't forgive you for." I flashed her my teeth. "I'll work on it."

"Work on that flabby ass too, bitch. No one calls me shallow."

I choked, grabbing my backside. Sanders swept into the room.

"Miss Sinclair, here is your—"

"Yum. I'll take that." Katie whisked my food off him and smooched my cheek. "Text me later. You're staying at my place this weekend."

I watched her go, as always, confused. *Fine. Call me a flabby-bottom bitch, invite me to hang out, then take my food. You can wake up in the maze tomorrow.*

"Hmm. I like the Chanel, but not with those shoes," Saylor said, stealing my attention. "Ugh. Hideous. Donna— Debra— Whatever. You, change into the Versace chain pumps."

The lady brushed past me to get the shoes. Saylor glanced up, fixing on me like she was finally deigning to notice my presence. "Sinclair, you came. We had a bet going that you wouldn't."

Sliding past her, I landed on Gabriella. This lady in particular reclined on the chair by the window, farthest from everyone. Huge, round heavy shades covered half her face, but not enough to hide her puffy cheek, swollen lip, or the black and blue bruise leeching down her nose. The updo, on the other hand, did a great job disguising the bald patch.

"Yep, I came," I replied lightly. "I endured the degrading routine at the gate, and then that silly show with three manservants running out to welcome me into your grand abode. If you're done trying to intimidate me with how rich you are, I'd like my ring back."

Saylor granted me a slow, curling smile. "That was no show. Every guest is treated the same. But it is interesting to hear you find my wealth intimidating. Any other pathetic insecurities you want to share?"

"Yes, sometimes I worry that no matter how long I pickle my heart in brine, it'll never get as sour and twisted as yours. On those days, I kiss a picture of you, Saylor, and remind myself that if you can be such a frigid bitch, I can too."

Ice frosted her stare. "You shouldn't worry about that, Dreg. You're already there."

"Saylor. Luna," Katie warned. "I know you're not here to trade insults, so get to the fucking point."

"Sticking up for the Dreg again?" Gabriella spoke up. "Gee, Katie, I'm starting to think you came here to protect her, not hang with us."

I narrowed on her. She had time to be nasty while her victim was in a hospital bed eating through a tube? Annika was no angel, but the Royals didn't have to prove every second of every day that they didn't give a shit about anyone else.

"She's not here to protect me," I replied. "She's here to protect you. Looks like someone kicked the shit out of you. Sorry I missed it."

Gabriella's lips disappeared in a thin line. "No one gave you permission to speak to me, you trashy, broken-condom mistake. Ironic you're talking about someone getting their ass kicked. The last time I saw you, you were crying in the dirt."

The models shuffled to the side, looking like they wanted to shuffle all the way out of the room.

I cupped my ear. "What was that? All I heard with that busted lip was *muh muh I'm trash, muh muh lower than dirt.*"

Gabriella flew off the chair.

"Enough," Saylor barked. "Sinclair, you are here for a reason, and it's not this. I had hoped with this week to reflect, you'd decided to make the right decision for everyone."

My hands curled into fists behind my back. "You mean breaking it off with Victor?"

"To start."

So the news hasn't gotten around yet. He already dumped me.

"What's the end, Burkhardt? Why do you care so much? And don't give me any crap about Everleigh or protecting the noble heir from a horrible match. Why do you want this so badly, you brought me here after getting me jumped, hitting me, and taking my ring? You had to know I was liable to come here and give you a face to match Gabriella's."

Gabriella bared her teeth at me.

"If you think you scared me into bowing and scraping at your feet, you're wrong. So tell me the real reason you brought me here, so we haven't wasted both our time."

Saylor leveled me a long, flat stare. It was impossible to tell what she was thinking beyond those light pools. Her coldly beautiful face gave nothing away.

She held up a hand. "You can go," she ordered her human mannequins. "Sinclair, follow me."

Saylor swept out of the room, slippered feet silent on the gold and red marble. I kept my distance behind her as we rounded the corner. A portrait loomed at the end of the hall. I recognized Saylor immediately. A little younger; cheeks slightly rounder; the same haughty twist to her mouth, and a coldness in her eyes. Some people are born bears.

An older man and woman stood behind her, each grasping her shoulder. The blonde hair and full lips gave away Saylor's mother, and the imperious brow on him screamed Daddy Saylor. The only person in the portrait who was smiling was the white-haired gentleman standing taller than them all, his arm around a handsome silver-haired woman. Her grandparents, I guessed. The people who spawned the fool who created Saylor Burkhardt. Which one of them took the brunt of the blame?

"What's the matter? Are you sad that your family portrait is you, a washed-up maid, a question mark, and a tombstone?"

"No, I was just thinking that your dad would've saved the world a whole lot of trouble if he shot you on the sheets."

"Well, he didn't, but at least he stuck around afterward. What's your dad's name again?" Saylor threw open the doors beneath the portrait. "In here."

I walked inside another sitting room—this one smaller, cozier, and occupied. A man sat before the fireplace, gazing into the flickering flames while sipping from a glass of amber liquid. I recognized him as one of the faces from the portrait. His hair was whiter, the lines on his face more pronounced, and the girth around his middle provided an easy resting place for his drink.

I flicked off him, taking in the rest of the space. Stepping in here was like stepping back in time to the grand Tudor manors of the thirteenth century. Dark wood covered the walls and floors, matching the intricately carved wooden panels, chairs, and tables scattered about the room—all arranged to face the roaring fire. Between the warmly glowing sconces and the fireplace, there was a romantic dreaminess about the room. It was the place you came to relax in the peace and quiet, reflecting the choices, people, and places where life took you.

"Grandpa, we need the room." Saylor and the Wilsons were cut from the same cloth. She didn't give the man a chance to think about it. She plucked the drink from his hands, set it on the table, and helped him up—leading him out.

He glanced at me as they passed. "Hello, dear," he said, and patted me on the head.

"Oh, hi. Nice to meet you, Mr. Burkhardt."

Saylor deposited him in the hall and shut the door behind.

"People know I'm here." I crossed to the fireplace, soaking its heat into my bones. "Just in case you were planning on killing me."

"Please. Does someone risk a life sentence by killing the disturbed weirdo who pees on their mailbox every morning? You're a disgusting annoyance but not worth the trouble of getting rid of you permanently." Saylor sank into the vacated armchair, helping herself to the whiskey. "At least you're not worth me doing it myself. There are more than enough Royals and Dregs happy to drive you out of Regalia U without me lifting a finger. A lesson you insisted on learning the hard way."

I hummed. "You'd like me to believe you're so unaffected, but the truth is you've never had someone clock you in the mouth for spewing your shit. I bet that's the first time your evil was met with consequences. Explains why you waited until I was already down to hit me back."

"You have me all wrong, Sinclair. I can take a hit." She crossed her ankles, flickering flames casting shadows on her slender legs. Ever the queen, she swept out a delicate hand inviting me to sit—as if I was waiting for her permission. "Curses, insults, sabotage, tricks, lies, and fights. I've gone up against it all... and I'm still here. On top.

"See, what you and all the outsiders don't understand is that nothing in Regalia is handed to you. Of course you come in here and see a bunch of silver-spoon babies waiting for someone to drop dead and hand them an inheritance. You don't know what we have to do to claim our place, and keep it."

Saylor rose as I sat down. Frowning, I watched her stop in front of the wall and stare at it. Reaching beneath a painting, Saylor tugged on something that gave a faint click. A wooden panel swung open, revealing a small compartment inside the wall.

"You asked why I brought you here." Saylor removed a long, delicate scroll about the length of her leg. "To do what no one else will: tell you the truth."

Saylor spread the scroll on the thigh-high table taking up the middle of the room. The table was the same size as the scroll end to end—a pedestal made for a single item.

My feet carried me on their own power, bringing me to Saylor's side. I skimmed the spiderweb of names, lines, and golden ink. The scroll was made of thick, yellowing paper, though I didn't believe it was much older than me. At first glance, it looked like a family tree spanning several generations, until a closer look showed me no two last names matched.

"What am I looking at?"

"The families of Regalia." Pride leeched into her voice. "Our history. Our legacy."

She traced the name at the top of the tree—the one from which all lines spread out: Burkhardt.

"Years ago, a Burkhardt bought the land that everything sits on and founded Regalia," she began. "There were some issues with the land's indigenous owners. They tried to reclaim it, cited treaties, and caused problems for the new settlers. Ansel Burkhardt didn't command an armed force at the time. He was a robber baron who favored negotiation that ended in bribes.

"When paying them off didn't work, Ansel gave his money to Elmer Wilson. Elmer and his militia slaughtered the entire tribe."

"Fucking hell," I cried. "That's the truth you needed to tell me? That Regalia has always been a breeding ground for the worst of humanity?"

Her calm expression didn't flicker. "It's not a story I'm proud of, Sinclair. It's evidence of what some have done to get where they are." Saylor traced a gold line down to the name directly below Burkhardt. "Elmer Wilson extracted a high price from Ansel in exchange for that atrocity. Two thousand dollars and a plot of land in Regalia that was his, no strings attached. Wilson Manor now sits on that plot."

Plot? Their land rivaled fifty acres.

"The money Ansel gave him funded the first business that became Wilson Industries," she explained. "They created an empire independent of the Burkhardts and it dominates every sector where we have no presence—transportation, mining, and construction. But when it comes to the industries the Burkhardts control—finance, real estate, healthcare, high-end retail, and not to mention, our senators and congressmen—they have failed at growing big enough to rival or even compete with us.

"They cannot beat us in business, and in Regalia where our name is woven in every blade of grass, they spread no further than the remains of a long-ago bloody deal. That's why their name rises higher than everyone else, but it'll never rise higher than us."

I gazed at the scroll with new understanding. The Wilson name edged slightly higher than the four names below: Alvar, Starling, Montana, Langford.

Lines connected the Wilsons to the Alvars, Starlings, and Montanas. All lines connected the names to the Burkhardts. But originating from the name Langford was only a single line from them to Burkhardt. Though Langford was in the same row as Saylor's other friends, her name stood apart—far in the corner.

"Why is Katie over there?" I asked.

"The Langfords are one of the rare families in Regalia that don't owe the Burkhardts their existence. Her family wealth was built on the jewelry business and we've never had a hand in that. Plus, her family was the Calderons before they became the Langfords—originating in Spain. Her family came to the Americas before us, settled in New York, then years later rented the home they're in now.

"The worst we could do is evict them from the property, but it wouldn't put a dent in their fortune or their position since they still maintain ties in New York and overseas. That's why the bitch walks around here like she's untouchable," Saylor said about one of her oldest friends. "Neither her business, status, future, nor position relies on the Burkhardts or Regalia."

I just nodded. A lot of things were making sense now. Why Katie didn't hesitate to stick up for me or call Saylor on her shit. Why everyone around here talked about their "status" the same way they spoke about oxygen—vital to their survival.

"So this line that connects the Langfords to the Burkhardts is what? What do all of the lines mean?"

"The line is the land," she explained. I didn't have to search my memory, this was the longest, and only, civil conversation I've had with Saylor since she cornered me on the terrace. "It represents what ties her to us. Alliances, marriages, business deals, land deals, etcetera. All the ties between the families to the Burkhardts, and the ties the families have between each other."

"But you said the Wilsons owe you nothing. Why are you two connected?"

Her smirk stood my hair on end. "Because we're connected by the strongest tie of all, Sinclair. Secrets.

"From the innocent lives the first Wilson slaughtered to get his hands on some money and land, to the many dirty deeds Wilsons have committed up and down the family tree." She sighed. "The trouble is the Burkhardts aren't angels either. The Wilsons know things that can destroy us too. Daddy plans to make a bid for president. If those things came out, it's political suicide. His career is over."

I pictured the Wilson family as it was today. One angry, drunk father; an overbearing beauty queen mother; a stepson fighting for independence; and a playboy ex-fiancé. These were the four with the power to bring down one of the richest families in the country.

"Mutually assured destruction."

"Exactly." She flicked my nose—the condescending ass.

I scanned the names and noted one thing in particular. Calais, Dumont, and O'Rourke were nowhere on it. They weren't even floaters in a corner by themselves.

The Rogues truly do stand apart from this world.

"But why are you showing me this?"

"So that you understand what you did when you went crying to Victor about Owen, Levi, Darren, Caleb, Silas, and Emmett." She pointed to each of their last names on the scroll—some farther up and down toward the bottom of the tree, but none of them less than three tiers down from the Wilsons.

My eyes hardened. *Saylor did fucking know about that night.*

"See all these lines between the families?" she asked, unaware of my darkening mood. "A business deal between the Maddens and the Von Housens. A marriage arrangement between the oldest Brown and a Morgan. The higher position the Thashers achieved five years ago due to Owen's mother, Karen, opening and funding the research clinic that created the vaccine. All of that," she cried, getting in my face. "Gone. Because of *you*."

I frowned. "What the hell are you talking about? I didn't do anything."

"You didn't. Victor did. Or I should say, his parents did at his request. They didn't share the details, but they told everyone that Owen and the others committed a terrible insult against their son's fiancée and anyone who refused to cut ties with them and their families, should consider themselves an enemy of the Wilsons."

My lips parted, and nothing came out.

"Since it was done after your official engagement announcement, they played the card that you're basically part of the family, and a strike against you is a strike against them." She flung out her hand. "You just fucked up dozens of people's lives, businesses, and futures. Members of their family who don't know who the hell you are or care, taken down because a couple of idiots went too far teaching a Dreg a lesson.

"This is partly my fault," she said, pacing the length of the table. "When I told the Royals you were fair game, I didn't believe this could happen. Victor's just a freshman. Eighteen-year-old jock with his head buried between a girl's legs every other night. If he's marrying you this soon, it's because you're pregnant."

"Hold on," I said, throwing my hands up. "You thought I was pregnant and you still had your friends *teach me a lesson*? Iris kicked me in the stomach."

Saylor rolled her eyes. "Oh, please. Like it wouldn't have done Victor a favor if you miscarried."

I shook with disgust, grip strangling my purse strap. Then more than ever I wished the guard hadn't found my gear. With perfect, grim clarity I saw Saylor seizing on the floor until she pissed herself... and that was to start.

"Anyway, I figured his parents were covering for an embarrassing mistake, and didn't give a shit about you. Definitely wouldn't care if someone handled the problem and got rid of you. But then my folks tried to intervene. Spoke to them about the impact marrying Victor to a Dreg would have and reminded them there were other ways to deal with knocked-up trash.

"It didn't go well. His folks got pissed, said how dare they imply his son was that irresponsible, and who they welcomed into their family was no one's business," she said. "I knew something wasn't right after they told me what happened, so I tried to head off disaster by impressing upon you why you should stay away from Victor. It wasn't soon enough to stop what they did to the Maddens, Johnsons, Browns, Joneses, or the Thompkins family, but from here on, you won't do any more damage."

I flicked from her, to the scroll, and back to her—brow climbing my forehead. "I won't do any more damage? Why is that, Saylor? Because I'm filled with remorse for the poor Thashers and Maddens who spawned the violent creeps who assaulted me? The same guys who may have lost a few lines on a piece of paper, but are still as rich, entitled, and privileged as the day before. That's the string you want to pull?" I laughed out loud. "Wow, you've been in this warped Regalia bubble for too long. You really think this little game of status matters to anyone else?"

Saylor waited me out, fingers drumming on the table. "No, Sinclair," she said, slow and mocking. "I'm not telling you to stop for them, I'm saying it for you. I brought you here to tell you the truth, so here it is: your sister wasn't targeted because she was a Dreg or because she turned Owen down.

"Winter was targeted because she became a problem to the system, and had to go."

Blood rushed to my head, making me dizzy. "What did you say?"

"If she'd gone on about her little Dreggy life and stayed out of people's business, none of this would've happened. Does this little game of status matter to anyone? Yes, idiot. In this warped Regalia bubble, it matters to *everyone,* and maybe if Winter realized that, she would've listened the first, second, and fifth time she was warned to get the fuck out of our town."

My breaths came in rapid pants. "What are you talking about?! What did you do?!"

"Me?" she said, shrugging. "Absolutely nothing. I didn't know or even care who she was when it all started. No Dreg has the power to take down a Burkhardt, but she did stumble into a secret that would've taken down"—her finger swirled over the scroll—"a family on this page. A secret, Sinclair. The only tie stronger than money.

"Winter wasn't smart enough to keep what she discovered to herself. She wanted to play their little game of truth or dare, but when the stakes got too high, she couldn't handle the penalty."

"She... No, Winter—"

"Look at the tree," Saylor snapped. "Messing with one family doesn't affect just them. Winter thought she was picking a fight with one person and ended up in a war. It seemed like the entire school was after her, but it wasn't. It was the families and allies she pissed off by threatening to take them down. Along with the Dregs who saw an opportunity to curry favor by driving Winter out.

"I don't think anyone intended for her to kill herself, but..." Saylor shrugged. "You shouldn't start fights you can't win. Which brings us back to you, another Sinclair-Bowden pain in the ass."

Her voice came from far away. I was small in my mind—hidden in the dark place that was spreading deeper, overcoming my soul. *That's why they chose her. This stupid game of pretend royalty... is what took my sister's life.*

"You would think the Wilsons' power play proves that you're untouchable, but it's just the opposite." Closing the distance, Saylor's forehead pressed on mine. "Owen, Levi, and the guys have nothing to lose now. The next time they come for you, they won't hold back. As for the other families of Regalia, you're not another Dreg sleeping your way to the top of the tree anymore. The Wilsons are willing to destroy families for you. You're an even bigger threat than Winter was.

"They'll do whatever it takes to get rid of you," she said. "They'll simply be smarter about it. The Wilsons can't take them out if they don't know who pulled the trigger—"

"You know, don't you?" The rasp ripped from my throat. "You know the secret. You know the person who basically took a hit out on my sister to keep it quiet."

"Well, yes," Saylor said, whipping her hair across my face as she spun away.

"Tell me."

She laughed. "Oh, please."

Slowly, I reached in my purse, closing over a single small object.

"I said I'd tell you the truth, but I'm not getting that honest. It's in the past. It's over. We're talking about you now." Saylor got something out of her pocket and tossed it to me. I caught it and turned my palm up. My engagement ring glittered in the firelight. "Dump him, Sinclair. Make it brutal and public to call off the families who think you're a threat, then pack up your shit and get out of town to get away from the ones who just want you dead."

I crossed to the end table, picking up the whiskey from where she left it.

"Despite your many digs," Saylor commented, "I'm not a callous person. I do feel for the maid who's about to lose both her daughters. That's why I'm still willing to offer you a deal. Jack Bowden can own his house and the land free and clear. You'll receive money to relocate to the other side of the world and agree to never come back here. Obviously, I don't trust your word and you don't trust mine, so we'll have a contract drawn up. The sooner, the better so—"

I tipped the glass over, spilling whiskey on the scroll.

"What the—!"

I flipped open Cato's lighter, the single weapon the guard didn't take from me, and tossed it on the table. The scroll went up in a flash—flames greedily devouring its whiskey-soaked prize.

Saylor's scream echoed through the manor.

Snatching the wooden handles, I lifted the scroll free and threw it in the fireplace, sensing that dark spot grow as it was consumed.

Saylor shoved me aside racing to save it. Falling to her knees, she clawed the remains out—the poker flinging embers and charred wood along with them.

"I want to thank you for inviting me tonight, Saylor." The voice that came from my lips wasn't my own. "I appreciate you telling me the truth, even though it was only as much truth that suited you."

"You stupid bitch!" Saylor flung the poker at my head. It went wide, clanging off the door. "That was the only copy!"

"I wouldn't worry about that. Since you refuse to give me a name, I have no choice." I got in her face, bonking our foreheads. "I'll bring the whole fucking system down—every family, every deal, every arrangement, every secret. If I get you all, the bastard who killed my sister will end up among the wreckage."

I straightened, heading for the door. "So you're welcome. By the time I'm done, you'd have had to throw that thing in the fire anyway."

I stomped through the manor, passing by Sanders and barking at him to get the guy with my keys.

Winter found out a secret and refused to back down. Less than a month since I returned to Regalia and I found out the kind of secrets the Royals kept in their closets—unpaid labor, massacres, arson. Whatever she discovered, there was no doubt in my mind she had a good reason for refusing to let it stay buried.

"It's all going to come out, sis. The Royals rule over Regalia ended the day the housekeeper's daughters came back."

"A SECRET," RAFAEL REPEATED.

"Something big. Something important enough that they couldn't risk it getting out." I wore a line in the living room carpet, making Cato's, Rafael's, Wilder's, and Lucien's eyes ping-pong in their heads tracking me. "You should've seen that scroll, guys. A million webs connecting all the families of Regalia, and severing one represents millions lost or lives ruined."

Rafael leaned forward half off the chair. "Do you remember the details? Where everyone is? Who's connected to who?"

"Not all of them, no." I threw up my hands. "Not even most of them. There were too many names."

Lucien snagged my hand as I passed him, enfolding it within his own. "It's okay, Luna," Lucien said, thumb caressing my knuckles. "It's incredible something like that exists. Or disturbing could be a better word—that the Burkhardts have been keeping such a close eye on the Royals."

"But that would explain a lot," Rafael said under his breath, eyes glazing at the wall.

I moved in front of him. "What does it explain?"

"It explains what Dad does for the Burkhardts." Rafael shared a look with his brother. "It's not about burying political opponents or burying bodies. To know the backroom deals, trades, affairs, and secrets of everyone in Regalia, it takes a full-scale fixer operation bigger than the four of us could put together. And the only man in Regalia with the skills is the man who taught me."

I fell to my knees before Rafael as that sank in, gripping his thighs. "But you said your dad wasn't a fixer. He's a hit man."

"He is a hit man. He's ruthless, efficient, and kills for the highest bidder. All qualities that look good on the résumé for a spy. Burkhardt hires him to get information, knowing he'll hand over the deepest secrets without a twinge of conscience. It's not Dad's normal gig, but for the right amount of money, he'll expand his skill set." His eyes suddenly latched on mine. "Where were we on the list?"

I shook my head. "You weren't on it. No Dumont, O'Rourke, or Calais."

They all nodded like this made sense. "Why aren't your families on the scroll? I get why the Dregs didn't make the list, but it's a document of how easily they can control everyone, wouldn't they want the families from the shady side of the street on it too?"

"I bet they would," Wilder replied, "but they don't control a single thing to do with our families, and that's not going to change."

"We don't rent property from the Burkhardts," Rafael said. "They couldn't tell you what property we do own. After our home was attacked and Mom was killed, Dad moved us to an unlisted address far enough away that the neighbors wouldn't see us strolling in and out—though we still went to school."

"The hospitals my descendants own aren't exactly listed either," Lucien admitted. "There isn't much need for their services in this quaint little town, so they split their time between Boston, Philadelphia, New York, and Washington, DC. We own a beach house outside the town limits. I bought it decades ago, thinking this would be a nice place to set up a simple practice.

"I left when people started noticing I wasn't aging, then returned years ago as my own grandson and enrolled in high school. To live a life like mine, you keep to yourself and don't make the kind of connections that get you on Burkhardt's scroll."

Picking through the bits of his story that could possibly be true, I pieced together that his folks set up underground mafia hospitals where crime was high. The little slice of the coast they owned was free and clear of the Burkhardts because this was their getaway. It was also a safer place to send their son to school.

"What about you, Wilder?"

"The Burkhardts don't know a thing about me or my family." He scoffed. "They don't even know what last name to write down."

"Wait. O'Rourke isn't your last name?"

He flashed me a look like the answer was obvious. Knowing Wilder, it should've been obvious to me.

I focused on Rafael. "But this is good. Saylor showed me that scroll thinking it'd intimidate me—prove how many Royals would take my ass down if the Dreg kept fucking with the system, but all she did was prove Winter wasn't the victim of random bullying. She was targeted because she knew something and the secret had to be about one of those five families, right? As in, she knew something about the Thompkins family, and the other guys came at her worse than everyone else because their families would be hit hardest if the Thompkins went down."

"I..." Rafael pulled a face. "I don't know, darling."

"What do you mean you don't know?" I cried. "It's the only thing that makes sense. Levi had her beaten black and blue. Wesley fucked with her brakes. Everyone else taunted and made fun of her, but the things those guys did bordered on psychotic. This is why."

"I'm not saying they didn't have a hidden ulterior motive for going as far as they did. Even one that affected their families or positions. But if it was so bad they'd resort to driving a girl to suicide, why wasn't it strong enough blackmail to protect her? Warning them it would all come out if they fucked with her, and then revealing it when they didn't listen.

"Luna, what could this secret be that she'd suffer in silence and, ultimately... take it with her?"

I sat back on my feet, cold cooling my fervor. Rafael was right. Winter's bullying went on for months. If it was all to do with some sordid secret, why didn't she out them? Reveal them for the cruel bastards they clearly were, and end her torment. Not even her letter said anything about some Regalia-destroying secret.

Except. It did.

Her words roared in my mind with sudden sharp clarity.

Do not go to Regalia University, Luna.

Beneath the pretty façade is a hideous nest of lies, secrets, and betrayal, and there are people here who'll do anything to prevent the truth coming out.

Do not share this letter with anyone, do not confront the men named, and <u>do not</u> mess with the Royals.

Any law thrown at them will fall short. Any fight will end with you losing everything, and them walking away without a scratch. They're untouchable, and more dangerous than you can believe.

"More dangerous than I can believe," I whispered.

That wasn't the kind of thing said about garden-variety bullies with mommy complexes. A hideous nest of lies? People who'll do anything to prevent the truth coming out?

Those are the kinds of descriptions used when speaking about monsters.

"Luna?" Cato's voice brought me back.

"You're right, Rafael," I said, gazing over his shoulder. "Winter could've used her ammunition. There has to be a reason she didn't—before or after her death. The only one I can think of is she was protecting someone. Herself, a friend, or our family. I've lost count of all the threats made against Jack since I've been here.

"Saylor even said something about ripping the land out from under Bowden Manor and tossing it off like airing out a sheet. Shaking a can of nickels outside the homeless shelter was also mentioned."

"There's also how Winter found out," Wilder spoke up. "I don't pretend I know everything about the Royals, but I've monitored them, hacked their emails, embedded bugs in their computers, and listened in on their conversations for years. I know more than you can believe about those five and their families, but if it was something so bad it'd take down five families and kicked off the war on your sister, I'd have told you already, Sinclair."

"What are you guys saying? That the five of them aren't involved? They tortured my sister for shits and giggles?"

"No," Lucien said. "There's more behind their cruelty. Maybe they were having fun. Maybe there was money or status involved. Maybe we don't know as much about the Royals as we think we do. We didn't know about the Burkhardts and their *scroll*, so signs point to the latter. But your sister did know something, and those five are the perfect ones to start with in finding out the truth."

A thought occurred to me. "Not just them. Saylor knows who's behind it and what they're keeping hidden. We can either get it from her, or the person who told her. Rafael, Cato, your dad—"

"No," the brothers sharply cut in.

"Why? Can't you ask him?"

"We can ask all day long," Rafael replied, "he won't answer. Dad doesn't give us details on his clients or the jobs he does for them—period."

"But if you tell him it's for Winter. That he fed the Burkhardts information about someone in town that ultimately got her killed, wouldn't he tell you then?"

Cato barked a short, harsh laugh. "Appeal to Papa's better nature? He'd have to have one."

"And he doesn't," Rafael finished. "He won't tell us the jobs he took or the enemies he made around the time of Mom's death, Luna, and she was our *mother*. He won't break his silence for your sister either. I'm sorry."

I couldn't tell if he was sorry. Rafael was curter and his expression harder than I'd ever seen him. Even if he wasn't sorry, he was serious. His father wouldn't help me.

"Would he do it for money?"

"You can't afford him."

Frustration strangled me. "Well then, one of them has to fucking talk!" I burst out. "Because the secret they tortured my sister to hide is coming out, and everything they protect is getting blown up with it!" I shot to my feet, glaring at each of them in turn. "I promise you. I swear it on the last drop of blood and breath in my body, I will burn this fucking town to the ground. Saylor will rule on a pile of ash."

I stormed out of the room, upstairs, and ran into Cato's bedroom. His had a door I could slam. It banged against the frame—splintering the wood. It rankled to have Saylor tell me something vital about my sister's death, and then for the Rogues to throw it back and say it wasn't useful at all.

Groaning, I spun around and tripped—legs tangling in the Christmas lights and pitching me on Cato's bed. Vision adjusting, I held still as though any sudden moves would make his room swallow me.

This was my first time in here. Cato was pretty territorial about the place, though he had no problem strolling into my bedroom and sliding beneath the sheets with me. This place was a type *A* person's nightmare. Like his library, there was no rhyme or reason to a thing that was happening in here.

Christmas lights spilled out of their boxes all over the floor beside a fish tank with water and decorations, but no fish. It looked like Cato was making something out of them—the lights arranged on his wall in half a design waiting to be completed. The wall next to it, on the other hand, was finished as long as the goal was to cover every inch of plaster with posters.

Movie posters, celebrities, bands, campaign posters, and affirmations, you name it. If you could blow something up and print it on glossy paper, Cato had it hanging on the wall sideways, upside down, or pinned over the poster underneath.

I pushed myself up on his black silk sheets, brows crawling at the black, charred objects covering his desk. One appeared to have been a pencil holder in another life. I could only guess, but I had the feeling someone gifted Cato a desk complete with holder, lamp, keyboard, and the rest, and he set them all on fire.

There wasn't a dresser. His television propped on an overturned hamper and his bedside table doubled as a milk crate. Actually, Cato seemed to like milk crates because he had another in his closet posing as his hamper.

I stilled as his door opened and Cato filled the entrance, landing on me with an unreadable expression. He made his feelings on me coming in here clear in his Cato way, and it didn't reassure me when he slowly closed and locked the door.

"Cato?"

Reaching into the pile of lights, Cato unearthed a lighter. The one thing he was ordered not to have, was the same item he made appear out of thin air like a magic trick. My mouth went dry as he lit the flame and bent over me, trapping me beneath him and the fire. It danced in his eyes, drawing me, a moth to the flame where a fate I wouldn't escape awaited me.

"Luna."

"Yes?" I whispered.

"We'll burn it down," he said, "together."

My lips parted—to say what, I didn't know. Face crumpling, a sob ripped out, taking a piece of me with it. Cato's arms encircled me, holding me all night as I cried. I fell asleep tucked under his arm, knowing my nightmares awaited me, but that Cato would hold them back.

I WOKE THE NEXT MORNING alone in Cato's bed. The faint smell of his soap clung to the pillow, and his phantom touch clung to me. It made no sense that I slept like a baby when his arms were around me. It wasn't that I felt safe around him. I knew he'd never hurt me, but it didn't stop my hairs standing on end when he snapped at me or looked at someone like he was waiting for the next time they were alone and he wasn't wearing his muzzle.

Stretching, weight pressed on my hand, making me check it out. On the finger where Victor's ring used to be, sat a massive emerald ring set in a gold band and rimmed with diamonds. We stared at each other for a full five minutes.

This was an engagement ring no matter how you looked at it. The question was, did Cato agree and did he believe slipping it on my finger in the middle of the night meant more than gifting me another pretty, likely stolen, treat?

I wandered downstairs, finding Rafael flipping a pan of home fries, wearing nothing but boxers.

"Morning," he called. "Sorry about last night."

"Don't apologize." I beelined straight for the tea cabinet and brought out the strongest one. "You guys were keeping it straight with me. I appreciate it. You tell me the truth."

"We made it seem like your conversation with Saylor wasn't a big deal, then I shut you down when you asked about my dad." Rafael came up behind me, resting his chin on my head. "For what it's worth, I will ask him. For you, I'll ask."

I melted against him, burying my face in his chest. "Thank you."

"I was thinking," he began. "How about I be your escort today?"

"Really?" I tipped my head back to see him. "I thought you were leaving that to Cato, Wilder, and Lucien because there was nothing in it for you."

"I'm holding out hope that'll change now that you called it off with Wilson. No ring on that finger, you're fair— Dammit," he cried, glancing at my hand. "What the hell, woman? Who proposed to you in the last twelve hours?"

I giggled. "It would serve you right if someone did. But no. This is a gift Cato slipped on my finger sometime last night. It'll pair well with the necklace." I shimmied out of his hold, heading for the kettle. "Be straight with me—these are all stolen, aren't they?"

"Stolen? Of course not." Rafael got busy with breakfast again. "He found it. Finds all that stuff."

"You don't *find* a ring with an emerald the size of an eyeball. You're going to have me walk out there and get tackled by the real owner."

Rafael grinned, standing there as the star of every woman's fantasy, and said, "They wouldn't get close, darling. No one will hurt you while I'm around."

"When you put it like that," I mumbled, "you can walk with me to class today."

"Sweet. What's my payment for *services rendered*?"

He loaded that with so much innuendo, my mind automatically summoned images of all the things I could do to thank him.

My voice did me proud and remained steady. "Once again, absolutely nothing."

Winking, he took his food and headed out. "Eh, I'll still do it. 'Cause you're cute."

This guy is going to be a problem. They all are, I thought, thinking of Lucien's lips on mine and my night in Cato's bed. *They're wearing away my defenses faster than I can build them back up.*

Pulling myself together, I finished making my tea and grabbed a quick breakfast. Rafael was dressed and ready to go by the time I finished my semiprivate shower and got dressed in my closet. We set off across campus, not saying much on the walk.

My mind went to Winter as it always did. Holding my hand over the letter, I listened to it crinkle as I thought for the first time of what it *didn't* say.

You said you wrote this letter to tell us the truth, Winter. The reasons why you did what you did. Why did you say it started with turning down Owen, if there was truly some secret you stumbled over?

"Luna." Something in his voice brought me back.

"What is it?"

"Look."

Scanning around, I noted groups of students huddled together. One group opened up and I spotted a piece of paper clutched in the guy's hands. He saw me, and laughed.

"Be careful in class today," Rafael said, voice tight. "Sit up front. In your professor's face if you need to. If someone's going to pull some shit, let them get caught doing it. Damn, I wish we were in the same class. I wish even more Regalia was like other colleges and you didn't have to see the same people in every class, all day."

"I'll be fine, Rafael." I rubbed his arm. "My veins pump pure spite and vengeance now. Like Lucien, I cannot be killed, taken out, or stopped. Not until I do what I came here to do for Winter."

"You're an odd one, Sinclair, but I like you."

"*I'm* odd? Have you met your best friends?"

He laughed. "Best friends? You make us sound like a sewing circle. They're cool. They know how to have fun. They're not like anyone else around here. That's good enough to hang with me."

"Ooooh," I drew out. "Didn't realize there were requirements."

"I'm a picky guy. You should hear my must-haves for sleeping with me."

I looked that teasing grin full in the face. "Maybe I should."

Surprise popped one brow up, then a smirk followed on its heels. "There's only two: Be. You."

My pulse galloped out of control, doing funny things to my head. Victor wanted nothing to do with me, and I wanted nothing to do with crying over a guy I never got the chance to fall for. The heat between me and Rafael had been there since I first saw him dance in the cafeteria, and I was very interested to know how those moves translated between the sheets.

If that's going to happen, this is the part where you say something flirty back.

"That's um... okay." *Smooth, Sinclair.*

I blushed harder when he laughed. "Definitely odd," he said, taking my hand as we stopped in front of the English building. He pressed a kiss to my fingertips. "And I definitely like you.

"Pick you up after class, Cloud Girl. Maybe then I'll hear your requirements."

He rounded a corner and released me from his hold, leaving me free to speed walk into the building, and run into Professor Anthony's class like Rafael was coming for those requirements now.

I skidded to a stop just inside, nearly running into Iris, Cynthia, and Rose—the Royals. Iris held a sheet of paper in her hands. The glee on her face was terrible to see.

"Good morning, Dreg."

Usually he was in before everyone, but that morning, Professor Anthony wasn't arranging papers at his desk or writing on the board. He wasn't there to catch them if they pulled something.

"I'm not interested, Iris." I sidestepped her and she jumped in the way, her friends crowding me on both sides.

"Not so fast, Sinclair. You don't fool me." She winked. "All this time, you were trying to piss me off for attention. Got a little girl crush, don't you?"

"What the fuck are you talking about?"

Clearing her throat, Iris held the paper in my face. "The truth about Luna Sinclair. Number one: she couldn't get off with a guy while in that boarding school, so she hooked up with half the girls on her floor. They dubbed her the Pussy Muncher.

"Number two: When her stepdad cut her off, Luna became a camgirl."

"What?" I shrieked. I made a grab for the paper and Iris jumped back, dodging me expertly.

"Keep reading," Alice shouted.

It was then I noticed almost everyone in the room had a list.

"Number three." This was the happiest I'd ever seen Iris. "Luna Sinclair was born seven months after her mother stopped working for the Cooperson family. Guess who Daddy is?

"Who is Daddy?" Iris asked. "David, Langston, or Roger Cooperson? Not that it matters since they were all married at the time. You came by your whorish ways honest."

"As honestly as you'll come by your hospital stay." I shoved her. "Don't I owe you a busted rib?"

"Hey!" A sharp, nasally bark cut off Iris's biting remark. "Do we have a problem here?" A short, stout man in a brown suit stepped between me and the three girls about to jump me—again. "I suggest you ladies take your seats."

Iris and her cronies went to their desks, and the stranger went to Professor Anthony's.

He's not here? Does that mean Victor didn't—?

My ex-fiancé blew in on a cloud of body spray. I held still as he passed me and claimed a seat in the third row, taking out his things like it was just another Monday.

I hesitated staring at him. We've been sitting next to each other for the last few classes. If I sat somewhere else, people would guess something's going on with us.

So let them guess. Something is going on with us, he dumped me. This game of playing pretend doesn't work for us anymore.

Climbing the steps, Branlon tossed his wadded-up paper at me, bouncing it off my ankle. I resisted the urge to pick it up. I heard numbers one through three. The rest wasn't likely to be better.

"Ah," Branlon crooned. "What's the matter, Pussy Muncher?"

"I have to see your fucking face so soon after eating breakfast. Hope you've got an umbrella"—I plopped next to Victor and behind him —"'cause I'm about to hurl."

"Bitch," he muttered.

Victor gave me a look like he was tempted to say the same. He opened his mouth.

"Victor, stop. Before you say anything, I want you to know it's not what it looked or sounded like. I can explain everything," I said, "but it's all right if you don't want to hear it. Everything's changed now. My mom— It doesn't matter."

I took a breath, slowing my babbling. Victor just watched me, expression hard.

"Turns out it was always going to end this way, but it didn't have to be this bad. That's my fault and I know it." Gathering up my things, I rose. "Meet me after class, so I can give it back to you."

I flashed my bare hand, indicating what I was talking about. Victor didn't speak. He didn't move. He didn't stop glaring.

I went up to my seat at the top and was hit with another paper ball to the head. Giving in, I picked it up and smoothed it out on my desk.

The Truth About Luna Sinclair

Number One: She couldn't get off with a guy while in that boarding school, so she hooked up with half the girls on her floor. They dubbed her the Pussy Muncher.

Number Two: When her stepdad cut her off, Luna became a camgirl.

Number Three: Luna Sinclair was born seven months after her mother stopped working for the Cooperson family. Guess who Daddy is?

Number Four: She tried to get into this school by cheating on the SATs. When that didn't work, she slept with the dean.

Number Five: The last person Winter Sinclair-Bowden called before she died was Luna.

And Luna didn't pick up the phone.

My lips trembled—pressed tight, the tear painted my mouth and dripped down, splashing on the crinkled page.

"Good morning, class. My name is Professor Ross. I will be taking over today as Professor Anthony is out sick," he announced. "I understand you start each week with a writing prompt. We'll do the same today, but with some adjustments. These papers will be graded, and I will see you again on Wednesday to present."

Groans filtered through the room, but none from me. I shook in my seat, wetness rushing down my cheeks to leech wetness from the horrible words.

Snickers floated up to me and got no response. Neither did my classmate, Oliver, setting that day's prompt in front of me.

"Luna? Luna."

I jerked, snapping my head up to an irritated Victor. Vision blurred, it took me a second to realize we were the last three people in the room.

"You have ten minutes before the next class comes," Professor Ross called as he walked out.

The only two people.

"Luna? What is that? *The truth about—*"

I snatched it up and crumpled it in my fist, throwing it as far as possible. I forced myself to pull it together as I stood. "Thanks for staying, Victor. I've got your—"

"Where the hell is your ring?"

"That's what I was about to say." I drew it from my pocket. "Here. Tell Martha the delay in getting it back was due to a vicious harpy stealing it off my finger. That should be all the information she needs."

Victor eyed the ring, making no move to take it. "Why are you giving that to me?"

I frowned. "Because we're over. I wouldn't feel right keeping this. It was your great-grandmother's."

Victor hitched his bag higher up his shoulder, jaw clenching as he looked away. "We're not over, Luna. The wedding's still on."

"But you said we were done."

"And you kissed my brother!" he exploded, blowing me back. "So we both said and did stuff that we shouldn't."

My head spun. "I don't understand. You're clearly still mad at me. Why do you want to go through with the wedding?"

"Because," he forced through gritted teeth, "I don't have a choice. Mother made it clear this wedding is happening, and I had to work this shit out with you. She won't accept another match. Won't accept it as in... I'll end up in the same place as Adonis."

I gaped at him. *Disowned? For not marrying me? What is wrong with this family?*

"So, put the ring back on. We're doing this." Victor looked me in the eye. "The only thing I want less than being with you, is losing everything because of you."

Anger bit at my regret. "I wasn't exactly falling over myself for your proposal, Wilson. I get why you're upset, but I didn't set out to hurt you intentionally. Actually, ever since we agreed to be exclusive, I've respected that—despite you not acting like a man I want to be committed to. You're even less that man today."

Something flickered in his eyes. It was gone as quickly as it came, leaving behind unreadable, frozen pools. "Then, this is your lucky day. We're done with the rules and the deals and all that shit I said. The two of us can do what we want, with who we want before *and after* the wedding. I don't need five years of pretending. This will never be more than what it is."

"Then, let me do you a favor you don't deserve, asshole." Victor paused turning away. "The wedding isn't happening, and Martha can't blame you. My mother changed her mind about everything. The engagement. My enrollment in Regalia U.

"She's pulling me out of school and the engagement is off. So, congratulations." I slapped the ring on his palm. "Now you can fuck your way around campus as a free man, instead of a bitter man trying to get back at me."

"Wait, she can't— Stop." Victor thundered down the steps after me. "She can't end the engagement, Luna. That's not how it works."

"Obviously it is because we're over for good this time."

"Luna, listen." Victor closed the door shut when I opened it, and got between me and the knob. "If this wedding doesn't happen, they'll come after your family—hard. These marriage negotiations are like contracts. Both sides have a lot to gain, and both have a lot to lose if it doesn't happen. Your mom may believe you and she can handle the fallout, but I have a feeling Jack Bowden will help her see she's wrong. This is Regalia. You're playing by different rules now."

He opened the door, stepping out, his eyes fixed on me. "Put the ring on, wifey. That's rule number one: never let them see you're cracking."

I stood there until Rafael came to find me.

What did any of this mean? I didn't push Mom because it'll break me if I set back her progress.

What'll it do to her if the Wilsons come after our family, and my mom can't save another daughter?

Chapter Twelve

I woke the next morning with Cato's arm snug against my stomach and his head resting between my shoulder blades. The guy didn't tiptoe into my bed. He climbed in and wrapped me up like a burrito, and I snoozed through it every time. What did that say about my awareness?

Nothing good.

Stretching, I slipped out from under him and started getting ready. I collected my homework off my desk and stuffed it in my pack. The list of my *secrets* tumbled out.

Rage flaring up hot and fierce, I snatched it up, ripped out my lighter, and set it on fire. Black crawled along the edges—devouring every horrid word so the only place it'd live is in my mind.

"I thought I only had to worry about Cato with a lighter in his hands." Rafael leaned on my doorframe. "You okay?"

I dropped the remains in my waste bin. "Fine. But I do understand Cato a lot better now. There's something satisfying about seeing the things you hate go up in flames. Orgasmic is the word."

"Oh yeah, I definitely have to worry about you too. But say orgasmic again anyway."

I gave him a look, though the corner of my mouth curled up. "What's for breakfast?"

"I made you something special. 'Cause of yesterday.'"

"Really? You didn't have to do that."

"Then, stop looking so happy that I did." He turned away, tossing over his shoulder, "Now I'll have to do it every morning to see that smile on your face. I've got shit of my own to do, Sinclair."

I giggled. "I'm sorry for your suffering."

I followed him and the heavenly scents downstairs. I found Lucien in the kitchen, lifting up pot lids and checking out Rafael's creations. "Would you like some?" I asked.

"No, thank you. I have my own breakfast."

"What is it you're drinking?" I blurted. "It's not blood. It can't be."

Backing toward the fridge, Lucien swept it open with a flourish. His mugs of red liquid innocently filled the doorway.

"Try it yourself and tell me."

Looking at him dead-on, I picked up a mug, popping off the top. Our silent standoff raged as I sniffed the contents and came away with nothing. It didn't smell like blood—which apparently smelled like rust. But it also didn't smell like raspberries or goji berries, anything that would explain why it really *really* looked like blood.

Lucien plucked a straw out of the drawer and popped it in. "Go ahead."

I wrapped my lips around the plastic, flashing back to his lips on mine. The heat of our bodies. The gentleman act dissolving in the fervor of clashing tongues. His fangs breaking my skin... and his smoldering hunger as he tasted my blood.

I released the straw, letting the drink drop back moments from touching my tongue. "Actually, Rafael went through the trouble of making me breakfast, so I should eat that." My face was burning up and my cowardice wasn't the reason. Lucien's knowing smirk said he wasn't confused about why either.

I ate my garden frittata with all the sides, talking to Rafael and Lucien while Wilder was upstairs doing whatever Wilder did. He was walking me to class that morning.

"Owen and Levi are back at school," Lucien said. "The other guys too. They all showed up yesterday in our last class."

My knife clanged too hard on the plate. "I see."

"They could've come back sooner," Rafael added. "I'm betting they begged off more time, so the bruises would heal and they could roll in like nothing happened."

"So, they spent the last few days kicking back poolside with the butler on call."

Rafael stroked my whitening knuckles. "Vacation's over."

"Damn right."

Wilder chose that moment to come downstairs. "Ready?"

"I'm ready."

I picked up my things and we headed out. That yummy breakfast turned in my stomach as we reached the main part of campus. Students crossed the quad—laughing, huddling, and passing a list back and forth.

Wilder veered off, advancing fast on a couple of guys in lacrosse gear. He snatched it out of their grip.

"Hey, man, what's your problem?!"

Wilder rose up, broad shoulders square. I swallowed from across the lawn seeing him tower over them. "I don't have a problem. Do you?"

They backed down quick. It was easy to mistake Wilder for a harmless nut, until you peeked that bodybuilder form and realized only half of that was true. "Nah, dude, chill. You can have it. There's a bunch more in the café."

Wilder came back to me, handing me the page. "What do you think?"

It wasn't my name written on top.

<u>The Truth About Giovanni Natale</u>

Number One: He pays a Dreg to do all his assignments.

Number Two: He has a coke problem. Stumble over him on a Friday night and you'll meet the original Snow White.

Number Three: He comes from a family of thieves. His grandfather tried to get credit for the Montana guidance system. When that didn't work, they stole the design of the Natale Telescope from the late Alvin Perry.

Number Four: He's been cheating on Annika with the daughter of his rival family, Gabriella Montana.

Number Five: And when Annika caught them, Gabriella pushed her off the bluffs and they both abandoned her to die.

"Now this," I said, "is more like it."

"Glad you approve."

We shared a grin I desperately hoped no one noticed or questioned.

"Let's see his lawyers butter him up and slip the bastard out of this one," I gritted.

"This is me going easy, Sinclair. Just wait until you see what I've got for the rest of them."

I folded up the page, sticking it in my pocket. This one I would not burn.

"Going easy isn't what I'd call it. Your truth list about me was inspired. Pussy Muncher? Seriously?"

"Some of those were just things I wished were true. I would very much liked to have met, known, and watched the Pussy Muncher in action."

I ducked my head, looking anywhere but at him. It messed with my head that someone could be so serious and threatening one minute, then so horny the next.

"The rest had to be brutal so no one would think you're behind it," Wilder continued. "The last one... I heard about yesterday. You spaced out of class. Did I go too far writing that about you and Winter?"

My throat tightened. "It was too far, but like you said, that was the point. It wasn't true, Wilder," I said to his fallen expression. "Winter didn't call me before she did what she did. To be honest, that's what crushed me. She didn't call me. She didn't call anyone. We didn't get a chance to talk her out of it. To bring her back to us."

Wilder laced his fingers through mine. "I'm sorry."

I smiled. "Don't be sorry for doing what I asked of you. Just promise me Owen is next."

"I hope he enjoys today, because by tomorrow, Owen Thasher will wish he dropped out of Regalia U."

I ATE RAFAEL'S BACON and spinach scrambled eggs the next morning, but Cato and I still strolled into the café that day. I only believed a fraction of what Rafael—and the other Rogues—said, but one thing I could not argue with was this: if Rafael was slowly poisoning me, I wouldn't ask questions or even care that much.

His food was the best damn thing I ever tasted. Better than the café food served by some of the top chefs in the country. If I had to die to eat his cooking, then so be it. Who knows if his mother was truly a poisoner, but if she cooked even better than her son, she didn't have to hide that she was an assassin. People would've updated their wills, kissed their families goodbye, and happily picked up their forks.

Inside the café, I squashed my grin down hard. Posters plastered the walls, covered the tables, and blanketed the carpet. I had no doubt someone would rush in, close the cafeteria, and get it all cleared away, but it wouldn't happen before the truth about Owen Thasher spread through the entire school.

I went to the drinks station, getting a mug of tea while Cato chased a couple out of our seats. I relaxed with my steamy cup of Earl Grey while I read.

<u>**The Truth About Owen Thasher**</u>

Number One: Owen steals things from his parents' house, sells them, then blames the staff when it comes up missing.

Number Two: His family got their Royal status by aiding in a hostile takeover that destroyed the Levine family. Then they turned on their coconspirators and bankrupted them. Owen likes to send them pics from the homes, boats, and cars they bought from them at auction.

Number Three: Owen, two Royals, and a Dreg were busted with drugs. The three of them pressured the Dreg to say they were his, promising they'd give him ten grand and a lawyer.

They lied. He's serving out a five-year sentence.

Number Four: He forced himself on the caterer's assistant and beat her when she said no. His folks paid her half a million not to press charges.

Owen didn't need five truths. Four were bad enough.

I set the paper down, pushing it away from me. I didn't delight in reading those things. That was a list of pain, vileness, and the deeds of someone who truly did not give a crap about the feelings of other human beings.

"Cato, is all of this stuff true?" I whispered. "I mean, Wilder made up my list."

Cato shook his head. "All true."

"My goodness. I knew they were monsters. I wanted the world to see their true face, and still, I'm horrified. Seems like the world already knows." I shuddered. "His parents discovered he assaulted an innocent woman and their first thought was pay her off. What if people try to find her to prove the story? Or Owen lies through his teeth, saying that someone is making up lies about him and tries to spin this to make him the victim?"

"Do you still want to do this?"

I looked at him in surprise. It was the first time one of the Rogues asked me that. It was the first someone suggested I could pull back, course correct, make a different choice.

"Is it weird that I didn't think this could hurt innocent people until now?" I asked. "I feel terrible about what happened to Annika, but I knew what I was doing when I sent her to that beach house. I didn't want her thrown off a cliff and left to die, but I daydreamed about her feeling a fraction of the pain she green-lit for Winter.

"This is different," I said softly. "Some kid rotting in jail. People working for a living branded as thieves. A woman recovering from assault." My gaze swept the café, and the shocked, laughing, and gossipy faces. "I wasn't looking to make their pain public."

"There are no names."

"No, but it wouldn't be that hard to look them up from these details. Maybe Wilder can leave all that out for the other guys. Be more vague."

Another headshake. "If it's vague, no one will believe it. What's the point?"

Cato was a man of few words, but they got straight to the heart of a problem. I couldn't argue with him. It's the details that make someone buy into the truth. Same for a lie. A list that said, "Owen got someone arrested. Owen assaulted someone," would be crumpled up and tossed in the bin. We were accomplishing what I set out to do.

So why did I feel so gross?

"Does it get worse than this?" I asked.

"Haven't gotten to Levi yet."

I bared my teeth. That shit had my sister beaten and set the Rogues' house on fire. He attacked me and almost carved his ownership on my skull. Those times he had witnesses and accomplices to his cruelty. If he had no qualms doing those things in public, it made me heave to think of the secrets he tucked away.

"I can't believe I'm saying this, but hopefully they crack before we make it to the end of the list—"

"Hey! Give me that, you Dreg fuck! Who did this?!"

My insides curdled. In an instant, I was transported to that night in my room—bound and covered with sores.

Owen burst into the cafeteria, ripping the list from everyone in sight. The time away from school did wonders for the bruises. His face was that of a classically handsome sociopath once again, if not for the snarl twisting him unrecognizable.

"Save it, Thasher, we've all read it." Lindsay rose from her table, arm folded and grin wide. "Sad thing is not one of us is surprised you're a twisted, rapist piece of shit."

He shoved through a pack of footballers, getting to her. "Yeah, and no one's surprised you caught gonorrhea," he snapped back. "Twice."

Lindsay's grin wiped away.

"But unlike your slutty ass, this shit ain't true!" He shoved a stack of lists off a nearby table, showering me and a half dozen people in the filth of his past. "Wake up, people. First, I'm attacked and hung from the ceiling. Then, those lies about the Daltons trafficking immigrants. Now someone prints up crap about Natale, and here they are coming for me.

"It's obvious to anyone with a fucking brain. Some Dreg coward is attacking the Royals, but they don't have the balls to do it to our face. Well, here's your chance!" Owen threw out his hands, chest puffed and face reddening. "Step up and say it to our face, punk. Better yet, come up with some proof.

"None of our servants were ever fired for stealing, and if something's missing from our house, this is the first time I've heard of it. What did I steal? If I got someone arrested, who was it? Huh? Huh!"

Notice you're not bringing up number four on the list.

"Whoever believes this fool has shit between their ears," Owen shouted. "Wake up, Royals. This is our school. Once we start taking this crap, letting Dregs trick and turn us against each other, we might as well give this town to the trash and be done with it!"

He stormed out, kicking up paper in his wake. I watched him go through narrowed eyes.

"I take it back," I hissed. "We don't let up on them. No names, and no mercy."

The corner of his eyes crinkled, giving away the smile behind that muzzle. "That's how we do it."

THE NEXT DAY, THE SHOWDOWN was held behind the music hall. Wesley Hill didn't eat anywhere else—the pretentious prick. That's why we were kind enough to drop a stack of his secrets on each table on the balcony.

Rafael and I ducked behind a tree, parked there as the sophomore Royals arrived to eat before their first class.

"—complete garbage," Gabriella said. "Me and Giovanni? Don't make me laugh. That guy isn't fit to lick my shoes, let alone my pussy."

"Hmm." Saylor led the pack, gorgeous as usual in a velvet rhinestone Armani dress. "I don't know. Lately, you've been disappearing on us. Saying you want a night in, or going on some trip with your parents for the weekend. Plus, we used to hear nonstop about your hookups. The last few months—nothing. A secret beau would explain a lot."

"But it's not true," Gabriella gritted. She, Everleigh, Piper, and Saylor claimed a table at the far side of the balcony and closest to us. Neither one spared a glance at the stack claiming their breakfast spot. "You four are my best friends. I tell you everything. If I was hooking up with Giovanni, you'd have found out way before these stupid truth lists."

She swept her hair back, ever the unfeeling vampire queen. "Besides, if you believe that, you're basically saying you believe I pushed Annika off the bluffs." She laughed. "I mean, come on. Like I would ever do something so horrible."

Gabriella cracked up. Her friends didn't join in.

"Annika ended up in the hospital around the same time someone messed up your face," Piper said, mouth turned down like that little tidbit just occurred to her. "Someone—not us, of course—but possibly the police could assume you got that busted lip from fighting Annika when she caught you bouncing on her boyfriend's—"

"That didn't happen," Gabriella shrieked. "I'm telling you, Owen's right. Someone is messing with us. The Royals are under attack by some hiding-in-the-shadows little bitch who doesn't have the guts to tell their lies to our face."

Saylor gifted her another delicate hum—neither agreeing nor disagreeing. If she truly knew the secrets of every family in this town, what were the odds she already knew about Giovanni and Gabriella?

Although, I'd bet she didn't. Saylor threw the secret about Katie and Piper's ex in her face so fast, my head was still spinning. She'd have found an opportunity to use that by now if she knew.

Or maybe this is her opportunity. Saylor is clearly enjoying holding back belief in Gabriella's version of events. She wants her supposed best friend to sweat.

"What is this anyway?" Everleigh asked, snatching a page off the top. She gasped. "Ooh, it's another list. This time about Wesley."

"What?"

"Let me see."

"Give me one."

"Guys, no," Gabriella cried. She tried to snatch the sheets off her friends. "We're not playing this sicko's game anymore."

"I don't know, Gabriella," Everleigh said. "I know everything he said about you wasn't true, but he was spot-on with Sinclair. That girl is the Pussy Muncher for sure."

Rafael smothered a laugh.

"Asshole," I muttered.

"That just makes him smart," Gabriella returned. "He tells the truth about Sinclair, so we believe all the lies coming after are true too. And I bet that wasn't even about Sinclair. This Royal-hater was actually trying to hurt Victor and the Wilsons by dirtying his new fiancée. How's it look that John and Martha are making their last heir marry some cheating skank who fucked the dean?"

The wind carried another delicate hum from Saylor. "You have a point," she said slowly. "Victor, Iris, Giovanni, Gabriella, Owen, and now Wesley? All Royals. All of them attacked or exposed by some unknown in the first month of school. Can't deny something is going on." Saylor plucked a page off the top, reading the latest Wilder masterpiece.

"I'm telling you it's some worthless Dreg," Gabriella said. "Maybe even some reject from the..." She dropped her voice, leaning over the table as she whispered to her friends.

My brows screwed up. "What was that? A reject from what? Rafael, did you catch it?"

Rafael simply pointed at his hearing aid. No, he didn't catch it either.

"She's really laying it on thick," I said. "Determined to make it look like some liar with a grudge is behind this."

"She would." We were careful not to let our voices carry. "She pushed a girl off the bluffs and couldn't be bothered to check if she was still breathing. Montana's going to fight till her hair turns gray, swearing up and down it never happened."

"—do something about this," Gabriella continued, drawing my attention back. "Who's this shit going to come after next? You, Everleigh? Or you, Saylor?"

Saylor delicately dabbed her mouth. "He wouldn't dare."

Wanna bet?

Voices carried over the balcony, signaling more of the sophomore Royals were coming with their breakfast.

"What's this?"

"Another one?"

They got louder and rowdier. Most of the sophomore crowd was there, and from the laughing, they weren't feeling the we're-all-in-this-together, band-against-the-Dregs vibes.

"Yo, read it out loud!"

"All right, all right." I spotted a crown of hair as someone climbed on the tabletop.

"The truth about Wesley Hill," he announced. "Number one: Wesley arranges accidents for people he doesn't like. The paint can that fell on Zaria Perez during rehearsal was him."

"What!" someone screeched.

"Damn, he did that?"

"What a psycho."

I nodded along, grip tight on Rafael's arm. *Thank you, yes. Now you're seeing these beasts for who they are.*

Rafael slipped his arm around me, pulling me in close. I was distracted enough that I let it slide.

"Number two: Wesley's made a hobby of causing accidents and pain. On the weekends, he used to test his traps on strays. He's been reported twice for animal cruelty but his parents covered it up."

"Fucking hell."

"What's wrong with him?"

Wesley wasn't on the balcony yet, or he'd yell and rant that it was all lies. It was good he wasn't there. Let the full, horrible truth of the bastard who cut my sister's brakes sink in. They didn't care when it was Winter suffering under his hands. Let's see if they care now.

"Number Three: Wesley rigged a hidden camera in the girls' locker room in high school. He makes extra cash selling naked pics of Royal girls online."

"He did what?!" shrieked Everleigh.

Wesley chose that moment to step onto the balcony, a tray under his arm while he sucked on a carton of milk.

"You disgusting pig!"

"Wha—?"

The girls flew at him, wielding their trays. Wesley disappeared under the mob.

"Stop! Get off!"

They were shouting so many things at him, the guy couldn't pick out what they were accusing him of. Rafael hissed as Piper landed a kick to his chest.

"We found out about the camera in high school and shut it off, by the way," Rafael said. "By then, the Royal guys were already passing the photos around like Pokémon cards. All the guys up there acting innocent deserve their heads kicked in too. It took Wilder a while to track the source back to Wesley."

"Joseph Collins. I'm starting to feel bad for the Royals. What went wrong while raising them that they became... this?"

"When you're raised by an army of nannies who fear upsetting you and losing their job, you're indulged way more than is healthy," Rafael said. "You start believing you own the world and everyone in it. Consequences don't apply to you, because there's no one strong enough or rich enough to hold you to them."

I blinked at him, shocked by the even, thoughtful reply.

He grinned lopsidedly. "At least, that's how Dad described it. He was raised the royal prince too. Not here in Regalia," he added quickly. "Our family is from Europe. My father was born into money, position, and titles—the real thing, Luna. Not this game of pretend they play here.

"He witnessed his father arrange the death of rivals and ruthlessly climb the ladder. You can imagine a man like that isn't the warmest, cuddliest parent. He raised my father to follow in his footsteps. Dad broke off and became his own man, but, uh"—he cleared his throat—"you can say the damage to his personality was done."

"Wow," I breathed. "I can't imagine growing up like that."

"My parents couldn't imagine us becoming one of these spoiled, rotten Royals either. They swore they would raise us differently, so we had to earn everything that wasn't food, clothes, or an education."

He noticed the expression on my face. "It wasn't like that. They were never harsh or violent. It was more like if we named all the deadly poisons in alphabetical order, we got to eat dinner in front of the television."

I kept my thoughts on that to myself.

"And when we turned eighteen, Dad signed a check for our first-semester tuition, then cut us off."

"Wait, he did what?"

Rafael's hand cleaved through the air. "Cut. Off. Bank accounts drained. Kicked out of the house. Credit cards cut up. He left home and became his own man, we're expected to do the same. Fortunately for us, we were taught a very specific skill set. There'll always be someone willing to pay for our services."

My jaw worked. I was still stuck on the "kicked out of the house" part. "Even so," I cried. "Did he have to go to those extremes? You can raise independent men without changing the locks."

He chuckled. "You should tell him that."

"I will. Introduce me to your father, I'll tell him exactly what I think."

"You would, wouldn't you?" Eyes softening, he tipped my chin, lightly kissing the tip of my nose. "The most dangerous man you or I will ever meet, and you'd tell him off. Nothing scares you, Luna."

I shivered under his touch. "I wouldn't... say that."

"I would. Cloud Girl," he whispered. "High above us. Fearless. Untouchable. Beautiful."

I glanced away, suddenly so sad I could cry. "You think too much of me, Rafael."

"You don't think enough of yourself. Right now, all you see is that you weren't there for your sister, and I can't pretend to know what that's like. But you know what I see? I see the person who's fighting for her now. Not your mom. Not your stepdad. You're here risking everything to make sure those monsters never hurt another Winter. That's amazing, Luna. You're amazing. You—"

I rose on tiptoe, crashing my mouth on his. His mouth closed instinctively at the shock, then it parted, moving hungrily on mine. Rafael wrapped my legs around his waist, spun and slammed me against the tree.

Yanking up his shirt, I glided over his pecs, indulging the fantasy playing nonstop in my head since we danced at the ABC party.

The kiss wasn't sweet, gentle, or loving. And it was perfect.

Rafael stripped me down to a bundle of quivering nerves, existing only to feel his soft lips. Delight in the faint aftertaste of dark chocolate on his tongue. Tangle in his silken strands.

All the things I read about while I was in the Catholic school *not* hooking up with my dorm mates, came to life with the Rogues. My pulse raced, air deserted me, and fireworks lit behind my eyes—telling of a different future than the one I was due.

What are you doing, Luna? The fierce, untouchable cloud, casting shadows over the men who killed your sister, don't come down to fall in love.

I broke away, pushing back on his chest. "Rafael, wait—"

"They're lies!" Wesley shouted. "I didn't do any of that stuff."

"Really?" Everleigh replied. "Because you fucked with Winter's bike and caused that little accident." Our heads snapped up. "Why should we believe you didn't give Zaria a concussion too? It happened the week she dumped your ass!"

"It wasn't me! I didn't do anything." Wesley shoved off the ground, stumbling against the double doors. The guy was a wreck. Blood dripped down his ripped shirt. Food covered him head to toe, and from him clutching his chest, that kick Piper dealt him was solid. "I'm telling you someone's fucking with us and you're all falling for it. They're probably laughing at the stupid Royals right now."

"Time to go." Rafael grabbed my hand and took off, racing around the side of the building.

"Do you think this is it?" I huffed. "The final straw."

"If it's not, it will be tomorrow when Wilder drops the truth about Levi Thompkins."

THURSDAY MORNING I slept in. Partly because I didn't have class until later. The other reason was Cato sprawled across my body, his head resting on my stomach. I was finding his weight and warmth too comforting to move him.

"Lady Luna." Lucien propped up in the doorway, watching me run my fingers through a sleeping Cato's hair.

"Yes?"

"If you've got time to laze around in bed, you've got time to practice. Up."

I groaned. "Between the bowing, hand-kissing, and Ladying, you'd never guess Lucien Calais is a vampire taskmaster."

"I've lived many years, my dear. I've had time to become many things." He clapped, waking Cato. Snarling, Cato leaped off the bed and tackled Lucien to the ground.

Shrieking, I jumped to help. "Guys, stop!"

Lucien flipped Cato off, using a roll, hold, and kick that he was working on teaching me. Cato hit the ground on his hands and knees, skidding along the hardwood.

"You're getting slow, Dumont." Lucien crouched low, circling my bristling Cato. "Aww, too tired? I've been up for hours."

"Lucien," I said softly, watching Cato's handsome face twist unrecognizable. "This is not a good idea."

"Worried about me, Lady Luna? Why? Dumont's not going to do a thing—"

Cato whipped his whole body around, sweeping his legs under Lucien. The pantaloon-wearing Rogue dropped flat on his back. Cato jumped on him, and the two started scrapping, trading blows all over the hallway floor.

"Lucien! Cato!" I struggled to get them apart.

Rafael came out of his room.

"Rafael, help me! I can't get them to stop—"

The oldest Dumont scooped me around the waist and carried me into his bedroom. He shut the door on the fight. "Don't concern yourself with them," he said over a furious shout from outside. "They'll stop when one of them draws blood."

"Rafael!" With the sudden shout came the knowledge that we were alone in his room, and we hadn't talked about that kiss since we took off running.

I slumped on his bed, wishing I could melt into his dark sheets and hide. The kiss was amazing—hot, passionate, electric, and a betrayal to my sister and what the five of us were here to do. Lucien was right to call me on impulsively kissing him to feel better after Victor, and I was right to end another impulsive kiss.

I never expected to have a life after getting Winter justice. The only future I envisioned was in a jail cell or on the run. Dangling boyfriends and a husband who hated me wasn't the fate the cards dealt me. Why pretend otherwise?

"Rafael," I began, "about yester—"

"Sinclair, look." He plucked a piece of paper off his desk, showing it to me. "Wilder dropped these all over campus this morning like Santa delivering goodies. What do you think?"

I read *Levi Thompkins* across the top. *The incredibly awkward conversation we have coming can wait a few minutes.*

"I don't know why you won't tell me the secrets beforehand," I replied, taking the list from him.

"Easy. So we can see the look on your face when you realize you've got nothing to doubt. You're about to destroy a living, breathing monster in human skin."

My lips parted to say something, whatever it was, it wasn't disagreement.

<u>The Truth About Levi Thompkins</u>

Number One: Levi carved his initials in a girl's skin after she rejected him, swearing she'd always belong to him.

Number Two: He siphons money from his dad's business account to pay for escorts that let him hurt them.

Number Three: Levi set fire to a building with people inside it.

Number Four: Levi Thompkins unplugged his grandfather's life support. A nurse found out in time and saved him. Levi threatened to destroy the nurse and his entire family if he told anyone.

Number Five: His grandfather died a week later from a stroke. Levi's parents inherited everything.

"See," Rafael said, voice hard. "That's the look."

"Oh my goodness, Rafael."

"After you told us what Levi tried to do to you that night, we went digging to find out if Levi got the idea to carve people up before." Rafael gestured with his chin. "The girl he did that to was his ex-girlfriend, Estelle. We left the details out because you were right. She went through enough while dating that piece of shit. We don't need to drag her into it."

"Thank you." I read it again. My stomach tightened further. "Do you really think he killed his grandfather?"

"There's no proof he did. The man wasn't well and he could've died from natural causes, but with the timing so soon after Levi *tripped over the plug* is too suspicious to ignore."

"Then, how did you know he did that if there's no proof?"

Rafael sat down next to me. "Wilder dug up the email Levi sent threatening the man. He said he tripped and if the nurse claimed otherwise, he'd ruin his life. There were no messages, threats, or emails after that."

I threw the vile list away from me. "But if Wilder had that email all this time, why didn't he report him... to the... police...?" I trailed off at Rafael's expression. "Holy hell, he did, didn't he? He reported him and the cops did nothing."

My heart cracked as Rafael nodded.

"That camera in the locker room," Rafael said. "Wilder found out about it when a photo of a friend of his got around. She was a Dreg, so no one paid attention when she swore it was a creepshot and she didn't take it.

"Wilder hacked every guy in our school looking for the one behind it, and discovered Wesley's *tests* on strays, the photos Owen sends to taunt the people his family ruins, and the email Levi sent to the nurse.

"It was him who reported Wesley for animal cruelty, and anonymously sent Levi's email to the police. Do I need to tell you fuck all was done about it after Mommy and Daddy flashed their wads of cash?"

"No, you don't," I gritted. "They pay for it all now, Rafael. Finally, there's someone willing to teach them consequences." I glanced at the list. "I wonder what Levi will say in defense of this."

"I'm sure I'll hear about it tonight." Rafael plopped his phone on my lap. "Giovanni called. The putzes have had enough and want to find the person ripping them down the Royal ladder. He set the meet for tonight, and he's bringing a few people."

"Are you serious?" I cried. "He called? It worked?"

He threw out his hands. "You wanted to drive those bastards into the arms of the Rogues. They jumped the curb and plowed right in it. It worked."

I jumped him, squeezing the mess out of him. The only one in his arms was me. "I can't believe they're so fucking stupid, they're begging their tormentor for help."

"Giovanni and Wesley don't have beef with me. Actually, we trade nods in class, and Wesley was my lab partner last year. They think we're cool." Rafael's hands slid down my waist, content to not let go. "As for Owen and Levi, those fuckers know we're not, but by making you the first victim of the lists, they won't think we got back at them for hurting you."

"Saylor's crew thinks my list was really about getting to Victor and the Wilsons. Spreading that theory around only helps us." I slipped out of his hold and opened his door. Making like I was checking to see if Lucien and Cato were fighting gave me an excuse to end the hug. The fact I did *not* want to leave his arms, was reason enough. "I'll be there tonight, Rafael. I want to watch them spring the trap."

"Normally, I'd say it's too risky, but I anticipated this request and already thought of a way to make it work. We meet at midnight tonight. You'll have to get there earlier," he said. "There's a side entrance..."

Rafael and I went through the plan, arranging where I'd be before and where to meet him after. We talked for so long, a random look at the clock warned me I was dangerously close to being late for class.

"I'll see you tonight, Rafa." I slipped into his nickname so easily.

He winked. "But I won't see you."

THERE'S ONE PLACE YOU never want to be. An empty school building in the middle of the night.

The halls hold the echo of the bustle, hustle, and noise of the day, and emit a moan or creak to call it back. Darkness pressed in on me as I slipped inside, recalling the building map in my mind's eye.

First floor. Class 156.

Tiptoeing through the hall, I jumped when the air-conditioning rattled on, blasting a wave of cold air on me. I shivered for the chill in my bones and up my spine. It was creepy here at night.

Class 156 loomed at the end of the hall. I tried the knob and cursed. *Locked.*

Lucien said it depended on who cleaned the classrooms that day. Some janitors locked up behind them. Some didn't.

I pulled out the lock-picking case he gifted me, dropping on my knees and getting to work. Lucien and I were focusing more on the self-defense than the breaking-in skills lately, and it showed.

I kneeled there cursing, dropping my tools, and rattling the knob for fifteen minutes.

Hurry up! It's after midnight. You're missing everything.

Taking a deep breath, I stilled my shaky hands. *Relax. Feel for the tumblers.*

I inserted the pin, gently eased it up, and turned.

Click.

The door swung in, creaking on rusty hinges that echoed through the lonely building. Slipping inside, I hugged the wall, making my way around to the window Rafael cracked open earlier that day. Voices filtered inside.

"—under attack. Every cent I put in my account vanishes, my car was blown up, and the police brought me in for questioning yesterday, asking if I'd like to *rethink* my statement about the night Annika fell!"

Rafael needn't have cracked the window. Giovanni could be heard loud and clear.

Though he told me not to, I edged closer, peeking through the window. Five figures gathered in the stairs in Rafael's preferred blind spot. No cameras. No guards. No chance of anyone sneaking up on them unseen.

Unless, of course, you snuck into the empty classroom building in the middle of the night and listened in.

"Shit's been happening to me." Wesley's bruised, swollen nose was obvious from my shadowed hiding spot. "The day peanuts accidentally get into my food is the same day my EpiPen goes missing. Then, I was locked in my room all night—music blasting me awake whenever I shut my eyes. My money's gone—"

"I can't believe you idiots!" The angry pacing figure that was Levi jabbed a finger at my silent, headphones-clad Rafael. "It's obvious who's behind it! It's him and his band of freaks. Who else is that stupid!"

Rafael's reply was light—almost amused. "If you believe that, why are you here?"

Levi got in his face. "To join in when they kick your ass."

"You're going to want to step three paces to the right, then one back. It'll be funny to fuck up that other leg and watch you penguin-waddle around campus."

"Oh, yeah? I'd like to—?"

"Levi, back off!" Wesley yanked him away. "Whatever problem the Rogues have with you, they don't have them with me. I told you not to come if you were going to start shit."

"He doesn't need a problem with you, dumbass. All he needs is cash." Levi whirled on Rafael. "I bet whoever's doing this is paying him."

Rafael leaned against the rail, stuffing his hands in his pockets. "You'd have to be a Royal to afford my rates. Is there a Royal that's got reason to hate the four of you and Luna Sinclair?"

Levi's puffed-up chest deflated. The four of them shared a look. Why did they just share a look?

"That's what we need you to find out," Wesley said. His voice dropped two octaves. "But if you are behind this, Dumont, I will—"

"I will have a personal problem with the next shit who threatens me. You dragged me out of bed in the middle of the fucking night. Have some respect!"

Flinching, I ducked out of sight. This was the first I'd seen the fixer in action. The night he blew Giovanni's car didn't count. Rafael was having fun then. He wasn't playing around now.

"Now," Rafael continued in their silence. "I assume you're looking at us because I've got a hacker in my crew. Not too big a leap for your small brains, but I read the secrets on those lists. If I knew you killed Grandpa or that you brain your ex-girlfriends, you can believe I'd use that information to my own advantage. I for damn sure wouldn't sprinkle prime blackmail material on the quad for a client. One or two secrets would've done the job of humiliating you just fine."

"I didn't kill my grandfather," Levi gritted. "Those *secrets* were bullshit."

"All lies," Giovanni echoed, though I noticed no one was accusing the Rogues of being behind it anymore.

"I also wouldn't risk prison for a client," Rafael said. "A bomb in your car and stealing an EpiPen could've killed you. Whoever is behind this more than hates you guys. Sounds like they want you dead, and they're happy for you to suffer on the way to your grave."

"See," Giovanni hissed, shoving Wesley's arm. "I told you this threat is real. We've got to do something now."

"What have you done already?" Rafael asked.

"I've hired—"

The final figure spoke for the first time. "We've answered enough questions, Dumont." Owen stepped forward as I chanced another peek. "Why don't you answer some? You know, just so we're sure we can trust you."

Rafael flapped a hand. "Go on."

"What's up with you and Sinclair?" My jaw clenched. "You beat the shit out of me and Levi for her. We've all seen you and your boyfriends walking her to and from campus, and I heard she's living with you too."

"You have and she is," Rafael replied without skipping a beat. "I normally don't give out this information, but it's not really a secret since everyone's seen us with her. Her stepfather hired us to watch her back. You didn't think they'd let their youngest daughter walk around this campus unprotected after what happened to Winter, did you? There it is again," he breezed, "those small brains."

"How do we know Bowden didn't pay you to attack us too?" he flung. "We all know what your dad does for money. Why wouldn't you risk prison for some cash?"

"Because what the hell would Jack Bowden want with Wesley and Giovanni? You two women-assaulting fucks I understand," Rafael said, waving at Levi and Owen. "What about you two? Is there something I should know? Did you do something to his stepdaughters—"

"I don't speak to the other one," Giovanni cut in. "And the guy wouldn't blow up my fucking car because I broke up with Winter. Especially when *your car* is sitting shiny and new in the student parking lot, Thompkins, and what you did to her was ten times worse!"

"Shut up!" Levi bellowed.

"No, you shut up!" Giovanni shoved him. "There isn't anything in that head if you think Jack Bowden is behind the lists. The first fucking one said his stepdaughter munches pussy, cheated on the SATs, and slept with the dean. If anyone believes it, she's fucked too. Why would he do that?"

Yes, you pretty, empty-headed fool. Argue in defense of the people who want you ruined.

"Exactly," Giovanni said to their silence. "But if you're so worried, Dumont will give us a name, and *after* we prove they're behind the attacks, we'll pay him."

"Actually," Rafael said, "you'll pay me half up front with the promise I'll have a name for you in a week or less. When you have your guy, I'll take the rest."

"Thirty percent up front," Owen countered, ever the vicious business-man's son. "And how can you promise it'll only take a week?"

"Because the guy's been smart, but he's made a few mistakes that'll give him away. He blew up your car, Natale, and the sale of explosives can be tracked—even underground sales. He hacked your accounts and set up an automatic withdrawal, likely into his own account. Wilder will trace the virus back to its source. Last, and most importantly, those lists had to be printed up and delivered. A security camera can tell you a lot about some-one even if they're hiding their face."

I nodded along. Damn, he's good at this.

"Now that you've told us that, we can have our own security track him down," Levi said. "Why do we need you and the freaks?"

"If your security was up to the task, you wouldn't be here. Also, it's now sixty percent up front, and if you insult me and my boys again, Thompkins, I'll find this guy and lend *him* my services. Don't think I forgot that we were number three on your list, so they're not all lies, are they?" The guys squared up. "Maybe a few other things on those lists are true."

"They're not." Giovanni got between them. "Levi, shut the fuck up, and I'm not telling you again. Dumont, you're hired. How much?"

I slipped away as they haggled, ducking out the door and melding into the shadows. I told Rafael this was the perfect recipe. Do everything right and their destruction is served up steaming hot on a platter.

Of course those fools didn't think Jack had a reason to go after all of them. They didn't know Winter left me a note naming every horrible thing they did to her. They didn't know she left notes at all.

The letter my mother received said everything about how much Winter loved her and was sorry for what she had to do, but mine said it all—telling the whole tragic story of the five men who drove her over the edge.

I did not let Mom see mine, or tell her I received a letter. My decision to kill Owen and the others was instantaneous—decided before I reached the final word. When they all turned up dead, I didn't want the first person my mother looked at to be me. Bearing the weight of one daughter's death and the other's fractured soul was too much for the woman I found in the bathroom with a razor only the day before.

Mom can't know what I'm about to do. She can't know that Giovanni just signed the check that'll lead to the loss of his girlfriends, friends, status, freedom, and ultimately, his life. They all have.

I left the building behind, setting down the sidewalk that curved around campus, came up behind Greek Row, and then led the way back to the Gallery. With Rafael wrapping it up with the Royal Bastards, I'd be the first one back to whip up the midnight snack. He deserved one after that performance. I'd replay Giovanni shoving Levi—the guy who had the situation right from the beginning—over and over in my head.

I can whip up something simple, sweet, and delicious for us. Caramel sundaes or brownies in a—

A branch snapped, heralding a curse from the depths of the trees. I spun as someone stumbled out.

Saylor swatted a twig out of her hair—annoyed at the thing for daring to mess with her style, then she landed on me.

"What are you doing here?" we said in unison.

Saylor stormed across the lawn, gossamer skirt swishing. "You're pathetic. Are you following me?"

I scoffed. "Don't flatter yourself. How was I supposed to know you spend your nights skulking around the woods like a skunk?"

Her eyes narrowed to slits. "And what are you doing here? Did you just leave your latest hookup? Some poor girl who hasn't figured out she can do better than the Pussy Muncher."

"Got it in one," I said brightly. "Now, if you'll excuse me, I've got better things to do than waste my time with you. Like literally anything. Sticking my head in a beehive ranks higher than dealing with you, no matter what your little scroll says— Oops." My smile widened as hers melted away. "*What* it said."

Her glare burned me where I stood. "You think you're clever, Sinclair. That you're tough and brave for standing up to me. All that makes you is stupid."

I walked away. "Tell your threats to someone who's afraid of you."

"Just because I haven't gotten you back yet"—something in her tone slowed me—"doesn't mean you'll get away with disrespecting me, my family, or our position. Rafael and I have unfinished business." She brushed against me, whispering in my ear. "I have to wait until he's shaken you loose and you're alone.

"When my opportunity presents itself, you'll find out what happens to people who fuck with Saylor Burkhardt. Sorry, I mean you'll find out again. The broken wrist and busted lip didn't get the message in."

I left without another word, ignoring her high, tinkling laugh following me into the night. Saylor could make all the threats she wanted. I was finally on the edge of taking my sister's killers down. She was done distracting me from my true purpose.

I thought that, but Saylor's threat hung over my head through the night and into the next day. She was clever about getting me alone the first time. Saylor was smart enough not to pull the same trick twice, so if her intent was to arrange another beating, pulling me out of class isn't it.

Then how exactly does she think she'll get another opportunity? I sat on the rim of the fountain, chewing my lip and distractedly enjoying Wilder making students veer away from the fountain with a single look. *I'm not accepting another invitation to her palace. Ambushing me in my dorm room won't go over so well now, and at least one of the guys is with me whenever I'm outside. From that tally, her threat is as empty as her chest cavity.*

"What the fuck are you looking at?" Wilder jumped up, fists balled and ready to go at two confused guys in glasses who came too close. "Look at her again. I dare you!"

They bumped into each other rushing away.

I flashed him a wry grin. "You enjoy scaring people, don't you?"

He shrugged. "It brings me a certain amount of pleasure. I won't lie." Wilder dropped next to me, propping his leg on the rim and slinging an arm over. "What's the update with your folks? Are they still pulling you out of school?"

Slumping, I blew out a breath. "The last I heard, Mom was making calls to the dean that haven't been returned. As soon as they can get a meeting, they're going to get his approval for me to transfer to the community college up the coast in the middle of the semester. I tried to remind Jack about our deal and that the Wilsons intend for us to hold up our end. All he said is he won't go against my mother's wishes."

"She is your mother," he said gently. "She raised you for eighteen years and he raised you part-time for four years courtesy of a boarding school. I wouldn't expect to win that argument against her either."

"He won the argument to put me in that boarding school," I snapped. "Why shouldn't he win this one?"

Wilder didn't say anything. He didn't have to. My internal voice berated me on its own.

Sighing, I said, "I didn't mean that. I know it's not the same thing. Mom is trying to protect me from the place and the people who took Winter. If I'm honest, she was trying to protect me when she sent me to France too. If I was anyone else's stepdaughter, crashing that boat would've gotten me a record, probation, and a label. I almost sent my life off track to impress..." I swept the quad. "People like this.

"Regalia wasn't good for me. France was. I'm glad that I left... but I hate that I wasn't here."

Wilder closed over my hand, squeezing my fingers. "I understand."

"I know," I whispered. "Thank you."

Wilder turned my palm up, pressing ours together as he slowly, deliberately, spread my fingers and laced his through. My heart thumped in my ears.

I swallowed roughly. "Can I ask you a personal question?"

"Haven't you learned by now?"

"You're free to blow the question off. Though, I'm curious how often you date when you refuse to hug a girl for more than five seconds?" I cocked a brow. "I'm starting to think there's a reason you've got so many computers in that room."

"They're queued up to play your videos every night."

I choked on a swallow. "Don't tease me with your lies, O'Rourke!"

He busted up. "Sorry. I'll answer the question you're dancing around. I don't *date*. No woman has passed the required background checks. But I'm not a virgin if that's what you're thinking. I get more ass than my boys Rafael and Lucien combined—if you'll excuse my crudeness."

My mouth hung open.

"It's all of this." Wilder waved a hand over all of *him*. "Girls say I look like Chad Michael Murray. I don't see it, to be honest."

"You're lying," I blurted. "Exaggerating. You never leave your room. What ass are you chasing?"

Wilder winked. "Just 'cause the door's locked, doesn't mean I'm on the other side."

Acid dripped down my throat. "Who?" I hissed. "Whose ass? Who are you hooking up with?" *While you're flirting with me.*

"A gentleman never tells."

"A gentleman gets his head dunked in this fountain!"

Wilder laughed so hard he wheezed, falling over onto my lap. "Whew, someone's jealous."

Oh yeah, he's going in that water. I'll let him up in an hour.

My phone buzzed. I got it out from under him and tapped the message.

Katie: Get his head from between your legs and get in the car. Five seconds or I'm leaving without you.

I glanced around and spotted Katie's car and driver waiting at the curb. "This isn't over."

Wilder mock shuddered, chewing on his nails like he was oh so scared. He was a second away from getting on the list.

I left the howling jackass behind and slid in the back seat with Katie. She had my phone out of my hand and a drink in it before I clicked the seat belt. "Cheers, Lu-Lu." She clinked her glass with mine.

"What are we celebrating?"

"Your disturbing, self-destructive knack for making everything worse. Saylor was spitting fire when she came from your little chat last weekend."

Spitting fire. Perfect word choice.

"Dare I ask what you said to her?"

I reclined against the leather, soaking into the cool, recycled air. "I reminded her that she is nothing but a golem—formed from mud and manure, then given life to serve her master, Beelzebub. Once I find the spell to destroy her, she'll return to the pile of rotting shit that she is."

"Yeah, that'll do it," Katie muttered. "Enough with your death wish. I swore I was having a fun year and I meant it. Next week, I'm throwing a party. My mom needs some chill time, so my parents are going to the beach house in the Hamptons."

I felt compelled to mention there was a beach a few miles to the west, but I squashed it.

"You're staying over to help me plan the food, drinks, decoration, theme—the whole thing." Katie clinked our glasses again. "Don't expect to get any sleep tonight because we're already behind. The party's only a week away."

"Ah, yes. So once again you've mistaken me for your assistant. Driver, pull the car over here."

Katie rolled her eyes, waving the driver off. "For fuck's sake, I'm inviting you over to taste-test my chef's finest, get tipsy, and fool around choosing themes. It's called having fun and getting shit done while you're at it. My goodness, you're so snobby."

I was so outraged at the comment, it struck me speechless.

The drive to Katie's place was short. We toed off our shoes on the welcome mat, padding inside her rent-free, lap of luxury. Flopping on the bed, Katie flicked the big screen on and called down to the kitchen, ordering the person on the other side to start bringing in the samples.

"Lu-Lu, mojitos or margaritas to kick off the night?"

I threw myself down next to her, landing spread eagle on the sheets.

"Mojitos." You know what? I deserved a night of fun. I had the Royal Bastards right where I wanted them—which was the only good thing happening. On the other side, there was Victor, Adonis, the threat of ending our engagement, Saylor, finding the truth about the secret that led to Winter's torment, and putting an end to all of that before Mom pulled me out of Regalia. Yes, I needed one night to bask in my single victory. There were many battles left to fight.

Twenty minutes later, Katie and I were knocking back mojitos and stuffing our faces on steak and blue cheese bruschetta while *Mean Girls* claimed the screen.

"Damn," I moaned. "Will your chef marry me?"

"Nah, but she's definitely down for a quick, no-strings hookup with the Pussy Muncher."

"Ugh. Must you?"

She laughed. "Tell me that list was a bunch of lies? I mean, no shame if you did get busy with your dorm mates. But tell me you didn't screw that uptight, wrinkled sack of prune piss to get into Regalia U?"

"I did *not*," I drew out. "That list was all lies. Written and posted by one of my many enemies, because apparently those come standard in this town. No one can live a normal life, going about their business without getting sucked into drama."

Katie plucked the last bruschetta off my plate. I was about to snatch it out of her mouth when her staff chose that moment to bring in the chicken and mushroom potstickers.

"If you wanted normal, you should've moved to Jacksonville. This is Regalia, boo. D-R-A-M-A is its alternate spelling."

"Can't argue with that." I grabbed the mojito mug off the tray. "More?"

"Top me up."

"Do you really need to go through all this trouble planning a menu?" I asked while filling up her glass and mine. "People come to dance, get drunk, and hook up. Fancy food ends up a puddle of vomit behind the couch."

"Eww," she said with a laugh. "Not behind my couch. I get why you think that, but in this town, the presentation is everything. Any old Dreg can set out a keg and a bowl of pretzels. For a Royal, every event we go to is the main event. A Katie Langford party, though, is the only kind worth attending."

"Am I invited?"

She pulled a face. "Duh."

"Are Saylor, Gabriella, Piper, and Everleigh invited?"

Katie flicked over my shoulder. "Michaelson, bring in the bacon-wrapped shrimp, please."

"Right away."

"No," she replied as the door clicked shut. "They're not invited, and before your head gets too big, it's not because of you. Annika woke up last night."

I shot up straight, potsticker slipping through the chopsticks. "She did? I didn't hear anything."

"There's a reason for that." Katie got up and locked her door. Michaelson wasn't getting back in with those bacon-wrapped shrimp. "The first thing Annika did after she woke up was confirm Giovanni's truth list is true."

My thoughts whipped through my head. *So that's why Giovanni was in such a state last night. With Annika confirming the cheating and abandoned-to-die thing was true, no one will believe the rest were lies. He's dying to get his hands on the person who sent his perfect life swirling down the toilet.*

"She did catch them cheating. Annika and Gabby got in a fight, and Gabby shoved her off the bluffs."

I gasped since that was the appropriate response.

"The Montana family lawyers were in her hospital room so fast, the cop's ink hadn't dried from taking her statement. They came down on her hard. I heard Annika burst into tears."

"Oh my goodness," I cried—that was genuine. "What did they do?"

"Gabriella's version of events, as relayed by her lawyers, was that Annika did catch them and they got into a fight. Annika beat her severely—the proof is in her banged-up face and bald spot. Gabriella ran to get away from her, but Annika chased her outside and *she* tried to push her off the cliff. Panicked and defending herself, Gabriella shoved her away too hard and Annika fell."

The potstickers turned bad on my tongue.

"Annika doesn't know what happened because she 'sustained a head injury' and her 'testimony isn't reliable.' After she fell, Gabby ran down to see if she was okay and then called the ambulance. She wasn't there when they showed up because she was in pain and scared for her life. A bomb did go off right outside their window."

Katie perched on the edge of her bed, an expression I'd never seen before clouding her face. It wasn't that it was disgust—she pulled that face plenty of times. It was that the disgust wasn't directed at me.

"Gabby's only crime was failing to come forward sooner. The true aggressor was Annika, and if she insisted on pursuing false charges against Gabby, they'd be forced to have her arrested for assault and attempted murder."

"Wow." I tossed my head in disbelief. "Yeah, I would burst into tears too."

"It's such bullshit. Sleeping with her boyfriend, tossing her off a cliff, then twisting everything to make herself the victim? Ugh! Who does that?"

I watched her close. "Hold on. Does that mean you don't believe Gabriella? One of your best friends."

"It's because she's one of my best friends that I don't believe her. I *know* Gabriella Montana. I'm not saying she's some sociopath who goes around throwing people off cliffs, but whenever she's in trouble, the only ass she's looking to cover is her own. Her parents busted us for drinking when we were fifteen. Gabriella turned on the waterworks so fast, sobbing that she didn't want to do it but I pressured her.

"Her mom still looks at me like I'm a snake that wandered in from outside. She's always telling Gabby to stay away from that *bad influence*. Worst part is she wasn't sorry then, or now. Nothing ruins her image of the shining heiress princess—not even her own actions. I can see Gabriella doing everything Annika said."

I saw Katie in a new light. She didn't have the nicest or cuddliest of personalities, but she saw people for who they were.

Sighing, Katie pilfered my last potsticker, stretching out on the sheets. "Saylor, Piper, and Everleigh know it too, but when I called Gabby out, they came down on me, saying I've been a terrible friend lately and how dare I call Gabby a liar. Whose side was I on?"

Wow. They made Katie out to be the bad guy when she was right up, down, and sideways. Gabriella's story about how Annika went over that cliff and what she did after was pure fiction.

Fiction she'll get away with because I can hardly come forward and say I was the one who called the ambulance after watching the fight I orchestrated and blowing up their cars.

"I'm sorry, Katie."

"It's whatever." Katie flipped over, facing the television. From the stiffness of her back and shoulders, it wasn't whatever. "I just need a break from them for a while, and since those bitches are convinced I'm a terrible friend, they can do with a break from me. So no, they're not coming to my party."

All of a sudden, it made sense why she was throwing this last-minute blowout bash. They gaslit and snubbed her. Katie would snub their asses right back... and I needed to be a part of it.

"Let's plan this party, my friend." I tipped off the bed, picked up a fallen notepad, and got to work. "Let that man back in here with my food, then tell me what you think of a carnival theme?"

A ghost of a smile tickled her lips. "I hate it. You predictably suck at this."

I laughed. "You're predictably ungrateful. How about roaring twenties?"

"How about we call it the basic bitch party and be done with it?"

I crossed that off as quickly as I wrote it down. "Alice in Wonderland?"

"Ugh."

"Slumber party?"

Katie halted with the denial on her lips. "Slumber party?"

"Maybe even like a super summer slumber party," I said, smirking.

"Hmm. Tell me more."

"Everyone dresses up in their finest, silkiest, sexiest pajamas."

Katie snapped her fingers. "Loving that."

"You could hand out personalized sleep masks and pillowcases—Oooh! We can build a giant blanket fort over the dance floor and decorate it with fairy lights."

"Inspired."

"We can serve fruity, yummy cocktails, and the food can be sleepover food. Popcorn, cupcakes, banana pops, and nachos."

"Yes, but whatever the high-class version is that my chef whips up. Music?"

I wiggled. "Fun, dancing-in-your-pajamas music. Oh my gosh, you know what we should do?" I cried. "You have a pool. What if we laid a platform from end to end, and people had pillow-fight battles to knock their opponent in first? Winner gets a prize. Loser has a penalty. They do a shot or have to strip an article of clothing. What do you think? Sounds like the best damn super slumber party there is."

A slow smile curved her cheeks. "Luna Sinclair, I knew there was a reason I let you hang around me."

I decided to let that slide. We spent the rest of the night planning every detail, assigning jobs, sourcing where we'd get the party favors, and deciding the guest list. Katie didn't blink twice at me scratching out Iris, Rose, and everyone who messed with me since the semester started. She was serious about me coming and having a good time.

Her driver drove me back to campus the next morning on two hours of sleep. I went upstairs, closed my door, and passed out on my rumpled sheets. It wasn't until I woke hours later that it hit me. Wilder put my door back.

He trusted me. Or he was starting to.

Chapter Thirteen

"**J**ack called this morning." I bounced on the balls of my feet, fists up and panting hard. "They've got a meeting with the dean scheduled for next week, Wednesday. He said there's nothing he can say or do to change my mother's mind. I should start packing my bags—"

Lucien jabbed. I blocked the hit and countered with a kick he blocked easily.

"—now."

He wasn't going easy on me, but neither was Lucien beating me as soundly as when we first started. I was starting to like him calling me a natural, and how his gaze wandered down the skintight fabric hugging my boobs and thighs.

It'd been days since my sleepover with Katie. Six to be exact.

Six days since we planned the party she was throwing that Saturday night.

Seven days since Rafael met with Giovanni, Owen, Levi, and Wesley.

Seven days. That night, Rafael would bring them to the same spot to conclude their business.

"What about the engagement? The deal was you marry Victor in exchange for attending the university." All the guys knew the truth. The deeper we got into this, the less I felt the need to keep secrets. "He's not holding up his end, you can't be expected to hold up yours."

"Victor said his parents aren't giving me, Jack, or Victor a choice. They threatened to disown him like they have Adonis."

"They have? But that's ridiculous. Why go to such extreme measures? What makes you the prized bride?" He inclined his head. "Besides the obvious."

"Oh?" I stopped moving. "What's the obvious?"

"You're beautiful, smart, funny, and ruthless," Lucien replied without skipping a beat. The man dropped all those compliments on my head like they were a fact of life and wouldn't embarrass me. He was wrong about the last one. "No doubt anyone who let you go is a fool, but kicking your son out into the cold for it is more than harsh. This is between you and Victor. Getting married should be your choice—not blackmail or to avoid a worse fate."

Lucien tossed his head. "Regalia is a backward town, and I lived through the eighteen hundreds."

"It is more than harsh. I saw Martha's face the night Adonis ate with them. She hated the fighting between her son and husband, and obviously wanted Adonis back. To then turn around and threaten Victor with the same thing? None of this makes sense."

"She might have no intention of going through with the threat," Lucien tried. "She's just using it to get what she wants: you."

I shivered. "Now I'm thoroughly creeped out. It's hard to believe Martha is so desperate for me to marry into her family. The woman never misses a chance to criticize me."

"Did Jack and your mother tell her the wedding is off yet?"

"Nope." I swung a left hook. Lucien blocked it naturally, though he praised my form. "Jack said they're handling one problem at a time. First, secure my transfer. Then, dump Regalia's most eligible bachelor. That he called it a problem says he's got no delusions about how this'll go over."

"I wonder what the exact terms of the deal are."

"What do you mean? I told you that Jack pays my tuition and—"

"Not the deal between the two of you. The deal between Jack Bowden and the Wilsons. The Wilsons get something in exchange for this wedding, and they want it desperately."

"I've asked Victor multiple times. He said it's because I'm the only girl willing to marry him this soon. He needs this marriage to show his father he's ready to step up in his place. Has to be more to it than that, right?"

Lucien's brows drew together. "Maybe that's why Victor was willing to do it. I have a suspicion his parents expect to get more from the arrangement." He dropped his arms. "Let's take a break. There's somewhere I want to take you."

"Take me? But I have class at ten."

He shrugged. "Blow it off today. Professor Gray follows the same syllabus year after year. Today is her fun lesson on the different death celebrations around the world. I'll fill in everything you need for the midterm."

"But where are we going?"

Lucien took my hand. "Trust me. I'll put your outfit on your bed. Be ready in half an hour."

Confused, I let him deposit me in the bathroom. The times Lucien and I spent alone together were confined to our strolls around campus and our time in the practice room. Lately, that alone time was haunted by the memory of our kiss and how poorly I reacted after it.

Speaking of handling a kiss poorly...

Rafael came out of the bathroom on a cloud of sage-scented steam. His towel hung low on his waist, giving a peek to the top of his cheeks.

"It's a hundred to stare."

I jerked my head up, blushing down to my toes. "I wasn't staring!"

"Liar." Rafael swayed his hips, thrusting and throwing his towel-clad middle at me. "Pay up, Cloud Girl. I'll take singles if you've got 'em."

I slammed the door in his face, hearing the thud from outside as the jerk fell on the floor guffawing.

Sliding down the wood, I dropped on the floor, head in my hands. Neither of us brought up the kiss or the bit at the end where I pushed him away. I was into Rafael more than I could say. Deep down in the place where I was honest with myself, I knew it wasn't an insult that made me push away Lucien, or timing that convinced me to end the kiss with Rafael.

When I was with them, I felt things I shouldn't feel. What kind of person was I? Flirting with guys, hooking up, and goofing around while my sister lay in a grave and her killers walked free. Every moment of my life now was dedicated to avenging her, because in that same honest place I was reminded that if I paid such attention to Winter when she needed me, none of this would've happened.

Resolve settling in my skin, I got off the floor and took a shower. My outfit awaited me on my bed.

"What the heck is this?" I whispered.

"Don't like it?"

I spun, holding my towel tight. Going so long without a door, I some-times forgot I needed to close it.

"It's not that, I just..." I took in the red-and-black corset dress with a high-low skirt. "Where are we going?"

He winked. "You'll see."

I flitted between intrigued and concerned. In the end, I chose intrigued and got dressed. The outfit was beautiful and something so pretty screamed for accessories. Black suede boots gifted my feet and teardrop pearl earrings dangled from my lobes. The earrings were another gift from Cato. I stopped asking where he got these things.

Lucien waited for me downstairs, handsome in an understated—for him—black patterned tailcoat and gray pants. He held an arm out for me to take.

"Can I get a hint?" I asked as we left the Gallery, crossing the expanse for the car.

"It's a place I've never taken anyone. One of Regalia's best-kept secrets. Not even Saylor Burkhardt has heard of it."

"Hmm. That tells me nothing, but does a great job hyping up the mys-tery."

Lucien laughed. "Trust me. It's worth the surprise."

I stroked his arm. "I guess I have to."

Lucien's car waited for us in the parking lot, recalling the night it lay open and searched as I awaited entrance into Saylor's manor. For all that she said she brought me there to tell me the truth and stop me messing with the system, I still wonder why she didn't shoot me an email. Why steal my ring, lure me into that windowless room, and reveal the scroll? A scroll not even the Rogues knew existed.

Like that's the oddest thing she's done. Saylor lives in the palace on the hill. Human mannequins parade around in her wardrobe, helping her pick out the next week's outfits. So what in the hell was she doing lurking around campus in the middle of the night, collecting dirt on her Versace skirt and twigs in her hair? She should've been snug in her bed while the servants fanned her with peacock feathers.

"Luna?"

I shook myself, pulling out of my thoughts. Lucien watched me from the driver's seat. Me, not the road.

"We don't all have an eternal life, Calais." I gently twisted his chin toward the window. "Sorry, I was out of it. Did you say something?"

"No, I just picked up on you having something to get off your chest. What is it?"

"I didn't tell you guys this," I began slowly. "With everything that happened that night, seeing her didn't make the headlines, but now that I think about it, it's strange."

"Seeing who?"

"The night Rafael met with Owen and the Shits, I was walking back to the Gallery and I ran into Saylor. The girl just tumbled out of the trees like that was a completely normal place to be lurking at midnight."

"She was where?" Lucien jammed the pedal, lurching me forward with a burst of speed. "Saylor Burkhardt? What was she doing there?"

"That's my question. She was pissed when she saw me too." I snorted. "Although, she's never been happy to see me, so that doesn't mean anything."

"Luna, you should've mentioned this before. Where did you run into her? Could she have been close enough to see Rafael with the guys?"

I was shaking my head before he finished. "She came out of the copse of trees by the library—nowhere near Rafael's spot. Something else brought her to campus in the middle of the night." I pushed up my lips. "Maybe a guy. Instead of putting her hookups through the pat-down or getting it on while his frat-mates howl from the other room, maybe Saylor takes care of business in the woods. It would explain why she looked so rumpled."

"Maybe," he said, but he didn't sound sure.

"What is it?"

"It's just that Wilder's collected info on Saylor and her habits over the years. Obviously, we don't know everything or we'd have known about that scroll, but we do know hooking up in the woods in the dirt isn't her style. She's a complete germaphobe. Haven't you noticed?"

I opened my mouth but nothing came out as our interactions came into sharper focus. I thought it was rich-girl vanity that explained why Saylor never had a hair out of place or a speck of dirt on her clothes. That's why she always looked at everyone like they were filthy. Why she hated to touch me when getting her posse to beat on me worked just as well.

"Now that you say it, it's obvious. If that's not what she was doing out there, what did bring her to campus?"

"Don't know." Lucien slowed to a reasonable speed. The trees crowded in on us, creeping closer to the road, and the road itself grew smaller as he turned onto the street leading us out of town. "Since we're speaking of Saylor, we can safely guess it's nothing good."

I flicked an earring on the tip of my finger, thinking of all the scenarios that could or have led me to a secluded area at night. Lucien was right—it was nothing good.

"What was it like in high school?" I asked. "I would've been there with you guys if I hadn't gotten myself shipped off to boarding school. I've always wondered what I missed. Is it like pretty much every high school movie ever made?"

He chuckled. "You're talking to a vampire frozen in the body of a nineteen-year-old man. I've lived every high school movie ever made. If you want a comparison, Regalia High was like... Forks High School in *Twilight*."

I gasped. "You've watched Twilight? Oh my goodness, is that like your soap opera? You throw popcorn at the television, yelling that a real vampire would *neeevvverr* do that."

Lucien laughed so hard the car drifted into the wrong lane. This is why the man didn't like getting behind the wheel. He was liable to drive his Porsche into a tree.

"I never thought of it like that, but now that you say it, it's obvious. That is why I watch vampire shows and movies—to laugh at all the things they get wrong. But one thing *Twilight* gets right is what it was like in our high school. There are the normal, average kids who study, goof around, do their homework, and hook up behind the bleachers.

"Then, there are the Royals. A group of impossibly gorgeous creatures gliding through the halls without looking left or right, because they don't notice or care that other people are around. They sit at their own tables, speak only to each other, and look around the place like they'd rather be anywhere else and you're lucky they chose to be there at all. That's high school in Regalia, and not just six years ago. It's every one I've been forced to attend over the decades. The idea that the rich and connected are better than everyone else has lasted a long time."

I nodded, soaking in his words. "I wish Winter and I went to high school together, but after hearing that, we would've been better off in a school that wasn't Regalia High."

"What was the Catholic school like?"

"Oh, well, I bet you've heard the stereotypes. Honestly, it was nothing like that. Some of the sisters were severe, though plenty were sweet, kind, and understanding of what it's like to be far from your home and family. On the weekends we would..."

Lucien and I fell deep into talking about St. Thomas's, Regalia High School, the life we've had outside of both, and how his was more varied and colorful than mine. I never knew what stories he was taking from someone else, or which were his that he set in a different time period—whichever it was, his stories were damn interesting.

"—three men were waiting for me around the corner. I knew they were there." He pointed to his ears. "Heightened senses. But I thought they were kicking back enjoying a cigarette. I had no idea they were there for me until they knocked me down and tried to put out their cigarette in my eye."

I hissed. "Did they really?"

"Oh, yeah. Their boss was brought to my clinic the week before. He got into a knife fight and it was"—he whistled—"nasty, Luna. Slashed across the face, ruining his left eye. He demanded I save it, but there was nothing I could do. Naturally, he decided if he didn't get to keep his eye, I didn't get mine."

"Wow. That's the kind of business that makes you opt for early retirement in Barbados."

He chuckled. "I was thinking about it. It does get tiring patching up you broken humans and getting a knife in the gut instead of a thank-you."

"They stabbed you?" I cried.

"One guy got in a lucky shot while I was twisting Cigarette Man's arm so far back, it snapped. With him howling in the dumpster, I snapped Knife Man's neck and fed on the last one. All three bodies were deposited on their boss's doorstep the next morning. Funnily enough, I never heard from him again."

"That's a badass story even if it's made up."

"All true, my lady," he replied, light smile gleaming in the rearview mirror. Lucien Calais could wear the most ridiculous getup. He could paint his face white and dress like a clown. Nothing would lessen the impact of that smile.

I was so caught up in our conversation, I didn't remember we were going somewhere in particular until the trees opened up, revealing the strip of bars, clubs, and beach hangouts that clung to the edge of town. Early morning on a weekday, there wouldn't be many people around and a single glance told me there wasn't. No one pulled up a stool at the beach bar or flitted from club to club, collecting a buzz, and yet the parking lot was packed.

"Where is everyone?"

Lucien parked half on the sand. Coming around, he opened my door, curling his hand over mine. "Let me show you."

Lucien and I crossed the parking lot into a charming open-air beach club called Damu. A tiki hut-style bar surrounded by white marble tabletops, plush cocoon chairs, and cabanas proved you had to get further away from Regalia to leave luxury behind. It was stunning, and completely empty. There wasn't a soul behind the bar, and from the silence, they weren't knocking around in the back either.

"Lucien, they're closed. Is it okay that we're here?"

"More than okay." Lucien led us around the bar, hand secured in mine. My confusion grew as we entered the kitchen, heading straight for the freezer.

"This is around the time you start dropping more hints."

"Here's one." Lucien pointed behind us. "The real walk-in freezer is over there."

"Wait, what—?"

Whipping open the metal door, a long black curtain greeted us.

"Um, did you convince me to skip class so you could drive me out of town and take me to your kill spot in an empty bar?"

The curtains swallowed him. "Come find out," floated through.

Parting the fabric, I slipped inside, foot coming down on the top stair. Scant light from the black-tinted wall sconces led way to... where?

Lucien climbed down with assured steps, stopping before a velvet-covered door. A keypad beeped under his fingers, drawing me closer—though a part of me was screaming *time to leave*. Reaching up, his hand sought mine. I grasped it without thinking—without giving my jangling nerves another thought.

I was here with Lucien. There was nothing to be afraid of.

A soft click sounded and we went inside. I gasped.

Black-and-red-swirling-patterned carpet clung to my shoes and spread around the long black columns, red leather couches, black ottomans, and dance floor. More velvet blanketed the walls and black crystal chandeliers worked half-heartedly to light the dim space. Gazing around the occupants, dark was exactly how they wanted it.

Lucien, Lucien, and Lucien as far as the eye could see. Men in Victorian dress, women in tight corset tops, chokers, pale skin, glasses of gleaming red liquid, and sharpened canines. They mingled by the bar, swayed on the dance floor, and greeted Lucien with nods and raised glasses.

It was a club. A vampire club.

"I never said I was the only one." Lucien grazed the small of my back. "What do you think?"

"I don't understand." I flitted about trying to take in everything at once. "You said you hated these underground vampire clubs. What happened to *those fools mock and exaggerate the torment of true nightstalkers*," I mimicked. "*Their silly little games are nothing more than foreplay for slightly taboo, but still bland, sex.*"

I no sooner finished the sentence than we rounded a couch and fell on a man with long, curly white hair spilling his drink down a woman's chest. She tore her dress, breasts springing free, and arched her back as the man licked every drop off her. I ran into Lucien beating a retreat.

Chuckling, he wrapped me in his arms, leading me to the dance floor. "All those things are true. In those clubs they mock us and they don't do it well." A soft, bluesy tune flowed from the speakers, calling us to a gentle sway. Lucien pulled me close, tucking me under his chin as we gave in. "So many things you've seen and heard aren't true."

"Like what?" I asked, resting my head on his chin.

"We don't chase virgins through the streets, sinking our fangs in their necks. At least, we don't anymore."

"Why not?"

"Same reason you get your meat from a supermarket rather than tromping through the woods with a rifle. With time comes modern conveniences—we call them blood banks. We also aren't bats in undead human form. We still prefer to sleep at night and wake during the day. For those without shaman-blessed talismans, they gather in places like this to escape the sunlight and be with our kind. And if we're all going to be here, we might as well drink, dance, and have a little fun."

I avoided looking at a couch in the back where a couple was having *a lot* of fun. "How often do you come?"

"Once a week, sometimes more. Just to hang out with friends," he said. "No need to be jealous."

"I'm not," I protested, though I relaxed in his hold. "You go every week but you've never mentioned this place. If this is something you keep just for yourself, why did you bring me?"

"Because you haven't stopped and taken a breath in five months, Luna." I blinked up into his eyes. "I know you don't think past crossing the names off your list. Your life stops after you've satisfied your vengeance, so why shouldn't it stop now? Why laugh, or love, or care?"

I pulled away. "Lucien, I don't expect you to under—"

"I do understand." He held me tight. "I understand so much more than you think, Luna." Emotion clouded his pools. "It's wrong to laugh, be happy, and go on with your life like nothing happened. It's like you betrayed them once when you weren't there for them, and you betray them again when you forget the pain of losing them for a single second.

"I understand, Luna," he said forcefully. "Besides all the jokes, the flirting, and kissing you because you looked so sad and beautiful, I couldn't stop myself."

"Lucien," I whispered.

He caressed my cheek. "Besides that, I don't expect anything from you that you aren't ready to give. Don't hold back or run away because you're afraid of what'll happen if you get too close. Nothing will happen, Luna.

Tell me what it is you want me to be for you and that's what I'll be until you say otherwise. I won't push. I won't ask. After we leave here, I'll give you the platonic, friendly relationship you want until you've forgiven yourself... because Winter's already forgiven you."

I swallowed through needles, starting to say something and giving up too many times. In the end, what I said was, "After?"

"After." Lucien spun me. Red and black whirled and then there was Lucien—his pools clear, his smile soft. "In this place, there's no judging or status. No rules, no games, no Royals, and no expectations. Once you step through those doors, you stop hiding and give in to every indulgence. Nothing that happens in here passes through those doors, so if you want, Lady Luna, indulge."

It took a minute for his meaning to sink all the way in, then I caught on fire. Or at least that's what it felt like as I watched all the couples *indulging* and pictured me and Lucien on a couch next to them.

Could he be telling the truth? One morning giving in to my wants, wishes, and fantasies, and then we return to Regalia U as though nothing happened. No pressure to give more. No guilt at pursuing the life my sister would never have.

How could anything end as cleanly as stepping out of a bar? It wasn't that simple, it couldn't be. We couldn't have a great love, but we could have a great friendship. Giving in to forbidden feelings in darkened underground clubs would change everything.

"Can we dance?" I asked softly.

Lucien circled my waist. We fit together like puzzle pieces—my arm around his neck and his face buried in mine. We moved in time to the tune, stepping as the other stepped, our hips connected in symmetry. My dancing experience was limited, but there with Lucien, it all came easy. Our bodies were meant to move in sync.

My pulse raced beneath his lips. Lucien didn't need to hunt his prey. They fell willingly on their knees, offering all of them in exchange for whatever sweet pain their time with him would bring.

"Can you kiss me?" I whispered.

Lucien licked my pulsing vein and pressed a kiss on my goose bumps. He burned a trail up my neck, along my jaw, and on the corner of my mouth—teasing the moment to the point of agony. Turning my head, I stole what was mine.

Our mouths moved hungrily, tasting each other's moans. Lucien didn't ask for entrance. He broke vampiric rule, slipping inside and tangling my tongue in a dance closer and more sensual than what was happening outside—only by a margin.

My thigh pressed between his legs, feeling him harden against me. Nipples rubbing on the fabric, my chest flattened against him, our hearts beating a wild beat on the other. His arm held me safe as he dipped me, kissing me thoroughly, completely, and pouring every ounce of the emotion we denied ourselves.

"Lucien," I breathed. "Can you make me feel... something new?"

He didn't ask what I meant.

Straightening, he grasped my hips, wining them down his thigh and up—the pressure in my core building to a fever pitch. He draped my leg over his arm, dipping me low. My head fell back, exposing my throat to his hot, biting kisses.

Beads of sweat prickled my heated skin—both for the people around us and Lucien, Lucien, Lucien. He thrummed in my veins, becoming a part of me as his hand slipped under my dress.

Lucien raised me up, our gaze locked. My leg slid down and wrapped around his waist. A pained gasp hissed between my teeth as he pressed between my folds.

"Relax, my Luna." His words were warmth on my ear. "You're safe with me. I'd never hurt you."

I melted against him, sinking down and driving him deeper. A ripple of pleasure contracted my muscles. I jerked, crying out, "Oooh."

"Just wait." He kissed me. "It gets better."

Lucien started moving, striking that spot we discovered over, and over, and over again. His thumb rolled over my middle and I moaned so loud, the music didn't hide a thing.

I arched my back reminiscent of the lady on the couch, trembling under his kisses peppering my chest and cleavage. I asked him to make me feel something new, and Lucien decided to make me feel *everything* new.

My skin tingled. My blood hummed. My mind wiped blank before the explosions bursting before my eyes. I was a stranger in this body, coming alive to sensations I imagined a thousand times, but never came close.

Lucien picked up the pace, ratcheting my cries to noticeable, attention-drawing levels.

I didn't care. No one else mattered but us—but him.

The pressure built, tightening my lower belly almost painfully. "Lucien!"

"Come for me, my Luna." He nipped my neck, breaking the skin. "Come, baby."

My nails pierced his long coat. Clinging to him, the dam broke, bowling me over in waves of pleasure that popped me out of my shoes and smashed me on the rocks. I was broken, destroyed, rendered into pieces, then made into a creature that was wholly new.

Wetness soaked his fingers and leg—the only evidence of the internal implosion that wrecked the girl who used to be Luna Sinclair.

"Holy fucking shit," I breathed.

Lucien chuckled. "A beautiful sentiment to end a perfect moment."

"End?" I kissed his nose, face, cheeks, and lips. "No way. Do that again."

THAT NIGHT, I CHANGED out of my damp, sticky dress, shedding the remains of Vampire Luna. I took back everything I said, and thought, about Lucien's nightstalker fetish. It was I who had it wrong. Underneath that beach club where they danced, drank, shed their inhibitions, and gave in to their desires was where the real living happened.

Up here where we scrounged and toiled just to end another day dissatisfied. Where we found pleasure not in our own happiness, but in stealing the happiness from others. It was being up here that made us dream of dark, wild strangers who whisked us into another world.

And for one day, that's what Lucien did.

I hugged myself, shivering remembering what we did on our own couch. Everyone else faded. We made out like there was a time limit, rolling around and nearly falling off three times. No one had to guess what we were doing. Bouncing up and down on his hand while my hand pumped furiously in his pants was a dead giveaway.

The sun going down and movement upstairs finally forced us apart after countless orgasms and thoroughly ruining his pants. We stumbled out rumpled and lips swollen—the reminders of our day taunting us during our silent drive.

I touched my lips, sighing. Lucien thought he was making this easier for me. One day to get it all out of our system, then I could focus on what we had to do. Lucien made me feel everything I'd been missing from lust, sex, and attraction. How could I set aside today and forget about it? How could I stop wanting more?

For now, you must. Tonight is for Winter.

Sobering, I forced myself to lock away our day, just for a while. I dressed quickly in simple jeans and a t-shirt, then stole into the night.

I picked the door lock again. It swung on rusty hinges, pinging creaks through the halls and my pounding chest. I held my hand over it, paper crinkling underneath.

We're close, sis. We're so close.

I ducked into the classroom, finding my spot by the open window.

"—got for us, Dumont?"

"First things first." Dark and deep, Rafael's fixer voice floated to my ears. "Do you have my money?"

"We've got it," Giovanni replied. "Give us a name."

My hand was still over my heart, and the letter.

After Giovanni stomped on my heart, I thought it couldn't get any worse, Luna. There wasn't lower for me to sink.

"I tracked the sale of explosives that packed enough punch to blow up a Lamborghini. It gave me a name that Wilder confirmed with the bank account hack and viruses in your computers. Both led to one person."

The funny thing is, as broken and humiliated as I was, Giovanni's betrayal wasn't the surprise it should have been. Looking back, there was something false in his kisses. Something too saccharine in his praise and compliments. I was so lonely, I pushed my instincts aside.

When it all came out, I hated him and myself, but there was still a part of me that wasn't beaten. I was pissed, hurt, and raging to make Giovanni and Annika feel the same. I wanted to fight, little sister.

Until he came along.

"You'll have to tell me if this makes sense," Rafael continued, "because what we didn't find looking through his shit was a motive. All I know is this is definitely the guy who's after you, and he's not done. Wilder found drafts of more truth lists—even worse than the ones already released."

"The first draft was lies and the second is too," Levi snapped.

"My contact also told me he put in an order for more bombs. Bigger bombs. The kind that takes out a building, not a car."

Levi didn't have a comeback for that. Silence smothered even the singing cicadas.

"What's his name?" Wesley rasped.

I had something left to fight for until he took it from me. Owen, Levi, Giovanni, and Wesley were my bullies, but my killer is Ashton Scott.

"Ashton Scott," Rafael said clearly.

The blowback was immediate.

"What?!"

"Ashton?"

"You have it wrong," Giovanni cried.

"I don't have anything wrong," Rafael returned. "It's your fellow Royal. Sits three seats behind us in statistics. What did you do to piss him off?"

"I knew it," a low voice hissed.

"Owen, hold on—"

"I knew it," Owen shouted. "Didn't I say it made no fucking sense that they were coming after us while Scott kicks back—"

"Owen, shut up," Wesley growled.

"—shooting the shit! I said it didn't smell right." Owen would not be stopped. "Could've saved us thousands if you listened to me! That fucker is cleaning up. Getting rid of us so he can have it all for himself."

My forehead wrinkled. "That fucker" was Ashton, but I didn't understand the rest he was accusing him of. Owen accepted the final name on my list with scary quickness because he believed Ashton wanted something for himself. What?

"Shut up!"

"We have to—"

"Enough," Levi bellowed. "Dumont, here's your money and..." Shuffling, then a thud. "Another two grand for you to forget that name and erase everything you found. You don't say a word about this to anyone."

"That's standard, Thompkins, but if you've got an extra two grand you want to give me, I'll take it."

"Good. We're done here."

"Gentlemen," Rafael said. His footfalls faded, and only his. The four hung back.

"Are we pretending we don't know what this is about?" Owen hissed. "The four of us *and* Sinclair. I should've called it from the beginning."

I pressed in as close as the wall would allow, straining to hear.

"Ashton coming after us?" Giovanni repeated in disbelief. "Doesn't make any sense. He has the most to lose."

"That's exactly why he's coming after us." Levi's tone was steel. "Don't you see? If he ruins us, our reputations, and our families, we're nobodies. We're Dregs. No one will listen to a thing we say against him."

Come on, my mind screamed. *Come on! Say something important. Why does Ashton have the most to lose? What do you think he's taking from you?*

"We weren't going to say a thing against him," Giovanni said. "He kicked this off for no fucking reason! Now Annika's in the hospital, Gabby won't talk to me, I'm out almost four hundred thousand dollars, and the professors found out about the truth lists. Professor Stone wants to meet tomorrow to discuss the *Dreg who does my assignments.*"

"He kicked it off unprovoked, but he had a reason," Levi said. "We all know what's at stake. The question is are we letting Scott get away with this?"

"Fuck no," Wesley hissed.

"Then let's go. Everyone, back to my place."

I could've screamed as their footsteps got further away and their conversation with them. They knew exactly what connected the six of us together, and believed Ashton turned for a reason. What was going on here, and why did Levi, Owen, Giovanni, and Wesley know more than me?

I STEWED THE WHOLE night—waking and sleeping. Poor Cato endured my tossing and turning, doing his best to soothe me back to sleep. It worked only for me to fall into nightmares about voices chasing me through the woods.

I was not my usual cheery self when I trudged into the kitchen. Wilder sat at the kitchen table, finishing up a bowl of cereal.

"Where's Rafael?"

"You mean where's his cooking?"

"That too," I muttered, checking the time. I had class in half an hour. If Rafael wasn't here, there went my plan to tell him what I overheard while we scarfed down his Nutella-stuffed pancakes.

"Ready to head out?"

"Yes," I replied. "I'll grab something in the café. Somehow I have a full day today. Katie is driving me back and forth to her place between classes, and then kidnapping me for another sleepover. We're getting ready for the party tomorrow night."

"The Royal hive is banging on about the party." Wilder and I grabbed our things and left the Gallery. "Almost every Royal got an invite and even a few Dregs. Which makes it a scandal that Piper, Everleigh, Gabriella, and Saylor didn't make the list." He tossed me a look. "I have no idea why you gave me one."

I shrugged. "I told Katie if I was planning, setting up, and attending this party, I got to invite my friends."

"You know I'm not going to this, don't you?"

"Why not?" I arched a brow. "Some of your hookups might be there. You can get some more ass."

He sighed. "This is why a gentleman never kisses and tells. It's not worth the regret."

I rolled my eyes. "How do you know the hive is buzzing? Still monitoring their communications?"

"All night and day."

A thought occurred to me. "Did you pick up anything from Owen, Levi, Giovanni, or Wesley last night around midnight?"

He shook his head. "Nothing. Why?"

"They all went off together after Rafael gave them Ashton's name." I grasped his hard, muscled forearm. "Wilder, I came on this campus with my sister's letter, believing I knew everything I needed to know. Now I'm not sure I know a damn thing. What's this secret? If it's something about one of the five, okay, but why haven't you or I found out what it is? We've both made it our life's mission to rip the skeletons out of their closets, so how come we can't unearth this one, and Winter did?"

Wilder grasped the back of my neck, gently kneading the muscles. The gesture both shocked and pleased me. I had a kink in my neck from a bad night's sleep.

"My guess is if there was a hole, they plugged it after Winter found out. Buried their tracks, got rid of evidence, paid off the right people. Someone found out a secret that kicked off all of this." The café came into sight. "They weren't about to let it happen again."

Shoulders slumping, I said, "Then how do I have a chance of finding out the truth? How can I be sure I've gotten them *all*? Winter was giving her last act of kindness when she sent us those notes—saving us months into years of wondering why. I need to know what secret my sister was tortured to keep. I have to."

"We're not at the point of giving up yet," Wilder said as we climbed the steps. "Saylor knows, and with the right leverage, we'll get her to give up the truth. If it doesn't work on her, it'll work on the guy who just acquired four enemies overnight and doesn't know it."

Ashton Scott.

"Whatever those four went off to talk about, it wasn't a peace treaty. They'll go after him and his family, sever the ties connecting them, drag them down the Royal ladder, and he won't know why. At that point, we can run the same trick on him—show up like the Rogues are willing to help in exchange for everything he knows."

"I don't know." Joining the line, my eyes found Ashton immediately. He ended up in the café at some point morning, noon, and night. A lifetime of chefs didn't prepare him for cooking for himself, and he wasn't about to start now.

I had something left to fight for until he took it from me. Owen, Levi, Giovanni, and Wesley were my bullies, but my killer is Ashton Scott.

"I can't stand the idea of letting up on him even for a second," I hissed. "That bastard doesn't get a moment of hope thinking someone will help him. From today to the end of his short life, he suffers."

"Understood." Wilder traveled down, grasping my waist and... hugging me. "We'll do whatever you want."

I laid my head on his chest, eyes fluttering shut. "Thank you."

Wilder knew what Ashton did. He knew everything.

Wilder stayed by my side as I covered a plate with eggs benedict and two slices of bacon. I had to eat fast, class would start soon.

I wonder if Professor Anthony is back yet. I owe him another apology, and maybe he could give advice on how to handle this situation with his parents. I still can't believe they'd give up their last son over marrying me.

Wilder and I sat down at a booth in the back.

Bang!

"Where's Scott!" Our heads swung around as Owen, Levi, Wesley, and Giovanni blew in. "Ashton Scott!"

Ashton looked up from his eggs, thick brows furrowing. Hatred burned my gut looking at him, even thinking about him—which is why I put him out of my mind while we went after the others. Ashton was the one I wanted to kill first, so in the original plan, I saved him for last, relishing his fear as he watched the others picked off one by one, asking himself if and when he'd be next.

Then came the night we blew Giovanni's car and Gabriella pushed Annika off the bluffs. Not the punishment I wanted for her, but seeing them gave me the idea for the lists and pinning the blame on Ashton. Why do this all on my own when the Royal Shitheads were just as capable of punishing each other as I was of punishing them?

The knife squeezed in my grip as they surrounded his table. *Now you'll finally get yours.*

"What?" Ashton grunted.

"Get the fuck up," Levi ordered.

His frown deepened. Ashton Scott was wealthy, privileged, and connected. What he wasn't was handsome. Small eyes set over a piggish nose and were covered by a pronounced brow. He had a tiny mouth nearly always twisted in distaste—like it was then. "What the hell is your problem?"

"You're our problem." Giovanni pulled something out of his backpack and tossed it on his breakfast, exploding eggs in his face.

Roaring, Ashton shot out of his seat, towering to all six feet three inches of him. The quarterback flung off the ruined letterman jacket, fists balling. "Is that my laptop? What the fuck, guys?!"

"Yeah, that's your laptop," Owen flung. "We couldn't believe it when we found out you were the one who spread those lists, blew up Giovanni's car, poisoned Wesley, and all the shit you've done to us. We *wouldn't* believe it unless we found proof ourselves."

"What are you—?"

"We paid a maintenance guy to let us into your dorm," Wesley said. "We got into your laptop and found the second round of truth lists you wrote. Not to mention the stack you already printed up and stashed under your bed!"

This show had the full attention of everyone in the room, including mine. I would be late to class that morning.

"Under my bed?" Ashton was not catching on fast.

"You were going after our families next. My mom. My brother." Wesley shoved him. "Where the fuck did you get that stuff? Huh? Huh! You been spying on us?"

"Don't put your fucking hands on me!" Ashton's shove sent slender, five-foot-five Wesley flying into another table. "I don't know what you're talking about!"

I started walking alone by the river at night, just to get some peace and quiet. One night I was sitting by the bank when I heard a noise behind me. I spun around, and Ashton was there.

"Here he is, Royals. We *told you* some coward was attacking us and spreading lies." Owen held out his hands, chest puffed out like the vindicated rooster. "Ashton Scott, one of our own, stole from us, almost killed us, and slandered the reputations of four important families."

"No, I didn't! You're the one who is lying, you—" Ashton charged him and was grabbed by Levi, Giovanni, and Wesley. "Agh!"

"He made the Royals a laughingstock. Dregs fucking spat on me! Calling me a thief and rapist. Want to know why? Because we know something about him that would destroy his life, so he thought he'd ruin us and our credibility before we got the chance."

Murmurs, cries, and angry whispers spread through the room. I took Wilder's hand under the table.

"The coward made our embarrassment public," Owen called. "Does everyone agree his punishment should be public too?

"Yeah," someone shouted.

"Traitor!"

"Liar!"

"Kick his ass!"

That was all the permission Owen needed. He reared, punching Ashton square on the nose. Blood spurted clear across four tables. The guys threw him to the floor, and started kicking.

He said I shouldn't take it personally. It was time for me to get the fuck out of Regalia University, and I wasn't taking the hint. I would after he was done with me. I didn't understand what he meant, until he unzipped his pants.

My fingers strangled Wilder, body jerking with every shout and cry from Ashton as their kicks landed. Hidden under my shirt, I held the letter.

"Stop! I didn't do anything!"

Students tipped their tables rushing to see the fight. The Dregs who craved watching a Royal beaten, and the Royals allowing a traitor to be punished. They packed in from all sides, blocking my view.

Neither Wilder nor I got up to move closer. It was good enough for me to hear his shouts and pleas for them to stop. After they all left him broken and bleeding on the carpet, and it was just us, I'd spit on whatever was left.

I don't need to tell you what he did to me. Pushing me facedown in the dirt, hurting me while I screamed and begged for him to stop. When he was done, Ashton walked away without a word like I no longer existed.

A plate or a glass smashed and his screams ratcheted higher. "Argh!"

"Okay, he's had enough," a guy said. "That's enough, guys."

A muffled grunt on the heels of a pained groan indicated they didn't agree it was enough.

"Ease up," someone else cried. "Stop before one of the cooks calls security."

"Nah, let him have it! Break his fucking nose!"

I crawled all the way to the infirmary. Nurse Geller helped me. She cleaned me up and called the police. I told them what Ashton did to me.

"P-please, st-top."

"Enough!" someone barked. "I outrank all four of you, and I say the fight's over. He's learned his—"

"When he calls you a murderer, Rivera, that's when I'll give a fuck about your opinion," Levi growled.

Suddenly, the crowd surged, moving in on the fight. To stop the fight, or to stop the people *stopping the fight*, we had no idea from where we sat calm and clear of the fray.

I expected him to be arrested. I waited days for the news that monster was hauled off in cuffs. Instead I was hauled into the dean's office.

"Hey!"

"Stop!"

"Get off!"

Chaos descended. Students shoved, ran, shouted, and tried to break up the fight. Amidst it all, Ashton was screaming.

Dean Simmons wasn't alone. Both the head of security and the school counselor sat at the other end of the table, looking at me with expressions I didn't understand. Then he spoke.

Simmons received the report of what happened to me and prepared to suspend and put Ashton on probation until the police concluded their investigation. That is until Ashton told them the "truth."

He never touched me. That night, he was holed up in Thompkins Manor playing video games with Levi, Owen, and Wesley. He was there all night. The guys and Levi's head of security would confirm it.

The whole thing was a scheme to extort money from him. I threatened to falsely accuse him of rape unless he paid me half a million dollars. He refused and I made good.

Simmons said he was disgusted with me. The counselor yelled, saying I shamed women everywhere and made it harder for true victims to be believed. They would see to it that Ashton pressed charges against me. A person like me had no business in Regalia University.

I was expelled.

"Break it up!"

"Aghh!" A scream ripped through the noise. "Oh my god! He's bleeding! Ashton's been stabbed!"

I jerked up, hand flying out of Wilder's.

The cry kicked off a stampede. Students knocked over tables, upended chairs, and shoved their friends out of the way fleeing. I forced through it all, running to Ashton.

It's over, Luna. They've taken everything from me, and I can't fight anymore.

All I can do now is say that I love you, take care of Mom, and be happy away from Regalia U and this cursed town.

Think of me the next time you eat jelly beans.

Signed,

Your loving sister

The crowd parted. Ashton curled on the floor—broken, bloody, hard pants spraying spittle. A knife protruded from his abdomen. "Help! Help... me." Screaming, he clutched the hilt.

Neither Owen, Wesley, Levi, nor Giovanni was around him. Actually, they were nowhere. Scanning the bobbing heads, I couldn't find them.

Hands seized me around the middle. "We need to go," Wilder hissed. "Now!"

I didn't fight him carrying me outside and escaping around the building as six security guards ran past.

"Shit, Luna." Wilder grabbed his knees, chest heaving.

"Why did you pull me away?" My voice was flat.

"Because one of them fucking stabbed him. I expected violence, but not a deadly assault in the middle of the cafeteria."

I arched a brow. "Am I supposed to cry?"

"No, you're not." Straightening, he took my hand, walking fast in the English building's direction. "You're supposed to be far away when stuff like this goes down. The last thing we need is the police calling you in as a witness, and your name connected to Ashton when he starts talking about being framed."

I nodded, barely hearing him. "Wonder which one of them did it. My money is on Levi. He was quick to pull a knife on me too."

"I wouldn't be surprised," Wilder said under his breath. Rounding on me, Wilder cupped my face and kissed me soundly on the lips. I gaped at him—my strange numbing mood blowing to smithereens. "That rapist piece of shit deserves everything he gets, and fuck if I'm not glad I finally got to see him taste a sliver of the pain he gave Winter. Your plan is genius, Luna. Whatever they did to you in France, they perfected you. You're amazing."

"I..."

"Go inside. Act like you know nothing and saw nothing. Classes will likely be canceled today. You were just another student kicking back in class when all this went down."

"Wilder..."

He took off, leaving me a red-faced puddle on the pavement. I stumbled into the building, touching my lips and the faint taste of Wilder.

He kissed me. The guy who sprung into attack mode when I hugged him, just kissed me.

And it was incredible.

No wonder he was out here snatching up sex. Call him all the things you wanted, the man knew what he was doing.

I tried to gather myself as I picked up the pace. I was ten minutes late and Wilder said I had to be sitting pretty in my seat with my notes out when the cops stormed campus. Closing on the knob, sirens sounded in the distance. I ran inside and skidded to a stop, darkness consuming me as the door swung shut.

"Hello?" I blinked in the gloom.

No one was here. Lights off, class empty. Somehow I missed that English class was canceled today. *Was there an email?* I turned to go.

The lights flicked on, flooding every corner of the class. Our gaze connected, and I screamed.

A girl in a floral blue dress and yellow cardigan hunched beside the light switch, a puddle of water growing at her feet. Soaked from head to toe, huge empty eyes stared at me through her curtain of dripping hair.

The asylum-white walls fell away, replaced by a wire window and glaring fluorescent lights.

"Take your time, Miss Sinclair." He squeezed my shoulder. "Whenever you're ready."

"Ok-kay," I wavered. "I'm ready."

He nodded to his assistant on the other side of the glass, standing beside the metal table bearing a still form beneath the white blanket. He pulled back the sheet.

It was Winter's favorite blue dress and yellow cardigan that I noticed first.

"No!" I screamed, shooting back and hitting a soft wall of flesh.

Spinning around, her wet, blue-tinged swollen face filled mine. Dressed in a blue dress and yellow cardigan, dripping apparitions appeared from the seats, behind the desk, and down the steps.

"No," I gasped, air punched out of me. "Stop!"

My nails cut my scalp, digging in under my crushing—forcefully holding my nightmares, my memories, the worst day of my life in.

I pitched to my knees, legs giving out, and they surrounded me. I fell over sobbing, Winter's death ripping me apart again, and again, until there was nothing left.

The apparition kneeled over me, her hair sprinkling droplets like tears on my cheeks. Through the horrible bloated makeup, she was unmistakable: Saylor.

"Nooooo!" I screamed endlessly, long after my voice gave out.

Chapter Fourteen

The door banged into the wall, denting the plaster. I saw them on a tour of the house, tucked away on every floor in case Levi Thompkins and his friends ever came back. Throwing open the hall closet, I seized the fire extinguisher and ran upstairs.

Locks, padlocks, and a keypad barred my entrance into Wilder's armory. Shrieking, I smashed the fire extinguisher on it all, littering the hardwood in metal bits.

Saylor, my mind screamed. *Saylor Burkhardt!* I redoubled my strength, denting my weapon on the final padlock.

"Hey? Hey! What the fuck is going on?" Rafael raced down the hall, grabbing my wrists as I reared for another strike. "Luna, what are you doing?"

"I have to get in! It's not enough. Stupid fucking zap phones and key chains aren't enough!" I ripped free and smashed the keypad. "Open the door!"

"Luna!" Spinning me around, Rafael wrestled the extinguisher from me. It clanged between us as we struggled. "You're not getting in that room until you tell me what's going on."

Dripping hair. Blue sundresses. Blank eyes.

"Get off me," I screamed, shoving him. "Stay out of my way!"

I ran at the metal, bashing my shoulder on the door again and again. I was numb to the pain.

He held my waist, dragging me back. "Luna, stop. Talk to me. Talk—!"

I jammed the heel of my palm against his jaw, wrenching his head up. Bellowing, Rafael released me and I made a run for it. I knew what would open the door, and it was right downstairs.

Bursting into Rafael's room, I stumbled over what I interrupted. His headphones lay on the carpet, belting out a tune, and his overturned tool-box littered equipment beside it. I reached for the bomb.

A hard force struck me off my feet. Together we crumpled on his bed, tangling in a mess of flailing limbs.

"Luna!" Rafael straddled me, pinning my arms above my head. "It's me. You're safe now."

The words pierced my heart.

"You're safe," he whispered. "No one is going to hurt you. I'm here." Rafael repeated it as my thrashing slowed—heart pounding in my ears. I stopped fighting, and the tears came. Loud, wrenching sobs that contract-ed my chest too tight to breathe.

I gasped into his shoulder, my strangle grip making him grunt and still he held me just as tightly.

"It's okay." Rafael kissed my cheek. "We can talk or not. Whatever you want, Luna. Just breathe. I've got you."

He made to kiss me again and I turned, catching his lips on mine. "Make me forget, Rafael." I kissed him harder—lips, cheeks, nose, fore-head—everywhere. "That's what I want."

The sheet drew back. The white daisies on her dress tinged green from pond scum.

"Make me forget." I scrambled at his belt.

"Whoa, whoa," he rasped. "Wait." Rafael curled around my hands. "Lu-na, not like this. You're upset. You don't want—"

"This is what I want!" Tearing free, I tossed my shirt over his shoulder. The rest of my clothes went with it. "Come on." I rested on my elbows, my naked body his to feast. "Take off your clothes."

"No. You don't know what you're doing."

"I'm not some innocent little girl," I gritted. "Lucien took care of that yesterday."

He reeled back, emotion flashing in his eyes.

I don't know if I said that to hurt or persuade him. Maybe both.

"I know you want to." I grabbed his belt again as raging waters dragged me under, tossing me to the depths where my nightmares awaited. "What's the big deal?"

"You!" His roar blew me back. "You're the big deal, Luna. I've wanted this for so long. Ever since you walked into that den of snakes, fearless and proud—my Cloud Girl. I held back while you were engaged to that brainless sack of shit, then I waited because you weren't ready.

"After all that, it's not going to happen like this. When you're angry and using me to feel something else, just so this can be another thing we don't talk about the next morning. Another reason to hate yourself."

My lips parted—the reply evaporated off my lips. Rafael's eyes were grave, but clear. He backed toward the door.

"When we're finally together, it'll be slow, gentle, perfect. I'll treat you like the royalty you are. The only one in this town of fakes and pretenders who's a queen. You won't use me to hurt you, Luna. 'Cause I'll do anything for you... but I'll never do that."

He turned to leave.

"Wait. Please, wait." I slid between him and the door, taking his face in my hands. "I'm sorry," I whispered. "Give me that, Rafael. Sweet. Gentle. The way that I imagined it too"—I kissed him slow—"with you."

"L-Luna." My name was a ragged cry from his throat.

"That's the same night it happened for me too. We danced, and for the first time in months, on the very night I planned to commit the act that would change me forever, you made me do something I swore I never would again: laugh.

"You don't hurt me, Rafael. You take the pain away. Make me feel like life can be worth living again, and I could live it with you. Before that feeling was too big for me to handle. It crowded out everything else and I thought I was failing Winter. Now I don't care... because I just want you."

He traced my lips—naked, open vulnerability etched into the lines of his handsome face. "You're very persuasive when you're naked."

I giggled. "See," I said, smiling softly. "There you go again."

Rafael pressed his forehead against mine, eyes falling shut. I couldn't say how I knew... that he was listening to the music.

He guided me toward the bed. The back of my knees hit the mattress and together we fell.

Rafael's clothes came off within a stream of moans and whispered sweet nothings. He rose up, taking my leg with him as he pressed lingering kisses on my ankle. I gulped laying eyes on the full glory of Rafael.

Wilder was thick, bulging muscles that made you sit up and take notice. While Rafael was lean and wiry. Underneath a surface of soft, tanned skin hid a ropey build that would not go down easily.

But I went down—trailing the dusting of chest hair to the defined *V* and where it met. My pulse picked up speed. The only thing that had ever been inside me were a few fingers, and those hurt going in. How would that long, hard, cut cock fit me without all the pain I swore I wasn't looking for?

Rafael kissed down my leg, making my skin tingle and prickle like a thousand static shocks. I stopped breathing as he reached my middle, mouth millimeters from my folds, and moved up, nuzzling my stomach instead. Frustration I didn't know I could feel squeezed a groan out of me.

He chuckled. "Patience, darling. You and I have nowhere to be for the next twenty-four hours. I plan to take my time."

Our fingers wove together—unbreakable. "Can you have sex for twenty-four hours? What about food? Sleep? Water?" I teased.

"What about this?" He kissed me slow and sweet.

I hummed. "Excellent rebuttal."

"Want to know my greatest regret?" he murmured against my lips.

"Tell me."

"That I didn't stick my head past that sheet and glimpse this sexy body *ages* ago."

"Rafael," I cried, smothering a laugh. "You regret not being a creeping perv?"

"Desperately."

If his teasing and wicked jokes were meant to relax and loosen my muscles, they were doing just that. I slid my arms and legs around him, so happy to be there with him I could bust.

"You have no idea how gorgeous you are, do you, Sinclair? These lovelies..." He palmed my breasts, squeezing them to the soft "ooh" that escaped me. "Two round scoops of caramel ice cream just waiting to be licked."

His tongue teased the tender underside of my breast. "Topped with sweet chocolate chips." My nipple disappeared in his mouth.

Wetness dampened my folds as he flicked the helpless nub, curling my fingers tighter. He kissed a burning line to my other boob and tortured it in kind. Traces of him glistened on me—proof of the lovelies' new experience.

Damn, why didn't he stick his head in? And then his whole naked body after it? After I got done yelling at him, I'm ninety-nine percent sure I would've given in to temptation and ended this dance long ago.

"Down here," he said, nose skimming over my belly button. "Is that where I get the hot, dripping fudge?"

Flames licked at my cheeks. My experience with sexy talk was at a zero, but even I knew this was creative. *Tempting me with food. You know me too well, Rafa.*

"Yeah, that's where you... um... the fudge is... okay." I reddened all over when he laughed, warm air tickling my clit and sending it into overdrive.

"You are so damn cute."

"Don't make fun of me," I squealed, covering my face.

"I'm not, I promise." Rafael gently reclaimed my hands and laced them how they belonged. "You're my little weirdo and I love it. I wouldn't change a thing about you."

"Oh, well, then it's a good thing I also love that you're my jerk."

Chuckling, his tongue darted out, licking a stripe between my lower lips. The gasp trapped between my teeth. "A jerk who always makes it up to you."

Rafael descended on my pussy—licking, tasting, lightly scraping me with his teeth. Whimpering, tiny sighs filled the room, and heat filled me, beading sweat on my sensitive flesh. I squirmed and arched and ran my heels on the sheets like I wanted to get away, but there was nowhere I should be than with him.

"Holy shit," I cried as he dipped in and out of me—expertly tongue-fucking a pussy newly discovering these sensations. Surging ripples of pleasure bowled me over again and again, knocking the breath out of me each time I caught it.

Throwing my head back, I came hard, clenching around Rafael and bobbing him between my legs as I jerked and writhed. I flopped in a heaving, sweaty heap.

"Wow. It's definitely not your first time."

"It's my first time with you." Rafael nipped my lip, distracting me while he got something out of the nightstand. "That's all that matters."

More kisses didn't hide the crinkle of foil. My nerves heightened as the full weight of what was coming next penetrated. I was going to lose my virginity to Rafael Dumont, bomb-making son of a hit man.

Condom on, Rafael hooked around my thighs, and flipped. Room blurring, I shrieked—suddenly finding myself blinking down at him, straddling his lap.

"All right, love." He cupped my ass, sliding me down where tip met entrance. "It's all you. Go slow. Go fast. I have a preference, but I'm good for you to decide."

"I didn't realize this is where I take over."

"Doesn't have to be." Rafael stroked my cheek. "But I know my Cloud Girl. You take control of your own destiny," he said with a wink. "Ride me, Luna. Bounce on my lap till you make me pop inside that tight little tasty pussy."

I shuddered, lower belly contracting hard. I wanted to do that very, *very* much.

"You're really good at dirty talk." I shook a little grasping his cock and positioning him. "You've got to teach me."

Rafael squeezed my waist, holding me firmly as I gently and slowly swallowed him. "All right, repeat... after me..." Voice straining, a deep groan rolled out of his chest. "I'm going to strangle your dick, baby, and milk it of every last drop."

I squeaked—both for the brief flash of pain and the thought of those words coming out of my virgin mouth. "That's expert level," I croaked. "Take me back to beginner."

"Okay," he said. "Tell me how it feels."

"How does this feel?" The sting faded as my body adjusted, stretching around all of Rafael Dumont, and the incredibly right sense of fullness. "It feels..." I moved—a little bounce on his hardness. "Ahhh," I moaned.

"You don't need me. You said it perfectly."

That was my green light. I rose on the balls of my feet, rocking up and down slowly at first, then faster when I found that spot Lucien discovered the day before.

Our grunts, moans, and cries intermingled, leaving no clue to where his started or mine ended. I rocked faster, impaling myself on him. Rafael grasped my bouncing boobs, tweaking my rock-hard pebbles.

My cries shot up to screams, breaking the sound barrier. "Ahh! Fuck yes, I'm going to milk this cock!"

"Fuckin—" Rafael froze stiff, rising off the sheets. "Holy shit."

Rafael came inside me. The feel of him warm and jerking beneath set me off. My nails dug into his chest as I screamed, coming so hard my vision blurred and I fell off his lap before I knew what was happening.

Rafael tugged me back, tucking me against his side. I rested my head on his chest, gasping, coming down from the high. "That was... the best first time ever."

"Damn, that was fucking fantastic." I felt no small amount of pleasure at how out of breath he was. "You definitely got the hang of the dirty talk toward the end."

Giggling, I climbed on top of him, popping a peck on his lips. "Thank you for turning the worst day into one of the best."

"I am yours any time." He folded his hands behind his head. "Consider me your sex toy."

"Hmm. How about my boyfriend?"

"Even better," he whispered, and kissed me till my toes curled. "But what about your fiancé?"

My eyes popped open, reality smacking me across the face. "Oh yeah... him." Rafael cracked up. "How are you laughing right now?"

"Because now I know you want me as much as I want you. And you, Luna Sinclair, take what you want. Victor Wilson is no threat to me."

"You can be confident for both of us. I can't believe I still have this whole mess to sort out with Victor. Not to mention what I did with Lucien yesterday. Or the fact I cuddle with your brother every night. Or that Wilder kissed me today."

He whistled, eyes closing like he was going to sleep. "Complicated for sure," he breezed. "Lucky me. All I have to do is lie back and wait for you to pick me."

Calling him a jerk was being kind.

I bit my lip. "Is it okay if I don't figure it all out right now? Putting aside the feelings that I have to sort through for Lucien, Cato, and Wilder, there's this mess with Victor. I have to figure out a way to end this engagement that protects my mom, and doesn't get Victor disowned. I can't have that on my conscience."

"There's no pressure coming from me, Luna. Take all the time you need."

"Thank you." I hid my smile against his chest. "I still want to call you my boyfriend, though."

He cracked one amused eye open. "You fucking better."

I lay on his chest, settling in to stay for twenty-four hours.

"Can I ask you something without it ruining the mood?"

My smile dimmed. "Is it about what happened today?"

"You took a fire extinguisher to a locked armory, then ran in here for a bomb. If I fall asleep, am I going to jolt up to the sound of an explosion?"

I searched myself for an answer. "No," I said honestly. "There's nothing in there that I need. My next strike has to take out every rotted b-bitch in that room today." My voice shook. "It's no good if I just get back at Saylor, then get thrown in prison."

Rafael's touch was warm on the back of my head. "What happened, Luna?"

I fixed on a point on the wall, holding on to the feel of Rafael's arms. "Saylor, Piper, Everleigh, Gabriella, Iris, and six other freshman and sophomore Royals dressed as Winter did the day she... died. They wet themselves down and painted their faces like they drowned."

He stilled, chest frozen as he stopped breathing. "They fucking did what?"

"It was evil." Wetness clung to my lashes. "A cruel, vicious, evil thing to do. And when I ran out screaming and crying... they laughed."

A low, menacing growl silenced the joking trickster. "I shouldn't have stopped you."

"No," I said softly, drawing him up and under the covers with me. "You did the right thing. I wasn't thinking clearly. Whatever I would've done to them after getting into that room, I would've regretted it. I will make them feel so much pain—so much anguish and despair—that they will never think of being unkind to another person again. Doing so will set off a reaction so traumatic, they curl up in a ball of urine-soaked pants." We faced each other across the pillow, hands linking under the sheets. "Will you help me?"

"Always."

"Rafael?" Wilder pounded on the door. "Rafael, you in there?"

"Wilder, hold up—"

He blew in, stopping dead at the sight of us. My mouth opened to say something—what I had no idea. *Wilder, that kiss was amazing and impulsive. As impulsive as what happened between me and Rafael? Please don't see this and make up your mind about us before we talk.*

Actually, that is what I should say.

"Wilder, that—"

Wilder shook himself. "Wait, you guys need to hear this first. I just found out the doctors couldn't stop the bleeding. Luna," he said.

"Ashton Scott is dead."

I POSTED UP AGAINST the wall, sipping on a red velvet cake martini. It was official: this was the best party I'd never get credit for.

The massive blanket fort pulled off even better than I imagined. Some wires and light constructing out of PVC pipes created a blanket castle, covering the dance floor on three sides, leaving an opening where I was gifted a view of Royals and Dregs dancing beneath the fairy lights in their pajamas and lingerie.

I missed out on party planning the day before, but that didn't stop Katie showing up at the Gallery that morning and demanding I come out. Thus ended my twenty-four-hour plan with Rafael, though we accepted this. It gave us time to put plans of our own into motion.

Fun, flirty pop music pumped from every speaker in the house. Outside over the outdoor pool—as opposed to the Langfords' second indoor pool—we placed the platform and a mountain of pillow weapons. But what I was most proud of was the food.

Of course we only planned the menu and the chef did the creating, but what we came up with was nothing short of a culinary masterpiece. Chocolate milk with vanilla mocha ice cubes. A hot pretzel bar. Cookie dough marshmallow crispy treats. Pizza paninis. Cookies and cream popcorn. Champagne gummi bears.

I moved from my spot in the entry three times to hit the dining room buffet table, bypassing amorous couples grinding and making out in every corner of the house. Despite Katie's insistence that the Royals had higher standards, every college party was about dancing, booze, and hooking up—not necessarily in that order. By those criteria, our party was a success. Especially since ours came with the bonus of half-naked coeds. Katie decided the pillow fight champion would receive a trophy and the losers would strip. Everyone accepted those rules easier than I thought.

Katie peeled herself off of Dean, running out of the fort up to me. "Lu-Lu, these walls are handcrafted by French masons. They don't need you to hold them up."

I laughed. "I'm just hanging out, drinking my martini clear of the flying butts and elbows. I'll rejoin the fun in a second."

"This party is my fucking masterpiece. Saylor called me yesterday and lost her mind, bitching me out for not inviting her for a full five minutes before I hung up." She posed for the imaginary cameras, gorgeous in her blue babydoll nightgown and matching heels. "I'm a genius."

"For letting me plan all this for you? Yes, you are."

"Oh, honey." She bumped my hip. "Who gets the credit? The underling who succeeded? Or the boss that saw their potential and hired them?"

"The underling."

Katie rolled her eyes like I was hopeless. "Ugh, whatever. Let's dance."

She tried tugging me away, but I stood firm, bringing her back. "Doesn't any of this seem weird to you?" I asked. "Partying and getting drunk when yesterday, a student was murdered on campus."

Katie's smile melted away. "Luna, of course it's weird. They shut down campus. After Owen was hung from the ceiling, Dean Simmons installed cameras in the café. They're going through the footage to try to find who did it, but I heard from someone in administration that it's hopeless. Too many people swarmed him. You can't even see Ashton on the tape, and there was so much chaos, no one saw who did it."

She glanced around. "I'll be honest, the reason you're not seeing anyone bawling their eyes out in a corner is because people didn't like Ashton. He was weird, aggressive, and creepy around girls. The kind of guy your instincts say to stay away from."

"I know exactly what you mean," I said flatly.

"If he really did all of those things—writing those lies about you, blowing up cars, poisoning people, then it's further proof we were right to stay away from the guy. Still, no one wanted him dead.

"We are all freaked out knowing that someone we go to school with every day is a killer. Half the people here called their lawyers before coming, because the cops are going to interview them. My parents are cutting their trip short. Between the bombing, Annika, and now this? Mom is supposed to be resting and it's just been one fucking thing after another!" Katie sucked in a deep breath, clutching her forehead. "We all get how serious this is, Luna. That's why we deserve one night—just one where we have fun and forget, because nothing will be the same from this point."

I squeezed her arm, feeling bad for her and her mom, though I felt none for Ashton Scott. Katie spent the last year facing the reality that life was short, and time with the people you love isn't guaranteed. She wanted to enjoy her college years, and more importantly, for her mom to spend the precious time she got back happy and relaxed. There was little chance of that with a stabber running around Regalia U.

But which one of them did it? My mind drifted back to the question as it did every ten seconds since Wilder told us the news.

My suspicions landed on Levi. The guy was accused of mutilation, arson, theft, and murder in those truth lists, and if he thought Ashton was behind it, why wouldn't he resort to violence when he's done it so many times before? But even though he was most likely in my eyes, it was a big risk to stab him within that mob of people. Anyone could've seen and confirmed rumor as truth.

Would he put his life and freedom on the line? Levi was a violent sociopath, but he planned all his other attacks. He planned the trick that got my sister beaten up. He may or may not have done something to his grandfather that can't be proven, and never will be. He's been smart and careful before. Does a person like that snap and plunge a knife in someone amid dozens of witnesses?

If not him, then who?

The reason I wanted to know wasn't because I planned to yell, berate, or bring the full force of the law on him. Owen, Levi, Giovanni, or Wesley—whichever one of them killed Ashton... did exactly what I wanted them to do.

Actually, they went further than I ever dreamed. I wanted Ashton Scott broken and bleeding on the floor, begging for it to stop. The plan was to set him up as the fall guy for all our crimes, and a few we made up. He'd end up ostracized, alone, and expelled. Then after enough strikes, when the bastards who gave him a fake alibi couldn't take it anymore, one of them would grant his final punishment and reveal him for the brutal rapist he was.

That was the plan, but killing him was so much better.

One down, four to go.

"I'm so sorry, Katie." I plastered on a sympathetic expression. "I know this is hard on everyone. We can all use something to smile about, because there won't be many of those chances coming."

I'll see to it.

"Let's just chill, have fun, and get two more of these martinis."

"Now that's what I want to hear."

I flicked over her shoulder. "Oops. I spoke too soon."

"What? What are you talking about?"

Standing in the entryway, shrugging off their coats and tossing them at the doorman, was Gabriella, Piper, Everleigh, and Saylor. Each of them wore matching satin short pajamas in different colors. They were here for a party.

My lips pressed to a thin, twitching line.

"What the hell?" Katie split a kissing couple apart, shoving them aside bearing down on her besties. "What are you doing here? You weren't invited."

"I'm always invited, Katie." Saylor flashed her a wide, smirking smile. "I'm Saylor Burkhardt."

"Yeah, the same Saylor fucking Burkhardt who said we needed space while I figured out how to be a friend. Are you on meds for that split personality disorder, or is everyone still pretending you saying one thing and doing another is normal?"

"Still pretending," she sang, bopping Katie on the nose.

"Ugh." Everleigh curled her lip. "A slumber party theme? We heard it but didn't believe it. We grew out of slumber parties when we were eight. So childish, Katie."

"Is that why there are twice as many people here than came to your stupid reality TV party? Wasn't that over by ten o'clock?"

"Because my parents broke it up," Everleigh snapped. "It was ten times better than this party that you basically stole from Saylor."

My gaze traveled off them, searching for and finding a handsome, sculpted figure in nothing but silk drawstring pants. Rafael winked at me.

"I am not doing this with you guys," Katie said. "If you came to start shit, turn around and walk out."

"The only one making a scene is you," Saylor said. "We came to drink, dance, and party. Stop being a terrible host and show your besties where the mojitos are."

"Find them yourself. I'm not the cruise director." Katie flounced off to the dance floor, plastering herself on Dean in a heartbeat.

Why did I so enjoy that Katie treated everyone, even Saylor, like a Dreg?

Looking around the party that was for sure better than a stupid reality TV theme, Saylor and her crew headed into the dining room. I caught Rafael's eye and nodded.

Of course Saylor and the Royal Bitches came. I sent them invitations just in case crashing and sticking it to Katie didn't cross their minds first.

Ten minutes later, they crossed the foyer loaded down with salted caramel cocktails, curiously sizing up the fort. They didn't think the party was childish at all. I knew envy when I saw it.

Saylor slowed down, fixing on Rafael. The man was standing there like a tall hot cocoa cooled with mocha sex ice cubes. She was looking where everyone else was, but Rafael was looking at her.

Crooking a finger, he tossed her a smirk that melted every panty in a ten-mile radius. Saylor promptly ditched her friends and slinked up to him.

I turned away, leaving them behind. That was my cue.

Outside, the pillow fights were in full swing, and I was surrounded by enough naked people to prove it.

Katie's backyard was a sprawling aquatic paradise. Between the Olympic-sized pool fed by six fountains, the water slide, two hot tubs, the pool house, cabanas, and the separate indoor pool, this was all the water park you needed.

Pillows claimed the lounger and partiers claimed everything else. They whooped, roared, and catcalled as two topless Royal girls battled it out for the victory of keeping their bottoms. The best thing about my ideas for the party: everyone was too distracted by boobs, wangs, and sex to give a crap about me.

No one glanced in my direction as I weaved through the crowd, coming out where concrete gave way to lawn, and clambering down the small dip to the path. My feet were soundless on the tickling grass. My breaths hot pants drying my lips. Anticipation swelled as I ducked into the indoor pool.

The space was as spectacular as the rest of the mansion. Molded after a Roman bathhouse, columns held up the second floor, and the pool's fountains were topped with resting lions. I scurried past the fellas to the back door. Cracking it open, I waited.

And waited.

And waited.

Goodness. How long does it take to—?

Giggles interrupted my train of thought.

"Shh. Over here." Rafael and Saylor stumbled into my line of sight—her hands all over him like she grew two other pairs. He stopped her within feet of the entrance, turning her back to me.

I slipped my phone out of my pocket. At least, it looked like a phone. The stun gun fit so easily in the palm of my hand. Why didn't everyone have one of these?

"Finally." Saylor draped her arms around my boyfriend's shoulders. "You played hard to get too long, Dumont. You almost missed your chance."

"I was waiting for the right time, darling. It's all about"—he flicked over her shoulder—"timing."

Straightening, my finger poised over the button. *You're about to wake up in your worst nightmare, Burkhardt.*

A hand clapped over my mouth.

Yanked back, the stun phone clattered on the welcome mat—replacing my shoes as they slid across the tile.

"Shh. Don't scream. I need to—"

I jabbed my elbow into hard flesh, ripping a grunt into my ear. His hold loosened and I broke free, racing for the stun gun.

"Sinclair, wait! You have to listen to me."

That voice stopped me dead in my tracks. Spinning around, I faced Giovanni Natale.

He hunched over clutching his stomach. Glassy eyes peered at me through wincing lids.

"What are you doing here? You weren't invited." Even as the words left my mouth, one look at him said he wasn't here for a party.

His *pajamas* were a ratty oversized paint-splattered t-shirt and pair of sweatpants. His hair, his most proud feature, pulled back in a greasy, haphazard ponytail. A shadow's dusting covered his normally clean-shaven jaw. The guy was a mess.

"Why did you grab me like that?" I snapped, widening the distance. "If you followed me in here for a fight, I promise you, Natale, you won't win this one."

"I'm not here to fight you. Will you just listen!" he burst out. "There are things you need to know."

I stopped backing toward the stun gun. "What are you talking about?"

"I didn't sign up for this." Giovanni clutched his head, pacing back and forth. "It was an easy dare. A simple one. Date some girl and dump her."

I froze. *Winter.*

"But I didn't sign up for this," he cried, thumping his chest. "No, not bombs. Not murder! Ashton fucking died for this shit and I will not be next. All I did was dump her. I didn't do any of the shit the others did."

I frowned following his rushed, agitated speech. "Giovanni... are you high?"

He laughed out loud, reeling me back. "Of course I'm high. My lawyers called this afternoon. I'm on tape starting the fight with Ashton, days after leaving my girlfriend at the bottom of the bluffs and walking away from an explosion. The police want to talk to me first thing in the morning," he said, laughing louder. "I'm their number one suspect. Can you believe that? Me."

"Yes." I plumbed those glassy, darting depths. "I can believe it."

His smile wiped away. "That's because you don't know the truth. But I do now. Ashton's death?" Giovanni shook his head roughly. "That was what they wanted.

"All because of T.O.D. Club."

"T.O.D.?" I repeated. "What is that?"

Giovanni threw up his hands. "It's the reason all of this started. T.O.D. Truth or dare."

"What about it?"

"It was a dare, okay? Someone dared me to date your sister, string her along for a while, then brutally dump her."

"A dare?" Bile rose in my throat. "A dare club? Is that what sick fucks like you do? Make a children's game out of people's lives! Dared you to break my sister's heart? Why didn't you say no!"

"Because the penalties for saying no are worse than anything I could've done to her," he shouted. "People get dumped every fucking day, Sinclair. How was I supposed to know what was going on?"

"Is that how you justify what you've done?" My nails pierced my palms. "Lots of people get dumped, so I can lie and manipulate my way into the pants of a sweet, innocent person."

"I didn't say I deserve a medal for it," he said, jabbing a finger at me. "I only did it because the reward was insane. More than has ever been offered for a dare in the history of the club. I had a feeling something wasn't right, but it was too much to turn down."

Closing the distance, I punched him in the face. "Argh!" Howling, Giovanni hit the floor, covering his eye.

"If you justify what you did to Winter one more time, I swear. You're a monster, Natale!"

"That's what I'm trying to tell you! I didn't mean to be!" He staggered to his feet, nearly tripping into the pool. "This is the kind of shit you do in T.O.D., Sinclair. You fuck with people—play pranks. It's not a club for pussies.

"I took the dare, but it wasn't until after..." Giovanni squeezed his eyes shut. "After I did what I did that I noticed Winter was getting it too hard. Too many dares were about her. Someone was in her face every day. When that video of her attack in the dorm went viral, I realized she wasn't just another Dreg who became the club's favorite that month. Someone wanted to teach her a lesson. I figured out what that lesson was—"

"—after she killed herself." I stumbled back, feet tangling and nearly sending me to the floor. "Someone in your little... *club*... dared you all to bully Winter till you drove her over the edge."

"I didn't know Winter's death was the goal, but *they* did." Giovanni spat the sentence. "They came to me after she died. Owen, Levi, Wesley, and Ashton. Said they all got specific dares like me, telling them to do something horrible to Winter for a huge prize.

"They had an idea who was behind it, but they needed me to get the proof. If we were right, we could demand so much more."

My lips peeled back from my teeth.

"Yeah, I went along with it, but it's not what you think," he cried. "I just wanted to know the truth. Someone made me a part of driving a girl to kill herself! Winter never did anything to me. I didn't want her dead."

"What does that matter now?" Wetness soaked my face. "Tell me you found out who started this. Give me their name!"

"No, no." He resumed his pacing—rubbing his eyes and tossing his head. "Who did it isn't nearly as important as why, Sinclair. It's about the secret Winter discovered."

I jerked. "Secret? You know what it is?"

"It's big," he breathed. "She found out and they used the club as their own personal hit squad. Now it's happening to us. Winter was bullied until she lost it. Now everyone who knows why is getting fucked up. Bomb in my car. Money stolen. Humiliated. On the edge of being expelled. I lost Gabby and Annika. It's happening to me, just like it happened to Winter.

"They got in his ear." Giovanni slapped himself, smacking his ears. The man was unraveling before my eyes. "Convinced Ashton to get rid of us and claim it all for himself. Now he's dead too, and they're not even sorry! That's just one less person who knows. But you."

I stepped back as he flew at me, finger in my face. "You can end all of this. Once you go public, it's over. There's nothing they can do."

"Giovanni." I held his face still, forcing his darting orbs to lock on mine. "Focus. You're all over the place. Give me a name, then tell the secret. Name and secret—the only words that you need to say."

He licked dry chapped lips. "If I tell you, will you protect me?"

"Yes." I didn't have to think about it. "After you tell me, the attacks on you stop. No one will mess with you again. You'll be safe."

"Okay." Shutting his eyes, he took a deep breath. "The name is... Sinclair."

"Wha—?"

"Sinclair, look out!"

I heard the footfalls behind me much too late. Electricity surged through my muscles, trapping them rigid. I crumpled, collapsing at the edge of the pool.

Black crept into my vision as two figures ran from me.

"—CLAIR? SINCLAIR!"

My eyes fluttered open, pain flooding in ahead of consciousness.

"Luna!"

I pushed myself up. A resting marble lion came into blurred focus. It came back to me—Giovanni following me, our conversation, and...

Reaching to massage my temple, I struck my cheek with a hard object. Looking down, I found the stun gun clutched in my hand. *How...?*

"Luna, holy shit."

Katie ran in. Rafael right behind her. Over their heads, half the wet and naked partiers crept inside, gasping and clapping their hands over their mouth.

"What's... going on?" I rasped.

"That's my fucking question," Katie cried. "Luna, what did you do?"

I had no idea what she was talking about until Rafael picked me up, and turned toward the pool.

Floating facedown in the water was Giovanni Natale.

Keep In Touch

Join Ruby's mailing list for news, teasers, and more: https://www.sub-scribepage.com/rubyvincentpage
Join Ruby's Facebook Reader Group:
https://bit.ly/3bNuCOq